# The Girl from the Workhouse

# The Girl from the Workhouse

Lynn Johnson

hera

First published in the United Kingdom in 2020 by Hera

Hera Books
28b Cricketfield Road
London, E5 8NS
United Kingdom

Print ISBN 978 1 80032 154 0
Ebook ISBN 978 1 912973 40 8

Printed and bound in Great Britain by Clays Ltd, Elcograf S.p.A.

*For Jane Richardson and Freda Tilsley*

## Prologue

A bang on the door. The clanging of a bell in the draughty corridor outside the bedroom. A key turning in the lock. Six o'clock in the morning.

*Noise everywhere.*

The bedroom is full of girls, some around her age, others younger. They go about their business and create huge black shadows that dance along the walls in the glow of the gas lamps at each end of the long rectangular room.

*All strangers.*

The panic in Ginnie's belly rises and flutters, as if full of butterflies. It happens when she's worried, but it's never been as bad as this. Before she came here, to Haddon Workhouse, she would run to Mother who could make the butterflies go away, but she doesn't even know where Mother is now.

She hopes Father's feeling better. He hasn't been very well and is ever so angry that he can't provide for the family. When her mother said the kids could help bring in more money, he said he could never be beholden to his kids. He'd rather kill himself. Ginnie hopes he'll be all right on his own – over on the men's side of the workhouse. One of the girls said to Ginnie that *her* father had died, and no one had told her for five days.

How will she cope, knowing that could happen?

There are no grown-ups. Older girls help the younger ones to dress, their hands fumbling, stiff with cold – otherwise there'll be no breakfast for them. Two girls sneeze heavily. Their racking coughs cause pain to Ginnie's ears. She wishes she could offer her shawl to the small girl with the large, frightened blue eyes, but it had been taken away. All Ginnie has to her name are her workhouse clothes, given to her yesterday after having a bath. in front of Matron. For the first time Ginnie had seen all the bones in her mother's back. That was before she was brought here, on her own, to the children's hostel.

The girls stumble towards the doorway, down two staircases and enter the dining hall for breakfast. Twenty pairs of feet, some shuffling, echo on the tiles and fill her ears with sound.

There's no talking. They are too tired to talk.

Despair such as she has never known fills her with dread. She wishes she could write down her feelings about the place, but she can't because she doesn't know how. She sits and leans her burning forehead against a window wet with condensation. Through it, she sees only a brick wall before her own breath fogs it up again.

Superintendent Hardcastle is in charge. He stands in a corner of the dining hall, watching them with narrowed eyes. Dressed all in black, he looks like an enormous bird, ready to swoop to catch one of them.

Ginnie's sister, Mabel, has gone to stay with Aunty Nellie up the road. She's going to try for a new job to bring in extra money. Aunty Nellie can't look after Ginnie, who is only eleven, because she has three little ones of her own. The workhouse hostel is the best place for her while her mother and father are in the workhouse. They said it wouldn't be for long.

Until then, she will have to be brave and do as she's told. After all, Clara manages it, and she's younger than Ginnie and has no one at all. Ginnie shares a bed with Clara. She hopes they will become friends one day.

But, for now, she's Ginnie: all alone.

# Chapter One

**After Haddon – May 1914**

Three years ago, Ginnie Jones had prayed for this; to be walking down the hill towards Burslem. Instead, she had walked up the hill to the gated entrance to Haddon Workhouse, with her mother and father, not knowing how long she would stay there. When she asked the question, she never received an answer. She'd wanted to stay with Mabel, at Aunty Nellie's, but Mother and Father said there was no room. Besides, she was only a neighbour, not a real aunty.

At first, she had been anxious, then worried, then frightened so that she could hardly breathe, and still no answers came. Eventually, she had grown used to the loneliness of life where family and friends were taken away and plans for the future had no place.

Today she walked down the hill, away from the workhouse, with her sister. Today was the beginning of her new life, her After Haddon life.

She caught her breath and turned away as Mabel gave her a sharp glance.

'You got a chill coming on, our Ginnie?'

Ginnie could only shake her head. If she had spoken at that moment, she would have begged her sister to take her back to Haddon Workhouse Children's Hostel. There had been lots of times during those years when she had longed to leave, but now it was happening, she felt such a fear of the unknown, and an unexpected sense of loss for there had been good times too.

4

She'd had friends to laugh with, and to cry with, when it all seemed impossible to bear. But, she reminded herself, friends made in the workhouse were rarely for keeps. They either left or died. She blinked and sniffed, then wiped her nose on the sleeve of her coat, drawing another glance from Mabel.

They passed a public house with tiny windows, too dirty to see through. Its dancing horse sign creaked in the early summer breeze. The house standing beside it had a huge chimney stretching towards the sky as if to compete with the hundreds of huge belching bottle ovens casting a pall over the horizon around the six towns of the Staffordshire Potteries.

She scanned the valley towards Burslem where she saw the black silhouettes of pottery manufacturers, their bottle ovens spewing soot over people going about their business. She knew that along any of the terraces of houses there would be a pottery manufacturer – a potbank, as they were known – and a public house on each corner where hard-earned wages could be spent on payday.

Over her arm Ginnie carried a red carpetbag containing all her worldly goods. A spare dress covered a couple of pairs of bloomers given to her by Mary Higgins who was in charge of Haddon Hostel. Underneath these were her tranklements, her bits and bobs, the things with the power to make her laugh or cry in an instant, special to her and no one else. She hugged the bag against her side as it bounced off her leg and tried to think of something to say to Mabel.

They walked towards the centre of Burslem, known by some as the 'Mother Town' of the Potteries, and her eye was drawn to the length of Waterloo Road in front of them. It reminded her of the serpent in Aunty Nellie's Bible, and a conversation she'd had with her father ages ago. The tramlines were backbones, and the people walking by, its scales. Ginnie didn't know if serpents had backbones and, when she had asked Father, he had said he didn't know either, but that serpents were like the snakes living out in the country. He also said the tramcars trundled all the way from Hanley, through Cobridge, Burslem, and Tunstall, to Goldenhill – less than five miles in total, and each town was packed with their own potbanks. She'd never been on a tramcar. The family couldn't afford it, and they didn't know anyone in those other places, only Burslem, so there'd have been no point.

Ginnie watched their reflections in the shop windows they passed: herself small and dark, scarcely reaching Mabel's shoulder; Mabel tall, elegant, and rather grand-looking in a wide-brimmed hat and long fitted coat. She looked quite different from the sister Ginnie remembered. Now, she was woman with a baby in her belly. They had grown up together until Ginnie went into the workhouse, with Mabel usually wanting her own way and Ginnie letting her get away with it. Would it be possible, now they were both older, for them to become friends?

They crossed a number of roads before turning into a narrow street of terraced houses straddled by another at the far end. Her old home had been just like these, one door among many.

'We'll be home soon, Ginnie. It's my job to look after you now.'

Mabel sounded pleased with herself. Ginnie didn't think her sister had given her comment a second thought but had made it sound as if it was a chore. How much better if she'd said, 'I want to look after you,' or, 'I want to care for you,' or even, 'because you are family'.

'See that house over there with the black door and the knocker? That's where me and my Frank live.' Mabel thrust out her chest, and there was a hint of a swagger as she crossed the road.

With its flaky paint and dirty windows, number twenty-five North Street wasn't the best kept house. Ginnie took a deep breath and followed Mabel inside. The door opened into a tiny front room, which some people called the parlour, and which was usually reserved for the minister and other important visitors. A settee and a square table with two chairs sat beneath a tall sash window, smaller than those she was used to at the workhouse. A dark oilskin covered the floor and the grate hadn't held a fire for a while. Nothing was out of place but, if she lifted the candlestick on the table, Ginnie was sure she'd find a clean circle surrounded by dust. The room felt bare, not at all cosy.

Opposite the front door, another opened into the back room, an altogether homelier place. even smaller than the first. A table and two chairs stood against one wall and two comfortable chairs sat on each side of the range which cooked food and kept the room warm. With cupboards and a set of drawers, a door leading to the stairs, and another to the scullery where dishes and clothes were washed, there was scarcely enough room for the two of them to stand side by side. Seven paces took her from the door to a window overlooking the backyard. Outside, a couple of shirts and a pair of trousers hung on a washing line attached to the house at one end and a wooden post at the other.

'This is my home, Ginnie, and now it's yours too. Well… take your coat off and sit yourself down.'

Now that they were alone in the house that was to become her home, Ginnie was overcome by shyness that burned her face and made her mouth feel dry. Mabel opened a cupboard on the left of the chimney breast and stretched to thrust coats and hats inside. Ginnie saw the small swelling of her belly, and quickly turned away. Catching Ginnie's stare, Mabel covered her stomach with her hand, and she flushed a becoming pink.

'Still can't believe I'm going to be a mum.'

Ginnie sat on the edge of her seat. Since her talk about monthlies with Mary, she knew where babies came from. Only recently one of the girls said she had been there when her baby brother came into the world. She'd hidden in a cupboard and saw the baby come out. It was horrible, she said, and she was never, ever going to have one. Mary said to stay away from boys and then there'd be no chance of it happening. Ginnie heard Mary whispering about morning sickness to one of the girls, but she couldn't find out more because she never saw the girl again.

Ginnie bent forward and fiddled with her boots to hide her embarrassment.

'You'll soon settle. My Frank'll look after all of us. Father came here when Mother died, but he had to go straight back to the workhouse afterwards.' Mabel rummaged in her pocket, drew out a handkerchief and blew loudly before carrying on.

The off-hand reference to their mother's funeral came as a shock. Even now, a year on, anger welled up inside making breathing difficult. Father had refused to let her go, said she was too young, but she believed he had not wanted her to be seen in her workhouse clothes even though he too lived in the workhouse. She hadn't seen much of him since but both Mabel and Father had asked her to live with them, within a week of one another.

'I have to tell Father about me coming to live with you 'cos he asked me an' all last time I saw him.'

'I've already told him you'll be living here so you've no need to worry.'

'You… you told him? When?'

'Saw him before I came to pick you up. He was angry – no, not angry,' she corrected herself as she saw Ginnie's face, 'more disappointed, I'd say. He thought as you could help take care of him so's he could come out of the workhouse if he could find somewhere to stay. I talked him round 'cos he knows I'll need help when the baby comes.'

Shocked that Mabel had taken it upon herself to give their father the message, Ginnie could have screamed. It was *her* life, and no one else's. She'd had *three* years of being told what to do in Haddon. But Mabel was nineteen and Ginnie supposed she felt she had the right. She closed her eyes and took a deep breath. Ever since Mabel had first come for her, Ginnie had questioned how it was that both her father and her sister discovered they needed her now that she'd officially left school. Father would need looking after and she could understand that it was her duty to care for him. Mabel could be selfish at times. He was alone in the workhouse and almost blind, whereas Mabel had a home, and a husband to rely on. But Ginnie still didn't know if she had forgiven him for refusing to let her go to Mother's funeral.

'It's worked out fine, hasn't it?' Mabel stretched her arms, contentedly.

'What's he like, your husband?'

'Frank's a good man. Works at Chamberlain's, same as Father used to. With the "saggar maker". Saggars are what the ware — the pots — get put in when they go to the kilns for firing. Good job an' all. Might not be long before we can afford something better.' Her eyes wandered around the room and she pulled a face.

*The dirty windows were nobody's fault but Mabel's*, Ginnie thought. *And surely a bigger house would mean more work?*

'Course, now you're here it won't be so bad 'cos you're going to help me.' Mabel shuffled to get comfortable. 'What was it really like in that place?'

'I hated it at first but then I got to know it and made some good friends.' Ginnie blushed, thinking of Sam.

'You'll make new friends now you're in a proper home again.'

Ginnie got the impression that Mabel would be happier to forget the workhouse altogether. However, she was no longer the girl she was Before Haddon, the girl who wouldn't say boo to a goose. She'd promised she'd visit soon, and a promise was a promise.

'Come upstairs and see your bedroom.'

Mabel opened the door in the corner. A narrow staircase rose ladder-like, with treads scarcely deep enough to hold even Ginnie's small feet. It was so steep she had to feel her way with her hands. Just like the one she remembered at her old home. At the top were two doors, one to the left, and the other to the right. Mabel opened the door on the right.

A streak of afternoon sunshine crossed the bed, lending the room a warm feeling. An old iron bedstead with a chamberpot underneath, a chest of drawers and a small wardrobe gave the room a crowded look, and the dull, dusty fireplace appeared unused. But, after all her worries, it wasn't so bad.

Mabel peered out of the window then turned and rested her backside on the ledge. 'It's yours till the baby comes. Course, you might have to share with a little nephew or niece eventually. I'd make the most of it if I were you.'

It was so quiet. At Haddon, even when the kids were at school, there was always somebody or something making a noise.

'Best start tea. Frank'll be home soon. Wants his meal put in front of him soon as he walks through the door. It's hard work on the pots. Come on, Ginnie.'

Ginnie made no move. Mabel grabbed her arm and pulled her towards the door. 'Rule one of a happy home. I've learnt that much.'

'Mabel? Is the… you know, outside?'

'The what?'

'You know.' She leaned over and whispered in Mabel's ear.

'The privy? I'll show you.'

They descended to the back room and Mabel pointed through the window to a small brick building at the bottom of the yard. 'We share with next door, so make sure as you bang on the door afore you go in otherwise you could get a proper fright!' She giggled and then laughed loudly.

This was the sister Ginnie used to know, not the elegant woman who was about to become a mother, who came to get her from the workhouse. Maybe, in time, that sister would come back to her. She relaxed. Even so, the thought of wandering down the yard on a cold, dark winter night in her shift was more than she was prepared to think about. Thank heavens for the chamberpot. Much better too than the bucket in the corner of the girls' room at Haddon.

She felt comfortable peeling vegetables as Mabel set the table and stirred a large black pot on the stove. Condensation trickled down the windows and Ginnie's face itched with sweat.

The front door banged.

'That'll be our Frank. Quick now.'

She took three bowls out of the top cupboard and laid them out to receive the contents of the saucepan.

'Hiya Mabel, love. Where's me tea then?' The deep voice sounded louder with each word.

'Coming, Frank. Dunner werrit.'

They placed the steaming bowls on the table just as Frank walked in, filling the room with his bulk. He gave Mabel a hasty kiss. Over her shoulder, his eyes met Ginnie's. He straightened. Moving Mabel to one side, his eyes travelled down Ginnie's body and back to her eyes again.

'And this'll be young Ginnie?'

His voice was deep.

'Yeah, and she's been a big help already, haven't you, Ginnie?'

Ginnie nodded, breathless. Frank's broad red sideburns and bushy eyebrows gave a strength to his face that worried her more than Mr Hardcastle, the workhouse superintendent, ever had. The room shrank even more.

He sat down and threw his cap on the chair by the fire. With his eyes still on Ginnie, he picked up his fork and shovelled food into his mouth without stopping.

Seeing him eat was worse than watching the kids she had supervised at mealtimes. At least they had good reason to rush. Mabel took small mouthfuls, and Ginnie copied. The food had more taste than she was used to, but she had to force herself to eat. *Living with Mabel was one thing, but Frank?*

'And she knows she's going to have to earn her keep?'

He spoke as if Ginnie wasn't there.

11

'Give over, Frank, she's only fourteen and a half,' Mabel laughed as she rose to clear the table. 'Besides, you'll have three of us to think about soon.' She spread her hands proudly over her belly.

He stared at Ginnie's face and then at her hands twitching next to her empty bowl.

She didn't know what he meant about earning her keep. She had assumed she would be keeping house for the family. Her jaw clenched but she had no excuse to move. Slowly, she slid her hands below the table.

Aware of the effect he was having, he grinned.

Mabel returned, wiping her hands on the bottom of her apron.

'I'm sure our Ginnie won't mind washing the pots.'

'Be glad to.'

She grabbed the dishes before Mabel could change her mind and hurried into the scullery pulling the door behind her. Her legs were shaking. Mabel was still talking.

'Don't go teasing her, Frank. I don't suppose she's used to it. By all accounts Ginnie hasn't been around men before.'

'Am only joking woman.'

'Course you are. But remember, she's just a kid.'

A chair scraped against the floor. The door opened and Frank appeared in the doorway, startling Ginnie into grabbing a cloth, and pretending to scrub the sink.

'Hey, duck? Your sister thinks I'm upsetting yer, but you know as I'm joking, don't yer?'

He reached over her shoulder to get a cup, his hot breath close to her ear, his eyes daring her to disagree.

'Ye-yes.' Ginnie's face was in flames.

He moved away, but not before his hand brushed the side of her cheek. Scalded, she jumped backwards. He had his back towards Mabel, who was chattering away in the background. Only Ginnie could see his sneering face. She quickly put her head down and rubbed the pot so hard the soap bubbles sprayed over both her and Frank. He sprang backwards quickly.

'What the——?'

'Sorry,' she muttered.

With her head still down, she smiled.

-

Later, Frank wandered off to the Flying Horse, something he did every Friday, according to Mabel.

They soon ran out of things to talk about and Ginnie, not used to long evenings, made an excuse to go to bed. She undressed down to her shift and squatted over the chamberpot, eyes glued to the door in case someone should walk in on her.

Sitting by her bedroom window later she glanced wistfully around the room. She hadn't known what to expect. The wallpaper was lifting in places. Tiny yellow flowers weaved their way towards the ceiling. A cross hung over the bed and brought to mind the minister who used to visit their house when she was little. She couldn't remember his name, nor what he looked like, but it no longer mattered. She hugged her knees. All in all, Mabel hadn't done too badly.

A vision of Sam shot unbidden into her mind. Her skin tightened. Her cheeks grew hotter. She closed her eyes to lose herself in the daydreams she always had when he wasn't around. She was too young to make plans for the future. They would have to find Sam somewhere to live when he got out. Would Frank help him to get a job? She doubted it. Besides, she didn't want to be beholden to Frank. Before he went out, he talked about his luck in sharing his home with two pretty women. His huge man's body, in the closeness of this tiny house, was overwhelming.

She opened the window, breathed deeply, and coughed on the smoke as it swirled through the air. She had no idea how long she sat there; it was one of the things she could decide for herself now.

She drew the curtains which just about met in the middle. Although it wasn't fully dark, she jumped into bed and pulled up the bedclothes until only her eyes and nose were showing. She'd never slept in a bed on her own before – her belly churned, and her breathing was shallow with nerves. She closed her eyes tightly. Her nose wrinkled at the musty smell of a blanket in need of a good wash. That'd probably be one of her jobs too.

Her mind roamed back to the days when she was last part of a family. Her eleventh birthday. In those days she hadn't given a thought to how lucky she was. She tossed and turned and, though she craved sleep, her mind wouldn't let her.

Now she was alone, she could take out her tranklements. She jumped up and slid the carpetbag from beneath the bed. Looking at her special belongings helped her to feel closer to the people who had passed briefly through her life; some good, some bad, some very, very sad. There was a red ribbon, a marble that Sam called a shottie, a purse, a comb with teeth missing, a dried carnation and a buttercup, a cobble of coal, a doll, and the carpetbag itself.

The doll. The doll Sam had made.

She laid it on the pillow next to her head, caressing the dress and the long, straggly hair. What did it matter if she was too old for dolls? She gathered it to her and kissed it.

'Night, night, Clara' she whispered softly. Clara and the carpetbag – links to her old life. Maybe Sam was awake and lying on his bed thinking of her. And what about Mary? It was true what Ginnie had said to her yesterday. Mary Higgins felt more like a big sister than Mabel could ever be.

Mabel. Her sister. Before she'd even heard of Haddon.

## Chapter Two

**Before Haddon – January 1911**

It's Ginnie's birthday and the best day ever because turning eleven in 1911 sounds magical. It's also the Sunday School prize-giving and she, Ginnie Jones, is going to get her first ever prize.

She bursts into song because she can't help it.

'Ginnie? Come downstairs. I need you.'

Mother is standing by the fire-grate holding out a dress and smiling. She's done little enough of that lately. Each time Ginnie asks if she's feeling all right, Mother says nothing's the matter. *Parents have to tell the truth, don't they? It's only right.*

'It's from Mrs Jackson for your birthday. You must thank her when you see her.'

Ginnie works in Mrs Jackson's laundry from time to time. A month back, Ginnie happened to mention she was getting a prize from Sunday School on her birthday. And now she has a new dress. It's quite the nicest frock she has ever seen; pale blue with tiny pink flowers, lots of folds, and a little white collar. Her old Sunday frock is tight under one of her arms. She *is* eleven after all.

'Can I put it on?'

'Best wait till after breakfast. You can't wear it to church if you get dirty.' Mother folds the frock over her arm.

Ginnie puckers her lips. 'But I won't.'

'I'll not have you messing it up and there's an end to it. Eat your breakfast.'

Ginnie picks up a piece of bread and dripping and closes her eyes. In her mind, she's striding through the town and everybody's watching the way her lovely new dress floats as she walks. A dress that isn't a hard-wearing hand-me-down from Mabel.

Father comes downstairs and drags a chair away from the table to get his long legs underneath and ruffles her hair. 'What's up, duck?'

Ginnie gives him her brightest smile. 'My new dress, from Mrs Jackson. I want to put it on, but Mother thinks I'll get it dirty before we go to church.'

'Have a heart, Flo. Let her get dressed up. It might never happen again.'

Mother's face has *that look*, the one she wears when she's trying to find a reason to say no. She rolls her eyes towards the ceiling.

'Go on then, and mind you're—'

Ginnie dashes into the living room where the dress is hanging on the picture rail. It slides over her head and floats down past her knees, soft and delicate. She whirls and twirls and the skirt spreads out like a beautiful blue flower. Soon everybody will be looking at her, and Mother and Father will be that proud. She returns to the kitchen overcome with shyness and can't bring herself to look at their faces.

Ginnie doesn't like Sunday School all that much but, at the beginning of last year, one of the other girls said she could get a prize if she went every week. She had forced herself to go and, if she doesn't get a prize, it will have all been for nothing.

Mabel wanders in and stares into the large mirror over the grate. 'Do I *have* to go?'

Ginnie pulls her face. Mabel's five years older and interested in boys. She's tall and slim, and her hair is brown and straight. She's always looking for spots and shrieks at any sign of redness. Ginnie hides a grin; *she* doesn't have any spots at all.

'Course we've got to go. Our Ginnie might get a prize.'

'I am… I am.'

'Ginnie! What did I tell you?'

'But I *am* getting a prize, Mother. I've been every week just like the other kids said.'

'Pride often comes before a fall, my girl.' Mother slips into her coat and beckons to Mabel to get a move on. After straightening her church hat and lifting a few curls, she turns to inspect them both. 'You'll do. Let's get gone then.'

Mabel glances towards the stairs. 'What about Father?'

'Gone for a lie down.'

Ginnie turns towards the stairs. 'Is he poorly ag—'

'He's had a hard week,' says Mother.

'Why do I have to go if Father isn't?'

Ginnie eyes smart, causing her to blink. Nobody in the family ever got a prize before. What could be better to a God-fearing family than a Sunday School prize?

'You're coming with us, Mabel, and there's an end to it.'

Mabel strides off as if she isn't with them.

Unfortunately, Ginnie's coat, with its frayed collar, covers her new frock, and she has to wear it because it's raining, and her teeth are chattering – otherwise she'd take it off so everybody can see her beautiful dress.

The houses are hardly visible through the mizzly rain. She'll have to sit in sticky dampness during the whole service. Already the folded paper she has stuffed into her shoe, to cover the hole, is sodden and mushy. Water trickles around her toes, freezing her foot to the sole. It'll be a relief to take off her coat and drop it on to her damp feet to warm them up.

Ginnie follows Mother and Mabel into a pew three rows from the back. Mother won't walk up the aisle where everybody can see them – she's funny like that. Ginnie will have to stand on the pew if she wants to see what's going on. She ignores Mabel moaning beside her and spreads out her frock. During the singing, she concentrates hard to show she *has* been paying attention for all those months.

On and on the minister drones until Ginnie reckons he's forgotten all about the prizes and her backside is nearly as numb as her toes. She wriggles. Mother glares, but Ginnie can't help it if her backside hurts. She folds her arms in a huff. If her toes freeze to death, *they'll* be sorry.

'And so, we come to the Sunday School prizes.'

Whispers buzz back and forth around the room.

'We have three little girls here today who have regularly attended classes throughout the year and I'm pleased to hand out a small gift from the church to each in praise of their fortitude.'

He waits for the clapping to stop. 'Miss Emmeline Bassett?' His voice rings out.

Ginnie wonders what 'fortitude' is and whether it'll matter if she doesn't have any. She climbs onto the pew and stares across the sea of heads in front of her. Ringlets bounce around Emmy's head like springs as she walks down the aisle and up the steps to the altar. She's even wearing white gloves like her mother. It's as plain as day that Emmy's from the rich end of the town.

Ginnie's new Sunday frock isn't a patch on Emmy Bassett's pale shining silk, and even Emmy's hair ribbon matches. Ginnie's excitement fizzles out. Her lovely dress is just an ordinary everyday frock. If only Emmy would trip up, or do something, anything, to wipe that smile off her face. The minister gives her a small book and shakes her hand as if she's a real grown-up. Emmy walks back to her seat with a red face, and her nose in the air.

Ginnie slides down into the pew dreading the moment when she will have to walk down that aisle. All those people… her face tightens… hundreds even.

'Miss Ginnie Jones?'

It's time.

Her backside *is* stuck to the pew, truly. She isn't clever like Emmy Bassett. Emmy deserves a prize. She reads from the Bible most weeks and takes the collection box round for the minister, Miss Goody-Goody that she is.

Mother nudges her but Ginnie's legs wobble like jelly. She can't do it.

'Ginnie Jones? Come on, lass.'

The minister strains his head looking through rows of people who, by then, have turned to look behind them too. She's about to duck when his eyes fall on her. He beckons her forward, but she isn't sure she deserves a prize any more.

Mother pats Ginnie's knee. 'Make us proud, lass.'

Ginnie's eyes fix on the minister, and she begins the long trek from the back of the church. The talking stops. Even though she tiptoes, her footsteps echo between the pillars and the stone floor. There's a whooshing in her ears. She closes her eyes. Maybe she'll faint… if she's lucky.

'Ginnie only missed one class last year, and so we have a special prize for her.'

The minister's voice grows louder, and there he is, beckoning her forward. Face on fire, she can't look at anyone but him. He smiles and gives her a large book. On its cover is a man, Jesus most probably, sitting in the middle of a group of smiling children. It's a beautiful book, and it's all hers. She takes it carefully; it's heavier than she expects.

The clapping starts, and she nearly forgets to shake hands. She can't take her eyes off the book as she returns to her seat, glad now to be at the back where the minister can't see her. She smiles as she turns page after page, fingering the pictures between the words. It's much bigger than Emmy's. She doesn't care who gets the last prize; she has what she came for. She even dares to ignore the odd shush from Mother.

Outside the church they wait to shake hands with the minister.

'Don't forget to thank him, Ginnie,' Mother whispers, giving her a nudge.

Mabel holds out her hand. 'Let me see.'

'No, it's mine.' Ginnie clasps the book against her chest and turns away.

'That's not what Jesus teaches us, Ginnie.' The minister takes off his spectacles, wipes them on his chest and returns them to his nose, sniffing.

Ginnie hadn't seen him coming and burns up with embarrassment. She meant to be so good today. Now it's all spoiled. What if he takes her prize back and gives it to someone else?

'Th-thank you for the lovely book.' She gives him her brightest smile and turns to Mabel. 'You can read it to me tonight if you like,' she says, to show just how good she can be. He'll think she's doing Mabel a huge favour, instead of the other way round.

'Go on then.' Mabel ruffles her hair.

'Don't.' Ginnie squirms away but remembers to smile for the minister's sake.

Mother holds out her hand to him. 'It's kind of the church. Ginnie's been on about today for ages.'

'Think nothing of it, Mrs Jones.'

He puts his hand over hers and, to Ginnie's surprise, her Mother's face turns pink.

'We aim to give our flock a good start in life and where better to start than the teachings of Our Lord?'

As they walk down the pathway, Ginnie notices Emmy Bassett staring, so she pulls a face, lifts her nose in the air, and turns away.

–

Mother can't argue when Ginnie spends all evening looking at her book; after all it *is* Sunday, and her birthday, *and* the book *is* from the minister. Mabel flops down beside her as the clock chimes eight. She reckons Mabel's come downstairs late on purpose, so there'll only be time for one story. But she's so looking forward to hearing it, she holds her tongue.

'Ready?'

Silently, Ginnie hands over the book.

Mabel's fingers run across the cover. 'It's a lovely book, isn't it?'

Ginnie nods, wishing she'd get on with it.

'Here we go then… it's called *The Children's Book of Parables*.' She turns to a blank page with a line of handwriting. 'It says, *To Miss G. Jones, For attendance. January 1911*.'

'That's nice,' says Mother, not looking up from her sewing.

Mabel clears her throat. 'The first story is called, The Prodigal Son.'

'What's prodigal?'

'You must've heard it in church?'

'But I didn't know what it meant. Now I'm eleven, I want to know.'

'It's about a ne'er-do-well son what leaves home and spends all his money,' butts in Mother, bending over a pile of mending. 'Then he goes home and asks for forgiveness.'

'He doesn't sound very nice.'

'Am I reading this story, or not?'

Mabel's about to throw the book down, but they all burst out laughing and everything's all right again. It's a nice story. It turns out the father loves the son who leaves, and kills a fatted calf when he comes back, and the other son is jealous.

'What's a fatted calf?'

'Something special. For parties, I think. If you keep asking questions, we'll never finish.'

Ginnie puts a finger over her lips.

At the end of the story, Mabel slams the book shut. 'Time you were in bed.'

'Read me another?'

'No.'

'Go on, please?'

'I said I'd read you a story, and I have.' Mabel flounces off.

Ginnie opens her beautiful book again to touch the pictures bringing to life the people in the stories. She can even guess which parable it is just by looking at the pictures. Her fingertip slips along the words – and she slams it shut. It doesn't matter how hard she tries. She can't read the words.

'Up to bed, young lady.'

Mother rubs her eyes and Ginnie's heart misses a beat. Does she have poorly eyes like Father? She's been working so hard under the dim light of the candle, so maybe she's tired. 'I loved today.'

'Hmm.'

'My birthday and my prize.'

'Make the most of today, duck,' Mother says, and turns away quickly.

Ginnie's smile reaches from ear to ear. On her way to the stairs, she kisses her mother's cheek.

Lying in bed waiting for Mabel, she gets the book out again and turns the pages slowly. For now, it's enough to feel them. One day, she will read *every* word.

# Chapter Three

## After Haddon – June 1914

Ginnie felt like an outsider staring in through a window; not a real part of the family. It was all too new. She did her work, made tea for Mabel, and listened to her endless chatter. It didn't take long for her to remember that Mabel's mind was quick to wander and that she preferred talking to doing.

She was getting used to Mabel's worries about the forth-coming baby too. Will the birth be painful? Will he or she be healthy? How many nappies will be needed? Ginnie was beginning to feel sorry for any poor mite who would have to depend on her sister for everything. Mabel even confessed that she didn't know if it would all be too much for her. It was a bit too late to think of *that*. Perhaps reassurance was all she needed, from someone older than her, and definitely not Frank. A woman friend.

Big, burly Frank, with his curly red hair and sideburns, Ginnie kept at a distance. She took care not to be alone in the back room when he was due back. Instead, she stayed in her bedroom, or in the scullery until they all sat down to eat. He had a disturbing manner and she had never had close contact with a man before, apart from Father.

By the end of the first week the house was spotless. Frank praised Mabel's sparkling windows. She never let on who had actually done the work. Instead, she smiled her thanks and buttered up to Ginnie when he wasn't around to hear.

Today, she was cleaning the outside window of the kitchen. Mabel sat knitting a matinee coat and talking loudly through the half-open back door. Ginnie stretched her back where a knot had formed.

'The house looks really nice now and I'll be able to keep it like that.'

Ginnie froze in mid-polish. 'Am I not doing it right then?'

A rustle followed. Mabel popped her head around the door and leaned against the wall. 'What *are* you on about?'

'Are you sending me back 'cos I'm doing something wrong?'

Mabel burst out laughing. 'Give over. I'm not sending you anywhere. Haven't I just said what a big a help you've been? Well, I don't get that sickness of a morning like I used to, so I thought as I could keep it clean and tidy.' She patted her hair in a satisfied manner. 'My friend said as all women get sick, but it'd pass. I didn't believe her because I felt that bad. But you're ok if you get through the first three months when you feel like your body's trying to get rid of the poor mite. Any road, it's gone now so you can do the washing and heavy work, and I can keep the house clean.'

Mabel's eyes had glazed over, as if her mind was somewhere else, and not in a happy place. '*The hard work of having babies must be worth it,*' thought Ginnie. '*What woman in her right mind would have more than one?*'

Ginnie's heart had skipped a beat at the thought of going back to Haddon. Much as she was glad to be free, seeing Sam and Mary again was all she could think about and she determined to visit as soon as ever she could. She opened her mouth to ask.

'Course, if I'm going to do the housework, you'll be able to get a job. You're old enough. I went down the registrar's and got a certificate of birth for you so's you can work in a factory. You'll need one 'cos you're not sixteen yet.'

Go to work? Get paid? Even better. She'd be proper grown-up with money of her own and she could scout around for a job for Sam so's he could leave Haddon, too. She jumped off the chair and carried it back into the house. 'I've never been near a factory, will it matter?'

24

'You went to school when you were in that place, didn't you?'

'Oh, yes. The workhouse kids went to school every afternoon, it's the law.' said Ginnie, carefully. No point in mentioning that she had preferred to help Mary look after all those kids back at Haddon. The bosses at the workhouse didn't care about them.

'We all have to start somewhere. I've heard they're taking girls on down Chamberlain's again. I was a sponger down there until I had to finish when I was sick of a morning. It's left us a bit short for paying the rent. A strong girl like you is bound to find something, and a few extra bob'll come in handy. Why don't we go down tomorrow and see what's going? Sooner we go, sooner you'll be paying your way.'

Obviously, Mabel didn't see cleaning the house and helping with the cooking as paying her way. Well, she *would* get a job, *and* put a bit by for the future.

'I'll do what I can to help.'

'You can give me something for your keep and I'll give you pocket money so as you can make some new clothes and get rid of them horrible rags.'

Ginnie glanced down at her dress. Mabel was right. She had been so busy cleaning she hadn't noticed the tear in the hem of the still too-long skirt. It would need stitching before it fell to pieces. She couldn't throw it away until she'd made one another one.

As if hearing her thoughts, Mabel chirped up, 'I'll go through mine tonight so as you'll have something half decent to wear when we go down there. If you look tidy and spritely you might get work. Frank says as it'll be good for you.'

She might have known *he'd* have something to do with it. She couldn't imagine it being Mabel's idea, what with her liking a bit of help and a natter during the day.

'I'll pay me way.' She held her head high. It would just be a different job than she was expecting, that's all.

'We'll go first thing tomorrow.'

Ginnie tried her best to put a smile on her face, but she couldn't really say that she succeeded. Housework, and cooking and now who knows what sort of job on the pots? Maybe she was right in thinking that Mabel's aim in life was to do as little as possible. Mabel could have got her out of the workhouse at any time once she'd settled down with a husband and a place to live. So, why now if not to send her out to work?

She spent the evening tacking up the hem on her borrowed dress. She had to admit that it was nicer than the dresses she'd brought with her. Her mind wandered back to the day her life changed, and the weeks that took her family away.

# Chapter Four

## Before Haddon – February 1911

When Aunty Nellie opens the door Mother just stands there, rooted to the spot, looking like a total stranger. She's soaked to her skin, with rat's tails of hair dripping into big staring eyes. She can't have come from home because it's only a couple of doors away.

'Oh, God Nellie, I don't know what to do. I can't hold it in no more.'

Ginnie's heart runs so fast she can't get her breath.

'Heaven and all the saints preserve us, Flo. Come in before you catch your death. We'll have a cuppa in the parlour. Put kettle on, Ginnie. You'll finish this load in no time.'

Mother holds fast to Aunty Nellie who pushes her gently towards the parlour and closes the door behind them.

*Why do grown-ups have secrets?* Yesterday her mother and father were whispering in the kitchen and when Mother saw her, she stopped talking. How's she supposed to learn if they don't tell her what's going on? *And, when things get bad, why do they always want a cup of tea?*

Back in the kitchen, she swishes clothes around the tub with the large wooden dolly peg. The weight of both mauls at her shoulders until she can't feel her arms.

Mothers don't cry, except when somebody does something special – like that time Father gave her a bunch of flowers after breaking her necklace.

Ginnie tiptoes over the red quarry tiles to the parlour door and slowly turns the knob. Her wet hands slide on its smooth, round surface.

'Lord above. He was fine last time I saw him.'

To hear the name of the Lord God Almighty taken in vain by Aunty Nellie is almost as horrible as seeing Mother breaking her heart against Aunty Nellie's huge chest. Aunty Nellie's eyes are closed as if she's praying to the Lord God Almighty for all she's worth.

'He doesn't want nobody knowing, Nellie. Not yet.'

'Won't ever ask for help, that man of yours.'

'He's been having headaches. His eyes are sore. Says the light's got a halo around it. That can't be right can it, Nellie?'

Mother's voice breaks between sobs. Ginnie's eyes are sore too. She wants to run away but she's rooted to the spot.

'We can't afford a doctor, Nellie. And if he loses his job, what then? The workhouse... I've dreamed about that place every night since he told me. I wake up crying and take myself off downstairs so's he doesn't see me.'

Ginnie opens the door a smidgen more. Mother's rocking back and forth on the chair. Tears threaten and Ginnie tries her hardest to stop them, her hand firmly against her mouth. She can cope with her own tears, for she knows they will stop eventually. But Mother's rasping breaths cause aching pains in her chest.

'I've watched them inmates and prayed to God it'd never happen to us. Fat lot of good it did.'

'It won't come to that, surely?'

'How else can it end?'

'Thought you was helping me with that washing, not listening at doors, lady.' Aunty Nellie's face is puffy and her voice sharper than usual.

'I... I...' Ginnie gulps and gulps again.

'Don't go fretting. We'll manage somehow, Ginnie duck.'

Mother opens her arms and Ginnie runs to her, to curl up warm and comforted. A hand strokes the top of her head.

'There, there, love. You're too young for all this. I wish I could make it all go away.'

They hold hands all the way home, but Mother never once looks at her, and never speaks. She plods on like an old woman, dragging one foot after the other.

They live in one of the two-up two-down terraced houses with alleys, tiny backyards and cold, dark, outside privies where spiders live. And always, there's soot from smoking chimneys and bottle ovens. Windows are buried under grime no matter how often they're cleaned. People walking in the rain end their journeys with black faces. Potbanks, such as Doulton's, McIntyre's and Wood's with their huge bottle ovens, are sandwiched between the houses. Chamberlain's, where Father works, make cheap pots for those who can't afford better.

They turn into Water Street and down the alley to their backyard. Mother bangs her backside against the gate until it opens, scraping grains of the dirt path with it. Once inside, she takes off her coat and puts on a shawl and tells Ginnie to do the same. Mother won't build another fire when there's just the two of them in the house even though it's early February and fit to snow outside.

Their home is tiny. It's said that the stairs in these houses are so narrow the upstairs windows have to be taken out to get new beds and coffins into the bedrooms. Most folk round this way can't afford new beds so the old ones stay put. Thankfully, she doesn't know any dead people so the bit about coffins could have been a fib.

It's Sunday, early April. Apart from Sunday School and Church, rain keeps them inside all day. Mabel and a friend are trying out fancy new ways of wearing their hair and arguing over who will have the long, shiny, bright red ribbon they found on the street outside Chamberlain's.

Father gets up and stands stock still shaking his head, then wipes his eyes with the back of his hand.

'Make a pot of tea, lass,' he says to Mabel, who is admiring her friend's black hair pinned up high and plaited through with the red ribbon.

'But, it's my turn to have my hair done,' she says to the mirror.

'I said we'll have a brew.' He bangs his fist on the table. 'I mean NOW.'

They very nearly jump out of their skins. Father moves slowly but still knocks the clothes-horse off its legs as it buckles under the weight of damp washing. He catches it before it tumbles to the floor.

'Got something in my eye,' he murmurs, his voice growing louder. 'Why the hell do we have to have the washing everywhere? Must've been dreaming when I thought we hadn't got two h'appennies to rub together.'

Nobody speaks.

His face is white and his eyes cold, avoiding everyone.

'Just stepping outside for a bit of air.' He slams the door and doesn't look back. Mabel's friend mutters something about having to call somewhere and disappears through the front door as if the house is about to crumble around them.

Mabel folds her arms in a huff. 'Oh, Mother, he's made me look proper stupid. I don't know what she'll say when I see her next.'

'Do as you're told for once, Mabel, and put the kettle on. Give her a hand, Ginnie.'

Mother's bones crack as she gets to her feet and follows him outside. He's leaning against the backyard wall and Mother pats his back as if he's just a kid. He bangs his fist against the wall and the hairs on Ginnie's arms stand on end. Their words float faintly up the yard.

'What the hell are we going to do, Flo?'

'Something'll turn up love, you'll see.'

'How? Where'll the rent money come from? A bloke what can't look after his family ain't a bloke no more.'

Mother pulls him towards her.

Ginnie blinks away her tears. She's always crying these days. Seeing Father, always so strong, falling to pieces, is much worse than watching Mother crying her eyes out at Aunty Nellie's.

'There, there, love. Mabel's trying to get a better job.' Mother strokes his black, curly hair.

'That's what it's come to then? Depending on me own kids for me next loaf of bread? I canna take it, Flo. I'd rather kill myself.'

'What kind of talk's that, Alf Jones? Don't you dare speak of such a sin.'

Mother crosses herself.

–

The next day Ginnie goes with Mother to see Mr Cox, the pawnbroker on Swan Street. The shop is small and dark, full of furniture, household stuff, jewellery, and all sorts of things that don't look new. The corners are dingy as if they've never seen a brush or duster.

'Morning, Mrs Jones, and what you got for me today?'

That's a surprise; her mother must have been to see him before.

Mother empties her shopping bag of small, easy to carry things, and hands them over. 'What'll you give me for these?' She smiles at Ginnie. 'We'll get them back soon... when times are better.'

One by one, he picks up a blue vase, four plates, Mother's church hat, and a doll. He looks them over, sniffing loudly. Ginnie's given the doll, the only one she has, to Mother to do her bit for the family. It has a scratch on its cheek where Mabel once dropped it. Ginnie smiles at Mother to show she isn't upset, but Mother turns away and doesn't look at her again.

Ginnie wonders whether she should've given more, but it's the only doll she has.

'I'll give you three bob for the lot.'

Mother opens her mouth, but he puts up a hand. 'Three bob, Mrs Jones. No more, no less. You know the rules.'

Mother shrugs and slips the coins into her purse along with the pawn ticket. 'Come along.' She pushes Ginnie out of the shop and never says another word.

When they get home, Mother pulls the bag of mending from behind her chair and sends Ginnie next door to help with their washing. Ginnie thinks she just wants her out of the way.

When she gets back, Mother is sitting in the dull light working on the last few clothes in the mending bag, her eyes puffy with strain. Ginnie stirs the pan of lobby on the stove. Fewer vegetables and pieces of meat mean the stew's easier to stir than usual.

Mabel breezes in and flops into a chair.

'Nothing else going at Chamberlain's, Mother. I went to others on the way home on the off-chance, but there's so many people looking.'

'Never mind.' Mother jumps up, pulls Ginnie away from the stove, and stirs the pan so hard that bits of carrot and potato spatter her hands. She licks her burning skin. It must hurt because it's already turning red.

'Early days yet, love. Summat'll turn up, you'll see.'

Ginnie can tell by the way Mabel sits, arms folded on the table, staring at the wall, that she doesn't believe Mother either. As the girls usually get a clout on the back of the head for leaning on the table, Ginnie thinks Mother must be in a world of her own too.

> Heart thumping. Can't breathe. Can't run. Can't hide. Black night. No moon. Where are you? Feet echoing. Help me. Help.

'Ginnie, wake up. You're dreaming...'

Alone. Help me. Feet echoing. Where are you? Let
go. Am I crying? Help me. Am I screaming? Heart
thumping. Can't breathe.

The black shadow holding her is Mabel. One hand smooths
damp hair from Ginnie's face and the other fumbles for the
candle.

'You're in bed, Ginnie. Shush now.'

Father bursts through the door. 'What the bloody—'

A flame, candlelight.

Dark shapes, soundless, fly from corner to corner growing
bigger and smaller with each flicker of the light sucking her
away from the dream. Distant words become louder as the dark
shapes fade into the remains of a dream, half-remembered.

'Our Ginnie's had a nightmare, Father.'

Ginnie shudders and picks up her damp pillow like a
comforter. 'I was all on my own… so scared.' She stares around
the room. Yes, everything is back in its proper place: the bed,
the wardrobe, the chair, even Mabel. 'I took fright.'

'You look all right now. Get back to sleep.'

Father rubs his hands through his hair and leaves the room.
He closes the door firmly to stop Mother coming in. They
argue, but the door stays shut, and their voices fade away.

'Maybe we can all get to sleep now.' Mabel pulls the pillow,
thumps it, and pushes Ginnie back with insistent hands.

Ginnie soon warms up with Mabel's legs curled around her
but she can't close her eyes and let the darkness back. She has
to be sure nothing is lurking in the corners to creep up on her.

Mabel starts to snore.

Ginnie closes her eyes and breathes hard like Mabel. When
she opens her eyes again, her eyelids feel heavy, but she's just as
wide awake, and it still isn't morning.

–

Ginnie hasn't been sleeping very well since the nightmares started. She tries not to wake Mabel but it's hard being awake when you've got bellyache from all the worry.

Someone's moving downstairs.

Ginnie slides out of bed slowly. In the darkness, she tiptoes towards the stairs and descends carefully. She opens the door to the kitchen just a crack. A small candle lights up the table. Mother's sitting in an eerie orange glow hugging her knees and making funny noises.

'Not the workhouse. Please God, not the workhouse.'

Her hair hangs loose. She doesn't look like Mother as she gets to her feet and hobbles across to the pantry and comes back with the bottle of gin somebody gave Father a few months back in return for a favour. They'd each had one small glass, 'a toast' they called it, and afterwards Mother put it away for a future celebration, except there'd been nothing to celebrate.

She places the bottle on the table and stares at it for ages before taking great gulps, spluttering and coughing. She wipes her lips with the back of her hand and cuddles the bottle like a baby.

'Oh, Joseph. My poor Joseph. I'm glad you can't see what our family has come to.' She's talking to the bottle as if it's a baby. *Who's Joseph? Has she lost her mind?*

Ginnie can scarcely take tear her eyes away. She thinks this is a private moment for Mother, something she wouldn't want Ginnie to see.

Ginnie lifts her nightgown and backs slowly up the stairs. Father has lost his job and Mother's taken to drink. Only bad people drink. She covers her head with the blanket to stop pictures she doesn't want to see rushing round in her head.

The next morning, she gets up with Mabel, who is off to Hanley again to look for better-paid work than she gets sponging the seams out of ware in the clay-end at Chamberlain's. Ginnie yawns and tugs carefully at her too-short dress, afraid she might tear it.

34

'Sit down and eat your breakfast, Ginnie. Mrs Jackson might have work for you today. God knows we need it else we'll never pay the rent this week. And I've got more stuff to take to the pawn shop.'

Mother looks pale but not too worse for wear after swigging back the gin. Nearly everything has gone, even the cabinet that used to get in the way when she sat at the table.

Mother goes upstairs.

Ginnie hisses across the table. 'Mabel, when we were all in bed, Mother was drinking.'

Mabel sighs and closes her eyes. 'Drinking what?'

'Out of that bottle in the pantry what we use for toast. Father got it from the man for the favour. Gin, I think.'

'Don't be daft, Ginnie. She doesn't touch the stuff,' Mabel hisses back. 'You were dreaming. Another nightmare or something.'

'Cross my heart.' Ginnie licks a finger and paints a cross on her chest. 'And another thing – she called it Joseph.'

Mabel looks up sharply. 'What do you mean?'

'She was rocking the bottle in her arms and calling it Joseph.'

'Don't ever mention that name again, Ginnie.'

'Joseph?'

'I said, don't say it. Never.' Mabel bangs the table with a fist. 'You must never tell nobody what I'm about to tell you, Ginnie. Cross yer heart.'

Ginnie crosses her heart.

'Joseph was our brother. He died when he was three.'

Ginnie's eyes grow so big she thinks they're going to burst.

'We never talk about him. He was the apple of Father's eye. Carried him round on his shoulders, he did. Thought the sun shone out of his – well you know what.'

'Didn't you like him very much?'

'Course I did. He was our brother.'

The sound of a box dragging across the floor came from the stairs.

'You must never, ever tell anybody what I've said. And the stuff in the bottle was probably medicine. That's what it'll be. Don't you go spreading lies. You'll get a clip round the ear if she finds out.'

Medicine? Ginnie isn't so sure. And *she* isn't the one telling fibs.

–

Ginnie shouts from the bottom stair. 'I'm off to Mrs Jackson's now, Mother.'

'Give us a hand with this lot before you go, will yer, duckie?'

The box for the pawn shop slides down the stairs but they struggle to get it through the door and into the kitchen. Mother pushes, and Ginnie and Mabel pull.

Mother pants rapidly and rubs her forehead. 'There's nowt else left,' she says, opening the lid.

Almost immediately, Mabel wails. 'You can't take my best coat.'

'I can, and I will. You can only wear one at a time.'

Ginnie spots her best Sunday frock with the blue flowers from Mrs Jackson, and *The Children's Book of Parables*. Much as she loves the dress, it's the book she reaches for, hugging it between crossed arms.

'Please don't give my prize away.'

'I know it's your prize, and I was proud when you got it, truly. But where'll we put it if we haven't got a roof over our heads?'

'But…'

'We all have to give things up for the good of the family. You know that, Ginnie. What good will a book be when you're in the workhouse? You can't even read. Don't be selfish.'

Ginnie's bottom lip trembles. Mother's never called her selfish before. Perhaps she's really worried and doesn't mean it?

The pain in Ginnie's belly is back. She clings to the book. It's hers and nobody else's and she *will* learn to read one day. When she doesn't have to do things for the good of the family, she'll read lots and lots.

But it's no good arguing. Between them, they carry the box into the front room, ready to go to Mr Cox. Ginnie opens the door to a commotion outside.

'Flo, have you heard?' A woman from the next street is standing outside their door swatting herself with a newspaper. 'Oh, dear, I've come over faint. I must sit down.'

'Heard what?'

'Mrs Grimshaw from that posh house up the street passed away last night,' she pants. 'Pneumonia, so they say. Only forty, she was. No age at all.'

'Lord above us.'

Ginnie's family might not have much to call their own, but at least they aren't dead. Ginnie feels sorry for poor Mrs Grimshaw. It goes to show that lots of money doesn't always keep a person safe. Perhaps she should be glad it's only a book that's being taken away.

A three-year-old boy named Joseph comes unbidden into her mind.

–

Mrs Jackson has been a laundrywoman for donkey's years and they work well together. Ginnie stokes up the fire while Mrs Jackson sorts the clothes. Once the tub's full of hot water, Ginnie tips in a pile of clothes and heaves the heavy contents around the tub with the large dolly peg. Mrs Jackson works the mangle, because it's too dangerous for young fingers. Each soggy rag is squeezed between its rollers. Once rinsed, the clothes go back through the mangle twice more and are laid out to dry. Ginnie then sets out more pots to boil as the outhouse steams and it starts all over again.

Ginnie had only been in school five weeks when Mother first told her she was needed elsewhere, for the good of the family. She loved being with the other kids. She could laugh and have fun. On the first day, she opened a book lying on the shelf beside the teacher's desk and wished she could read the words but could only guess at them from the pictures. The day after, Mother had taken her out of school, saying that some things were more important than reading and that she must play her part in keeping the family together. The birthday before last, when Ginnie was ten, Mother had said that what schooling she'd had hadn't been much help if she still couldn't read. Ginnie thought that wasn't very fair. Mabel could read, so Mother said it stood to reason she must be cleverer. Mabel got to go to school so she could get a job when the time came. When Ginnie went back, her teacher had promised to thrash her if she didn't go every day because she was breaking the law, but Father had a quiet word and she never said much after that – just looked down her nose at Ginnie.

Now, when Mother speaks of work, Ginnie keeps her mouth shut, for the good of the family. Each time she goes back to school it's more difficult to remember what has gone before. The little voice in her head tells her she's not as clever as Mabel and she has pains in her belly every time she walks to school. It's easier to work for Mrs Jackson.

At a little after half-past six she trudges home from Mrs Jackson's, too tired to run. In her hand are a few sweaty coppers because Mrs Jackson's a bit short herself this week. She pushes the gate hard and opens the back door.

They all stop talking.

Head held high, she walks to the fireplace and stretches onto the tips of her toes to take the blue-ringed jug down from the mantelpiece. She drops the sticky coins inside and puts it back. The clock chimes the half hour.

Mabel bursts into tears.

'Sit down, our Ginnie.'

Mother strokes away the loose strand escaping from Ginnie's plaited hair and takes her hand.

Suddenly, Ginnie doesn't want to know why Mabel's crying. She tries to cover her ears but Mother grips her hands tightly.

'You need to be grown up and strong, Ginnie. It's not as bad as it seems.'

'I… I'm not a child,' Ginnie's mouth says, but she wants to run upstairs and burrow under the blanket on her bed.

Mother smiles, just a little. 'Your father has tried to get work but there's nowt about at the moment and lots of blokes are looking. We can't pay the rent… so we… we have to go away for a while.'

She smooths Ginnie's hair the whole time she's talking. The ticking of the clock grows louder again.

'Go? Go where? Father…?'

'Can't do it, Flo. I can't…' Father mumbles and rushes outside, slamming the door. The money jug wobbles on the mantelpiece.

'You, me and your father will go to the workhouse tomorrow.' Mother's words rush out in one breath. 'Won't be for long.'

'But I brought you some money tonight. You saw—'

'Yes, love, and it'll be very handy. But there's still not enough to pay the rent, and we need money for food.'

'Well, I don't need much.'

Mother puts a finger to Ginnie's lips. 'I know. We have to go till we get more money coming in. Father'll get a job soon and we'll be home before you know it. Mabel'll go to Aunty Nellie.'

'But I can go an' all. I'll find work.' As soon as she says the words, she stops. Mother and Father will go away and she'll be with Mabel and Aunty Nellie. She'd miss them so much. Wouldn't she be better staying with Mother, even in that godforsaken place?

'You're too young. Mabel's much older and she's bright too; she'll get a better job soon. Besides, Aunty Nellie hasn't got room for you. You'll come with us.'

The workhouse. That horrible place that has frightened Mother for so long. Scenes from the night Ginnie had seen her drinking something that might have been medicine rush back.

Father is alone in the yard, yelling. Through the window, she can see him thumping and kicking anything he can get hold of.

# Chapter Five

## The Red Ribbon

**Haddon – May 1911**

*Don't think about it and it won't happen.*

Ginnie stares at the houses they pass, jealous of the people living inside who don't have to worry about walking to the workhouse. They don't know how lucky they are.

Last night Mabel had given Ginnie the shiny red ribbon she'd argued about all those weeks ago. She tied it into a beautiful bow just above Ginnie's ear and Ginnie had felt like a proper lady as she glided around the kitchen, all of them watching and laughing. Then Mabel spoiled it by crying and saying she'd never forget her.

Ginnie slips a hand into her coat pocket and the silky ribbon wraps itself around her fingers. It shows that even though she will stay with Aunty Nellie, Mabel will be hurting too.

They stop at a narrow road near the top of the hill. Ginnie thinks Mother needs to catch her breath, but she doesn't. Ginnie follows her dull eyes to the huge building still some way off, standing alone among fields abutting the skeleton of deserted colliery workings running as far as the eye can see.

When Mother speaks, her voice matches her eyes. 'They can't bear the thought of it being near decent folk. Why do they have to make it so bloody hard?'

Ginnie drags wet, smarting eyes to the clouds moving across the sky, a streaky grey with the smoke from all the chimneys, as if they're crying too. The sick feeling lingers in her belly and threatens to explode.

Then, the sun slips out of the clouds. Fields of green, brown and yellow come alive. The grey hills in the background look closer. Ginnie has never seen views without any houses. In a field close by, two men stride through long grass, each carrying a sack and a shovel. Two others are waiting beside a hole in the ground. The men dump both sacks and shovel soil over them. Then the clouds cover the sun, and the greenness dies.

'Are those men planting taters?'

Mother pulls Ginnie away. 'No love, they're not planting taters.'

Ginnie asks no more questions and Father's face gives nothing away as they arrive at the workhouse gates. Suddenly, the sun reappears from behind a cloud and the shadow in front of them shows three figures behind bars.

Father opens the creaking gate, straightens his jacket, and takes off his cap before knocking on the door of the first building. An old man wearing thick grey trousers and a flannel shirt shunts them into a tiny room with no windows and a musty smell of sweat.

'Wait here. There's a mighty big palaver going on at the moment.'

The door bursts open. A man younger than Father looks them up and down, and shrugs.

'Follow me,' he says sharply and runs his fingers through his thin, dark hair.

A scruffy man with a long beard and a flat cap hobbles behind them, pulling a face as if it hurts to walk, one of the poor people. Mother used to say that layabouts, those who couldn't hold down a job and wanted money for nothing, were called the 'undeserving poor'. Ginnie had asked who the deserving poor were. Mother said they were the old people and the sick. But Father isn't a layabout, 'cos he wants a job, and they aren't old or sick neither. She quickens her step and bites her nails. And what about the workhouse kids? Are they the undeserving poor?

She tries to remember their route in case they need to leave in a hurry, but all the corridors look the same. Supposing she can't find a way out and she dies, and they bury her in the ground at the front where they aren't planting taters?

She gags but carries on all the same.

The man they're following shuffles them into a room with a desk beside a grimy window and eases himself into the large padded chair beside it. They stand in a row before him and he studies each of them, splaying out his fingers as if making a church with a steeple. Ginnie reaches for Mother's hand and pulls her coat into her chin.

'Three of you looking for a bed tonight?'

Father waits before speaking. 'Yes, sir... maybe a bit longer.'

'Can't say as we'll have room tomorrow. Board of Guardians will decide soon enough.' The man taps his fingers on the desk. 'Got any money?'

'No.'

'Any of you sick?'

'Oh no, sir,' blurts out Mother.

Ginnie squeezes Father's hand, hoping it might calm his short temper.

'We're all fit and well. We were all right until Alf here—'

The man holds up his hand. 'Haven't got no time for your life story, Missus. Give me a chance to say my piece and I'll be happy. We'll give you a bed, but I can't promise how long for. Like I said, Guardians'll decide, make no mistake.'

His watchful eyes narrow as Mother sways and Father has to hold her up.

'You sure you're not sick?'

'Yes, sir.' Mother pushes Father away to prove it.

There's a knock on the door and a woman in a grey woollen dress and white pinafore walks in and stands next to the man.

'Ready, Mrs Hardcastle?'

The woman nods without smiling.

'You two stay here with Matron. You,' he points at Father, '… come with me.'

Ginnie tries to keep hold of Father's hand, and Mother makes a grab for him too, but Matron pulls them both back and shuts the door behind them with a foot. Her striking white hair is scraped back from her face leaving deep wrinkles around her nose and mouth, and not a glimmer of a smile.

'Doctor Roberts'll see you now. Strip to your shifts.'

Ginnie expects Mother to refuse but she doesn't. Her shaking fingers struggle to undo her coat. 'Do as you're told, Ginnie,' she whispers.

'Get a move on. Doctor's waiting,' says Matron, tapping her foot loudly on the dark wooden floor.

Mother keeps herself covered as long as she can. Redness climbs up Ginnie's cheeks. She hunches her shoulders and turns away, struggling with the fastenings on her frock. Matron tries to help but Ginnie pushes her hands away. They shiver in the middle of the room as Matron knocks on the door opposite.

Ginnie was never embarrassed sitting naked in the old tin bath before the fire at home. Her and Mabel often took turns. But today, seeing Mother in such a state is shocking and she can't bear to look.

The doctor is fat with a moustache that curls up at each end. He looks daft and, if things had been different, Ginnie would have giggled. But today, she can see all the bones in Mother's shoulders and nothing seems funny any more.

'No lice? Nits? Temperature?'

'Certainly not.'

Mother sounds proper put out but Ginnie knows there are lots of children with nits. That's why Mother always plaits her hair, so the nits can't get in.

He taps their chests, asks a few more questions, and that's that. He leaves without saying another word.

'You can get dressed now,' says Matron.

Mother pulls her dress over her head. 'Who was the man who brought us here?'

'Mr James? He's the Relieving Officer. Nobody gets in without seeing him first.'

Ginnie's none the wiser, but he sounds important.

Matron takes them to a room called the Receiving Ward, a room full of beds where people have to wait until their case is put to the Board of Guardians, and they are allowed entry into the workhouse.

'You're lucky your case is being considered tomorrow 'cos there isn't another meeting until next week,' she says, bustling away.

A bell will sound for supper, someone in workhouse clothes tells them.

Most of the beds are full of women and many have little ones. Some can't stop crying. Ginnie huddles against Mother on the bed. At least they're together. She only hopes that Father is coping on his own.

*How is it possible for an afternoon to last so long?*

When the bell finally rings the ward is full to overflowing. They follow a woman with a loud mouth who seems to know where she's going. 'Expect nothing and you'll not be disappointed,' she says to anybody listening. Ginnie gets into line and stares at the feet of the woman in front, waiting for her turn to move. Slowly, the line shunts forward.

The inmates are already seated as Ginnie's group arrives in the huge dining hall.

There are no men.

Matron bangs a piece of wood on the table. The chattering stops. She puts her hands together to say grace and when it's over, spoons hit metal bowls. Nobody speaks until every bowl is licked clean. Kids a lot younger than Ginnie cry and ask for more. She tries to eat but gags on the smell of something that looks like broth before it reaches her mouth. She doesn't hold her nose because it might look disrespectful.

Although it isn't dark when the lights go out, sleep is all they can do. Mother's arms creep around her. Ginnie holds on tight, trying to close her ears to the sounds of women and children coughing, snoring and sometimes spitting, but most often crying.

She tosses and turns in the narrow bed and waits for the sun to rise.

—

A bell jangles.

Last night she prayed she'd wake up and they'd all be back home. She promised she would *never ever* complain about helping Aunty Nellie or Mrs Jackson, or not going to school.

But she's awake and the nightmare's still going on.

The dining hall is just the same as last night, but noisier and still there's no sign of Father. She's hungry and swallows her breakfast without chewing so she doesn't have to taste whatever is in the bowl.

By ten o'clock most of the women have left and there's little to be done except lie on the bed and watch the ward fill up again. It's late afternoon when Matron comes through to tell them the Board of Guardians have accepted them into the workhouse. Glancing at Mother's stony face, Ginnie finds it impossible to tell if this is good news or not.

'What about my—'

'Him too, but you'll not see him for a while. This isn't a boarding house.'

Mother grows paler at the news. Ginnie bites her lip. She's sure Mother wasn't expecting that. Her chin feels wet. Automatically, she wipes it and there's blood on the back of her fingers.

They follow Matron up a flight of stone steps to the next floor. She opens a door and waits for them to enter. In front of them is a large iron bath, much bigger than their tub at home, a sink, and a wooden chair.

'Strip off.'

'What, everything?' Mother's voice comes in a funny little squeak.

'How else are you going to have a bath?' Matron disappears into a room next door and returns with grey bundles in her arms. 'The dresses and pinafores are what all the inmates wear. You'll get your own clothes back when you leave, all washed and disinfected.'

'Disinfected?'

'We have to make sure you haven't got nothing what's catching.'

Even Mrs Jackson didn't disinfect clothes.

Matron turns on the taps. 'Best undress now. I have to be here when you take your bath. Workhouse rules, not mine.'

Ginnie has never seen Mother with no clothes on. The water in the bath doesn't even cover her ankles. She's all hunched up to cover the parts she doesn't want Ginnie to see. More embarrassed even than yesterday, Ginnie turns away until the splashes stop, and Mother steps out again, wrapped in a towel hardly big enough to go around her.

Matron changes the water. 'Your turn,' she says and beckons Ginnie to the bath. She makes a move to undo her dress but Ginnie shakes her hands away; she isn't a kid any more.

Mother picks up the longer of the two dresses and holds it in front of her. Both dresses are made of the same grey material that all the women inmates wear. A white pinafore covers most of the dress and, with a bonnet on her head, she no longer looks like Ginnie's mother.

Ginnie tries unsuccessfully to work up a lather from a bar of smelly old soap full of deep ridges. She soon steps out of the bath again and Matron rubs her dry because her whole body is shaking with fear. She pulls on her dress, and an apron that buries her.

'Not so bad, was it?' Matron drains away the water and scoops up their old clothes. 'Have you got any more?'

Mother shakes her head.

'Like I said, you'll get them back when you leave.' Matron stuffs them into a bag.

'Wait! Please Miss?' Ginnie drags the bag from her and kneels on the floor, fumbling inside.

'Ginnie, what on earth are you doing?'

She takes no notice of her mother's cry. She tips the bag until everything is strewn across the floor; she had nearly forgotten the silky red ribbon from Mabel. 'There it is,' she cries, and forces the clothes back into the bag as best she can before handing it back to Matron.

'Finished?' barks Matron with a scowl. 'You'll need these too.' She holds up some wooden blocks with straps. 'Clogs. We can't afford boots for the likes of you.'

The clogs are hard and make loud claps as Ginnie walks. She can't bend her foot, and the toe end catches the floor with each pace.

'Step lively. Superintendent Hardcastle needs to see you. He's my husband, and he's in charge of the workhouse. A very important man.' Nose in the air, Matron heads off down the corridor, knocks on a different door, and beckons them in.

Ginnie has never seen a room so big. A large, highly polished table with lots of drawers stands against a wall with a picture of Burslem Town Hall hanging above it. A man breezes in. He reads the workhouse rules from a torn brown paper and tells Mother she'll be working in the sewing room. He fingers the chain of his pocket watch as he speaks. Instinctively, Ginnie reaches for Mother's hand.

'Well now, Ginnie Jones. We can't keep you in this building because it's for women and little children, and you're not little any more, are you?'

The pains start. She can't hold her belly because that'll mean letting go of Mother's hand.

'We've got a special place for the likes of you.'

'But you can't just take her away—'

Superintendent Hardcastle holds up his hand. '*I* can do precisely as I like, Mrs Jones. Ginnie's eleven. She can't stay here because that's the rules. She'll go to Haddon House Children's Hostel up the road. All the children go there. She'll work, but she'll get schooling, and be with others of her age. Much better than staying here with all the down and outs, wouldn't you say?'

It's another kick in the ribs for Ginnie. Gone: Mabel, Father, and now Mother. Nobody said she would be parted from her family. She shakes her head, frantically.

*They didn't say, they never said.*

'Please, sir, let her stay. I beg you. She's too young to be on her own.'

'I can't do nothing about the rules.'

Matron studies her hands.

Ginnie pulls at Mother's arm, begging her to run. Run from this awake-nightmare.

Mother falls to her knees beside Ginnie, arms around her, firm like ropes.

'Don't let them…' Ginnie tries to hold on but Matron prises Ginnie's fingers open.

'It'll not be for long, Ginnie love.' Mother shakes free of Matron's clutches and kneels in front of Ginnie, hands on her shoulders. 'And you'll go to school too.' With trembling lips Mother can hardly get the words out. 'You like school, don't you?'

Ginnie's hands are wet with a mixture of their tears. 'I don't want no school. I want to stay with you. Don't let them take me away. I'll go to Aunty Nellie's. I'll be good, I promise.'

'You'll get to see her from time to time, Mrs Jones.' Superintendent Hardcastle turns away, his work done.

Matron heaves Ginnie towards the door.

'No, not yet. It's too soon.' Mother cries out.

Panting and red-faced, Matron tries to avoid Ginnie's punching fists.

'Mother! MUMMY!'

Ginnie screams, kicks and claws at the woman holding her. The last thing she sees is Mother, on her knees, crawling towards her, arms outstretched as the door bangs shut.

Ginnie's new clogs rub the skin on her feet as Matron pulls her along the street, back through the emptiness separating the workhouse from the town, to the crossroads where people out walking stare at her. She has been warned not to make a scene for her own good. Bad behaviour only reinforces the perceptions of passers-by, she's told.

Haddon House Children's Hostel lies back from the road up a dirt track squeezing its way between two terraces of houses. Bushes along the track, grown wild with sharp thorns, separate the house from folk who are their betters and people could be forgiven for not knowing of its whereabouts. The house itself is imposing, three storeys, with identical wings on either side. Somebody important might have lived there once. Now it's a home for children without one.

Matron unbuttons her coat, lifts a key from a chain around her waist, and jabs it into the lock underneath a large, round brass knob. The door creaks open. At once, Ginnie's ears are assaulted by loud voices from an open door. but Matron takes no notice. She pulls off her gloves and hurries to the end of the black and white tiled passage, stopping at the door next but one to the end.

It opens into a small room with four chairs, each covered by grey woollen blankets with deep red fringes. A small red rug lies on the polished wooden floor. It isn't cosy like Aunty Nellie's; no pictures decorate the walls, there are no photographs on display. A sob catches in Ginnie's throat.

A tall, thin woman gets to her feet, patting her wavy brown hair. She might have been pretty if it wasn't for her long nose and worried frown. She's younger than Mother because her hair isn't grey, but older than Mabel.

'Oh, it's you, Matron.' The woman wipes her hands down the front of her pinafore and spots Ginnie. She closes her eyes and gives a deep sigh. 'Not another one?'

'Afraid so, Mary. And before you say anything, there's nothing we can do about it so don't go making a fuss.'

Matron folds her coat and lays it on a chair, places her gloves inside her hat and rests it on top of the coat. She sits on the chair next to it with a groan and mutters about her poor legs.

Ginnie waits.

'This is Ginnie Jones. She's eleven and a half nearly. Her parents have just gone into the Big House. She's a healthy-looking girl. A good, capable pair of hands, I'd say. She'll be useful to you. Turn around for us, Ginnie.'

Ginnie feels like a piece of meat hanging in the meat market. Reluctantly, she obeys.

'Where's your manners, girl?' Matron bellows. 'Say hello to Mrs Higgins.'

Still Ginnie can't speak.

Mrs Higgins folds her arms. 'Cat got your tongue, I suppose.'

'When can I see Mother?'

'Bide your turn,' says Matron. 'There's lots of kids here and they all want their mams – those that've got one, that is. You'll soon settle down.'

'Where am I to put her, Matron? I've got no room, you know that.'

Matron rises, groaning, and slips into her coat, jamming the bodkin through the hat with such force it's a wonder she doesn't stick it right through her head and out the other side. She pulls on her gloves.

'You'll manage. She can't stay in the workhouse. You know the rules as well as I do. I'll take my leave now and see myself out.'

She opens the door without looking at either of them. Shouts and laughter from the kids in the corridor fill the room.

'Quiet! Quiet… this is a home, not a fairground!'

The thunderous voice grows fainter as she heads towards the front door. There is a loud bang, and then all is quiet until the chatter starts up again, followed by snorts and giggles.

'Best go upstairs and find you a bed.' Mrs Higgins walks towards the door. 'Come on, girl. I haven't got all day.'

Back in the passage, Mrs Higgins orders the children to be quiet, but she doesn't have the same effect as Matron. Ginnie hides behind her, frightened they might laugh. At least they're all wearing the same dowdy clothes so they can't make fun of her dress and clogs. Children of various shapes and sizes step aside to allow them to pass through.

A wooden staircase off to the right leads to a large landing with several doors, all closed. Instead, Mrs Higgins heads towards a flight of steps leading to a second, much smaller landing with three doors. She opens the nearest.

'The girls' room. You'll sleep in here.' She walks swiftly between two rows of tightly packed beds and stops at the last but one. 'This'll be your bed, but you'll share for the time being.'

The beds are wrapped in the same grey blankets Ginnie had seen in Mrs Higgins' room, each separated by a small wooden cupboard. The blanket feels rough beneath Ginnie's fingers. The room is neat and tidy, but empty.

'Put your coat in the cupboard. You'll share with Clara Woods. She'll put you straight about how we do things. She's been here a good while, has Clara. Any road, it's nigh on teatime. Come on.'

Mrs Higgins bustles out of the room and back to the landing, pointing to a door opposite. 'The bathroom. You'll get a bath a week, whether or not you need it. You'll be told the day and time soon.' She opens the last door. 'Sheets and blankets are kept in here, so take heed. Making beds'll be one of your first jobs.' She herds Ginnie back to the stairs.

'Where do the boys sleep?'

'That's no concern of yours. And I'll thank you to keep well away from them, mark my words.' She wags a finger at Ginnie's nose, causing her to lean backwards to avoid a poke in the eye. 'They're in a wing on the other side of the house. We don't want no trouble here.'

In the now empty corridor at the bottom of the stairs, a bell rings and children reappear from nowhere.

'Quiet now. Single lines into the dining hall please.' Mrs Higgins claps her hands. The talking stops. Children file by, eyeing Ginnie up as they pass.

Three long tables with benches on both sides hold loads of children, talking, laughing, swearing and heaven knows what else. Ginnie counts twelve girls on one table with an older girl in charge. She stands next to Mrs Higgins at the middle table which holds eight sniggering boys. She crosses her fingers behind her back hoping she won't be sent to *their* table.

Before she can count the girls on the last table, Mrs Higgins claps her hands hard.

'*Silence!*'

The talking stops. All eyes are on Ginnie. She wants to wriggle. She rubs the back of her leg with her foot, wobbling on strange clogs, and stares at the floor to avoid the sea of faces.

'Everyone, this here's Ginnie Jones. She'll be with us for a while. Make sure as you tell her where everything is. Clara Woods?'

A girl on the first table rises. Her white-blonde hair straggles a heart-shaped face. She looks no more than nine or ten.

'Look after Ginnie. Away you go, Ginnie.'

Mrs Higgins pushes her towards Clara and waits, foot tapping, for her to shuffle between the benches.

'Sorry... sorry,' Ginnie mumbles as she squeezes down the line.

With her hands together and eyes closed, Mrs Higgins lowers her head and waits for the talking to die down.

'For what we are about to receive, may the Lord make us truly thankful. Amen.'

'Amen.'

Clara grins like a doll and, although small, she's what Mrs Jackson would call 'wiry'. Slurping every last mouthful, Clara licks the inside of her bowl clean. Ginnie puts a spoon to her mouth and swallows something watery with bits in.

'They call it broth, but it's the water the meat was cooked in, and there's not much of that. There's bits of carrot and taters. We get it most evenings. I'll have yours if you don't want it?' Mouth open, spoon half raised, Clara is ready to devour the contents of the bowl.

Ginnie pushes it over and watches her gobble it up surprisingly quickly. With all minds on food, it's safe to look around. The room is full. A woman stirs a big copper and slops a ladle of broth into each bowl as it passes. Only when the bowls are empty do the voices grow loud again. Each child clears away their own dirty bowl although, in Ginnie's eyes, they look as clean as can be.

The children march out of the hall and into a room scattered with stools where they are told to sit still and hold their tongues. The older ones grab the stools leaving the slow ones, Ginnie included, to sit cross-legged on the floor.

When all is quiet, Mrs Higgins reads out the parable of the widow's mites from the *Gospel of St Mark*. Ginnie had heard the story in church lots of times because it was the minister's favourite. A woman gives away her last bit of money to help someone in need. The minister had said they would find favour with God if they too gave away what they could to someone even less fortunate than themselves. She likes the story but doesn't believe the bit about finding favour with God. If you've nothing left to give, how can you ever find favour, and what does finding favour mean, any road?

In no time at all they're sent to bed although it's still light outside. Ginnie follows Clara upstairs. Windows are pulled shut and girls rush about making ready for bed, rubbing their hands briskly up and down their naked arms to keep the blood circulating. Most take off their dresses and sleep in their shifts. The end of spring is still cold. Stockings will keep their feet warm until the heat from the girl sharing their bed thaws them out.

Ginnie waits beside the bed, shyly.

'Do you want to sleep that side?' Clara, already in bed, opens the bedclothes.

Ginnie sits on the edge of the bed and slips her legs under the rough blanket, feeling an urge to scratch. 'Thank you.'

She turns her back and tries to take up as little space as she can so she can pretend it's Mabel lying in bed next to her, but it's Mother she's unable to get out of her mind.

A tall girl from the other side of the room walks between the rows of beds. 'Come on, you lot… into bed. And no talking, else I'll tan your backsides.'

Ginnie stares at the ceiling. She traces a crack from the wall behind her to the corner near the window, a thin spidery web. Everything has changed.

*I won't cry, I won't.* She blinks and blinks again. Yesterday, she had a home and family, and today she has nothing. Missing school and working for the good of the family has got her nowhere.

Coughs, sniffs and the odd loud whisper from girls further down the room keep her awake for ages. She had shared a bed with Mabel all her life, but this is different. In the dark she can hear them all breathing. The world beyond the blanket petrifies her. Monsters under the bed. Beasties inhabiting the dark corners of the room. She doesn't know what safe is any more.

A sob escapes. No one comes to dry her eyes or give her a cuddle. Is this God's punishment for doing something really bad? Because if it is, she can't for the life of her remember what she's done.

'It's all right,' whispers Clara in her ear. 'I'll look after yer.'

Ginnie pushes a strand of hair out of her eyes. Her forehead feels hot, and her cheeks wet. She's glad the room is dark.

'Our Mabel, my big sister… I used to share a bed with her.' After a moment Ginnie says, 'When did you last see your family?'

'I haven't got nobody.'

'No mother? Or father even?'

'Don't think so. I was left here when I was a baby.'

'And you've never been nowhere else?'

Clara shakes her head. She doesn't cry and Ginnie feels very, very small.

# Chapter Six

**After Haddon – June 1914**

The grimy smoke of Burslem collected in Ginnie's throat as she strode through the crowds of workers with Mabel the following day. Carts of bread and milk trundled by, delivering to the big houses at the top of the bank. People jostled past trying to get to work on time. The wheel of a carriage grated on the cobbles behind her and she jumped into Mabel.

'Sorry,' she murmured. Her voice sounded unnaturally formal, as if they'd only just met.

Soon she'd be one of them – the workers. Mabel seemed confident enough that she'd get a job. Even so, Ginnie couldn't help feeling she'd need a barrel-load of luck if this new life was to become anything like the life she had at Haddon. *But it had taken a long time*, she reminded herself.

They turned into a side street and walked towards the entrance to Chamberlain's Pottery, a long building with two rows of small, dirty windows. Set in the middle was a large archway flanked with open iron gates. A queue of men pushed and shoved each other as they shuffled slowly towards the entrance, alternately cursing and pleading for work.

'We're not taking on no men today. Gerroff 'ome, lads.'

The gruff voice grew louder as a man worked his way down the line.

'No work today I say, so bugger off.'

When he reached Mabel, he took off his cap and wiped his face with the back of his hand.

'How're you doing, Patrick O'Malley? You awful busy?'

'Hiya, Mabel, love. Dunno whether I'm coming or going. These blokes won't take no for an answer. Can't say as I blame them, but it don't make my job no easier.'

His voice lost the hard edge it had when speaking to the men. Ginnie suspected he was younger than he looked. Clay dust had tinged his hair white.

A youngish man pushed his way into Patrick O'Malley's face. 'Give us a job. I'll do anything. Got a baby at home and another due any day.'

'Sorry mate.' Mr O'Malley's voice was gentle, but firm. 'Wish I could help, but I canna. Try one of the other potbanks. You might get lucky.'

He patted the man's shoulder and turned him slowly on his way, shaking his head. 'What's the world coming to heh, Mabel? Grown men begging to feed their kin; how can one be more deserving than another? And dunner tell me you've come for your job back in your condition?'

Mabel's cheeks turned a fetching pink and when she smiled, her face lit up. Ginnie had to admit that she was quite pretty. At least she doesn't have to worry about spots no more.

'Course not.' She gave him a soft punch on his arm. 'My Frank's the breadwinner in our house and won't have it no other way. It's our Ginnie here.' She pulled Ginnie in front of her. With one arm around her shoulders she said, 'She's my little sister come to live with us. It's her what wants a job.'

'Didn't know you had a sister.' He shook his head. 'Sorry love, but you heard what I said to all the blokes. Wish I could help, but there's nowt going. The gaffer only wants mouldrunners and that's a job nobody in their right mind would want. Smart young wenches like yourselves would be after getting a better class of work, decorating end maybe?' He winked.

Mabel lapped up his chatter. 'Oh, no, Pat. We're not expecting nothing like that. Our Ginnie would do anything, wouldn't you, duckie? Smile for Mr O'Malley.'

'Yes. And I'm quick, so I'm told.'

'Mouldrunning's a bloody awful job, I'll tell thee that right now. Worst job on potbank, if you ask me.'

A glance at Mabel told Ginnie what she needed to know – a job was a job. Mabel had worked on the pots; she knew what a 'mouldrunner' did. Even if what Mr O'Malley said was true, she was positive Mabel wouldn't let it get in the way.

Before Mabel could open her mouth, Ginnie jumped in. 'I'll do it, Mr O'Malley. I'm a hard worker. You'll not be sorry if you take me on.' She stood tall as she could, her head held high.

Mabel appeared impressed. So, it seemed, was Mr O'Malley. Mabel linked his arm. 'You'd be doing us a big favour, Pat.'

'I'll give the lass a try out. Canna promise more'n that.'

'Thanks, Pat. You're a good man.' Mabel reached up and kissed him on the cheek.

Now the matter had been decided, Ginnie fought the urge to run. It was one thing going for a job, but quite another getting one that nobody wanted.

She couldn't believe she had just done that, and him a complete stranger. Maybe it would've been better to have kept her mouth shut, but she needed to take control. She had a feeling it would've happened anyway, but now, she felt she'd had a hand in it.

'Be ready to start at seven sharp in the morning. Can you fix her up with an apron too, Mabel? The bigger the better.' He turned back to Ginnie and wiggled his finger right under her nose. 'And you'd better not be late.'

–

She spent the rest of the evening preparing herself for the big event of becoming a worker. She didn't consider the jobs she'd done in the past as proper jobs. They were just fillers to help the family, for coppers. This was her first job as a real worker. So, she had to look her best.

'No, you can't wear my frock. It's a dirty old place you're going to. You can wear the old thing you got from that place until you can make yourself something more presentable,' Mabel said, when she asked for the favour. 'I've got a couple of dresses I was going to throw out. You can do something with them.'

Disappointed, Ginnie set to with a needle and ran up a couple of skirts, shortening them and taking them in at the waist, nothing special. It hardly mattered. Her apron would cover all but the hems.

She was starting out afresh and was determined to come through it.

–

Ginnie ran along the cracked, wet pavement at half past six the next morning to be sure of getting to work on time. It didn't take as long as she had anticipated. Her heart was in her mouth as she stopped momentarily at the iron gates. In this light, Chamberlain's looked as much a prison as the workhouse ever was. Most of the people milling around were taller and strong-looking. She was buffeted from pillar to post and felt very young amongst the experienced workers. It reminded her of her first day at the school the workhouse kids attended, knowing no one and alone in the world. She wouldn't want to go through that again for all the pots in Burslem. She almost turned to go back to Mabel's.

A large man with a black beard bumped into her, almost knocking her over. Desperately, she fought for something to hang on to. He let out a stream of curses as she stumbled.

A hand grabbed her by the scruff of her neck and pulled her to one side. She lashed out with all her might ready to fight, and bite, if necessary.

'Bloody hellfire and damnation. The little she-cat hasn't even started work and already I'm regretting it.'

Ginnie swung round and came face to face with Mr O'Malley.

'Sorry, sir. I didn't know it was you. Beg pardon, sir.' Her anger fizzled out as quickly as it had come.

'God help me for taking you on. Don't make me wish I hadn't, my girl. I'm taking you to the casting shop in the clay-end. You'd best look sharp.'

Her legs buckled with relief as he let her go and strode off through the crowds, muttering something about a pain in the arse. She ran after him, wishing his legs were shorter, or hers longer.

The buildings in the yard were black with soot. Two bottle ovens stood in the centre of the courtyard like giant skittles surrounded by buildings with the familiar small, blackened windows. All the potbanks had them. Rickety stairs climbed the outside walls to the upper floors. She stumbled over the uneven cobbles in an attempt to keep pace with Mr O'Malley. He never once turned to check her progress. She felt like shouting, screaming at him, but now was not the time.

He gave the lodge keeper her name. In return, the lodge keeper gave her a yellow card.

'Your clocking-on card. You'll need it if you want to get paid.'

She panicked briefly when she thought they might ask her to read it and very nearly turned to run back through the gates.

'See the number at the top there, that's you. You get this card stamped afore you start work otherwise you won't get paid.'

Mr O'Malley put his own grubby card into a machine and pulled the iron handle down with a strong forearm to stamp the time and waited, tapping his fingers, for her to do likewise.

'If you're more than ten minutes late, lodgekeeper'll close the gate and you'll not get in for another two hours. That means no pay for you. And if you can't get in, it'll cost me money, and I'll give you a good belting, make no mistake.'

She glanced at him sharply, unsure whether or not he was joking. It was then that she dropped the card. She scooped it up and had to use both arms to pull the lever. Mr O'Malley rolled his eyes and tutted. She came to the conclusion he meant everything he said.

Then they were off again. The rhythmic clunking of the engine house sounded like a sleeping giant, snoring, breathing heavily, in and out. It would've been nice to ask about the machines, but Mr O'Malley was striding across the yard and had opened a door in the far corner. She scurried after him before he could have another go at her.

They entered a large room. Slowly her eyes became accustomed to the dull gas lights. The walls were lined with shelves so full of pots and funny-shaped boxes and the like that the space left to walk in was little more than a corridor. Men, boys and women were setting up, women wearing aprons spattered with grey clay, and bonnets to keep the dust out of their hair. Boys clad in aprons topped with flat caps strutted about like little old men. She hid a grin lest somebody thought her daft or an idiot, or both.

Fumes from the lamps mingled with the sickly-sweet smell of damp clay. Already, grit ground between her teeth. She gagged, desperate to hold her nose but not wanting to show any signs of weakness. She shivered in the long, unheated room they called The Shop.

'Me, am a fast worker, see?' Mr O'Malley put on his cap and apron and approached a well-worn bench with a tall machine sitting on it. 'I work this old lump.' He gave it a sharp slap. 'It's a jigger and it helps me make the plates – what's called flatware. So, I'm called a "jiggerer". I'm on piecework and that means I gets paid for what I make. It's your job to make sure I don't run out of moulds, because, guess what?'

'It'll cost you money?'

'You catch on quick for a wench. And if it costs me money, it'll cost you too, because I pays your wages, see?' His nose almost met hers.

'Yes, Mr O'Malley.' The machine stood tall but didn't look overly complicated.

'I expect you to get the stove going and have me bench cleaned and the clay waiting, ready, like. Your job is to keep me stocked up with fresh moulds. And what happens if you don't?'

'It'll cost you money.'

'Got it in one, lass.' He handed her a box, round with a lid. 'Glad we understand each other.'

He took his hand away and she was surprised at the weight of the box, even though it was empty. She very nearly dropped it.

'This here's the mould and after I've filled 'em you gotta take 'em to the drying room and bring me back the empties so's I can fill them up again. It's 140 degrees in there so get out quick. You'll be my mouldrunner and that's what I expect you to do – run!'

His face swam so close she jumped violently.

He sighed. 'You'll be working with George Mountford here.' He pointed to a small lad not much taller than her.

Ginnie paled. That name set her teeth on edge. The face that turned towards her, so instantly recognisable from school, made her feel sick. The bully who had made her life a misery. Why him? Why now?

'Show the wench what to do.' Mr O'Malley strode off to get some water. 'And listen well, lass.'

'What the hell are you doing here?' spat out George.

Surely he wasn't going to cause a scene before she'd even started? She decided to stick to the truth and keep it simple. Hopefully things would be different here in the grown-up world.

'My sister asked him for a job, and he said yes.'

'He only ever pays one mouldrunner normally and O'Malley's always one for a pretty face. You'd better not be after my job, 'cos if you are, you'll be sorry.'

Ginnie put her hand to her collar and dragged it away from her neck. Why should he be worried about someone being after his job? Any road, Mabel had done all the talking.

'I haven't come for your rotten job.'

She held her chin up high and pretended she didn't care. His nose almost touched hers. She hated it when people did that but she chose to say nothing. She had learned to fight only if she stood a chance of winning, but she refused to back away.

'Don't you go causing trouble, workhouse girl. Bet you didn't tell him where you came from when he gave you this job, did you?'

He went to spit but changed his mind as one of the women sauntered by, curious to discover what was going on with the new girl.

'Get in my way, and I swear I'll tell everybody you can't even write your own bloody name.'

Ginnie glanced behind her, searching for Mr O'Malley. He had never asked if she could read or write and, once he'd offered her the job, she didn't dare tell him. After all, she'd rather be Ginnie Jones, mouldrunner, than Ginnie Jones from Haddon Workhouse who couldn't read. Would Mr O'Malley care? So far, she hadn't needed to read anything.

He came back and George moved away quickly. 'Get working, you two. Ten inch today.'

A lad standing beside Mr O'Malley took a wad of clay and batted it into a flat round sheet. When Mr O'Malley was satisfied with its thickness he placed it on the top of the revolving head of the plate mould and shaped it like cutting pastry to fit a pie dish. Then he took the clay off the head and placed it beside him and reached for a new mould.

'Get going, George. Ginnie… follow him and take heed.'

She trotted behind George as he carried two full moulds to the drying room and pushed the door open. The heat threatened to scorch her eyebrows and burn the inside of her nose. She held her breath for as long as she dared. Within seconds, sweat trickled down her back.

George laid the moulds carefully on empty shelves and turned to those on the opposite wall containing moulds that had baked overnight.

'Take the ware what's dried out of the moulds and stack 'em in bungs like this, then take the empty moulds back to Pat. Don't take any old thing. Check for cracks 'cos they'll leave a mark on the clay and ruin the ware. Make sure they're clean and free from dust 'cos that causes the same problem, and you'll be in trouble.'

Armed with empty moulds, they closed the door and hurried back. The air in The Shop felt much colder after the shock of the drying room. She picked up the first full mould and tried to balance it on her hip while picking up the second.

'It's not a job for a weak wench. Each one weighs a good five pounds,' George chimed up.

It seemed easy enough but, as she tottered after him, she soon changed her mind. Before long her back screamed with the sheer effort of standing, never mind lifting the heavy weights. She stretched, trying to undo all the knots.

'You ain't got time to stop,' snarled Mr O'Malley as he banged another mould down on the bench next to her.

She rushed to pick it up and slipped on a small pool of water, almost losing her balance. George sniggered as she limped to the drying room terrified that one of the moulds might slide through her too-small hands and crash to the floor in a thousand pieces as she struggled to open the door. No way was she going to ask *him* for help, but neither did she want him to see her getting a beating.

On one of her visits to the drying room she met the "tow-er" going in, a lanky lad named Fred, who had a permanent whistle. It was his job to collect the bungs of dry ware, sand the edges of the plates with horsehair and put them into saggars for first firing. He grinned at her.

It was the first welcome gesture of the day. His hair curled around his flat cap, covered with clay dust. Even his eyebrows were thick with it and he had a habit of blinking that Ginnie felt a sudden urge to copy.

She smiled warmly. He nodded as he passed, and the whistle started up again. How much better it would be if George was more like Fred.

Back in The Shop she placed an empty mould on the bench and shivered as she waited for the next full one to come her way.

'If you're cold you're not working hard enough, is she, George?'

George sniffed, picked up a couple of moulds and gave a triumphant smirk.

She lost count of the number of journeys she made, alternating between the intense heat of the drying room and the sharp coolness of The Shop. Never once did she let George see how tired she was. She had to impress Mr O'Malley to please Mabel.

At last, the bell sounded and, as Mr O'Malley put on his coat, his face relaxed for the first time.

'You done all right for your first day seeing as how you're new to the pots. You'd best come back again tomorrow.' He walked off, buttoning his coat as he went.

Relief flooded through her. He was a man of few words and that was likely to be as much praise as she could expect. She took off her dirty apron and slipped on her coat with a smile. He wasn't so bad really.

George planted himself in front of her, hands on hips. 'And where do you think you're going? *We* haven't finished yet. We got to clear up all this mess first and get sorted for tomorrow. Unless you want to come in at six o'clock in the morning?'

Sighing, she removed her coat and they worked solidly, not speaking until everywhere was as tidy as a dirty shop could reasonably be. It was past six, and she could hardly drag one foot in front of the other as she headed back to Mabel's, longing for a bite to eat and a comfortable chair.

'You manage all right?' Mabel asked as she walked through the door.

'He said I can go back tomorrow, so I think so.' Ginnie yawned loudly and stretched.

'Good. You can help me finish tea off and there's a bit of ironing needs doing before Frank comes in.'

Ginnie felt a trifle miffed.

–

The 'bit of ironing' turned out to be three of Mabel's dresses, two shirts, four pillowcases and two tablecloths. Also thrown in were some baby clothes that had been freshened up ready to put away for the big day.

Mabel's question about how she got on in her new job was merely a polite link to her housekeeping tasks. It was as if the housekeeping was Ginnie's job and mouldrunning was purely a means of keeping her occupied during the times she wasn't cooking or cleaning.

Ginnie could hardly see as her feet took her upstairs and she fell into bed, but weary bones were the least of her problems. It had been a shock to see George Mountford working there. If she had given him any thought at all, she would have expected him to be working somewhere much grander. Mind you, he always did have something to say for himself.

She tossed and turned, but sleep didn't come. The thought of seeing George tomorrow filled her with foreboding and threatened the fragile confidence she was slowly building.

# Chapter Seven

## Haddon – July 1911

Afternoons are spent at the Board School on High Lane. In their workhouse clothes, the workhouse kids will stand out from the locals. Arguments and fights happen most days, so they say. Ginnie wouldn't have been too worried about going to school if she could read but, in her mind's eye, she could see herself surrounded. The laughs, the butt of jokes, the hurtful words.

So far, she has kept herself busy in Haddon and has avoided school. Mrs Higgins is so rushed off her feet she's never even noticed. The promise she made to herself to learn to read niggles her, but how can that matter when she doesn't have her lovely book any more?

The second month starts much the same as the first but, on her way out of the hall after dinner, Mrs Higgins stops her.

'Ginnie, the schoolmaster, Mr Latham, wants to see you before school starts. Don't go wandering off like you usually do. I'm not blind, you know.'

A flush climbs Ginnie's neck. Her skin tingles. Her mouth's dry and she can hardly swallow.

'We'll set off at half-past one, and don't you forget.'

Ginnie's ready a good ten minutes early and shuffles around waiting for the others. The sun is shining, and she would have enjoyed it if she wasn't dreading the next few hours.

Mrs Higgins leads the straggly line of kids, holding hands in twos. People on foot stop talking and stare as if it's a show put on for their benefit. Creeping along doesn't work because of the pounding of their clogs on the pathway. Some older boys bang their clogs out of step to make even more noise.

At the school gates, Mrs Higgins pushes Ginnie forward.

'He'll be in the schoolroom. Best be quick.'

Ginnie hurries past some lads who point at her and smirk behind their hands. Dressed in neat but old trousers and jackets, they're not workhouse boys. One of them holds his nose. Ginnie glares and sticks out her tongue when Mrs Higgins isn't looking.

She doesn't care. They have no right to laugh.

It's dark inside after the sun and she blinks a few times. Along one wall are rows of neat coat pegs separated by two doors which, on investigation, turn out to be cupboards. She stops outside the only other door she can see, takes a deep breath, and knocks.

No answer.

She moves from foot to foot as quietly as she can, unsure whether to knock again. The door opens. A tall man with white hair and spectacles on the end of his nose, glares down at her.

'Yes?'

'Mrs Higgins from Haddon House told me you wanted to see me.'

'And who might you be?' He cups his ear towards her.

'Ginnie Jones.'

'Well, come in then, child. Why didn't you knock?'

'I… I… did.'

She's talking to his back and has no choice but to follow him to the large desk at the front of the schoolroom. Bits of plaster have broken away from the cream and brown walls where chairs have been pushed backwards too hard. High windows allow the sun's rays to reach only the top third of the walls. Thirty-five small desks, with hinged lids and long thin legs, are set out in five tightly packed rows. Behind each is a plain, wooden, upright chair.

'What did you say your name was?'

'Ginnie Jones. I came to Haddon a month back.'

'In that case, why haven't I seen you in school?'

'Didn't know as I had to.' What else can she say?

'But it's the law. You must attend.'

She doesn't want to get anybody into trouble, especially Mrs Higgins. She stares down at her clogs, another tell-tale sign she's only a workhouse kid.

He takes off his spectacles and wipes them on a large white handkerchief he flips from his breast pocket. 'Never mind, you can start today. You *have* been to school before, haven't you?' He stops mid-wipe.

'When I didn't have things to do for Mother.' Judging by the deep frown on his face, it's not the answer he's expecting.

'I shall expect you in school in…' he pulls out a pocket watch, '… five minutes. Off you go.'

Ginnie raises her head. He has picked up his pen and is writing in a large book, clearly expecting her to leave. She closes the door as quietly as she can. It hadn't been so bad to meet him although she can't rightly say what has taken place.

'What did he want to talk to you about?' asks Clara.

'He asked if I'd been to school before.'

She nudges Clara and points across the yard to where boys and girls have gathered in small groups sniggering at the workhouse kids. One boy stares straight at her. He sneers and says something to his friends. It's the boy she had made a face at earlier. She wishes she hadn't. It isn't a good idea to make enemies before making friends.

Clara pulls Ginnie away. 'That's George Mountford. He treats us all like that. He hates workhouse kids but expects every girl will swoon all over him. You can't trust him so, whatever you do, don't get on his bad side. He's not worth it.'

Ginnie closes her eyes and groans. Well, it can't be helped; what's done, is done.

A bell rings and the school doors open. Minor scuffles, lots of chattering, and the odd dig in the ribs go on as Ginnie stands by Mr Latham's desk waiting for the kids to take their seats.

'Sit down and be quiet.'

The scraping of chairs on the wooden floor sets Ginnie's teeth on edge. The sun has gone in and the room is dull. After a stern glance from Mr Latham, everyone folds their arms on the desks.

'Good afternoon, children.'

'Good afternoon, Mr Latham,' they chorus.

'We have a new girl in class today. Ginnie Jones.'

His hand presses down hard on Ginnie's shoulder as if he expects her to run away. The kids stare. There are no mirrors in Haddon so Ginnie can only picture what a sight she must look by inspecting other Haddon girls.

'Ginnie, you may sit next to Sam White at the front where I can keep an eye on you.'

He turns her to face an empty desk at the front and pushes her towards it. Her clogs sound like drums beating. George Mountford whispers behind his hand to the lad sitting next to him. Ginnie flushes and creeps to the empty seat, burying herself out of view. Has Mr Latham told her to sit next to a boy deliberately to make fun of her?

Lessons begin with sums. Ginnie copies the rest and takes a slate out of her desk. Mr Latham reads out numbers from a book and the kids write them on their slates. The room is quiet except for the sound of his voice and the scratching of chalk. She licks her lips as she concentrates and writes down the answers.

The boy, Sam, grins whenever she looks at him. She recognises him from Haddon. He has only written a little on his slate but doesn't seem to care. She smiles back. He has clear blue eyes and, like all the Haddon boys, his head is shaved. He seems nice and is the only one who has given her a kindly glance. She carries on writing and tries to ignore him. She doesn't want to fall behind.

'Put your slates down.'

Sam is still grinning like an idiot. Ginnie wishes he wouldn't. Deliberately, she turns her back on him.

71

'Read out your answer to the first question, Ginnie Jones.'

She jumps. Heart in mouth, she reads out her answer, turning hot and cold at the same time. Mr Latham nods and turns to Sam. Her thumping heart steadies and she lets out a noisy breath.

'White, what is fifteen take away seven?'

Using all his fingers and thumbs, Sam counts slowly. 'Is it ten?'

'Come on, White. You know that's not the right answer. Think about the numbers again. Pretend they're apples. If you had fifteen apples and ate seven, how many would you have left?'

'Dunno,' says, Sam. 'Never seen fifteen apples. Mam would've crowned me if I ate more than one any road. And I'd likely as not have the bellyache.'

Everybody laughs. He winks at Ginnie. He's probably telling the truth, but she isn't sure about the wink. It's rude to do that in class.

'Quiet. I will not have my class disrupted.' Mr Latham glares at him. 'That'll do. Leave it for now.'

Mr Latham continues round the room but the next time, he leaves Sam out. Sam stares at the wall. He even calls out an answer from time to time in a dull, subdued voice but Mr Latham tells him to hold his tongue, which isn't fair because he's only trying to get to the right answer.

The bell rings for break.

Ginnie places her slate carefully into her desk and gets to her feet. She had thought Sam was younger than her but when he stands up he's as tall as she is.

'Eight apples,' he says over and over as he follows her outside. 'That *would* be a basket full.' He pretends to juggle with his hands and laughs, winking again. *So he does know the answer.* Ginnie can't help smiling.

Clara catches up with her and whispers in her ear. 'Sam's strange in the head. Mrs Higgins says he's a bit slow, but I've heard Matron say as he's mental. I don't know if it's true. I don't talk to him very much – him being a boy.'

Ginnie gazes up at the soft white clouds barely moving in a sky as blue as Sam's eyes. Her face burns at where her thoughts are heading and she deliberately turns her back on him, linking arms with Clara instead.

In no time at all they're back inside.

'That's enough sums for now,' says Mr Latham. 'You will each come to my desk and read a page from this book to the rest of the class.' He waves it above his head as if swatting flies. 'Is that clear?'

Judging by the groans, Ginnie isn't the only one wishing school was over. She makes herself as small as possible in her seat, swallowing to stop sick rising towards her throat. She tears a strip off a nail and blood oozes out. Quickly, she licks away the blood but stops when she realises she's sucking it like a baby. Instead, she uses a finger to stem the flow.

He chooses kids at random so it's impossible to tell when her turn will come.

'Clara Woods.'

Clara squeezes behind the chairs and walks steadily to his desk. She reads quietly, tripping over the longer words, but finishes the page and receives a smile from Mr Latham for her efforts. She raises her eyebrows in relief and grins at Ginnie as she returns to her seat. 'You'll be all right,' she whispers.

Two boys and a girl read their pages quickly. Three boys, dressed in workhouse clothes, are sent to the corner where the dunces gather, fidgeting and scratching their heads. One young boy, who has stood alone in the corner for ages, is still shaking under the sniggering gaze of the rest of the class. Ginnie keeps her head down and swallows constantly. It's easy to imagine herself standing next to him.

'Ginnie Jones.'

Her arms turn to stone, too heavy to lift off her desk. She bites her lip to stop herself from blarting. It will never do to be a cry-baby *and* a dunce who can't read.

73

'Jones? You're next. Come to the front when I tell you.'

The room is silent. Swaying, she gets to her feet and hopes she might faint. She doesn't. Instead, she makes her way to the front of the class, wincing every time her clogs bang on the wooden floor.

She picks up the open book. Groups of letters swim across the page. She recognises small words like 'the' and 'but,' but the rest may as well be tea leaves in a cup.

Never has she felt more alone. She risks a quick glance at Clara sitting wide-eyed waiting for her to start, her small teeth holding fast to her bottom lip.

Ginnie takes a deep breath and points at the first word with a sweaty white finger. It sticks to the page. She tries to swallow but her tongue's too big for her mouth. And she can feel tears slowly making their way down her cheeks.

'The... the...'

The room is deathly quiet, all eyes on her. 'I can't,' Ginnie whispers into the book.

'Speak up, child. I can't hear you?'

'I can't read,' she mumbles, louder this time. 'I can't... *read.*' She spits out the last word and glares at him for making her say it. Buzzing voices fly around the room. Now she's said it, she wants to say it over and over to shut out the tittering. She hates herself and the whole world for what has happened today.

'Not any of it?'

She grits her teeth and shakes her head, unable to speak.

'You'd better join the others.' Mr Latham points to the dunces' corner with a look of disappointment. Once again, she has failed.

Head down, she crosses the floor to join the small group huddled there. Even with her shoulders hunched, she's easily the tallest. She stares at the floor so she can't see the faces laughing back at her.

Mr Latham clears his throat. 'Next? Oh, it's you White. You can stay where—'

'No, sir, I'll do it.'

At hearing Sam's voice, Ginnie sneaks a glance. He jumps out of his seat. To the sound of titters, he stands beside Ginnie's empty chair and make a big thing of moving it out of his way. He trips over the leg and ends up in a heap on the floor with a puzzled look on his face. It takes time for Mr Latham to regain control of the class.

'I don't know why you're in such a hurry to read, Sam White, when you obviously do not have the skills to do so, but I suggest you join the others in the corner. And, if you can oblige us by getting there in one piece without tripping or falling, we might continue with the class.'

Sam swaggers across the room, hands in his pockets, and gives Ginnie a wink. Despite everything, she turns away as a giggle threatens to explode from her mouth, glad the class has someone else to look at. Then she catches sight of George Mountford jeering, and lowers her gaze.

The afternoon lasts forever. Her legs ache but she daren't move and bring attention to herself. Clara's eyes are full of sympathy and Ginnie prays that she will still want to be her friend.

Standing there, itching to scratch her nose, her anger builds. She… *hates*… Mr Latham. Even in her mind, she can hardly get the words out. And when the bell rings for the end of school, she storms out, wanting to run as fast as she can, vowing never to look at his hateful face ever again.

Clara runs after her. 'Lots of people can't read or write,' she pants. 'We've been reading that book for ages. We know what the words look like, that's all.'

Ginnie slows and squeezes Clara's hand, appreciating the feel of friendship. Clara knows she's a dunce who can't read, and still wants to be her friend. Even Sam grins and pats her back.

'Dunce! Dunce! Where's your silly hat?'

It's George Mountford.

A small group have gathered around him, egging him on. The workhouse kids stand behind Ginnie, their hands in their pockets. Ginnie lets out an uncontrolled gasp. Her instinct is to run but Clara has linked her arm and refuses to let her go. And so they stand, workhouse kids united.

'Hey.' Sam steps in front of her. 'Watch me lips, George. I'll only say this once.'

His voice is slow and quiet, and it comes to Ginnie that he isn't mental at all. He knows exactly what he is doing as sure as eggs is eggs.

'We're all here for learning. Keep your big mouths shut. All of you.' Sam waits for his words to sink in. ' 'Cos if you don't, I'll give you something to talk about.' He raises his arm and the boys back off, whispering and sneering.

George shakes his fist and Sam makes a move towards him, but Ginnie grabs his coat. The boys saunter off with George, sneering, and giving the occasional whistle.

Ginnie turns on Sam. 'You shouldn't have done that. You'll get into trouble.'

He shrugs. 'They had it coming.'

'But they'll go on at me all the more now…' she wails, '…and they'll laugh at me. I have to stand on my own two feet.'

'Your mam isn't here. Who else'll look after you?'

Ginnie's bottom lip trembles. 'I have to do it myself.'

He grins. 'That's what friends is for.'

'No, Sam.' She holds her head high. 'I've got to fight my own battles from now on.'

She runs through the yard and out of the school gates, startling an old woman walking by. The woman shakes her fist, but Ginnie carries on, too upset to say she's sorry.

Clara catches her as they arrive at Haddon. 'Why did you scarper? We aren't allowed out on our own.'

'I couldn't stand no more.'

'You should've waited for me so we could come back together. Why is reading such a big thing?'

Ginnie stares for a moment. 'You don't know how it feels. Everybody knowing you're one of the dumb ones. I couldn't go to school very often. I had to work – when I could get it – for the good of the family.'

She pulls away sharply. 'I *hate* Mr Latham. I'll *never* go back. And you can tell Mrs Higgins, for all I care.'

She shoots up the stairs to the first landing. Checking no one's watching, she squeezes herself onto the window ledge behind the long, thick curtains. With her head resting on her knees, she hugs her legs and closes her eyes. The tears she couldn't shed when everyone was looking splash onto her knees.

# Chapter Eight

*A Tanner*

**After Haddon – June 1914**

'Best get up unless you want to be late.'

A loud rapping shook the bedroom door and the unfamiliar sound of a man's voice so close had Ginnie sitting on her pillow fighting for breath and holding the bedcovers tightly around her. She trod carefully as she walked down the stairs trying not to yawn, painfully aware of her aching legs and leaden shoulders.

'Too much f'yer was it?'

Unsure of the best way to deal with Frank's sarcasm, she ignored him. It didn't feel right, just the two of them in the kitchen, his eyes watching her as she made her snapping for dinner time – a bit of dripping spread on a chunk of bread. In future she would make it up in the evening, before Mabel went to bed. Then she could get up after Frank had gone to work and she'd have the place to herself.

'Yer not bad-looking, yer know,' he sneered. 'And you've got a job an' all. Maybe we'll… get on all right.'

Ginnie burned hotter, first from shyness, then anger. 'Make one move towards me and I'll swear to God, I'll tell Mabel.'

'My word. You've a bit of gumption too. I like that. And what makes yer think *she'll* believe yer? You've only been back in her life five minutes.'

He moved closer and his eyebrows rose when she didn't back away. She glared, willing her mother's voice inside her head, to give her the strength to stand her ground.

'I came 'cos Mabel asked me to.' She took a deep breath and held her chin high. 'I'm not afeared of going back to Haddon. And if I go, *you* can tell *my* sister why.'

She felt she was being tested but it was Frank who backed away.

'I was only being friendly. Besides, it'll be your word against mine.' He picked up his snapping – a hunk of bread and a bit of cheese – and placed it in his bag, whistling. 'I'll be off then. I'll see yer later.'

She didn't relax until she heard the front door slam. Slowly, she sank into a chair. With shaking hands, she thrust her own snapping into her bag. He wouldn't want to cause trouble with Mabel in her condition, surely?

Frank preyed on her mind on her walk to work and she ended up running part of the way. She dived through the gates and clocked on. At least she knew where she was going today. She took off her coat moments before Mr O'Malley breezed in.

'Right, Ginnie, lass. You've had it fairly easy so far.'

She didn't know him well enough to disagree.

'But you're on yer own today, so you got to be on yer toes.' He scowled from behind the jigger.

Her heart missed a beat. Where was George?

'George? Where the hell's that lad now?' He stared over Ginnie's shoulder. 'There you are. You'll be doing a bit of mould making today. Jump to, lad.'

George was standing behind her, his usual scowl replaced by a huge grin. For a brief moment she actually thought she *had* taken his job, but it turned out that he'd gone up in the world because another bloke had been taken poorly. If *she* hadn't been mouldrunning, *he* might not have been given the chance, so *he* should count his lucky stars.

Judging by his face, Mr O'Malley doubted she could manage on her own, especially when she panicked and dropped a mould. Burning with embarrassment, she muttered a quick apology, scooped it up, and busied herself so as to keep out of his way. At least he hadn't taken a swipe at her for being clumsy.

She worked better when George wasn't close by, quickening her pace and hardly speaking to anybody as she flew between The Shop and the drying room. Later in the day, Ginnie watched as George crept up behind Elsie. He untied her pinny and when she bent over her bench, the top fell into the wet clay. Spying him laughing, Elsie hurled abuse at him, and Ginnie couldn't help but laugh too.

Surprisingly, George winked at her before sidling off out of sight. Ginnie felt Elsie'd had it coming to her, making up to him, and then pushing him away. She straightened her face as she caught a scowl from Elsie, who'd worked at Chamberlain's for years, and could make things difficult if she had a mind to.

Now he wasn't mouldrunning and not under Pat O'Malley's thumb, George appeared more relaxed, chatting with the lads working at the next bench. Even so, when she got behind with the moulds, he sidled up to her and prattled on about wenches not being strong enough. She ignored him, and that didn't go down too well either.

'I'm no bloody mouldrunner now and I'm damned if I'm gonna help you.'

'I don't want no help. Any road, you should thank me.'

'What d'yer mean?'

'If I wasn't here, *you'd* still be mouldrunning. So, think on, George Mountford.' She lifted her nose in the air and flounced off.

'Wha— I mean don—'

If he said anything else, she didn't hear him.

She worked quickly. She didn't want a telling-off in front of everybody. She guessed that Mr O'Malley would have preferred having a boy working for him and had only taken her on to please Mabel. She would give him no cause to regret it. She glowed when he dropped a few words of praise in her direction and worked even harder. She'd heard it said that he was always fair. Some bosses didn't think twice about punishing mistakes with their fists.

She began to take notice of her fellow workers. The man on the next bench was a "jolleyer", making perfect bowls, beautifully smooth. His mouldrunner was also small and fast and Ginnie competed with him, matching him for speed, even though her moulds were heavier. To him it was just a game; he'd pretend to run and change his mind. But Ginnie had something to prove to herself as much as to the rest of them.

Each night she helped Mabel prepare the evening meal, wash the pots and pans, and generally kept the place tidy while Frank disappeared down The Flying Horse on the corner of East Street until his money ran out. Mabel put her feet up most evenings.

The tiredness didn't go away but Ginnie managed to stay awake longer in the evenings as she grew accustomed to her new life. If it hadn't been for Frank and George, she could have settled more quickly. Mabel was teaching her to knit a scarf but she found it difficult to follow. There were more holes in it than in a net curtain. Mabel said it would do her good to keep at it but had indicated firmly that she didn't want Ginnie to knit for the baby.

Mabel was basically idle and left much of the housework to Ginnie, who tried to give her the benefit of the doubt, but couldn't help thinking that other women didn't have the luxury of someone else doing their housework even when they were expecting. She hoped Mabel wasn't just using her until the baby was born.

Mabel always asked Frank about his day over tea and was ready with sympathetic words at just the right moment. She threw in her half-pennyworth about all the jobs that needed to be done around the house, but never actually said who would do them. The first time it happened, Frank pointed his fork at Ginnie.

'Make sure as you help your sister as much as you can, else you'll have me to answer to. She's got enough on her plate what with the baby coming. She can't be running around after you, not when—'

'No, Frank.'

Mabel's tone was surprisingly firm and stopped Frank in his tracks. Ginnie gazed at each of them, but Mabel had her head down, moving peas around her plate. Frank changed the subject. It was difficult to catch what he was saying because he had taken a mouthful of food and bits of it flew across the table as he spoke.

*What had he been going to say before Mabel stopped him*, Ginnie wondered? *Something serious?* Mabel, it seemed, still had *some* power over him.

He hadn't made a move towards her since those first couple of days, much to her relief. She might have misread his intentions. Perhaps it was the novelty of sharing a house with two women that had led him behave as he had at the beginning. It seemed strange to think of herself as a woman, though. She was the girl from Haddon, and always would be.

—

At the end of the week Mr O'Malley picked up his wages from the lodge and counted out the coins at the of back of The Shop ready to dole it out to his workers. Ginnie was the last to get hers and, by the time he got around to her, she could hardly keep still for excitement. For the first time in her life she would have money to call her own that didn't have to go into the blue-ringed pot on Mother's mantelpiece.

'Ginnie! Over here.'

She took the coins from his rough, dirty hands and counted them. Six shillings and thruppence – more than she had ever seen before, and *she'd* earned it.

George came up behind her and sniggered. 'Think you're rich now, do you?'

'I'm not complaining,' she said, refusing to let him spoil the moment.

'You aren't worth much, a young wench like you. That's why he took you on. You're cheap.'

'S'only right. You've been working longer.'

'That's nowt to do with it. You're just a wench. If you work all the hours in a day you'll never be worth eleven shillings.' He shook the dust from his cap and put it back jauntily.

Eleven shillings. Her six shillings was a piffling amount. Why should lads be worth so much more than girls? She stuck her tongue out at him and then wished she hadn't as a huge grin spread across his face. She cossed herself for letting him get under her skin. *I'll make you eat your words, George Mountford*, she vowed.

The cleaning was finished in record time. With the coins safely in her pocket, Ginnie hummed as she put on her coat, determined to keep the excitement of her first week's wages alive. It would all be worth it if she felt this good every week.

'I'm off to the Red Lion with the blokes. You'd best get off home, back to your mummy!'

'I haven't got no mother... she's dead... if it's any concern of yours.'

She fastened the buttons of her coat and brushed past, leaving him tongue-tied for once. Her wages were far too precious to drink away at the pub. She would give some to Mabel for board, put some by for Sam, and still be able to buy dress material, she hoped.

It was good to be alive. Sam felt particularly close tonight. Maybe Mabel would let her visit Haddon on Sunday. It would be good to see Mary too. She'd earned one day off.

By the time she arrived back at North Street, the coins in her pocket were hot and sweaty. She skipped into the kitchen, straight into Mabel and Frank having a row. They jumped apart when they saw her, Mabel tearful and Frank angry. She glanced from one to the other, hands still in her pockets, not knowing whether to take off her coat. Frank sidled towards her and she backed away, not taking her eyes from his approaching hands.

'See here now, Ginnie. We was just discussing how much you're going to give us for your board.'

Her hand closed protectively around the coins deep within her coat pocket. Was he going to take them all?

'Show us what yer got.' His hand splayed out like a shovel and a finger beckoned.

She sent a frantic gaze to Mabel, but she'd turned away. Ginnie slid one of the coins out of her hand and let it sink back into her pocket as she lifted her clenched fist. Slowly, she opened it; a few shillings, tanners and coppers sat in her palm. Frank scooped them up and counted.

'Not much for over sixty hours! You sure this is all you got?'

'Yes.' She crossed her fingers.

'Course she's given it all to you, Frank. She's just a strip of a girl. She'll not get much yet.'

Ginnie shot Mabel a grateful smile. Frank glared at them both.

'S'pose it'll have to do. But if I ever find as you've been cheating me, I'll make sure you wish you hadn't. Do you hear me?'

Ginnie could only nod.

'Here's a bit of pocket money. We don't want to take everything, do we, Mabel?'

Unexpectedly, he tossed her two silver tanners which she failed to catch. She scrambled under the table to search for them. With her eyes full of tears and her newly found pride in tatters, her hand closed over the coins. Slowly, she eased herself backwards and got to her feet. It was all she could do to keep control, to stop the words she wanted to scream at him, to hold back the hands that were itching to hit him. This then was the price of his humiliation when she told him to keep away from her. Well, she could cope with him taking her money better than him treating her like a street girl.

Mabel looked genuinely upset. Ginnie, concerned for the baby, kept her mouth shut. Pity Mabel hadn't stuck up for her, though. Nose in the air, she walked past her sister and up the stairs. As far as she was aware, Frank hadn't moved.

Their voices carried on, but quieter.

In the safety of the bedroom she stared at the coins she had left. All were sweaty and hot, two tanners and a penny. In one fell swoop he'd managed to do what George, for all his ways, couldn't – to take away her spirit. It was true what she had told Sam; good things were almost always followed by bad.

She slipped one silver coin into the carpetbag. She wouldn't spend it, no matter what. It would be a token of her freedom. Out of the rest of her money she would have to buy material to make a new dress before she started looking indecent. Once she'd done that, she'd be penniless again and all because of Frank. To him she was nothing but a wench feeding off the goodwill of others. Maybe Sam was right about them taking her as a servant. Next week she'd take some money out of her pocket before she got home and find somewhere to hide it. And then, when she had enough put by, she would leave, hopefully with Sam.

There was a knock and the door opened. Ginnie jumped to her feet, but it was only Mabel.

'It's all right. Frank's gone out.'

Ginnie sank on to the bed, surprised how wobbly her legs felt. As their eyes met, Mabel's pale face flushed.

'Why didn't you stick up for me?' Ginnie's voice was little more than a whisper.

'Once he gets used to you being here, he'll come around. He was only joking about the money.'

Ginnie turned a stony face towards Mabel. 'For all that you think Haddon was a terrible place, I never felt as bad as I do now.'

'I'm so sorry, Ginnie. He doesn't mean it, you know.'

They were just words and words held little comfort when the person who spoke them didn't believe them either.

Day followed day in a similar pattern. Early rise, work, house-keeping, and sleep. Just like the workhouse. No freedom. Freedom was something people have who are lucky enough to choose what they do with their lives.

She was getting on reasonably well with Mr O'Malley. He never complained about her and was more like a strict father figure than the rest of the bosses. She still hankered after trying out some of the machines but decided to bide her time. She had seen the girls from the decorating end going into work, smart young ladies walking briskly, going about their business. People from the clean-end didn't talk to the common, clay-end women.

The end of June turned warm and bright. After tea at the end of the week, they sat around as usual. Mabel was knitting a bonnet, her tongue caught between her lips in concentration. The wool had been bought with the money Ginnie had paid for her board. She knew that because the wool appeared two days after Frank had taken the money from her. It made her feel better somehow.

Frank was reading *The Staffordshire Sentinel*. Ginnie hadn't seen him read anything else. If *she* could read, she would have lived in another world where people had dreams, and dreams came true. In real life she couldn't read, and dreams never came true.

Frank whistled through his teeth. A duke had been killed in a foreign country and all hell had broken out. Some countries were already fighting, he said, but England wouldn't join in. Why go looking for trouble? The fighting was in Russia and Austria, and the English Channel separated England from all the goings-on over there.

# Chapter Nine

### The Red Shottie

**Haddon – October 1911**

Ginnie is the oldest dunce in the class apart from Sam, and *he* doesn't know how old he is. Mother and Father had said she wasn't as brainy as Mabel. And they were right. She'd been so proud to get the Sunday School prize but all she'd had to do was turn up. So here she is, Ginnie Jones, the only girl in the school who can't read. Nobody, not even Clara, can understand how lonely *that* feels.

Clara has promised to help and is as good as her word. Almost too good. Every evening she's there, book in hand, until Ginnie feels like screaming. Clara has spent all her life at Haddon and can still do something Ginnie can't. Panic sets off pains in her belly for being so stupid.

Somehow, she has to take Clara's mind off the reading, if only for a day or so. Ginnie stares at Sam across the other side of the room until he looks up. She pulls a face and shrugs towards the ceiling and then at Clara. Seconds later he wanders off, and then he's back.

'Fancy a game of shotties?'

He croodles on his knees beside them holding a small draw-string bag.

'What's that?'

'You've never heard of shotties? Marbles?'

Ginnie shakes her head. 'Is it a boy's game?'

'Well, girls are not as good as boys mostly,' he grins. 'I'll show you.'

He unties the string and lots of glass balls tumble out, their bright colours catching the light as they roll across the floor. He holds one up to the lamp and it glows like a star.

Clara flashes the book at him. 'Go away, Sam. Can't you see we're reading?'

'How do they get them colours inside?' Ginnie reaches for a bright yellow ball. 'They're beautiful.'

'Dunno, but you can have it if you want. Don't play with it till you think you can win else you'll lose it.'

She rolls the shottie round her hand and watches the reflections dance across her palm.

'You're never going to learn to read if you don't stick at it,' says Clara.

Ginnie feels ashamed, but the reading is so difficult and the shotties are so beautiful. She hands it to Clara. 'Look at it. See all the colours, ever so pretty they are.'

Clara shrugs her shoulders. 'If that's what you want…' She lowers her voice. 'But don't blame me when we have reading classes again.'

She wanders off, muttering to herself.

'Right, watch what I do.' He takes a long piece of string from his pocket and places it in a circle on the floor. 'I'll lend you some shot…'

'Slow down, Sam.' She lays a hand on his arm and he stops, mid-word. Maybe he doesn't like being touched by a girl.

'I ain't started yet. We put the shotties in the circle but keep some back: they're the shooters. We each take turns to flick the shooter and knock shotties out of the ring. Whoever's got the most at the end wins.'

'Sounds easy.'

Sam snorts. 'See how far *you* get if you think it's so easy.'

Ginnie picks up a shooter and flicks her thumb. The shottie falls to the floor with a thud and rolls away from the circle.

She tries again and the same thing happens. She can't even play shotties. She backs away.

Sam grabs her hand. 'Here, I'll show you again.'

He places the shottie on her thumb. It's strange being that close to a boy. He feels hot and sweaty.

'Watch… now.' His thumb flicks at hers. The shottie jumps into the circle and comes to a rest. 'See?'

'How'd you get so many?'

'Won some. Brung some with me when I come. Found the rest in the yard at school.'

'You must be good.'

He shrugs.

'How long have you been in here?'

'Mam died when I was naught but a kid. I think I was seven or thereabouts. She worked on a potbank at the bottom of Burslem. She was a "dipper's girl" – what dipped the ware into the lead glaze before it went for firing. Made it nice and shiny. She hated it but she couldn't do nowt else. It gave her bellyache. All the dippers had belly pains. They reckoned it was something in the glaze. Every morning she drank some white stuff. It put a lining on her stomach she said, so's it didn't hurt so bad. It kept her going. She worked hard and didn't let it stop her till near the end. Made me promise never to work in a potbank though.'

'What about your father?'

'Last I heard, Dad worked away at sea. Ran away from home soon as he was old enough to work. Couldn't stand being cooped up inside. Don't really know how him and me mam got together – him being away all the time. Must've come back one time and found her. When he was at home they rowed. I was always glad when he went away again. God knows how they managed to get hold of him when Mam died. Ma Ford, from next door, must have known, I think. I used to go to her house while Mam was at work. Dad come home for the funeral and hardly said a word, apart from asking Ma Ford to look after me while he sorted things out. Said he was going to ask about Poor Relief. He scarpered. Didn't want to be saddled with no young-un's. Ma Ford couldn't take me in for keeps when nobody was paying, not with five kids of her own. That's how I ended up here. Wasn't nobody else.'

'How old are you now?'

'Eleven or thereabouts, I think. Nobody ever told me.'

'Same age as me,' she smiles. 'Do you ever see him?'

He shakes his head.

'My father was a potter.' Ginnie's bottom lip quivers. 'He lost his job because he couldn't see properly.' It was the first time she'd told anyone at Haddon. It struck her that her story wasn't the saddest she'd heard. She *did* still have a mother and a father.

A clap of hands behind them makes them jump.

'Let's be having you in for tea. Unless, of course, you don't want any?'

It's Mrs Higgins. There's a scramble for the door. Fighting breaks out as two lads try to be first out of the room only to have their ears boxed for their trouble. Ginnie follows the rest and watches Sam make his way to the middle table.

'Hey, lads. Guess who's been playing with the wenches?'

Sam lurches at the lad who has spoken and receives a frown from Mrs Higgins.

He's not hard like the others. Ginnie slips her hand into the pocket of her apron and clasps the yellow shottie hard until it feels as if it's burning a hole right through her hand. Reluctantly, she pulls her hand away in case it melts into her fingers.

Mrs Higgins claps her hands for silence. 'I'm going to the Big House tomorrow, and I'm taking Fred, Sarah, Alice and Ginnie with me.'

The Big House is Haddon Workhouse where the grown-ups live. Ginnie claps her hands and bounces up and down in her seat, unable to stop herself. The waiting is nearly over. She has lots of news to tell Mother and Father – about her new friend Clara, and Sam who might be her friend if he wasn't a boy. He's looking at her now. She grins back.

'Hey, Sam? You staring at the wenches again?' says another of the boys.

Sam leans over and boxes the lad's ears. 'Shut your mouth. It's nowt do with you, any road.'

'Maybe he wants to sit with them. Just look at his face!'

'Dunner be daft. I'll have your tea if you don't watch it.' Quick as a flash Sam grabs a bowl and threatens to tip the contents over his tormentor's head.

'Hey, wotcha…'

Ginnie smothers a grin. Mrs Higgins has come up behind him and clouts the back of his head sharply with an open hand. He ducks now in case a second one follows.

'Sam White… If you haven't finished eating in five minutes, I'll give it to somebody as wants it.'

The talking stops and the bowls are emptied soon after.

—

It's fun sharing a bed with Clara, better than sharing with Mabel. They whisper to each other long after the rest have gone to sleep. Mabel never wanted to talk in bed. What did *she* have to say to a little sister?

Ginnie is unable to take her mind off the visit tomorrow and sleep feels a long way off. 'Wonder what our Mabel's doing?'

'Sleeping, if she's got any sense,' Clara mumbles into her pillow.

'Don't be daft. They don't go sleep this early on the outside.' Ginnie turns over and lies on her back staring at the crack in the ceiling and follows the spidery pattern. Will it grow and grow and cover the whole ceiling like a big, bare, wild plant?

'Mabel said she'd come and see me. I wish she would.'

'Wasn't she looking for extra work?'

'Are you saying she's too busy? Oh Clara, I can't wait to see Mother and Father,' she mutters at the crack in the ceiling.

'You'd better go to sleep or else you'll get really, really tired. Just like I am right now.'

She sounds cross. Ginnie tosses and turns trying to get comfortable and catches Clara with her knees.

'Ouch!' Clara gives her a dig at the bottom of her back in return.

The next time she turns over, Ginnie tries to do it as slowly as possible so as not to wake her. How long till morning?

–

Ginnie scrubs her face so hard it goes all blotchy, or so says Clara. And she's brushed her hair so long that it flies out like a black halo around her head.

'Do I look all right?' she asks for the umpteenth time. 'I wish we had a mirror.'

'Whether you look good or not, there's nowt you can do about it. Just be thankful as you've got a mam and dad to meet.'

Clara's eyes are misty, too bright. Ginnie had clean forgotten poor Clara had nobody. How could she have been so wrapped up in herself? She hugs her friend. 'Sorry for going on about it. You must think I'm a real pig.'

'It's your mam and dad. S'only natural isn't?'

There might be a tear on Clara's cheek. She's never seen Clara cry. She gives the impression that she can look after herself. Maybe she just has a different way of showing her true feelings. Ginnie vows to be especially nice to her when she gets back.

By the time she arrives in the hall by the front door, the other three are waiting. Mrs Higgins is wearing her best coat and struggling to get her hat on straight. She stabs a pin through it firmly and opens the door, muttering about being late as if *they* were the ones at fault.

The small, wiry man, who opened the door to Ginnie and her parents when they first came to the Big House, lets them in. On seeing Mrs Higgins, he grins broadly, showing uneven yellow teeth.

'How do, Mrs Higgins? It's a while since we've seen you in these parts.' He sweeps off his cap and gives a lavish bow.

Ginnie thinks he has a fancy for Mary but she can't imagine the two of them together, him being a bit on the rough side. The look on Mary's face is enough to send him packing. Ginnie smothers a grin.

'You know why I've come, Ephraim Tolley; I'm here most weeks, as you well know. Be good enough to tell Matron I'm here with the children.' She draws herself up to her full height and turns her back on him, fussing about the kids and re-checking hands and faces. Mr Tolley frowns and disappears through the door opposite.

As usual, Matron's voice is heard long before they see her, ordering Mr Tolley back to the porter's lodge, and giving instructions about tea to somebody. She herds the children into the huge dining hall where rows upon rows of tables line up between wooden benches, all facing in the same direction. Disinfectant can't mask the smell of sweat and cabbage.

A group of people wait at the far end. Forgetting how grown-up she planned to be, Ginnie screams.

'Mummy! Mummy.'

Arms come around her.

She holds on until she can't breathe, tears pouring down her cheeks.

'It's right good to see you, our Ginnie.' Father's voice wobbles as his arms sweep around them both. The three of them stand there, entangled in a hug, none of them wanting to be the first to break away.

Ginnie lifts her head and gazes into his watery red eyes, touching his face to make sure he's real. He gives her a quick pat and ruffles her hair as if it was only yesterday since he'd last seen her. Mother drags her from the rest to sit on a bench.

Ginnie has no idea when she will see them again. She takes in everything, their smiles and tears, and how they held hands before reaching out to her. How thin Mother looks.

'Are you all right, duckie? Have you been good? Are they looking after yer? What have you been doing with yourself? Oh, come here,' Mother pulls Ginnie on to her lap, touching her eyes, her nose, her mouth, her hair.

'Give the wench a chance to answer, love,' says Father, but the hand he lays on Ginnie's shoulder is shaking.

'Wish I could be with you. When can we go home?'

Mother squeezes her hand hard. 'Are you all right, duck?'

Father grabs Ginnie's other hand. 'What have you been doing with yer'sen all this time?' he asks gruffly, as if he has a sore throat. She tells them all about Haddon and her special friends, Clara and Sam, hastily reassuring them that her new friends could never take *their* place, because she misses them *all* the time. She keeps quiet about school and being picked upon by Mr Latham and George Mountford because she can't read.

'I'm glad you've got friends, Ginnie. I hardly get to see your father. Maybe once a week if we're lucky. They say they don't want us getting too comfy.' She glances around and shakes her head. 'So, it's just as bad for us.' She pauses, hunting for something more to say. 'Our Mabel come to see us last week. Her's got herself a new job, still with Chamberlain's, but pays more. She's still at Aunty Nellie's.'

'She's forgotten about me.' Ginnie tries to be brave, but the tears come anyway. 'She promised, but she never come.'

'Nay, Ginnie,' says Father. 'Her's not forgot. Our Mabel's a good lass.'

'Why can't *I* stay at Aunty Nellie's? I'd be ever so good.'

'You know her's got no room. We told you afore.' Father rubs his nose. 'We'll be out of here before you know it.' He turns away before she can catch his eye.

She wishes she could believe them, but she knows now that grown-ups don't always tell the truth.

Mother smiles. 'Are you going to school?'

Ginnie nods, crossing her fingers behind her back. She *has* been a few times.

When she gets back to Haddon, she can't remember what else they talked about. She knows too that the sight and feel of them, for just an hour, will never be enough.

Over the weeks that follow she only sees them twice more because Mary Higgins is busy and can only take a few kids each visit. Whenever she asks, she's told to bide her time. How can she? And Mabel *should* come to see her. She's the only one who's free. But she doesn't.

—

Autumn creeps towards winter. Getting up in the dark and going to bed in the dark is much better than going to bed when it's still light outside. Once the key turns in the lock, they often get up again, but dare not make much noise, else Mary will tan their hides. The lamps give no more than an hour of light and if too much is used in the evening, they will be falling over each other as they dress in the morning.

The windowsill behind the curtain on the first landing is still Ginnie's favourite place. It's somewhere she can hide when the world is cruel and where she can pretend she isn't part of it. Sometimes she stands on the sill and opens the top window just to feel the wind on her face. On a clear day she can even see the trees in the park at the bottom of the hill.

December comes cold and wet, and the damp brings coughing, sickness and sore throats. She doesn't care how long it takes for them all to get well because she has volunteered to help Mary rather than go to school. What Mr Latham will say when she goes back, she doesn't know.

'What happens at Christmas?' It comes into Ginnie's mind one day when she's scrubbing the kitchen floor with Clara because the three who usually do it are laid up. 'I mean, if I'm still here?' A sudden pang hits her belly. *Will Mother and Father be together on Christmas Day, without me and Mabel?*

Clara stops work and leans on her mop. 'What d'yer mean?'

Ginnie blinks hard. 'Is it the same as every other day?'

'Well, we have meat for dinner...'

'Trust you to think about your belly. I know we won't get no presents. Never got them when I was at home. Mother would bake a cake and we'd play games after tea because Father didn't have to go to work the next day. Afterwards Father would fall asleep and we'd tiptoe around the house so's not to wake him.'

Clara thinks for a moment. 'As I said, we have a nice dinner and, yes – a bit of cake. Workhouse Friends come around so we have to be on our best behaviour, else Mary'll give us what for.'

'Workhouse Friends?'

Someone's coming. They stop talking and mop the floor as if their lives depend on it. When the footsteps clatter past the kitchen door, Clara leans on her mop.

'Workhouse Friends are stuck-up ladies what come for a look at us. *Doing their duty*, they call it, thinking we got no ears as well as no family. They bring baskets of fruit – oranges or something. Just enough to go around. They don't stay long, but I expect it makes them feel better.'

'Suppose we should be thankful they give up their time at Christmas.'

'Oh, they don't come Christmas Day.'

'When do they come?'

'Beginning of January, sometime.'

'That's daft.'

'It doesn't really matter. Pity the poor kids what come in at Christmas, expecting something grand. The only thing they can be sure of is that they'll have a full belly.'

She sounds really clever sometimes.

–

Christmas comes to Haddon House on Saturday, 6th January 1912. Christmas food will be on the table and Workhouse Friends will bring each kid a small present, Ginnie is told.

She's been rushed off her feet for days what with bread-making, baking and helping Mary so *she* doesn't have 'one of her heads'. Clara and some of the girls have made paper chains to string around the dining hall. Paper ringlets, stuck to the ceiling, dance every time the door opens. Lads have been out cutting holly branches, some with berries, which are laid in the middle of each table. The hall looks festive, almost cosy.

Sam stands on a table, reaching high above his head to pin up the remaining chains. Clara bites her nails and shouts orders from below.

'Does it look nice?' she says.

It sounds as if the whole of Christmas rests on her shoulders. Ginnie hugs her. 'Oh, Clara! It's just like fairyland – only real. Nobody's going to have a better Christmas this year.' She realises then that she wants it to be true because it's the only way she can get through it.

'Except they've had theirs and we're still waiting.'

'We can pretend, can't we? In this room it *is* Christmas Day and we're going to have meat and taters and pudding and presents…'

'They're not presents really…'

'It's not like you to be so mopey. What's got into you?'

'It reminds me of all the things I'll never have.' Clara shakes away tears vigorously. 'Oh, tell me to shut up.'

'You'll have a proper Christmas someday.'

Clara shrugs. 'If you say so.'

Sam jumps off the table. 'We could give each other something, couldn't we? Then it would be Christmas proper.'

'What with?' Clara kicks out at a chair.

Sam's eyes lit up. 'We could make each other something.'

'What with? Fresh air?'

Ginnie really feels like telling her to shut up. 'He's right.'

'Think about it. You do the mending, Clara, so you must have cast-off cloth and stuff.' Sam turns to Ginnie. 'You help in the kitchen, so there must be scraps of food left over? I'm in the garden and there's lots of wood and stuff nobody'll miss.'

'Oh, yes.' Ginnie claps her hands. She has never had a present from a friend before. Then she stops, the smiles gone. 'It's too late now. Why didn't we think of it before?' She thinks for a second or two. 'We can easily put stuff by during the year and make presents next year, can't we? Something to look forward to?'

It's the first time it has crossed Ginnie's mind that she could be in this place for a long time, until she's grown-up even. So far, she has got through each day by thinking she'll be going home soon. She watches her friends cutting up more decorations and swallows hard. Well, if she *did* happen to stay here until next Christmas, she would have a present to look forward to, wouldn't she? And even if she has no family, she'll have her friends.

'Do you really think we could?' says Clara.

Spying the time's right, Ginnie presses on. 'Try and stop us. I can't hardly wait. Real presents from special friends.'

Sam climbs back onto the table and stretches as far as he can reach.

'Not there, Sam, it isn't level,' shouts Clara.

Ginnie sighs. Next Christmas is *ages* away.

–

By the afternoon everything's ready. They've been told to stay in the living room, to keep themselves clean, and not to get into trouble until the Workhouse Friends have left.

Mary stares through the window and dashes back and forth to the kitchen to stir pots and check for signs of burning even though Mrs Gladys Piper, the helper, is in there fussing too.

The first to arrive is an old lady dressed in black, walking with a stick. A girl, also in black, maybe the same age as Mabel, links her arm. The girl is dressed in a coat reaching to her knees and has a small posy of flowers pinned to her chest. A gathered skirt almost covers her polished black boots. She struggles to carry a huge basket of fruit, and a large brimmed hat with a posy is sliding off the back of her head. The flowers are so pretty, and a sweet smell follows her as she passes.

'That's Mrs Copeland and her daughter, Miss Constance,' Clara whispers. 'They live in a big house up the hill on the way to Sneyd, so people say.'

'Sneyd?'

Clara shrugs. 'Don't ask me. I've never been nowhere.'

The visitors pass the open doorway where Ginnie and Clara are watching. Ginnie waits for the snigger, or the quick rising of the nose. Instead, she receives a smile. She grins back like an idiot with nothing better to do, but the green eyes twinkle. Ginnie is dumbstruck that one such as Miss Constance would take any notice of her. She even winked like a proper friend.

They're waiting for two very grand-sounding people, Lord and Lady Percival, who are to say grace at the Christmas dinner. If they don't come soon the meat will be as tough as old boots and the vegetables too soft to spoon onto plates. They would have to use bowls and who's ever heard of eating Christmas dinner out of a bowl?

'Why do I bother?' Mary mutters, banging pans and metal plates on the table with such force Ginnie worries they will be full of dents, and not fit to eat off. A rustling stops her in her tracks. She turns quickly. Miss Copeland is standing in the doorway. There are no signs of winks or smiles now.

'Mrs Higgins,' she says in a strong, clear voice. 'Mother says you are to serve the food directly. If Lord and Lady Percival choose to arrive later, *she* will speak to them personally.'

Even though she doesn't look old enough to be a woman, it's obvious Miss Constance is used to people doing as she bids.

'The children have waited long enough for their Christmas meal.'

Ginnie gets the feeling she isn't just talking about the wait today.

'Thank you, Miss Copeland.' With relief written all over her face, Mary nods to Ginnie. 'Ring the bell will you, duckie.'

'Yes, Mrs Higgins.' Ginnie rushes across to the door and stops because Miss Copeland is blocking her path.

'The bell, Ginnie? Ring the bell. Didn't you hear Miss Copeland say as they're ready?'

When she realises she's in the way, Miss Constance steps quickly to one side. 'I do beg your pardon.'

Ginnie gives her a quick smile and curtsey. She picks up the bell from its place on the shelf by the door of the dining hall and rings it furiously.

The noise quietens down, and Mrs Copeland says grace. The vegetables, when they arrive, are soft and mushy and have little taste and, although the meat's tough, it's very welcome. In minutes, satisfied groans echo around the room. It takes Mrs Copeland longer to eat than anyone. There's a lot of fidgeting and the talking grows louder.

As soon as the old lady lifts the last morsel to her mouth, Mary jumps to her feet and claps her hands for silence. 'As Workhouse Friends, Mrs and Miss Copeland are partly responsible for helping to make today special, and we appreciate the time they spend with us as they share our Christmas dinner. Time they have given up so that we might have a celebration to remember. Thank them, children.'

It's the longest speech Ginnie has heard her make.

'Mrs Copeland, would you like to say a few words?' Mary's awkward curtsey turns into a bow when she realises there's no room to move.

It doesn't deter Mrs Copeland. She rises slowly as if her joints are stiff and painful. With the help of her chair, she reaches for her stick.

'Children, it has been a pleasure to spend some time with you today. My daughter and I…' she turns to Miss Copeland, who smiles and drops her eyes to the table, '… have a small present for each of you. We hope you enjoy them. Constance, will you help me, my dear?'

Miss Copeland picks up the large wicker basket from the floor beside her and moves from table to table handing one piece of fruit to each child, mainly apples and oranges, but also some long yellow things. Ginnie scowls. Just her luck to get one of those. What are they, and what in heaven's name is she supposed to do with it if one should come her way? As the basket passes in front of her and she puts out a hand to receive her present, she notices its redness is creased with dirt from the vegetables. She snatches it back and wipes it on her apron under the table. When she's given the only red apple left in the basket, she glances up quickly to say thank you. The green eyes smile back. *It goes to show that the likes of them can be just as nice as the likes of us*, Ginnie thinks with surprise.

'Thank you for your hard work today.'

'Th-thank you, Miss...' Ginnie tries to say, but Miss Copeland has moved on.

Soon after, the Copelands get ready to leave. Ginnie follows them into the hallway.

The doorbell sounds. Mary's face drains as she opens the door to a gentleman and his lady dressed in all their finery. Behind them, a smart, black carriage waits. A man in uniform is holding steady four snorting black horses.

'Lord and Lady Percival,' squeaks Mary. 'Oh, my word. I don't know what to say.' Her trembling hand pulls frantically at her neck.

The newcomers hold their heads high and sneer at poor Mary as if she's dog dirt.

'For goodness' sake woman, stand aside,' the man grunts in a deep voice. 'It's perishing cold out here.'

Mary sways and reaches out to hold on to something, anything. Ginnie pushes forward to stand beside her, whether for moral support or to catch her if she should she fall, Ginnie can't say.

'Don't worry yourself, Mrs Higgins. I'll attend to this.' Mrs Copeland moves forward surprisingly quickly for an old lady. She brushes past Ginnie to stand between Mary and the late-comers.

Leaning on her stick, she speaks loudly. 'Lady Evelyn, Lord Henry, so good of you to spare the time out of your busy lives.' She hooks her free arm through that of Lady Percival and ushers her gently back towards their carriage, leaving Lord Percival blustering behind. 'I'm so sorry we couldn't wait for you to arrive. The children were really looking forward to their luncheon and it would have been unfair to make them wait unnecessarily, don't you think?'

Ginnie almost bursts out laughing at the shock on their faces. For a weak old lady, Mrs Copeland seems mighty strong. She hears a chuckle as Miss Constance comes to stand beside her.

'Mother hates inconsiderate people, whatever their station in life.'

All in all, it has been a funny old day: Christmas in January, a present from someone she has never met, and meeting a toff who winks at her as if she's one of them. Father always said, 'Never trust a toff'. Maybe he was wrong about that, just like he was wrong to tell her she'd be back home soon.

—

'Ginnie?'

She glances around but sees no one.

She has taken a short cut through the wild garden to get to the kitchen. Her mother and father have been on her mind a lot since Christmas. And so has the thought that she might still be at Haddon for the next one. Just because she's settled with her new friends doesn't mean she thinks any less of those she has lost. She hadn't even remembered her birthday until Mary caught her in the corridor and told her she could visit the Big House as a present.

'Ginnie? Over here!'

She has to stand on her tiptoes to see Sam over the spiky brown hedge. 'Why are you hiding?'

He beckons to her. She spies a gap in the bushes and forces her way through. Sharp spikes catch her hair and hold it tight and she scratches her hand trying to pull free. Annoyed, she inspects the resulting red mark as she walks towards him.

He stops grinning when he sees her hand. 'Hope that didn't hurt?'

'It did, Sam. Thank you very much for asking. This had better be good.'

'I heard Mrs Higgins say as it's your birthday and I wanted to give you something. Only a little thing. I know you like red and you really wanted a Christmas present but a birthday present's next best thing.'

'A present... for me?'

He claps his hand down on hers and runs off, jumping over the vegetables as he goes. In her hand sits a beautiful shottie. As she rolls it around her palm the colours captured in the glass ball change from pink to blood red. It's beautiful, and all hers. Sam's so nice. This is even better than Christmas.

Compared to the little girl she was when she first came, twelve sounds quite grown-up, and her present too precious to play with. An idea comes to her. She could start a treasure box where she could save all her very nicest things – presents and stuff that mean something. She still has the red ribbon Mabel gave to her, so that's two things already.

She runs up to the girls' room and carefully wraps the shottie in the red ribbon and places it under her coat for safety. She will play with the yellow shottie he gave to her earlier and save the red one for keeps.

# Chapter Ten

**Haddon – March 1912**

Clara wasn't at all well yesterday. Springtime has sent a warming sun but she is often blue in the face with coughing and retching. She's off her food and that isn't like her. Each time Ginnie asks her to eat, she's waved away.

The rest of the sick children are soon back on their feet and Ginnie no longer has excuses for missing school. Her numbers are coming on fine, but her reading and writing are as hopeless as ever and her belly pains are back. No matter how hard she tries, the letters on the page mean nothing to her. She has to content herself with sitting with Sam and the littlest ones in the class.

Since Sam put George in his place he hasn't bothered her but whenever Ginnie is made to stand at the front, he always smirks and whispers to the other lads and they smirk at her too. She keeps her head down and tries to think about nice things like the yellow of the primroses, dandelions, the buttercups beyond the veg patch, and the bird she heard singing just the other day.

Let Mr Latham think her miserable and slow. He'd given her a piece of his mind for missing school but then calmed down when she told him she had been taking care of the other kids because there was no one else to do it. It's easier for Ginnie to step in and help Mary than it is for her to read because Mr Latham just makes everything ten times worse.

In nearly a year, she has seen Mother and Father only half a dozen times, and Mabel not at all. Each time, they have less and less to say. She tells them again about Clara and Sam, and how she's helping Mary Higgins, but after that the words dry up. Mother and Father barely talk to one another. Their clothes hang on their bones and they look as if they have given up. Last year, when she was young, the first thing she asked when she saw them was, when will we be going home? Now, she knows better than to ask.

–

It's raining.

With no excuses for being outside, the kids are cooped up in the living room. It's so noisy Ginnie can't hear herself think. A group of boys play tiddlywinks at the table while most of the girls have joined in a noisy clapping game, 'Have you ever, ever, ever in your long-legged life seen a long-legged sailor with a long-legged wife?' A couple of lads lie on the floor whispering and snorting over something, and swear loudly at anyone who trips over them.

Clara has been coughing on and off for a few days. Today, they are sharing the same chair for a bit of reading practice. Three more children, all under ten, are due in the morning. Mary and Ginnie have tried to squeeze another bed into the girls' room but it won't fit and now Mary's in her room having one of her heads. She's had a lot of them this winter.

A loud scream shocks everybody into silence. The clapping girls stop, their hands frozen in mid-air. Everyone's staring at the corner where Sam had been sitting on his own. Ginnie had been meaning to go over to sit with him but doesn't know whether he'll like that for fear his friends might rib him.

She pushes through the muggle of girls. With a sharp intake of breath, she sinks beside him as close as she dares.

Mary comes running, breathless. 'Whatever's the—?'

Sam's lying on the floor, his body stiff, jerking. Out of control. Eyes wide open, staring.

Mary touches his arm, but he doesn't notice. His tongue falls out of his mouth and almost touches his cheek. He looks a bit loopy; his arms thrash out and his legs kick uncontrollably. One kid screams and covers her eyes. Another girl grabs her arm and gives her a cuddle before pulling her away from the crowd around Sam.

He doesn't even look like Sam.

'Stay where you are. Leave him alone.' Mary ducks under his flailing arms and pulls him on to his side.

Ginnie stretches forward to touch him. 'Sam?' This is worse than her very worst nightmare.

'I said leave him alone.'

Mary's face pales, giving the impression she doesn't know what to do even though she's a grown-up.

'Why don't you help him?' Ginnie shouts.

'Let him be.'

Mary's voice, now firm, calms everyone. They watch Sam's rigid, shaking body. Beads of sweat cover his forehead. His eyelashes flicker. Then, when Ginnie thinks she can stand it no more, he stops moving. His staring eyes close.

Someone screams.

'Is he… dead?' The words are out before Ginnie can stop them. If he is dead, she'll *never* forgive him. *Please God, let him not be dead.*

'I think he's fitting.'

Just at that moment his head moves. His eyes open. He shakes his head and tries to sit up.

'What are you lot staring at?' His voice is unsteady. He wobbles as he tries to get up.

'Stay there, Sam.' Mary forces him to lie down with one hand and lays the other across his forehead. 'Do you feel sick?'

He shakes his head again and must've wished he hadn't because he screws his eyes up. Ginnie rubs his hand as if she's trying to bring it back to life. 'Sure you're all right?'

'Think so. Me head feels right queer.'

He sounds drunk and speaks more slowly than usual.

'What happened? Did you take a funny turn? What were you doing?'

Ginnie feels like telling Mary to shut up. She's asking so many questions. He probably doesn't know which to answer first.

'Dunno. It all went black. Me heart was racing and I was sweating like a pig. Can't remember nowt else.'

Ginnie steadies his arm as he tries again to get to his feet. His eyes are bright; she can see panic in them. She ignores the sniggers behind her, and the word 'loopy'. She doesn't care; he's her friend even if he *is* a boy.

'I'll see to him now. The rest of you carry on with what you was doing.' Mary helps Sam from the room.

Ginnie chews her nails and returns reluctantly to the chair where Clara's still sitting. There's no way can she concentrate on reading now. She keeps looking over her shoulder hoping to see Mary coming back.

Clara coughs so loudly it brings tears to her eyes. 'Me chest's on fire,' she mutters hoarsely.

Ginnie rubs her bony back until the coughing stops. 'Feel better?'

'What was that all about?'

'Mary said he was fitting.'

Ginnie's heart may have returned to normal speed but her mind is racing. *Can fits make you die?* Sam's her best friend ever. More than Clara. Even more than Mabel. She can't lose him.

–

It's a relief to see him back on his feet the next morning.

'Feeling any better?' She checks his pale face for signs of the boy with the staring eyes and the tongue hanging out.

'Why shouldn't I be?'

'Can you remember *anything* about last night?'

'I was flicking through the pictures in that book what Mr Latham give us to read. Then Mrs Higgins was tucking me up in bed. The lads have been going on at me. They say I'm loopy in the head.' He gives an unsteady grin.

'Don't talk like that. Any road, you're better now. That's all that matters. If I hear anyone say different, I'll give them what for.' She gives him a light punch on the arm, and then another until he smiles again.

Halfway through breakfast Gladys from the kitchen bustles in and whispers in Mary's ear. She gets up straightaway and hurries out. Moments later she's back and beckoning to Sam. He points at his chest and she nods back. He follows her into the corridor.

'I can't just stay here and wait. Let me out, Clara.' Ginnie climbs over the bench and catches her dress on a rusty nail. She pulls sharply, tearing the hem. *Damn and blast, more mending.*

'What's up?'

'Won't be long. Tell you later.'

Once in the corridor, she listens carefully. Most likely they'll be in Mary's room. She checks there's no one about, takes off her clogs, and tiptoes past the partly open door. She presses her ear against the crack and can just about hear the low voices. She's certain it's the doctor with the silly moustache she had seen when she first came to Haddon.

'If it's catching, I don't know what we'll do.'

'Not now please, Mrs Higgins. Now, Sam, breathe in for me. Hm. Hm. And again. Hm… now cough, try a deeper one.'

*Please God, let him be all right.* Ginnie crosses her fingers as tightly as she can, as if the strength of the tightness matters.

'He gave us such a fright, Doctor.'

Ginnie pushes the door very slowly, praying it doesn't creak, until she can see a little. Doctor Roberts is bending over Sam, staring into his eyes.

'Look up, lad. Ok, look down. Now to the left, and to the right.'

He grunts after each order, giving no clue on whether Sam is doing well or not. Next, he holds up three fingers and asks Sam how many he can see.

'Three, I think.'

'Ok, that'll do, Sam.'

Sam jumps up. 'Don't worry, Mrs Higgins, I'm all right. I keep telling you.'

'Course you are. But we have to check.'

'Well Sam, you'll do for the time being,' says Doctor Roberts as he walks over to the sink to wash his hands. Sam moves swiftly towards the door, leaving Ginnie hardly time to lurch backwards to avoid being seen. She squashes herself down between two visitor's chairs and lowers her head to her knees. Sam saunters out, whistling.

Once he's gone, she moves quickly back to the door, hoping to find out more. Sam had left it open, but the occupants must've moved because she can't see them. She screws up her eyes so as to concentrate and listens again.

'You're right about possible epilepsy.'

*Oh, God, no.* Ginnie pushes her fist into her mouth.

'Has anything like this happened before? To any of them?'

'Not while I've been here, Doctor. Is it catching? Will it happen again?'

'Calm yourself, Mrs Higgins. It's not catching, and it's something he might grow out of. However, I can't confirm that.'

Ginnie hears a sharp intake of breath and holds on to her heart which is about to fly off. She's sure Sam has gone away with the idea that he's better.

'I'll report the matter to Superintendent Hardcastle, and we'll see. He'll need close watching for the next few days.' Doctor Roberts paused. 'I'll try to see him again tomorrow.'

A groan from the chair warns Ginnie he's getting ready to leave. Quickly, she tiptoes back to her hiding place between the chairs.

He stops in the doorway, his back to Ginnie. 'I'm sure Mr Hardcastle will want to discuss the matter further.'

'But what if the lad fits tonight?' Mary runs alongside him, arms outstretched to stop him from leaving.

Neither of them see Ginnie.

'Leave him on the floor, then he can't fall.' He opens front door. 'He might lash out so keep everyone away from him. It's safer that way.'

Mary closes the door after him. She stands there for ages, not moving. Pins and needles run up and down Ginnie's leg and it's all she can do to stop herself from crying out. At last, Mary fiddles with the collar of her dress and walks into the dining hall.

Ginnie gets up slowly, rubbing her legs to get the feeling back. She slips into her clogs and follows Mary slowly into the dining hall.

There's no sign of Sam.

–

Ginnie watches Sam constantly during the days that follow. She listens to how he speaks, and looks for signs of illness, as she had done with her father. The world she has built around herself has become unsafe.

The doorbell interrupts her reverie. Thinking it might be Doctor Roberts come to attend to the young patient she is caring for, she runs down to the first landing but it's Superintendent Hardcastle's deep voice she hears in conversation with Mary.

'You should have said you was coming, Mr Hardcastle. I'd have poked up the fire and put kettle on.' Mary's voice rises and falls as she hurries to keep up with him. 'Is it about young Sam?'

'Not here, Mrs Higgins.'

Ginnie tries to listen at the door again but the voices are too low. She's boiling cloths in the kitchen when they emerge.

'It'll go to the Board of Guardians on Friday. I'll send the porter round at eight on Saturday morning. Mind you don't keep him waiting.'

Even if Ginnie had been standing there as bold as brass she doubts Mary would've seen her. She looks proper mithered.

Ginnie finishes her cloths and quickly hangs them on the rack to dry. She takes off her apron and smooths her dress before tapping on Mary's door.

Determined, she walks in.

Mary's eyes are closed but she opens them at the sound of the door. She shakes her head. 'Not now, Ginnie.'

'Mr Hardcastle came about Sam, didn't he?'

Mary closes her eyes again and sinks lower into her chair.

'Is something bad going to happen to him?'

Mary rubs her face with both hands as if trying to wake herself. 'I said, not now.'

Unable to get any other response, Ginnie moves towards the door.

'Ginnie?'

She turns hopefully. 'Yes, Mrs Higgins?'

'I'm so sorry.'

–

'Come quick.' Ginnie puts her arm around Clara's shoulders and urges her inside, refusing to say anything until she's sure they're alone in the girls' bedroom. Clara and the others have arrived back from school and Ginnie can't wait any longer.

'Superintendent Hardcastle was here just now about Sam.'

'Why?'

'Something to do with going to the Guardians on Friday.'

'Why would they want to know? There's always somebody poorly.'

Ginnie slumps onto the bed. 'D'yer think they'll send Sam away?'

'They can do what they like. Two girls got sent away before you came. Who cares tuppence about us?'

'What happened to them?'

'Dunno. They just went.'

'Who'll work the veg patch if Sam goes?' It sounds lame to Ginnie, but someone'll have to do it.

'They don't give a toss.'

'We can't let them send him away.' She glances through the window and sees Sam working in the garden. She should've realised that's where he would go. 'Stay here, Clara,' she says. 'I'll try and get something out of him.'

She rushes out through the kitchen door and heads over to the far side of the veg patch.

'Hiya, Sam,' she calls. Her clogs sink into mud, and water squelches between her toes. Once on dry land again, she lifts her dress and shakes each foot vigorously. 'Damn, damn, damn.'

'What you doing out here?'

'Never mind me. Have you seen Doctor Roberts again?'

He bends to clean the head of his spade. 'Yep.'

She bites her tongue in frustration. 'So?'

He turns the spade over and carries on cleaning it. She slaps his arm, forcing him to look at her. 'Sam, what did Doctor Roberts say?'

'Asked how I was feeling. I said all right and he said good, he was glad to hear it.'

She can't bring herself to tell him about the Superintendent's visit. Instead, she says, 'You would tell me if he said anything else, wouldn't you?'

'When have I ever kept anything from you? You'd clip me round the earhole,' he grins. 'I could never tell you an untruth, Ginnie.'

Ginnie's face is hot as fire.

—

'Won't go. You can't make me.'

Sam crashes through the door of Mary's room and pushes through the kids waiting for their tea outside the dining hall. He takes the boys' staircase, two steps at a time, his face white and his mouth pulled so thin Ginnie can hardly see his lips.

Mary flaps after him. 'Sam, wait! Sam!'

He ignores her.

'You can go in now but be good. And no fighting,' Mary pants over her shoulder to those waiting, and pushes after him.

Whispers buzz like bluebottles up and down the corridor. Ginnie grabs Clara's shoulder. 'There's trouble brewing. Come on.'

They pound up the boys' staircase. At the top, Clara doubles up and clutches her belly.

'Stop. Gorra stitch.'

Ginnie rubs Clara's back and strains her ears for sounds of either Sam or Mary. As Clara's breathing returns to normal, they press on more slowly. They reach the top of the second staircase to find Mary rattling a doorknob and shouting through the keyhole.

'Open the door, there's a good lad. Let me in.' She rattles the knob again and pushes against the door with her shoulder. 'Sam… please?' She sees Ginnie and Clara and puts a finger to her lips.

'Is he locked in?' Ginnie whispers.

'Course he is. And you two shouldn't be up here.' Mary sags against the door wearily. 'But seeing as you are, you can help. Push.'

Ginnie hangs back. Whatever Mary has to say to Sam, it's clear he doesn't want to hear. But if he doesn't open the door she'll never find out, and he could stay in there for ever.

'It's important, Ginnie.'

Ginnie nods. 'Sam? It's me.' She waits. 'We want to talk to you. Open the door.' She turns the knob and the door gives ever so slightly. He must be leaning against it. 'You've got to tell us what's up, Sam. Open the door.'

There's a scraping sound. Something moves. The door flies open, catching both Mary and Ginnie off balance and together they fall into the room. Sam paces up and down the gap between the rows of beds, running his hands over his spiky scalp.

He glares at Mary. 'Why have you let *her* in?'

He sinks onto a bed and Ginnie's flesh goes ice cold to see the hate in his eyes.

'I've told you. I won't go. You can't make me.'

'Oh, Sam.' Mary is beside him in a flash, hugging him, but he shakes her away.

'I never asked for you to go, I promise.' Mary's next words get caught up somewhere in her throat. 'It won't be the same without you. You're my right-hand man,' she ends with a smile.

'Go?' says Ginnie. 'Go where?'

'It might not be for long. Happen you'll learn a trade.' Mary never takes her eyes off him, but he refuses to look at any of them.

Ginnie glares at Mary. '*Where* are you sending him?'

'Up north, Manchester way. It's a colony especially for people like Sam. Doctor Roberts's instructions. They can take care of him better than we can.'

'Because of his fit?'

'We'd keep him here if we could.' Mary sits on the nearest bed and places her hands on her knees.

'You didn't waste much time.' Ginnie spits out the words.

'It's for his own good.'

'Superintendent Hardcastle says they can't cope with me here. I don't know but I never needed no special looking after before.'

'I have to report anyone that's poorly, but I never said we couldn't take care of you.' Mary strokes her knees, picking fluff or something off her apron. She looks quite small sitting there, almost as if she's one of them. But she isn't.

'Doctor Roberts is worried the fits'll come again. Sam needs to go somewhere where they have nurses they can call on.'

Mary's last sentence is almost a whisper. 'Like I said, you'll learn a trade, Sam.'

'You can't just send him away.'

'I can't,' Mary walks to the door, '… but Mr Hardcastle can. He has to do what the Guardians tell him.' She stares at Sam. 'I swear I didn't ask for you to go. You have to believe that.'

Nobody speaks.

She opens the door and disappears through. She doesn't even send Ginnie and Clara back to the girls' room.

Ginnie picks up his hand and squeezes it.

'Was I really bad when I had the fit?'

She can't lie. 'We were ever so worried. We didn't know what to do.'

'I can't remember.'

'You were on the floor and your whole body was shaking. Stiff, like you was having a bad dream. Your eyes went right up into your head and your tongue was hanging out.' A tear slides down her cheek. 'I thought you were dead, Sam.'

His face drains. 'What happened then?'

'When Doctor Roberts came later, he said if it happened again best thing to do would be to leave you on the floor so you couldn't hurt yourself.'

He walks up and down again and turns sharply. 'They can't make me go.' His eyes are bright.

'It mightn't be for long.'

'You want rid of me?'

The anguish on his face almost has Ginnie in tears. 'Course not. You're my friend.' She grabs hold of Clara's hand too. '… both of you. Why would I want you to go?' It's comforting holding his hand. Right, somehow.

'That goes for me too,' whispers Clara and picks up his other hand.

Ginnie thinks for a moment. 'Where's Manchester, any road?'

'Am blowed if I know,' says Sam.

Sam looks older dressed in his outside clothes, handsome even. He lifts his foot to show off the polished black leather boots that have replaced his clogs.

Ginnie grins back. He must've been working on them half the night to get them that shiny. He looks calmer today, as if all the talking had gone out of him yesterday, and he has nothing left to fight with. She needs to talk to him. Blast the rule about girls not sitting with the boys.

The doorbell rings.

Everyone stars at Sam, open-mouthed, wondering what he'll do. He picks up his bowl and puts it carefully in the small bag with the rest of his belongings and leans back in his chair. The stare comes back – the one he wears in class when Mr Latham takes no notice of him.

'Come along, Sam. It's a nice day for a ride,' says Mary.

The blankness in his eyes is shocking to see. Mary flushes and lowers her eyes. Ginnie is sure she sees a tear fall. That horrible Ephraim Tolley, the porter from the Big House, appears at the door flashing the few yellow teeth he has left. His eyes light on Sam.

'Come along, lad. I've brung the cart with me so as you can take a nice ride to the Big House and show off to these wenches.'

Seconds slide agonisingly by.

Slowly, Sam gets to his feet.

Ginnie rushes to stand beside him. 'I'll be thinking about you,' she whispers before anyone else comes near. She holds out her hand and then drops it, unsure if he'll want any fuss. It isn't for his sake she needs to feel his hand.

They walk toward Mr Tolley.

'Wait, Sam.' Mary runs towards them. Out of breath and shaking, she places a flat cap, made from a green woolly material, on Sam's head. 'There you are.'

She shakes him.

Ginnie thinks it's because Mary wants to hug him and can't. Her hands hang on to his coat just a little too long. As she watches, the blankness on Sam's face disappears until all that's left is fear, and a terrible sense of loss.

'You can't make me go!'

He ducks and twists but Mr Tolley's been in the job too long and is ready for him. His grip is strong even though Sam is taller. He drags Sam cursing and swearing to the cart. Even the sight of the huge brown and white carthorse fails to excite him. He wipes his face angrily with his free arm.

'Leave him alone, you bully.'

Ginnie rains blows across Tolley's back as he manhandles Sam up the step and into the arms of the other man, sitting waiting like a jailer. With one arm the man grabs Sam and pushes him on to the bench seat at the front of the cart. The other shoves Ginnie away with such strength that she falls to her knees in the dirt of the drive.

She's past caring what the rest of them think.

'Sam, *Sam!*'

He tries to turn but the man holding him tightens his grip. The wheels of the cart make a rasping sound as it jerks off, leaving two dark lines in the dirt. Through her tears, Ginnie can just make him out, boxed in between the two men, turning back for one last glance.

'Back inside everyone.' Mary claps her hands to round them up.

A hand touches the middle of Ginnie's back as she struggles to her feet. She shakes it away, empty inside, like when they took her from her mother.

'Leave me alone. I hate you.'

Without a backward glance she walks into the house and straight up the stairs. Nobody comes after her, for which she's thankful. She hasn't known Sam that long – *it shouldn't ache so much.*

In the evening she can't help searching for him, even though she knows he's not there.

'You might work harder at your reading now.' Clara tries to laugh but fails miserably. She squeezes Ginnie's hand instead. 'Sorry, I'm only joking.'

Ginnie could've slapped her. She doesn't need more reasons to feel bad just now. She could've hidden herself behind the curtains on the first-floor landing or fought Ephraim Tolley harder to stop him taking Sam. So many things she could've done.

'I hate it here.'

She had begun to think of Mary as a friend. Well, she was wrong. She can't say who she hates more: Mary, Superintendent Hardcastle, Ephraim Tolley, or Sam himself for getting sick in the first place. That night, for the first time in ages, Ginnie cries silently into a wet pillow. For losing her family, and for losing Sam, who will haunt her thoughts like no other. She had opened her heart to her new friends and now it's breaking.

# Chapter Eleven

## A Purse and A Comb

### Haddon – November 1912

It's months and months since Sam went – eight, to be exact – and Ginnie has missed him more than she had thought possible. It's difficult to explain how she feels. Lost, maybe?

On the days she isn't needed at Haddon and school is her only alternative, she sits in class, motionless. When Mr Latham raps her knuckles for not doing her homework, or for not joining in, she ignores him. Why should she care? Even when George Mountford keeps up a banter about 'good for nothing workhouse brats', she refuses to be drawn. Anger and fighting are not the only roads to survival. Cutting herself off numbs the pain. Only Clara is allowed to enter her world.

'It's nearly Christmas.' says Clara, as they make the beds.

'So?'

'We can start planning.'

'Without Sam?'

'He wouldn't want us to miss out.'

'It won't be the same.'

It's a whole year since he had first talked about presents. Who'd have thought he wouldn't be around to join in?

'I started making one for you before Sam went away,' says Clara. 'Haven't done much lately, 'cos I didn't know as we'd still be doing it.' There's a gleam in her eye. 'You could come up with something if you've a mind to?'

Clara's like a dog with a bone sometimes.

'So, why don't we? We'll each have something to keep forever and nobody else need know.'

It's those words, 'keep forever' that make Ginnie's mind up; a present from Clara will be another treasure for her little collection. And Clara would have something from her.

'Ok.'

A pincushion's easy enough and won't take too long to make. It might be just what she needs. Clara spits on her hand and offers it to Ginnie.

Ginnie hesitates, then shrugs.

'Come on, you two. These beds have to be finished if you want any tea today.' Mary claps sharply as she comes up behind them.

Startled, they jump, and grin at each other, pulling funny faces. Christmas *is* coming, after all.

Most of last year's decorations are still useable, but the twigs and holly had been thrown away. Although Ginnie blames Mary for what has happened to Sam, she's slowly coming around. It's difficult not to if she wants to be Mary's helper. She's discovered a liking for tending to the younger kids.

In preparation for Christmas in January, they all work together, sorting out the food, chopping wood, cleaning the places the Workhouse Friends might visit, and cutting new greenery for the tables.

The big day arrives. A sheepish Clara gives Ginnie her present — a pretty little patchwork purse with a large button to fasten. She must've put a lot of time into it. The stitches are so neat compared to those in Ginnie's pincushion that she very nearly doesn't give it to Clara. But she does.

'It's beautiful,' Clara's eyes open wide. 'I never got nothing like this before.'

'Good job I made it for you if you're going to do more stitching. You'll need somewhere to put all your pins.'

Ginnie's purse has a little 'G' embroidered in the corner. 'This is lovely, Clara. You're so clever. All I need are coppers to put in there.'

Clara was right. Life has to go on.

The Workhouse Friends, Mrs and Miss Copeland aren't here this year so it looks as if their world has moved on too.

–

Clara's the only one, apart perhaps from Mary Higgins herself, who knows how upset Ginnie really is about Sam going. Ginnie is beginning to appreciate the size of the hole he has left behind. She keeps herself to herself doing the jobs Mary hands out, and more if she can find them. Much better than having time to think. Mary must be in agreement because she lets Ginnie off school more often that she should. She tells Ginnie she's worried about her state of mind, and that work may be the answer, rather than sitting daydreaming in school. It suits Ginnie to let her think so.

Nippy March winds bite sharply. Bare trees silhouette starkly against grey skies, and draughts whistle through ill-fitting windows.

There has been a change in Clara. The mischief has gone out of her dark-ringed eyes. Just lately, there have been days when she doesn't want to get out of bed, complaining when Ginnie tries to get her up that her legs ache to her bones. Her temperature goes up and down like a yoyo. She mutters on about the cold and then, after wrapping herself in the blanket, throws it off, fretting that she's too hot and can't breathe.

Ginnie groans at the sound of the bell but has a good stretch, rubs her arms hard to get the blood going.

'Are you getting up today?' she says to Clara over her shoulder. 'We've got to clean out them cupboards in the kitchen again, because the Workhouse Friends are coming.' There's no reply, so she carries on. 'Mother used to be like that. I remember her wanting to tidy the house before we went out in case we had robbers. That's a laugh, isn't it?'

Still no sound from Clara. Ginnie turns to chivvy her along but Clara's eyes are too bright and her cheeks too rosy. With hardly a crease in the sheet, it's as if she hasn't moved all night.

'Don't leave me.' The faintest of whispers.

Ginnie lays her hand on Clara's clammy forehead and bends closer but can't make out what her pale, blue-tinged lips are saying.

'You've got to get up. Please, Clara.' She searches under the blanket for Clara's sweaty hands.

Clara's eyelids flutter briefly. 'My head hurts.' She struggles to sit up but flops back, groaning as her head hits the pillow.

'Lie there, and don't do anything. I'll get Mary.'

She tucks the bedding in tight. With a quick backward glance, she can make out Clara's lips moving although the words don't come out. Ginnie sprints down the stairs to the kitchen.

'Mrs Higgins? Mrs Higgins,' she shouts. 'Come quick.'

Mary is coming out of the pantry with her hands full of pans and glances around for somewhere to lay them. 'Here, lass, take these, will you?' She pushes the pans into the arms of the girl helping her.

'Whatever is it, Ginnie? You shouldn't be wandering about in your nightclothes. It's not right. One of the lads might see you—'

'You have to come. Oh, please…'

Mary grabs Ginnie's shoulders and forces her to stand still. 'Take a deep breath and talk slow. I can't make head nor tail of what you're saying.'

'Clara's poorly. She's really bad,' she pants, pulling Mary along the corridor to the stairs, desperate to get back. 'Please come.'

'Hang on. You'll have me over.'

They hurry up the stairs and Ginnie pushes her way through the crowd of girls gathered around Clara's bed, not caring who she knocks out of the way.

Mary places her hand on Clara's forehead. 'She's got a temperature for sure. I don't like the look of those cheeks,' she murmurs. 'Come on girls. Get dressed, all of you. You'll be late for breakfast. Mrs Piper, in the kitchen, will see to you.'

She turns back to Clara, feeling her under her chin and down her neck. Everyone, except Ginnie, moves away whispering among themselves. 'Get her a drink of water. She'll need plenty. Ginnie, the water... now.'

Ginnie takes one more peep at Clara and flies from the room. Her hands shake so hard she has to fill the cup twice before she can leave the kitchen.

'Poor Clara. You're not feeling well at all, are you, duckie?'

Mary's words are low and comforting as Ginnie walks in, her eyes glued to the cup of water so as not to spill a single precious drop. Carefully, she passes it to Mary who gently raises Clara's head and holds the cup to her lips. After the tiniest of sips Clara turns her head away. Tutting, Mary covers her up and tucks in the blanket.

Ginnie's world spins. She should've done a much better job of caring for Clara, instead of moping about Sam when there's nothing she can do about it. Some friend she's turned into. She straightens the blanket where Mary had been sitting as if it makes a difference. 'Got to look after her. Don't let her get more poorly.'

'Whatever are you doing, child? Get dressed and stay with her till I can get Doctor Roberts to come. And mind you keep her covered up.' Mary gives Clara a long stare before hurrying out.

Ginnie throws on her clothes and settles herself on the bed, her arm across Clara's chest. 'Don't worry. I'm going to keep you nice and warm. Doctor'll be here soon. He'll make you better.'

'I'm so hot.' Clara struggles to move the blanket.

Ginnie stays Clara's hand. It feels scaly and rough as though her skin is falling off. 'Mary says I've got to keep you warm.

You wouldn't want to get me into trouble, would you? It's the cold what's making you so hot.' How funny that sounds. She daren't laugh else she'll start crying and won't be able to stop.

*Please let the doctor come soon*, she prays, over and over even though she doesn't believe he'll come all that quick for an orphan in the workhouse.

Mary hurries in and out, picking up Clara's hand and clucking to herself. She lets Ginnie stay, although, as the day draws on, she orders her to go down for a bite of food. Ginnie ignores her, knowing she'll be sick if she tries to eat. Mary doesn't push. Instead, she brings up a plate of bread and cheese. Ginnie nibbles at it but it tastes dry and stale and she can't swallow over the lump in her throat. And the belly pains are back.

Shadows grow longer until there is hardly any light left. Clara's breathing becomes more ragged. Sometimes she's awake and sometimes she isn't. Ginnie's glad they are on their own during the brief moments when Clara opens her eyes and smiles. The other girls must have been told to leave them alone. When Ginnie speaks, Clara doesn't always answer, so she holds her friend tight to pass on some of her own strength. Even when the arm around Clara has gone to sleep, Ginnie won't move. She has no idea of the time. Now and again, Clara whispers something. Ginnie puts her ear close to Clara's lips, but can't make out all the words.

When Dr Roberts eventually arrives, Mary waves Ginnie off the bed. He lifts the tangled hair to feel Clara's clammy forehead then reaches under the covers to catch a pulse. Ginnie tried to find Clara's pulse earlier and found tiny butterflies moving beneath her skin.

'Sit up for me, Clara.'

She tries to rise but Ginnie has to hold her as the doctor listens to her lungs. His face gives away nothing.

'Cough for me, will you?'

The cough, once it starts, is difficult to control. Ginnie rubs Clara's back and glares at the doctor, panicking that he doesn't know what he's doing.

'All right, you can let her rest.'

Ginnie lays her down gently. 'Please make her better, else...' She can't go on.

'What'll I do, Doctor?' Mary straightens the covers and pats Ginnie on her back.

Ginnie smiles back, comforted that Mary really does care for them both.

'Keep her warm. And plenty to drink, Mrs Higgins. She's got a fever. She can't stay here. I'll ask Mr Hardcastle to take her into the Big House infirmary. That young lass should go too. She could be infected.'

Mary sees Dr Roberts out. When she returns, Clara is asleep and Ginnie is lying fully clothed on the bed beside her.

'Get off the bed right now. You are not to share a bed with her tonight, do you hear me?' In a kinder, quieter voice, she says, 'She's got pneumonia. Dr Roberts is going to send both of you to the infirmary at the Big House. He thinks you might catch it too. Best to be safe.'

Ginnie gets off the bed. Clara seems to be shrinking before her tear-filled eyes. 'She will get better, won't she?'

'I don't know, duckie, but I do know as she'll be better over there than here.'

Ginnie wraps her arms around herself, hardly taking in what's happening. First her family, then Sam, and now Clara. It's all God's fault. He never answers any of her prayers. *It isn't too much to ask, is it? To keep one friend in all the world?*

The covered cart arrives very quickly. Mary gives Ginnie an old laundry bag to carry their second dresses, and another chemise for Clara because the one she's wearing smells of sweat and stale milk. Thankfully a big man, who isn't Ephraim Tolley, picks them up. Ginnie couldn't have borne it if *he'd* come.

Once they are at the Big House, they are taken to a small room at the end of a large ward full of women. Some are lying in bed, asleep and snoring, while others sit on their beds laughing, for all the world as if there is nothing wrong. When the door closes only muffled sounds tease their way through.

'You mustn't leave this room. Do you hear me? You could be infectious.' A woman with red hair and a red cross on her apron moves around the room and checks on Clara, who has hardly said a word during her journey. 'We don't want you contaminating anybody else.'

Ginnie has no intention of leaving Clara's side for a moment longer than necessary. She climbs on to Clara's bed because it feels right to be there.

'And you're not to share beds.'

Never, in Ginnie's experience, has a night lasted so long, not even when she was waiting to go to the workhouse and had the nightmares. The red-haired nurse comes and goes, bringing in first gruel and then bread and cheese but Ginnie can eat neither. She offers Clara a sip of water, but she turns her head away. The thought of food makes Ginnie feel sick. She walks restlessly around the room, biting her nails, rubbing her gritty eyes and praying over and over that God will help the only friend she has left.

Clara drifts in and out of consciousness all day. As the room darkens into evening and the shadows in the corners grow longer, Ginnie notices a funny noise at the back of Clara's throat.

Not caring about getting into trouble, Ginnie climbs onto her bed again.

'You all right, Clara?'

'I... can't sleep...'

'Do you feel any better?'

Clara shakes her head, wincing. She licks her lips as if they're too dry to talk.

'I'll get you some water.'

'No, stay with me, Ginnie. I'm frightened.'

Ginnie's heart hits her belly with such force she cries out. 'Let me fetch the doctor. Please, Clara? He'll help you.'

'Get… into… bed, please?'

Clara's small, blotched hand tries to move the blanket like she had done on the first night they had shared a bed, but this time she has no strength to turn the covers. Ginnie stops her hand and pulls them back herself. Never mind what that nurse says. If Clara needs her then that's where she should be. Clara's hand closes over hers and she lies with her head against Clara's bony shoulder. 'Do you want to talk?'

'No… just stay with… me.'

The words make barely a sound. She pats Clara's hand to show she understands. 'I'll never leave you, I promise.'

–

She doesn't know how she knows because she's never seen a dead person before. It might be the silence, the stillness next to her. She opens her eyes slowly. She doesn't want to, because then she'll know for sure.

She lays her head on Clara's heart for the last time and closes her dry eyes until they come for her.

Why does everyone leave her? What's the point of having friends if they don't stay? She might as well be dead too.

The scream, when it comes, sets her throat on fire.

They come to take her away and she fights them all until the world goes black.

She doesn't know how long they keep her in the infirmary. It doesn't matter any more. They wouldn't even let her see her mother because it might make *her* sick. Once they confirm she's not going to spread germs over everyone there's no time to see her.

She is sent straight back to Haddon House.

–

Her bed feels different. It has been stripped down, given a good scrub, and fresh blankets laid. She breathes in deeply but, try as she might, she can smell only bleach. A new girl waits beside it.

Ginnie points to the other side of the bed without speaking then turns and bends down to put away her clothes. Sharing with another girl makes everything final. She has seen death and it's horrible.

'Is this yours?'

Dangling from the girl's left hand is Clara's comb with several teeth missing.

'Don't you dare touch that!' Ginnie lunges for the comb. Alarmed, the girl throws it onto the bed. Ginnie scoops it up. A couple of strands of Clara's white-blonde hair thread their way among its remaining teeth. She reaches into her cupboard for the purse that Clara made which holds the red ribbon and the shottie and adds the comb to keep it safe.

Clara's passing, so soon after losing Sam, is too much. She rolls up into a tight ball so that nobody will be able to hurt her again. She tries to stop breathing, thinking it might help the pain go away, but it hurts the back of her throat when the air comes rushing back. Even that's better than the other type of pain that comes when she thinks about the people she might never see again. Never again will she let anyone get close to her, she resolves. The world is too cruel.

The night goes on forever. In the dark, black shadows creep all around her. The girl lying beside her sniffs, but it isn't Clara, and Ginnie finds it hard to care.

Images of her friend lying in the blackness of a box, or a bag like them that got put in the ground at the front of the Big House the day she arrived. She knows now what's in those sacks, in the ground, with beetles and worms, all alone.

Over the next few days Mary orders Ginnie about and Ginnie's brain does as it's told. She peels vegetables, washes pots, mends clothes, makes beds, and cleans floors. Eating makes her feel sick and brings back memories of Clara's last days. Mary says Clara is one of God's chosen because he has taken her so early. Ginnie doesn't want to think of God no more because, of one thing she is sure: when *she* sends Him her prayers, He isn't listening.

# Chapter Twelve

### A Pamphlet

**After Haddon – July 1914**

Saturdays were half days on the potbank, and a tired Ginnie was buying food for tea. She wandered past the rank smells of the meat market and noticed a woman standing on an upturned box close to the bandstand. Although the woman's voice was strong, Ginnie couldn't make out the words. Most people walked straight past her, but some had gathered and were shouting. A woman made her way through the watchers handing out pamphlets. Ginnie moved closer.

'Give women the vote!' shouted the woman on the box. 'Women are strong enough to bear you, feed you, clothe you, take care of you when you're ill. Women work and take care of your children. All of these things they do, and you might not even notice – until they don't get done. Are these women not good enough, intelligent enough to vote?'

Close up, the woman on the box looked older than Ginnie had first thought, judging by the silvery hair escaping from beneath her hat. Wearing a long black coat, there was an air of quiet determination about her. Ginnie hadn't thought about whether women should vote before and neither, she suspected, had most of the jeering crowd who were barely listening. She vaguely remembered Father talking about women causing trouble in the streets, 'women what should've known better'. This woman didn't look like a bad person. She looked ordinary, although standing on a box in the street wasn't quite so ordinary. Ginnie moved closer.

'Go home and cook your husband's tea,' one man sneered, waving his fist. 'Unless you're too gobby to have one?'

'Your husband needs lessons in how to control his wife.' Another man joined in. 'I wouldna' want a wench like her, would you?' He pointed to some men in the crowd.

'I don't need no vote, my husband takes care of me and the kids,' shouted a woman at the front. 'Don't have time to—'

The woman on the soapbox leaned forward sharply. 'Make time. You have a right to a say in what happens to you in your world.'

The girl handing out the pamphlets thrust a sheet into Ginnie's hand.

'I-I,' Ginnie was about to give it back when a pair of green eyes met hers and lit up. It was Miss Copeland, the girl she had met during her very first Christmas at Haddon, the daughter of a Workhouse Friend, who had given her a red apple. Surely *she* couldn't be a troublemaker?

'I know you.' The girl, now grown into a woman, caught hold of Ginnie's hand. 'I'm sorry but I can't remember your name; how awful of me.' Her unmistakable green eyes with their amber flecks shone above her dark, hollow cheekbones.

Surprised by her reaction, Ginnie stammered, 'Ginnie Jones from—'

'I know where you're from,' Miss Constance interrupted. 'Sorry, that sounds awful. But I *do* remember you. You're quite grown up now, Ginnie Jones.'

Ginnie smiled and turned to go, but Miss Constance put out a hand to stop her. 'Please, stay. I'd very much like to talk to you.'

Ginnie looked behind her, thinking she was talking to someone else. She wished she had a job in the decorating end and went to work poshed up and not wearing a pair of old trashers on her feet. But now she thought about it, she was fed up of keeping quiet – about Haddon, about mouldrunning, about her life in general.

'Please stay. I've nearly finished.'

The woman on the box continued to speak but her voice was drowned by shouts from the crowd who were beginning to look fierce. Miss Constance, smiling, pressed pamphlets into unwilling hands.

'Can I interest you… please take this to read…' Ginnie heard as Constance moved through the crowd.

'It's all right for your kind. But that's me husband's job,' cried a woman, arms folded, 'What would he have to say about it?'

'Why should husbands speak for their wives when we women have a voice of our own? And what about women with no husbands?' came back the woman on the box. 'Who speaks for them unless they have the opportunity to do it for themselves?'

Excitement bubbled up in Ginnie's chest. Women *should* take care of their own futures. With talk of war overseas, women needed to be prepared.

Ginnie watched, fascinated and a little concerned. Men gathering on the edge of the crowd pushed forward. The crowd parted to allow them through, not wanting to risk getting caught among the troublemakers. One man, catching his wife reading the pamphlet avidly, snatched it off her, screwed it up and threw it at the woman on the box. He pulled his wife away, cursing and swearing. Constance was so brave to put herself at risk in such an obvious way, handing out pamphlets supporting votes for women. Supposing some of the men took against her?

Two constables moved forward, arms wide. 'Come on, lads. No fighting. Nice and peaceful now. Let them have their say and we can all go home.'

His words sounded condescending. Listening to women going on about their rights was probably not what he joined the force to do. The woman on the box ignored it all.

'You women out there. It's time to take control of your lives. Listen to what's going on around you. Don't wait for someone else to speak for you. We are half the population. Why should we be silenced?'

Indignation at the crowd's hostility replaced Ginnie's excitement. She could cheerfully have helped to give out pamphlets at that moment, but she held back. She had no idea what they said. If someone asked a question, she'd look daft.

Miss Constance smiled sweetly at the two constables. 'Such a shame you didn't come earlier. You might have discovered more about us.'

How could women succeed if they had to battle with their men all the time? How many would go against their husband's wishes? *Not many*, thought Ginnie.

At last it was over. The woman stepped down from the box. She sagged and dabbed her brow with a delicate lace handkerchief. Now that she no longer had the authority of the box, she seemed to become very small.

'See you on Monday, at noon, Sarah?' said Miss Constance quietly. Sarah smiled wanly and gave a quick nod. The constables moved to follow her, but Miss Constance stepped out and thrust pamphlets at them.

'Would you be interested in more information, Constables?'

Both men shook their heads. 'Got no time for that, lady. Our job is to make sure everybody behaves, nothing more.' The man speaking had one hand on his whistle, ready to call for assistance. 'Can't you just go home and find something else to do?'

'And what would you have me do, Constable? Sit and read a book? Practice my music?'

The smile on Constance's face belied the acid in her voice.

'No concern of mine, miss. But you women shouldn't be out shouting in the street. It's not right.'

'And you speak for *your* wife, do you, Constable?'

He poked his finger under the strap holding his helmet in place as if it had become too tight. 'My wife wouldn't—'

'Oh, but have you asked her, Constable? And have you ever listened, really listened, to what she has to say?'

The green eyes blazed and Ginnie overflowed with admiration. She had never heard a woman speak to a man in such a manner. How proud she was to know her.

By the time Miss Constance let them go, Sarah had disappeared through the crowds and even though Ginnie had been watching, she couldn't have said which way the woman went. She had just melted away.

Miss Constance gave Ginnie a hug. 'Sarah's been through so much and yet she never gives in. She's been on hunger strikes, and forcibly fed. Held down while they pushed tubes into her mouth and sometimes up her nose. It made me ill just hearing her speak of it.' She shuddered. 'She's out of prison until she's well enough to go back to finish her sentence. Damn Cat and Mouse Act! It's cruel. I couldn't do it to my worst enemy.' She whispered in Ginnie's ear. 'She's even worked with Mrs Pankhurst.'

'What's the Cat and—'

'If we go on hunger strike in prison and become too weak, they let us out, but once we're better we have to go back to finish our sentence. Barbaric, if you ask me.' She shook her head.

'If you don't mind me saying, Miss Constance. I think you're so brave,' said Ginnie shyly, as she wondered who Mrs Pankhurst was and how talking about women in prison came so easily.

Constance laughed outright. The green eyes danced. 'That's the nicest thing anyone has ever said to me. Please don't call me Miss Constance. I'm Constance to my friends.'

Ginnie's mouth fell open as Constance linked her arm and led her down the street. She had no idea where they were going. It didn't matter. She, Ginnie Jones, was out walking, *with a toff who was a suffragette*. Something else Father would've mocked.

They crossed the cobbled street and carried on walking until they reached the park and passed through the wide, intricately decorated iron gates more than three times as tall as she was. Flowers, both bold and fragile in full summer bloom

– geraniums, violas, foxgloves, white, blue, red and yellow – dazzled her while gentle scents drifted on a light breeze. She forgot where she was, who she was with. There was no room in her head for anything but the sight and scent around her. She wished she had come here before now. How calm it was. No wonder Sam loved working the veg patch.

'Let's sit down.'

Constance pulled her up the stone steps to a wooden seat overlooking an empty bandstand. Ginnie had a mind to come back here on her own and walk in the gardens for the pure pleasure of it.

'So, how are you, Ginnie? You've left Haddon House, I presume?'

Nervously, she dragged her eyes away from the beauty surrounding them to hear what Miss Constance had to say. Her hand fluttered to her hair and she hoped she looked presentable.

'Been gone a couple of months now, Mi… Constance. Am living with our Mabel, my sister. She's married now.'

'You've got family? I'd assumed you didn't have anyone.'

'Mother and Father were in the Big House… but Mother died.' Her eyes welled up as if it was only yesterday. She cleared her throat noisily. 'Our Mabel came for me 'cos she's expecting.' A nervous laugh escaped her lips and, embarrassed, she carried on. 'Well, not really 'cos she's expecting, although I suppose it does her good to have a bit of extra help about the place. I've got a job down Chamberlain's potbank. Nothing much.' She couldn't bring herself to say that she had a job that nobody wanted. 'But I want to do something different if I can.'

'Good for you. You've done well to get a job at all.'

Ginnie let her eyes wander, overcome with a contentment she had not experienced in her life so far. Heaven itself couldn't be more beautiful than this.

Aware that Constance was speaking, she shook herself and returned to her companion. Unsure exactly why Constance had taken her aside at all, she felt obliged to say something.

'You were mighty busy just then.'

'Oh, that. It's my bit for the cause.' At Ginnie's confused frown, she said, 'I've been a member of the WSPU for a while. After Emily Davison went under the King's horse... did you hear about that?'

Something stirred in Ginnie's memory and, although it was tragic, she couldn't remember why it was important.

'She was killed. It was truly awful.' Constance paused. 'But it got everyone talking about the rights of women. I think that's what she would've wanted. I couldn't just stand aside and wait for the wheels of state to turn.' She lowered her voice. 'I was arrested once.' She lowered her voice even further and leaned forward to whisper in Ginnie's ear. 'I even went to prison.'

Although looking shocked at her own behaviour, Constance sounded rather pleased with herself.

'Sarah's in a terrible state when she comes out. You wouldn't think the authorities would treat an old lady so badly.'

'What's the WS...?' she couldn't remember the rest.

'I beg your pardon,' Constance flushed. 'My tongue's running away with me. It's the Women's Social and Political Union. We believe women should be treated as men's equals. We pay taxes but we aren't asked for our opinions on how things should be run. We're treated like children who don't know what's good for them.' She stopped abruptly, and then smiled. 'Sorry, I'm getting on my high horse. I can't help it.'

'Anyone can see it matters to you.' Ginnie's chin came up. Constance didn't act like someone from another class. She talked like a friend. Ginnie hadn't had a friend, who was a girl, since Clara. She missed having someone to talk to, compare thoughts with, tell her greatest wishes to.

'How old are you, Ginnie?'

'Four—nearly fifteen.' She flushed. She wasn't a kid after all.

'Come with me.' Constance linked her arm again. Together they strode down the street. 'I need to catch the tram soon.'

Ginnie hoped she wouldn't be expected to climb aboard. She had spent all the money she had on a bit of scrag end for tea.

'Maybe we can meet again soon? I want to know all about you. It's all very well having women stand up for women against men who presume to speak for their wives, but if women do exactly the same for other women, then we are just as bad as the men.'

It sounded quite logical, although Ginnie didn't see how it would help, or why Constance would want to know more about *her*. She was just a working girl: a nobody. 'And you can tell me a bit, maybe, about you?' she countered bravely.

Constance smiled. 'I suppose that's fair. Meet me next week, same time. I shall be here again with Sarah and when we've finished, you can tell me all there is to tell about Ginnie Jones, and I shall tell you about Constance Copeland.'

As the tram left, Ginnie started on her way home. She still got a thrill from saying the word even if Frank had spoiled it for her. She didn't really know what Miss Constance would talk about next week and wondered what she might say to sound interesting to a rich girl who wasn't afraid to stand up for herself and other women.

–

Although Pat O'Malley had kept her busy all week, the time dragged slowly by, leaving her frustrated and ready to speak out if someone were to take advantage of her. Someone like George. He egged her on, telling her to get a left-handed screwdriver and a bucket of hot air for Pat, knowing that her mind was elsewhere. Even Mabel commented on her dreaminess.

So, it was with some relief when Saturday arrived, bringing with it the freedom Ginnie had been waiting for. She stood next to the box, as arranged, waiting for Sarah to appear. She hadn't told Mabel, who believed that class was important and people shouldn't stray beyond their boundaries. Not for the first time she wondered why the likes of Constance could possibly want to spend time with her. In her mind she was back in the workhouse, hiding grubby hands from the young lady with green eyes.

Her thoughts turned to Sam, as they so often did when her hands were idle. What was he doing? Was he thinking of her? Every night when she went to bed with her doll, Clara in her arms, she whispered to him about what she had done all day and asked how his day had been, just like Mabel did with Frank, like she thought Mother had done with Father.

'If anyone asks any questions, tell them to speak to me.' Constance appeared and thrust a pile of pamphlets into her arms, nodded and moved on.

Ginnie took a deep breath but, before she could refuse, a woman sidled up to her and took one. She whispered, 'You're so brave doing what you're doing. I just wanted you to know.' She patted Ginnie's shoulder and fell back into the crowd.

Ginnie stood erect. Constance smiled at her across a sea of faces and Ginnie felt she could do anything.

'What the hell do you think you're doing, woman?'

A man had grabbed hold of the friendly woman and raised his hand as if meaning to strike her. The woman tore up the pamphlet and tossed the shreds of paper over her shoulder.

'Just having a laugh, Jim. Yer don't seriously think as I'd want to read that muck, do yer?'

He lowered his arm and dragged her away through the crowd of heckling men. She never looked back.

Constance threaded her way through to where Ginnie was standing, open-mouthed, her heart thumping. 'We come across all sorts. Ignore him. Keep in mind the good we are trying to do.' She patted Ginnie's shoulder.

It would be safest to stand near to Constance, Ginnie decided. The crowd, mainly men, had grown. Although the majority heckled, some appeared to be listening. Two police constables standing in front of the meat market watched but made no move to intervene.

It was then that Ginnie noticed George Mountford standing on the edge of the circle of people around Sarah. His eyes burned into hers. Damn him. Something else he could talk about. He might be tempted to report back to Pat O'Malley. She could even lose her job. When she looked back, he'd gone.

Once the pamphlets had been distributed, they headed towards the park again and watched the ducks quacking and squabbling in the water. Neither spoke but it didn't matter. She didn't know what Constance wanted to talk about, so it felt safest to leave it to her to start.

'I could sit here all day, Ginnie. It's so beautiful surrounded by the flowers, the scents, and the colours. Don't the birds sound wonderful?'

Ginnie didn't like to say that she was usually too busy working or doing household chores to come to the park to stare at flowers. 'I had a friend in Haddon,' she said dreamily. 'He used to work the veg patch, but he loved flowers. After my friend Clara died, I never had nobody else.'

'How awful.' Constance spoke softly. 'Your face tells me he's special, isn't he?'

Ginnie hung her head.

'You're so lucky, Ginnie. I don't have anybody like that.'

How could she be lucky when she had lost so much? The memories packed away in her carpetbag were precious to her but maybe the time had come to concentrate on what she had rather than what was lost.

'What is his name? I would like to meet him.'

'Sam White. Ever since I first met him, he's been there for me. I'm hoping he'll come out soon.' She looked away. Talking so frankly didn't come naturally. Mabel hadn't asked her anything about Sam. In her eyes, he didn't exist. Ginnie's eyes blurred. She would to go to Haddon at the first opportunity she decided.

She needed to move the conversation to something less painful. 'What about you? I mean, I know you're doing this suffragette thing, but…' her mouth was suddenly dry '…if you don't think I'm being nosey, that is.'

'Of course not. It's only fair. What can I say?' she thought for a moment. 'Father managed a cotton mill in Manchester and Mother came from a very refined family. In fact, they were quite upset when she married for love and not money.' She snorted in a most unladylike manner.

'Manchester was where Sam was sent when he had a fit.'

'And Manchester's where the Pankhurst's hail from. That's how I came to get involved with the suffragettes. Mother always felt she had a duty towards the poor. I was more interested in the plight of women. When Father left the company, we moved to Sneyd, near Hanley. That's when Mother became a Workhouse Friend. We've been living at Holmorton Lodge, just out of Burslem, on the Sneyd Road, ever since.'

Ginnie smiled tentatively. '… and do *you* have a special friend… a boy?'

'Actually…' Constance paused as if trying to decide whether to say something or not. '… I do have a gentleman friend. His name is Matthew, but we've only recently become acquainted. He says he likes the idea of a wife with a brain in her head.' She giggled.

'What does he think of you being a suffragette?'

The giggle disappeared as quickly as it appeared. 'I haven't exactly told him… everything. He knows I give out pamphlets with Sarah; he's seen me do it.' She looked away. 'I might not have told him yet that I spent a month in prison.'

'You've never told him?'

'It was last year. It happened in London, so it wasn't reported in *The Sentinel*. I promised Father and Mother I wouldn't do it again.' She grimaced. 'I met Matthew two months ago. Father said I mustn't say anything if I want to keep him.'

Ginnie's mouth fell open. 'Well I never—'

Constance jumped up. 'I don't know why I told you. Father's hoping I snare a rich husband before he discovers my shameful past. I think Mother was secretly quite pleased. I must have more of her blood in my veins. Anyway, It's early days.'

Just in time, Ginnie remembered her mouth was still wide open and promptly closed it.

'Going back to you again – I'll ask Mother. She's still a Workhouse Friend. She might be able to help in some way.'

Ginnie grabbed Constance by the hand and shook it, over and over, grinning with delight.

They agreed to meet again in a week's time and Ginnie would help to distribute more pamphlets.

'If you are going to help me, you'd better read it,' said Constance, passing her a copy.

Ginnie slipped her fingers around her collar, which had suddenly begun to choke her. She lowered her head and pretended to read as if engrossed.

'Don't bother now; save it until you get home.'

Back in her room, she lay on the bed and stared at the ceiling. How long would she be able to keep her secret from Constance. Apart from that, the day had turned out well. If only Sam could get out of Haddon and find a job, everything would be perfect, and she would never ask for anything more. She sat up, tugged out the red carpetbag and dropped the pamphlet inside. Remembering seeing George at the meat market, she felt her belly ache with worry… would he tell Pat O'Malley what he'd seen? Was she about to lose her job just as life seemed more hopeful?

-

Back at work on Monday morning, she was quiet, relieved she hadn't yet crossed paths with George and worrying about what to do about the situation. Pat shouted at her for loitering and threatened to hurry her along with his boot if she wasn't careful. It was after snapping time when she was able to speak to George. For once, he didn't look angry and wasn't sneering.

'George? I…er, about the other day?'

'It's all right. I won't blab.'

'You won't?' She couldn't believe he was going to keep quiet. Would he make her pay later?

'Just be careful what you're getting yourself into.'

He didn't follow it up with a threat, nor did he suggest they spend some time together. She decided to give him the benefit of the doubt and smiled.

'Ta, George.'

They heard Pat bellowing at someone and grinned at each other. She was about to walk away when George held her arm and whispered in her ear.

'You looked real good standing there. At home, like.'

For the first time, he had been nice to her and she had to acknowledge that he could be quite charming when he wanted to be.

## Chapter Thirteen

### A Carnation

**Haddon – April 1913**

Superintendent Hardcastle rarely appears at Haddon these days. In his long black cloak and bowler hat, Mary calls him 'a harbinger of doom'. Ginnie isn't sure what a 'harbinger' is, but the 'doom' bit is enough to keep her out of his way. When, in early April, she is told to present herself to Mrs Higgins and Mr Hardcastle in Mary's room, Ginnie's heart sinks. She keeps herself to herself pretty much these days and has done nothing bad that she can think of. She knocks on Mary's door, surprised at how nervous she feels.

'Come!'

It's as if she's eleven again, Mr Hardcastle fingering his watch chain and Mary upright on a wooden chair. Ginnie fixes her face with a blank stare.

'Ginnie...' Mary's eyes blink as if something is lodged in one of them. Ginnie's sure she's been crying. The pounding of her heart grows stronger. It's the concern on Mary's face that frightens her most of all.

'... Ginnie, Superintendent Hardcastle has something important to tell you.'

Reluctantly, Ginnie turns towards him. Put off by her stare, he stutters and fidgets and she's glad she can make *him* feel as uncomfortable as she is.

He clears his throat. 'You're a big girl now, almost a woman.'

He stops abruptly and turns to Mary. She opens her mouth to speak and stops too.

*What are they trying to say?*

Mr Hardcastle clears his throat and tries again. 'Yer ma's not been well.'

'What's wrong?' Her voice sounds unnaturally loud and her collar's choking her. Mother must be very poorly to bring Mr Hardcastle on a special visit.

'Look at me, Ginnie, I need to see as you understand what I'm saying,' he says.

She wishes he'd get on with it. He's just making everything worse.

'Sit down, lass.'

She sits.

'Your ma's not been well. She was let out of the Big House for the day a few weeks back. Said she was going to look for work… she came back drunk.'

Ginnie bursts out laughing. She wouldn't normally have been so disrespectful but they obviously don't know Mother. 'It's a sin to have a nip, never mind get drunk. You've got it wrong, Mr Hardcastle.'

'I saw her with me own eyes. She was drunk, I tell you.' His sympathetic voice has gone. He clenches a fist.

'Ginnie Jones, you're never calling the Superintendent a liar, are you? It's not for you to say what you want. If Mr Hardcastle says as your ma was drunk, then drunk she was. You should know better.'

Mr Hardcastle coughs. 'It's not the first time. She went out of the Big House a couple of months back. Trying to find work. She was drunk when she came back then an' all.'

Ginnie covers her ears to stop their lies but it doesn't stop a memory flashing through her brain of that night, long ago, when she saw Mother in the kitchen taking swigs out of a bottle that might have been medicine.

He looks pointedly at Mary, but she's staring at the wall.

'We don't know where she got the money from but there was some bother with the police.'

'No. No. No.' Ginnie jumps up and runs to the door.

'Ginnie!'

At least Mary isn't studying the wall any more.

He continues. 'When she came to, she refused to work and was taken to see the magistrate. She can't just waltz into the workhouse paid for by the people of the parish and refuse to earn her keep. As she weren't feeling too good, the magistrate bound her over. He said as she had to get back to work soon as the doctor said she was fit. That was three week ago.'

Ginnie shakes her head unwilling to believe her ears and trying desperately to fight the memories of Mother in the kitchen rocking the bottle, which she now realises probably was gin.

'Your ma had a sore throat and was feeling sick. It got worse and then the fever come. We got the doctor to look her over.' He continues in a gentler voice. 'It was the influenza she had, duckie, and bronchitis.'

The silence hurts her ears.

'Ginnie, your ma died last night.'

Ginnie's head explodes into white lights, flashing bright. The world swims. Someone catches hold of her and stops her getting up. A strong hand on the back of her neck forces her head down between her knees. She fights for air but the hand stays firm.

'Stay like that, there's a good girl.'

Mary's voice comes from a distance. Another white light and a whooshing inside her head. Voices mix together; mumbles surround her.

'There, there, lass. Take it easy.' A man's voice this time.

Slowly, the grip relaxes. Ginnie lifts her head, her voice barely a whisper. 'I want to see her.'

'She'll be moved out of the infirmary soon, if she hasn't gone already.'

'But I've got to see her.'

'She's infectious, lass and like I said, she might have already gone.'

'Then I must go to Father.' She jumps up.

'He knows. I might be able to squeeze you in for a quick visit in the next day or so given the circumstances.' He struggles out of the chair, avoiding her eyes.

Mary's knees crack as she rises. 'I'll see you out, Mr Hardcastle. Ginnie, stay there and don't move.'

Ginnie does as she's told, aware of their muffled voices moving down the corridor and then the rustling of Mary's petticoat and the patter of her shoes bustling back into the room. The door closes. Mary sinks into the chair opposite.

'This is a to-do and no mistake. You haven't half had a lot on your plate, girl. Maybe this'll see an end to it.' Mary takes her hands and rubs them to bring a little feeling back. 'Why don't you lie down for an hour? Shock can do strange things. Happen you'll feel able to cope when you wake up.'

Without answering, Ginnie allows herself to be led up to the bedroom. She can feel Mary's eyes on her, but she keeps hers shut. She hears the door creak and close quietly and feels it's safe to open them again. She traces the crack in the ceiling above her bed and her thoughts turn to Clara who will never see those patterns again. She imagines her mother lying somewhere all alone, whose hand she will never hold.

The door opens wide, letting in the chatter of voices. The returning girls must have thought the shadowy room was empty because someone squeals, causing a momentary stir. They crowd around Ginnie's bed chattering.

She ignores them.

'What's the matter, Ginnie?' asks the youngest.

Ginnie turns away and covers her face with the blanket.

Mary hurries into the room and claps her hands several times. 'Come on now, girls. Ginnie's had a shock, so leave her be.'

A cold hand presses gently against Ginnie's forehead.

'You don't feel so bad. No cause for worry.'

It's just too much trouble to open her eyes.

'Downstairs, everybody. Time for tea. You too, Ginnie.'

Mechanically, she gets out of bed, pulls the bedclothes straight, and follows Mary downstairs. She walks to her usual seat and lays her head on her folded arms. Mary says grace and asks everyone to say a little prayer for Ginnie's mam who is no longer with us. Before she came to this place, Ginnie would have put her hands together and joined in. Now, she knows better.

–

She sees Father the following afternoon. During the walk to the Big House she concentrates on her clogs. She's so used to the clunking she might even miss the sound if it wasn't there. Mary walks beside her, for a bit of company she says, but they don't speak.

The porter, Ephraim Tolley, grins as they pass through the gates, but Mary ignores him. Ginnie does too, for his part in Sam leaving. He pulls a face and disappears inside, appearing moments later to tell them to go along to the dining hall. Mary says she has to speak to Matron, so Ginnie waits alone.

Father shuffles through the door, his shaved head peppered with tiny white hairs and he's thinner than she remembers. He reminds her of the old tramp she used to see in Victor Street in the days when she ran errands for Mother. She can't remember the tramp's face, only the shape of him as he propped himself against the wall next to the shop.

She runs and nestles in his arms where it feels safest. Her family is smaller now.

'There, there.' His lips are in her hair as he hugs her. 'I've missed you that much, our Ginnie.'

'Oh, Father.'

Even the smell of sweat doesn't put her off, and his chin, spiky and rough against her face, makes her cheeks itch. He's old. *He* could die any time. She holds him even tighter.

'Sorry about your mother.' His bottom lip trembles and he runs out of words. He stares at the wall behind her and starts again. 'Mabel came t'other day. She says your Aunty Nellie's not been well neither.'

Ginnie leads him to a bench and, once he's sitting comfortably, sits beside him up close so he can feel her next to him. 'Mabel's never come to see me.'

He stares at his hands and stretches his fingers. She wonders if they're just a blur.

'Her ain't forgot you, duckie. I suppose she's busy what with working all hours and the like. She came 'cos of the funeral.'

*It wouldn't have hurt her to spare some time for me too*, Ginnie thinks.

'We sorted out the arrangements and the wake, Ginnie. It'll start from Aunty Nellie's and she'll be buried in St John's on Monday. They've given me a pass out for the day.'

'I'm coming too.'

'Nay, duck. Funeral's not for the likes of you. You're too young.'

Mary had told her that funerals are the last chance to say goodbye. *I have to go. How can he say no?*

A huge sob escapes, even though she has promised herself she won't cry.

'Funerals are for grown-ups, and there's an end to it. Besides, I've got to come straight back here soon as it's over. She'll not be buried a pauper, thanks to Nellie and our Mabel.' He holds his head high, but his bottom lip quivers.

'Father, I'm thirteen.'

'And that makes you a kid in my book. When you're old enough you won't want to go, believe me. No kid of mine'll turn up at a funeral in workhouse clothes.'

*He's ashamed of me, that's why he won't let me go.* She is sick and tired of being told what she can and can't do by people who say they will do what's best for her. She knows from experience that once her father's mind is made up, no amount of pleading will change it. She clenches her fists and hides them in the folds of her dress.

In her mind's eye, she and Father would huddle together, helping each other, but now she feels cut off by more than the workhouse.

'Please, Father.'

He continues to stare at the wall.

In no time at all, Mr Tolley comes to take him back. Ginnie stands erect in Father's arms when he hugs her, her arms by her side. She remembers Mother calling him a bloody-minded bugger because he's a man, and men don't change their minds. As he's led away, he glances over his shoulder even though he can't possibly see her. Then he's gone.

Ginnie blinks away angry tears. The trembling won't stop. She has no idea how long she sits waiting for Mary, wrapped in a world of her own, a place where she thought nothing could hurt her. She should've known better.

Voices shout to each other, becoming louder. Somewhere not far away, a deep-throated machine whirs to a regular rhythm. Anger bubbles up so strong she feels she'll burst. Why is Father so bloody proud of not changing his bloody mind? Because now she bloody hates him too. Swearing makes her feel good. Mother used to threaten them with a good hiding if she caught them swearing. She doesn't know when she'll see him again but at that moment, she doesn't know that she even wants to. How can she fight *him* after all she's been through?

Mary appears at her side. 'Finished already? Come along then, duckie. We've got to get you back to Haddon.'

Ginnie puts on her coat without a word.

'You're not the only one to lose your mum, you know,' Mary says, quietly. 'I was your age when it happened to me. Only I lost mum and dad at the same time – in an accident. I didn't know what to do with myself. Workhouse was a lot worse in them days. A lot worse, I can tell you.'

Ginnie has never thought to ask Mary why she works at Haddon. She had assumed it was just a job. She knows nothing about Mary's husband, whether he is alive or dead. It might be wrong to ask.

Mary clams up again.

'Father won't let me go to Mother's funeral.'

Mary throws her a sideways glance. 'Why ever not?'

'He says I'm too young.'

'On the outside you wouldn't be far off working now.'

Ginnie shrugs.

Mary links her arm and nothing more is said. They carry on walking but, in that brief moment, Mary has become her friend and not her jailer.

—

'Mrs Higgins, did you go to the funerals of your mother and father?'

'I did, and I can't tell you no lies, I'm glad I went.'

'Then you know why I've got to go?'

'Why is your father being so difficult? Maybe, in his mind, he still sees you as his little girl and wants to protect you.'

'And once he's made his mind up, he won't unmake it. He doesn't want me there in workhouse clothes, that's what he said.' Ginnie catches her bottom lip with her teeth. 'He's ashamed of me.'

'That's a bit like pot calling the kettle black. Maybe he's ashamed of putting you here. Have you thought about that?'

It doesn't help.

'Once your mum's in the ground… well, that's it.'

'You think I should go too?'

Mary hesitates. 'I don't see how you can if he doesn't want you there.'

'He can't see, can he?'

'You mean you'd go without telling him?'

Ginnie steels herself. *She* has to make things happen now, no one else. 'Father isn't the only one who can make up his mind and stick to it. There's nothing anyone can do to change my mind.'

'I don't see how—'

'If you don't want to help, you don't have to. Just don't tell nobody.'

'Course I'll help, child. Seems mighty tough on you.'

Ginnie throws her arms around Mary and hugs her until the stiffness softens. The hug she gets back is so tender she very nearly bursts into tears there and then.

–

Mary has arranged that Gladys Piper, from the kitchen, will come in early to tend to any sick children not going to school. The plan would be that Mary and Ginnie leave early to stock up on medicines from the pharmacy. The funeral is at half past two, which means they can take the kids to school, walk down to the church for the funeral, call for the medicines and be back at school to collect the children. Mary picks out a black, wide-brimmed hat for Ginnie and a scarf which, between them, will cover most of her face. Hopefully, no one will look twice at her.

The old church, built of weathered stones darkened with soot and green damp from the trees, is surrounded by gravestones, weather-beaten over the years, carrying messages too smooth to be made sense of. The grey stones match the grey rain, adding to their grey mood.

Ginnie gazes around the churchyard. 'I wish the sun was shining. It all looks so sad.'

'There's still time to change your mind.'

Ginnie stares at the church door. They have found a place between a tall, rather grand tombstone on one side and an angel on the other, protected by two trees, where they can watch unnoticed. They dare not enter the church for only half a dozen mourners have gone in.

The coffin arrives, flanked by the bearers. Father walks behind with a white stick. Ginnie covers her mouth to stop herself from crying out. Mary's arm links hers, locked in place lest she should fall, or decide to run. Behind Father walk Mabel and Aunty Nellie, their arms around each other, Mabel's face hidden under a wide-brimmed hat. At eighteen, *she* is a grown-up.

Ginnie makes a move towards them but Mary pulls her back sharply.

'We're not supposed to be here, remember. You'll get me into trouble if you let on. Please, Ginnie.'

Ginnie freezes. Her need to be part of this final goodbye fights with her gratitude towards Mary. If it hadn't been for Mary, she wouldn't be here at all.

The mourners walk slowly into the church and the heavy door closes behind them. She can do nothing but wait.

The colour of the soil changes to dark brown as the grey rain starts again, bringing with it a moist, sweet earthy smell. People walk through the graveyard huddled in long dark coats adding hardly any colour. Some sign of life, a ray of sunshine, or maybe the twittering of a bird or two would have helped. Today, there is none.

The church door opens and the slow journey towards the grave begins. As the procession moves steadily closer, Ginnie and Mary pull back behind the tombstone. The words of the minister are too low for Ginnie to make out, but it doesn't matter. She's been thinking of this moment ever since Mary agreed to let her come and has her own prayers ready.

When it's over, Mabel puts her arms around Father and turns him towards the lych-gate. Together, they walk away. The family Ginnie has left doesn't want her there. Whether or not it's for her own good hardly matters.

When they're certain everyone has left, Ginnie and Mary move towards the surprisingly small grave. Two little posies lie each side of a small, wooden cross. Now the time has come, she is more aware of Mary's presence than she'd thought she would be. She whispers the words hoping, for Mother's sake, that God will know what's in her heart. Her problems with God not listening in the past are still in her mind but she hopes He will hear her now.

> Oh Lord, they say as you are wise and all-knowing. Please look after my mother, Florence Jones, a good God-fearing woman. Who took care of me and our Mabel, and who has brung us up the same. Who never hurt no one. Who was full of love for everyone. Help her as she has helped others. Bring her joy in Heaven and help her to look after us what's left behind. And bring her peace. Amen.

She had memorised the words a line at a time, adding the next line when she could say the previous one. It had taken all her waking moments to get what she wanted to say fixed in her head.

Mary's hand squeezes her arm tightly and Ginnie's glad she isn't alone. A tear splashes onto her cheek. She dashes it away.

'Amen. That was lovely, Ginnie. I'm sure He'll take care of her.'

'You heard?' Ginnie isn't sure how she feels about Mary hearing her most private words.

Mary sniffles. 'I never heard anything more beautiful. It must have been very hard to think of all the words and remember them.'

'What do you mean?'

'I'm not a fool. I know you can't read.'

'H-how?'

'That's why you won't go to school, isn't it?'

Ginnie stares at her feet. 'No.'

'Are you sure?'

'I don't want to go to school because I can learn more by helping you than by sitting in class with Mr Latham.'

'You must go, Ginnie. There will come a time when you'll regret it if you don't.'

'All I want is for someone to want me. Where's reading going to get me? Better if I can look after them when they're poorly.'

'Oh, Ginnie, love. That's a hard lesson to learn so early in your life.'

Ginnie had wanted to keep the words to herself, but now she's glad Mary has heard them too. She really is a very nice person even if she can be bossy now and then. *Who else would've done what Mary has just done for me?* Ginnie throws her arms around her and then they're hugging each other.

'Thanks, Mary. Oh…sorry… I know I should call you Mrs Higgins…' The moment had been so personal she just said the words that were in her head.

'I think Mary sounds much nicer.'

Mary squeezes her even harder and Ginnie is disappointed when they finally break apart.

'Come on. We'd best go and pick up the medicines and get the kids from school, duckie.'

Before they leave, Ginnie picks a flower off one of the posies to add to her treasures, and gently puts it into her pocket.

Mary fusses about like a mother hen but Ginnie doesn't care. She has seen a different Mary today, a mother and a big sister rolled into one. She holds Mary's hand because she wants to, and that makes all the difference in the world.

–

Ginnie grows up a lot in the days following the funeral. There's only two people she can rely on in this life – herself, and Mary, who has risked so much in going against Father's wishes. Haddon's her home now.

At thirteen and a half, Ginnie has more responsibilities in helping the younger ones, making sure they have clothes to wear, taking them to school, and supervising them at table and bedtimes. They want cuddles when they first arrive, and when they get sick, and that means she's in control. The moment they can fend for themselves, she distances herself, telling them they must learn to cope without her. How can she grow to love them, knowing they will be taken away? It's the only way she can protect herself.

She doesn't feel grown-up yet, although the 'thing that must not be mentioned' began a short time ago. The blood terrified her. She had so much pain in her belly the first time it happened that she went rushing to Mary, thinking she was dying. Mary chortled, saying it's nothing more than women's monthlies, a curse she'll have to put up with from now on.

'Every month? How long for?'

'Until you're too old to have babies. That's how long.'

Maybe when Mary went on about having 'one of her heads', she really meant she was having one of her 'monthlies'? Ginnie feels very wise.

'Does that mean that I can get a baby now?'

Mary takes her to one side and whispers in her ear. Ginnie can't believe what she says but supposes it must be true; she has no one to talk over such matters with. Special friends either leave or die. It doesn't matter how they leave because the hurt is just the same.

She expects Father to send for her after the funeral, to make it up to her in some way but when she asks Mary if she's heard anything, she shakes her head.

The minister calls twice after Mother's passing. Each time he comes they sit in Mary's room. He asks how she's coping. How can she put into words the emptiness she feels inside? She says, 'As well as can be expected, thank you.' It stops all further conversation dead, to the relief of both of them.

'Think of your father. He needs someone to care for him. Maybe, when you're older, you'll be able to look after him, as every good daughter should.'

# Chapter Fourteen

## The Buttercup

**Haddon – August 1913**

It's dinnertime and upstairs, Ginnie is feeding a child with a sore throat. She has been up most of the night and can hardly keep her eyes open.

The faint sound of the front doorbell has her peeping through the window. The cart from the Big House is outside and mumbled voices and laughter leave her curious. She tucks the bedclothes around her patient and runs down to the first landing. She stretches over the bannister as far as she can. A large group has gathered near the kitchen and is moving slowly towards the dining hall.

She runs down the stairs. Stops. Rub her eyes.

And again.

Her feet won't move. Her mouth can't find the words she wants to shout out. *If it's a dream, please let it carry on forever.* She shuts her eyes and opens them slowly, peeping between crossed fingers. The view is just the same.

It's him.

Laughing and hugging anyone who dares to get close to him, a little thinner, but most definitely Sam, head and shoulders taller than everyone else. He coughs and splutters as a lad thumps him between his shoulders and Sam pretends to thump him in return. His head turns this way and that until his eyes fall on her. A huge a smile spreads from ear to ear.

She clutches her cheeks to cover the burning flames shooting up her neck. 'Sam… oh, Sam!'

She claps her hands over her mouth and runs towards him, not caring who sees or what they think. She touches his breast, squeezes his arms. He seems solid enough.

'Ginnie duck.' His voice is warm and low, speaking only to her.

She swallows, over and over. 'You're not a dream?'

'Does this feel like a dream, lass?'

He grabs her hand and pulls her into his arms, swinging her round and round. Everyone jumps out of the way, some laughing, others moaning. Her feet return to the floor and, reluctantly, her heart returns to her chest.

'I thought they might send you away before I came back,' he whispers in her ear, still hugging her.

The tenderness in his eyes fills her to the brim with emotions she's missed for so long. He's the first person to go out of her life and come back again. She keeps touching him to make sure he's real. Others gather around them, the shock on their faces enough to make her burst out laughing. Some are probably wondering who the tall handsome lad is who makes a sullen girl like her giggle and dance and lose her senses.

'What's all this?' Mary's loud voice is followed by several sharp claps. 'Sam White! You've only been back five minutes and here you are causing me all sorts of problems. Let's be having you all in your seats before your dinners get cold.'

'Why didn't you tell me, Mary?'

All eyes are on Ginnie, and Sam's arm, draped around her shoulders as if he's forgotten he's left it there.

'I wasn't too sure when he'd turn up, and I didn't want to raise your hopes, duckie. It's good to have you back, Sam.'

A twitch appears about Mary's mouth and quickly disappears as she tries to remain stern. She folds her arms as if to avoid touching him, but Sam lurches at her and traps her arms in his. He swings her off her feet as if she weighs nothing, all signs of their disagreement over his leaving now forgotten.

Ginnie laughs uncontrollably as a flustered Mary straightens first her dress and then her hair, tutting all the while, but her face holds the ghost of a smile. Ginnie isn't too sure if it's because Sam is back, or because he's made her feel young again.

-

Ginnie refuses to be parted from Sam for a single minute and so they sit side by side at the tea table that evening, and Mary lets them. Neither touch their gruel. Ginnie can't take her eyes off him for fear he might disappear again. She's happy enough just to listen to him talking.

She hasn't told him about Clara yet. She wants to keep it to herself for a time lest she should start blarting but when he eventually asks her outright about the kids he used to know, she tells him. Stunned, he drops his head into his hands. She tells him about her mother too, and how unhappy her world has been.

'You've been as lonely as me?'

She can't speak. She blinks to clear her eyes, trying not to let the floodgates open. It's too soon, too raw in her memory.

'You need looking after, wench. No wonder you've grown so skinny while I've been gone. Just you wait until I get to work on them vegetables.'

She forces a smile and the smile grows into a laugh. He takes her hand and tucks it beneath his arm, joking that they'll have to take care of each other from now on. At least, she *thinks* he's joking. She holds on to his arm tightly.

She can't stop giggling. Every time she straightens her face and looks at him, she starts all over again.

-

'What really happened in Manchester, Sam?' They're alone and she's desperate to know.

'When Ephraim Tolley come for me, I was scared out of me wits and worried I might never come back again.'

She squeezes his hand, spirited back to that awful day, seeing his face as he's bundled into the cart. She squeezes his hand again, although this time, it's more for herself.

'Me and two other lads was put on a train, with Old Tolley, to make sure as we didn't scarper. Never been on a train before and it was grand, watching the steam pouring out of the chimney. Bet the blokes what drove it worked hard to keep it going. I stuck my head outside and the smoke nearly took it off. But what a feeling it gave me. Couldn't breathe when I pulled back inside, and nearly coughed me guts up. Took me mind off where I was going, any road.

'The train pulled into a station and we got shunted off. There was nowhere to hide, just a few houses and then fields and fields. Didn't know there was so many fields in the whole world as that. We didn't cut loose. Where would we go? Langho Colony has big houses built in fields as far as you can see. Gave me the jitters. It would've been easy to go there and never come out again. Some of them colonists had been in there for donkey's years. They told me at Haddon that if I didn't go there they'd have no choice but to send me to a lunatic asylum and that I was very lucky to have this chance so I shouldn't muck it up.

'We were in a world of our own. There was no call to go anywhere 'cos there was kitchens and farms and a hospital and gardens, laundry and even a mortuary, and a chapel in the hall, so even if you died you still got to stay.'

Ginnie can only give a half laugh. Death has followed her such a lot recently. She loves hearing him talk and wouldn't mind at all if he carried on talking into the night, although she suspects Mary will have a different view.

'I was put in Home Three, and the other two in Home Five, but they was all the same as far as I could tell. It would've been easy to put yourself to bed in the wrong one if you wasn't watching what you was doing. Although there was lots of work to keep the gardens and farms stocked, they didn't let us use tools what would have made life easier for us. They thought it'd do more harm than good having machinery about people what's having fits. Wasn't so bad 'cos it meant we got more animals to look after, cattle, horses, chickens and pigs. We could never go nowhere by ourselves, there always had to be two blokes with us, one in front and the other at the back.

'I worked mainly in the kitchen garden 'cos, after working at Haddon, I could tell the difference between a tater plant and a nettle. Sometimes, when the farms were really busy, I'd go down and help them. It was hard work, but I could see things grow and that was better than road-making any day. We started work at eight and worked through till noon and finished at four, so we had some time to kill before tea. They liked to keep us moving, so we played football or bowls. Some of the blokes played in the band, but I didn't know one end of a whistle from a trumpet.

'It was like Haddon, only better. Blokes and wenches were kept apart just the same, even in the gardens there was places where us blokes couldn't go for fear of bumping into lasses. If you was caught with a wench you'd lose what they called "privileges", like sweets or baccy, and entertainments. I found out later that them what looked after us was told that if two of us got together and had kids, then they would most likely have fits an' all. Each home kept a book of fits so as they knew when and how many fits each of us had. They didn't believe me at first when they looked me up and found as I hadn't had any since I come in, and they said I must've had them in me sleep. Well, how would I know about that?'

'Sounds a good place. Why did you come back here?'

The saucy grin's back. 'Missed you lot, didn't I? Langho wasn't so bad, except they wouldn't let us go anywhere by ourselves. I could've put up with it if you was there. I missed you more than I've missed anybody. In the end, I told them I wanted to come back here 'cos I've never had another fit. They wouldn't normally take any notice, but the colony was packed, and they was glad to get rid of me. They said the fit might well have been a one-off. So here I am.'

Ginnie's heart somersaults.

–

The long hot summer of 1913 turns out to be the best of all summers. Ginnie is determined to pull her weight, just like Sam, lest they try to send her away next. She likes bossing him about. If he talks to a girl too long, she pushes between them until the girl moves away. He enjoys having someone looking out for him, he says, even it is only a lass.

She loves the special way his eyes light up when she comes into a room. He'll often sit on the edge of a group listening to her telling the stories she has learned from Mary. He pretends he isn't listening. Sometimes she stops deliberately and chuckles at the annoyance he can't show. She loves this power over him but always carries on before he moves away.

It's wonderful to share her thoughts with Sam, but she needs to talk about her new feelings for him, and that's when she misses Clara most of all.

Whenever she can, she slips out from the dark pokey room where she sits with the other girls working through the pile of torn clothes, sewing on buttons and darning stockings, and races out to the vegetable grounds. She loves watching the blue sky, the sunshine and the banks of buttercups, dandelions and daisies running along both sides of the walled garden. They're such happy flowers, even though Sam says they're weeds because they haven't been planted in that spot but have chosen to grow there. To Ginnie, that makes them extra special.

Most of all she loves watching him. When he gets too hot and takes off his shirt, she can't take her eyes off him. Over the summer his arms grow muscular and his white chest takes on a golden glow. Sometimes he catches her watching him. Hot with embarrassment, she either picks fault with what he's doing, or busies herself with weeding, even though she doesn't always know which plants she's meant to be pulling.

The kids are at school today and she has time on her hands before helping Mary with tea. She takes off her apron and wanders outside to find him. She knows he wants to finish weeding the last corner of the vegetable plot and sits nearby making buttercup chains because they're his favourite flowers.

'Somebody told me ages ago that if you hold a buttercup beneath your chin and a yellow glow comes, you'll soon marry.' She stares wistfully at the flower in her hand. 'Not that anybody'll want to marry me.'

He laughs outright. Resting his arms on the handle of his spade he watches her hands as she carefully picks the flowers. 'That's downright silly. How can a flower know when you're going to get wed?'

'Dunno. I'm just telling you what she said. And there's no need to laugh, Sam White.' She turns her back in a huff. She still doesn't like being laughed at, especially by a boy telling her she's silly. She probably *will* get wed one day because everybody does, unless they're very unlucky. She glances across at Sam. Her face burns when she sees he has stopped work and is watching her.

'You don't have to ask them flowers… 'cos I'll marry you.'

Ginnie's hand hits her cheek and breaks the stem of the buttercup. 'You'll what?' Is she that simple he can read her mind now?

'I'll marry you. I was going ask you when you was older, any road. If the buttercup says as you're going to get married, then you'll need a husband, won't you?' Still leaning on his spade, with head on one side, he waits for her answer.

She can't, daren't, answer. She gets to her feet slowly, then bends to pick another buttercup. As if in a dream, she walks towards him, and lifts her chin. 'Well?'

His face is deadly serious as he leans forward just as slowly. 'Yeah. I can see a spot of yellow.' His eyes move from her chin to her lips, and then to her eyes and back to her lips.

She can't move. The world is quiet.

He reaches for her hand and takes the buttercup and lifts his chin in the same way. 'What about me?'

For a moment, the sun shines in her eyes, causing her to squint. He reaches out and his touch sends a shock flashing through her body. The cat's got her tongue. She can only nod.

'Then we'll have to get wed to please the buttercup.'

The lightest of kisses brushes her lips, oh so softly. The world belongs to just the two of them. She feels dizzy as he lets her go. His arms come around her. She's in exactly the place she wants to be, has wanted to be ever since he fell over her chair in the classroom.

He plants a huge kiss on her cheek and grins, knowing the effect he's having. The air feels lighter again and the moment is lost. She punches his arm and pretends to laugh. It comes out squeaky and uncertain. But something between them has changed.

They sit planning a wedding with lots of laughs about where and when it will be, and who will help them celebrate. Blushing madly, they speak of how many kids they'll have. Memories of Mary's talk about monthlies flood Ginnie's mind and her face grows even hotter. She's never had much to plan for. She has a warm feeling in her belly knowing there will be someone in her future who cares for her.

'Ginnie? You out there?'

It's Mary.

Ginnie jumps up and pushes her hair behind her ears. 'Coming, Mary,' she shouts back. 'Gotta go, Sam.'

'Best get a move on, lass; you're keeping me from me work,' he says in a pretend gruff voice. He winks as she brushes past him.

They smile at each other, not wanting to be the first to leave. She tries to skip away in her clogs and when she falls over neither of them can stop laughing. She knows he's still watching as she runs into the house. She doesn't go straight to the kitchen but up to the bedroom to stow the buttercup, with a broken stem, away in her little purse with the 'G' on the flap.

That evening at tea, they send knowing smiles across the dining hall, and turn away quickly in case others discover their secret. But she can't stop the rosy flush rising on her cheeks each time she thinks about that kiss, nor the sparkle lingering in her eyes.

'You look mighty happy these days,' says Mary as they wash the pots later.

'Hmm. Suppose so.'

'Young Sam's grown quite handsome don't you think?'

'Hmm.' Ginnie wishes she'd shut up. She isn't yet ready to talk about her feelings because she isn't really sure herself. It's much too soon to share with Mary.

If only Clara was here…

—

The coldness of winter seeps into the bones of those with little strength to fight. Ice forms on the tops of cups of water left out for the poorly ones, and frozen pipes leave Haddon with no running water for three days. Buckets are set out in the girls' bedroom and in the bathroom ready for the thaw, whenever it comes.

Ginnie's almost fourteen and it's her job to make sure all the girls are in bed by eight o'clock. Most are tired and cold, so it isn't difficult. After a bit of backchat, she usually has little difficulty in herding them upstairs. She circles the room checking all is well before turning in herself. Tonight, she advises them to wear both their dresses and two pairs of socks to keep warm. She tells the four youngest to share a bed, and they do with lots of giggles, which is fine so long as it doesn't go on for too long. Sometimes her diplomatic skills are known to turn to temper but she's fair, and they know it. She tucks everyone in and checks for signs of illness which can often take hold in the long dark hours of winter nights.

She shares a bed with thirteen-year-old Ada who arrived at Haddon two weeks ago. Ada likes to chat but Ginnie tells her to hold her tongue if she knows what's good for her. It keeps Ada on her toes. Tonight, when Ginnie finishes her checks and finally makes her way to bed, Ada is sitting in the middle rubbing her toes and poking out the bits of dirt between them because her bath night is still a couple of days away.

'Will you stop doing that?' Ginnie pulls hard on the blanket to cover her shoulders but Ada's body is in the way.

'Me toes are itching like mad. Can't stop.'

'You'll rub the skin away and make it much worse.' Ginnie lowers her voice. 'Peeing's best for taking the itches away.' She turns over and lights the candle. She almost bursts out laughing at the astonished look on Ada's face.

'Peas? How do peas help?'

'Not peas. Peeing, you know, in a bucket.'

'Dunner be daft, Ginnie. How's peeing going to stop me toes itching?'

Ginnie explains in the same low voice. 'Next time you pee in the bucket, rub some on your toes and it'll take the itches away. Try it if you don't believe me. I don't care.'

'You're fibbing.' Ada screws up her face in disgust.

'No, I'm not. If it's itching that much, why not give it a go?'

'Will I have to put me hand in the bucket?'

'I'll show you.' She holds out her hand and they scurry off to the bucket. Kneeling in front of Ada, whose eyes are like saucers, she says, 'Lift your foot up so's I can see your toes.'

'You sure?'

'Do you want it done or not? I'm not sitting here all night waiting for you to think about it.' She stands up and taps her foot lightly on the floor.

'Go on, but don't tell nobody; don't want them laughing at me.'

'Course I won't.'

Ginnie kneels again, holding her breath against the smell of the bucket. Ada places her foot reluctantly on Ginnie's thigh as she smears the 'medication' across her toes. 'Course, you'll have to do it a few times to make it work.'

Ada watches the beds, checking no one is spying on them. 'What'll they do if they see me? Laugh their heads off, I shouldn't wonder.'

'Well, don't let them see you then.'

When it's over, they run back to bed and shuffle beneath the blankets. Ginnie snuffs the candle. She stares at the ceiling as Ada squirms about in the narrow bed, still grunting.

'Will you stop? It's like sharing a bed with someone with nits.'

Ginnie folds her arms around Ada to control the flailing arms, hoping the extra warmth will benefit them both. Minutes later the door opens and Mary casts a light around the room. Apart from the odd cough and sniffle, all is still. Satisfied, Mary backs out of the room and closes the door.

Ginnie can't stop smiling. Many moons ago, someone had told her about this way of fighting chilblains, although she's never tried it herself. But she was willing to try anything to put an end to Ada's itches.

More snow has fallen during the night. Girls shiver in their sleep-crushed dresses. Clogs offer no protection for cold toes. Ginnie swears she only knows she still has feet because she doesn't fall over. Sam and another lad are given the task of clearing snow before more falls and they're cut off from the road.

As she creeps between the bedcovers that night, Ada shuffles up to her and puts her arm around Ginnie's shoulder. The cosy warmth of lying next to someone helps bring a contented sleepiness to her tired body.

'How's your toes?' says Ginnie over her shoulder, her eyes half closed.

'Heh?'

'Them chilblains! They was itching, wasn't they?'

'Oh, them have all gone. I did as you said, and my toes are right as ninepence.' Ada's voice is full of admiration. Ginnie's relieved she has her back to her for she'll prattle on and on, if she's a mind to.

'That's all right.' Ginnie turns her head away quickly to hide the laughter building up. She would do well to remember that cure for future patients.

'How do you know all that stuff?'

'What stuff?'

'Peeing and chilblains. Who told you?'

'Another wench what was older than me, I think.'

'I bet as you know lots of things. You always help out so you must be good at it.'

'Ada! Will you shut up and get off to sleep? You're giving me a right headache.'

Ada stops speaking and, instead, starts to whistle. Ginnie sits up pointedly and punches her pillow with a loud grunt. The whistling stops and soon the sound of gentle breathing beside her is all she can hear.

If the truth be known, she's rather pleased to know that someone thinks she's mighty clever.

# Chapter Fifteen

## A Cobble of Coal

### Haddon – April 1914

In the spring of 1914, Haddon House is crowded to the gunnels. After a long and bitter winter, both Mary and Ginnie feel sour when they are told to expect yet another small family of two girls and a boy.

'Don't they know we've got no room?' Ginnie bangs the knife down on the draining board.

'Course they do, but there's nothing we can do about it, so stop your moaning.'

Mary scrubs the kitchen table, teasing dirt from the soil-caked potatoes out of the wooden top while Ginnie slices up the rest of the vegetables in an attempt to stretch them out amongst twenty-six mouths.

'Hmm.'

'We'll cope,' says Mary, and scrubs even harder. 'We always do.'

Ginnie isn't so sure. There will come a time when coping is just not possible. Mary's eyes look dark, as if she hasn't had much sleep. Ginnie worries about her.

'Don't forget we're taking some young un's to the Big House this week.' She glances at Ginnie over her shoulder, 'And your father wants to talk to you.'

'Father?'

'Yeah. You've still got one, remember?' The more harassed Mary is, the more sarcastic she becomes. Ginnie has learned to take it with a pinch of salt.

'Dunno as he'll want to see me.' Ginnie keeps her head down and mutters from behind the lock of hair that has escaped from the bunch at the nape of her neck. She concentrates on clearing the table of peelings and other scraps so Mary can finish the scrubbing.

'He wouldn't let you go to the funeral but that doesn't mean he cares less about you.'

Ginnie rounds on Mary. 'Mabel went. Why is he suddenly remembering he's got another daughter?'

Mary washes her chapped hands and dries them with the end of her apron. 'She's grown up now and he's still your dad, so you'll come along and see what he has to say. About time too, if you ask me.'

Later that evening she asks Sam what he thinks her father might want to talk about.

'How can I say? I've never met him.'

'But if you had to guess?' She knew he couldn't really say, but it helps to talk.

'Perhaps he wants to say he's sorry.'

-

Ginnie helps three excited little girls to get ready for the visit to the Big House. Mary sends two boys back to wash away the grime from an early morning spent clearing out rubble from the garden where a wall has fallen in. It's now half past ten, and they'll have to hurry if they're to stand any chance of getting back for dinnertime. They leave Gladys Piper, who has recently become the cook, with instructions about timings in the event they are late returning.

As they walk up to the gates, Ginnie's eyes are drawn to a black stone glistening by the side of the track. She lets go of the two girls on either side of her and tells them to follow Mary.

When they are safely inside, she picks up the small lump of coal, a cobble, smooth and dull. It leaves a trail of black dust over her palm. She turns it over and it glistens, black as black, flashing like a precious stone. She slips it into her pocket and runs to the door, rubbing coal dust from her hands, glad her black coat won't show the dirt.

Voices work their way along the corridor and the door swings open. A young couple dash forward and throw their arms around two of the girls. Squeals of delight are followed by tears which are soon dashed away with fists because they aren't cry-babies. Ginnie turns her head away. *Her* meeting isn't going to be like that at all.

Her father edges his way forward with his white stick, stopping to listen after a few paces.

Ginnie can't move.

Mary nudges her. 'Go to him, Ginnie. You must or you'll never forgive yourself.'

It's odd standing in front of his near sightless eyes, not knowing what to say.

'That you, Ginnie?'

Even his voice sounds frail. 'Yes, Father.'

'How are you, duckie?'

'All right.'

Of course he *loves* her; they just don't see eye to eye on funerals. A hysterical laugh builds in her chest at the thought, but she manages to calm down before it erupts. More than likely, it's just the stress of the meeting.

She steers him to a bench a little way away from the rest of the group. They sit side by side. She could ask him anything – what he's been doing, if he's been well, who he talks to – but she doesn't. She could tell him about Haddon and Sam coming back, but she doesn't.

'You're just sitting there.' He slaps his hand hard against his thigh, startling her. 'You've got to speak 'cos I canna see yer.'

'Sorry, Father.' Her conversation has taken place inside her head. He has no idea what she's thinking. 'It's been a long time,' she says finally.

'It wasn't my fault you had to go away.'

'I never said it was!' Her words come too quickly. She's grateful he can't see her discomfort.

'I know you blame me. You can't even talk to me, can you? Speak up, wench. I need to hear yer voice.'

'I *am* talking.'

'Yes, but you're acting like a wench with nowt to say. I want to know what you've been doing with yourself these past months. Have yer got any friends? Who's been looking out for you? I want to feel I know you.'

*But I've already told you*, her brain protests, *but you never listen*. She starts the painful re-living of her history at Haddon. 'I had a friend once. She died.' She tries to say more, but her tongue is too dry. A sob comes from nowhere.

It's his turn to feel uncomfortable. He sniffs and rubs his forehead. 'Sorry. Poor mite.'

She doesn't know if he's talking about her or Clara. Although he doesn't know it, he's gazing at the blank wall opposite. Ginnie studies his profile, the sharp nose, thin lips. He used to be handsome. Now he's just old.

She can't read his thoughts. She carries on talking. 'Her name was Clara. She was even younger than me. She shared my bed at Haddon. Then she got sick and they took her away. That's when she died.'

'I'm mighty sorry, love. Did you get sick as well?'

'Not like Clara was.' She can't tell him that her own sickness was in her head and in her heart.

'That's all right then.' He draws a long breath, as though he feels he's done his duty. 'Come here, lass.'

He rubs his nose on his sleeve before holding out his arms to her. She feels a stirring of something. Things might be different in the future.

'You'll come to see me again?'

'Do you want me to?'

'Course I do, silly wench. What man wouldn't want to see his own daughter?'

She thinks of the long wait since the funeral. 'I can't just drop in while I'm at Haddon.'

'You'll be working soon. You'll be able to come whenever you like.' His words come faster. He moves his hand up Ginnie's arm to her neck and lingers at her jaw, his voice husky. 'Growed up you may think you are, but I can only see my little wench, in here.' He points to his head. 'Ah, Ginnie lass, I wish I could see yer now, proper like.'

It's just as Mary said. He still sees her as the child she had been, but there's love in his voice. She moves closer to give him the hug she has held back.

He clears his voice a couple of times. 'Well, I've news for you, lass. I'm going to get wed soon. That's why I wanted to see yer.'

Her arms fall to her sides, the hug forgotten. Has she heard right? If he got wed it'd be like Mother never existed.

'Dunno whether I'll ever get out of this place. I've all but lost my sight, but my brain's still working. I'm not daft. If I do get out, I'll need somebody to look after me. You can come and stay. We'll be a family again. You'd like that, wouldn't you, Ginnie?'

'You want *me* to come and live with you and somebody else?'

He carries on as if he hasn't noticed. 'She's called Ellen. She lives here in the Big House. Her husband died a few months back. Haven't asked her yet but I'll need someone to look after me if I ever get out of here, and she'll need a home.'

'Has she got any family?'

'Grown up and left home. She doesn't know where they are.'

'But, what about Mother?' A spark of jealousy runs through her, but whether it's for her mother or herself, she can't say.

'No amount of wishing's going to bring yer mother back, Ginnie. I have to plan, like I said. I'll never forget her, never.

She was a good woman, but she was taken from us. I've got to look to whatever future I've got left. I can't manage on me own. I know that.' A smile crosses his face. 'We've got to be practical, and we can go back to being a family again.'

'What about our Mabel?'

'Her's got married.'

'Married!' Ginnie's eyes bulged. 'Why wasn't I—'

'Not long after yer Mam died. It was quick, couldn't be helped.' His voice is almost a whisper.

'Where?'

'Somewhere up Hanley.'

'You didn't go?'

He purses his lips as if he doesn't like Mabel's new husband.

'What's he like?' She can't imagine her sister married.

'Not good enough. And before you ask, I'll not be living with them, and there's an end to it.'

She waits for him to say more, but he clams up.

Something else she's missed out on – her own sister's wedding. Was she too young for that as well?

The bell rings and it's too late to talk. What's the point? He's made up his mind again and that's that.

None of them have a mind to talk on the way back to Haddon. Even the boys sniffle and wipe their snotty noses on their coat sleeves. Mary looks her way but Ginnie refuses to be drawn into conversation. She has too much to think about. Her father and a woman who isn't Mother? It's only when she's back at Haddon and taking off her coat that she realises she never asked him when he's planning to get married and thus when she might have to leave Haddon.

*He's got no money to live on. How can he leave?* Her reaction shocks her, but she has new friends now. No one should ask her to give them up – not again, not after all she's been through. In the beginning, she had hated her life at Haddon. But she has Sam and Mary. They're her family now.

Ginnie says nothing to Mary about her visit. She wants to be clear in her own mind how she feels. When Sam asks how it went she says they had an argument about nothing in particular, that she was very angry, and that the workhouse makes it difficult to patch things up.

She's scrubbing the floor of the kitchen when Mary bustles in. Something about her entrance makes Ginnie stop and look up. Mary has a huge smile on her face.

'You'll never guess. Seems as your sister's been asking after you.'

'M-my sister?'

'Mabel isn't?'

'Mabel?'

'Yes child, and for goodness' sake, stop repeating everything I say.'

Ginnie sits back on her heels 'Mabel's asking for me?'

'You're not taking it in, are you? Remember your sister? We saw her at the funeral?' Mary pulls her on to the small wooden stool used for reaching into the high cupboards.

*My married sister*, Ginnie corrects her silently. 'Course I do. What's she want?'

'Ephraim Tolley's been with a note from the Big House. She's been asking after you. She wants to see you, duckie. That's good news, isn't it?'

'She wants to see me? Here?'

'There you go again, telling me what I've just this minute told you.'

Ginnie jumps up and grabs the mop propped up against the door and looks wildly for the bucket of water. Gently, Mary takes the mop out of her hand and pulls up a stool.

'Mabel wants to come here to see you after dinner tomorrow afternoon. You'll get on fine once you put your mind to it.'

*What'll we have to say to each other?* Ginnie shakes her head. She knows nothing about Mabel and what she's been up to since the family parted, apart from her getting a new job and getting wed. What does Mabel know about her? And, why now?

Amid her anxiety there's a spark of curiosity. All the waiting, and it's finally going to happen. She paces about the kitchen, wringing her hands as if kneading bread. 'What shall I say?'

'Ee duckie, I don't know. The Lord moves in mysterious ways. She wants to get to know you again… maybe.' The 'maybe' hangs in the air. 'I thought you'd be pleased. See what she's got to say for herself. No point in second-guessing and upsetting yourself. She's coming here later tomorrow so you'll find out soon enough.'

'That's too soon.'

'You have to see her. She's family. You'll be all right.'

'Will you be with me?'

'For heaven's sake, child! It's your sister we're talking about, not some vagabond off the street. You moaned when she didn't come, and now you're moaning because she wants to. No pleasing some folk.'

'What if she doesn't like me?'

'Course she'll like you, you silly girl. Who wouldn't?' Mary's voice softens. 'Don't worry, I'll be here. Maybe you won't want me when you get talking. She'll love you because you're her sister.'

That's not necessarily true, but Ginnie can't help feeling guilty when Mary puts it that way. She *should* be excited. Clara had nobody. Perhaps *she* doesn't deserve a sister.

Mary pats her on the back and smooths her apron before walking off towards her room. Ginnie reaches for the mop to finish the floor. She won't tell Sam until after she's seen Mabel. No point in getting *him* all worked up too.

That night she thinks about the tall woman she saw at the graveyard. Mabel will be about nineteen now. As the night grows longer, Ginnie's anxiety about the following day grows stronger. *What happens if we don't like each other? Why now?*

At three o'clock prompt, the doorbell rings. Ginnie drops the duster she's using to put the finishing touches to Mary's room, where the meeting is to take place. She has waited nervously for the bell and, as a consequence, it sounds much louder than normal. She's brushed her hair vigorously and hopes she looks tidy and presentable. She strains to catch the unfamiliar voice, but it's too low.

Mary ushers into the room a tall, smart woman wearing what looks like the large brimmed hat she had worn at the funeral, now decorated with a thin band of green ribbon around its crown. Ginnie stands beside the fireplace, arms at her sides, hardly breathing.

Close up, Mabel is quite pretty, with a pointed nose like Ginnie's, and her eyes are the same deep brown with the dark lashes she remembers. Where Mabel's eyebrows are smooth and delicate, Ginnie's are dark and bushy. In her long black coat, her sister appears tall and grand, and her black boots are polished. Ginnie, conscious of her own well-worn clogs and workhouse dress, wants to hide.

Mabel moves a small black bag from one hand to the other before taking up Mary's offer of a seat.

'Hiya, Ginnie. Been a good while, hasn't it?'

Ginnie manages a nod. Mabel's voice spirits her back to the days when they argued and fought together. She feels calmer.

Mary speaks first.

'Have you come far, Miss?'

'I walked from Burslem, and I'm *Mrs* Mabel Farmer, by the way. But you can call me Mabel.'

'Beg your pardon. It's a good walk, isn't it?' Mary smiles and nods encouragingly.

'It's not that far,' Mabel blurts out. 'I like a good walk.'

*Then why take three years to come and visit?* She must've pulled a face because Mary glares at her as Mabel looks around the room. The rhythmic tick of the clock in the corner is oddly soothing.

Mary glances from one sister to the other. Shaking her head, she gets to her feet and walks to the door. 'Best leave you to it. There's things need seeing to. No, Ginnie, you stay put; you've got a visitor. You girls must have a lot of catching up to do. I'll not be long.'

The silence and the clock take turns to thump in her ears. Every time their eyes meet, they turn away self-consciously.

'It's a cosy little room, isn't it?' says Mabel.

''S'all right, I suppose.'

'Are they looking after you?'

'Yes, I'm used to it. I've been here a good while, after all.' She can't resist the little dig.

'You wouldn't believe how much I've missed you.'

Ginnie's head shoots up. *Why not come sooner then?* It would sound disrespectful to say the words out loud and Mary wouldn't be at all pleased.

'Remember I went to live with Aunty Nellie when you went away with Mother and Father?' Mabel clears her throat and slowly paces around the room. 'Well, I was all right until October. That's when I met my bloke, you see.' She flashes out her hand to show a thin gold band on her finger to prove it.

Ginnie tries not to mind that she wasn't a bridesmaid. After all, what would she have worn? 'Father told me. He says he's thinking of getting wed too.'

Mabel carries on talking as if Ginnie hasn't spoken. 'It was all done in a rush and so it wasn't in church.' Her face reddens. 'Father wasn't too happy. Still, I'm one less person he has to worry about now, aren't I?'

Ginnie can't think why Mabel wants to tell her all of this when her wedding has already taken place and she wasn't invited. She makes her mind up there and then not to go to Father's wedding… if Mother isn't there. A wave of hysteria washes over her. If Mother *could* go to the wedding, then there'd be no wedding because they'd still be married. So deep is she in her thoughts that she misses some of what Mabel is saying.

'... name's Frank. He's a "caster" on the pots. We got married in December. Am expecting now.' Her hand moves automatically to her stomach.

'Father never said.'

All this time with no family to speak of and now she has a married sister who's having a baby and a father who is thinking of getting married again.

'I haven't told him yet. We weren't on speaking terms at the wedding.'

'Wh—?'

'Am going on three months now.'

Ginnie's eyes drop to her sister's belly but Mabel's coat is still buttoned up. Mary said babies were carried for nine months. Ginnie counts the months on her hands locked under her knees. Whatever problem between Mabel and Father, it wasn't 'cos she had to get wed because she was having a baby.

Her face must show her concentration on counting because Mabel flushes violently. She drops to her seat again. 'It's good news about me and Frank, isn't it?'

'A baby sounds nice. Will I be an aunty?'

'Course you will. You're the only aunty my baby'll have. Do you like babies, Ginnie?'

The question hangs in the air, as if her next words are really important.

'I think so.'

Mabel visibly relaxes as if the hard work is over with. 'I was wondering...' Mabel picks up both of Ginnie's hands. '... actually, me and Frank was wondering, if you might like to come and live with us for a while?'

Ginnie very nearly falls off her chair. 'With you and your husband and your baby?'

'It'll be so good, you and me together again.'

Ginnie's head swims. All those years of being on her own and now two offers in no time at all. If only Mabel had come when Clara passed away and before Sam came back, she'd have jumped at the chance. But, now? She can't imagine living anywhere else but Haddon.

'Father said I could live with him after he's wed.'

Mabel rushes on. 'You could help me with the baby and everything. We want you to come and live with us, Ginnie. You're family. I think I'll need you more than Father after he's married.'

'What about Aunty Nellie?'

'Aunty Nellie's not been too well herself. She's gone to nurse her brother who's been taken poorly.' Mabel's face turns into a frown. 'She never liked my Frank. Thought he wasn't good enough.'

*Is the baby the only reason for Mabel's visit*, she wonders? Over the years, Ginnie has learned not to show her feelings to anyone especially when she's not sure of them herself. With Aunty Nellie gone, Mabel will probably need all the help she can get.

Mary's return at that moment is a welcome relief. She gives Ginnie a sharp glance as she sits between them. 'Now then, what's to do?'

'I've asked our Ginnie to come and live with us, Mrs Higgins.'

It's Mary's turn to be shocked. 'You've asked Ginnie to…' Her eyes swivel towards Ginnie who makes no attempt to fill the silence. 'Well, you could knock me down with a feather. Isn't that good news, Ginnie love?'

*Leave Haddon? Sam? Mary? This is my home now*, her brain protests.

'I'm sure she's over the moon. She isn't one for saying much. She just needs a bit of time for it all to sink in. As a rule, kids like her what's been here a long time, don't get offers like that. They stay till they get a job. Ginnie, what do you say?'

Mary's sharp voice requires a response.

'Thanks,' Ginnie mutters through the folds of her hair, her fingers crossed.

'We can't hear you, Ginnie.'

'Do I have to go?' She blurts it out before she can stop herself.

'Ginnie! Don't be so ungrateful.'

'I'm sorry, Mary.' Ginnie tries again. 'What I mean is, do I have to say yes now?' *Things are going from bad to worse.* 'Only Father's asked me as well,' she finishes lamely.

'I thought you didn't want to live with him? Your sister's offering to take you in, child. Surely that must make you happy?'

Mabel must've thought she'd be on her knees, begging. But all she wants is to choose for herself. Does that make her a bad person?

'Well, if that's all the thanks I get… I never expected you'd want to stay in this God-forsaken place when you could have a real home, our Ginnie.' Mabel marches towards the door, nose in the air.

'It's not a God-forsaken place. It's my home.' It's the first time Ginnie has spoken out, and it gives her confidence. 'Did you ever think of me when they put me here? I was eleven, Mabel.' Ginnie gets to her feet and holds her head high. 'I was that lonely.'

Mary slides between Mabel and the door. 'Don't go, Miss… Mabel. She wasn't expecting such news. Let's sit down and talk calmly.'

Mabel glances at Mary, and then back to Ginnie.

The silence lengthens.

'Ginnie, your sister's offering you a home. You should be grateful. You can't want to stay here forever. Not when you've got a chance to be part of a family again. You have to grab it and be thankful 'cos there's lots of others in here would snap your hands off.'

Dreams of going home had stopped for Ginnie when she realised nobody was coming for her and now the dream has become a reality, she doesn't know if she wants it any more. The butterflies are back and playing havoc in her belly. *What if it all goes wrong?* Will she be able to come back, like Sam? The protective walls she has built over the years are crumbling. *And what about Sam?*

'Right,' said Mary taking charge again. 'When can you take her?' The colour has returned to Mary's cheeks and she's back to her practical self.

'I suppose she'll have to agree to come with me first, although I have to say, Mrs Higgins, she doesn't look too pleased. Thought she'd jump at the chance. Shows you never can tell.'

'You're family. She doesn't have no say. The parish'll only pay her keep if there's nobody else to do it. If she's got any sense, she'll be only too pleased to go with you.' Mary glares at Ginnie, daring her to contradict.

Ginnie sinks lower into her seat, beaten. If Mary won't let her stay, she has no choice at all.

'I thought you'd want to come. I wanted to get you out after you left with Mother and Father. But I couldn't, not until I was wed, with somewhere to live, could I? There wasn't enough room for us all at Aunty Nellie's. I came soon as I could.'

A solitary tear reaches Ginnie's mouth before she knows it's there.

Mary croaks. 'Ginnie's overwhelmed. It's been a big day. She'll come round soon enough, duckie. How soon did you say you can take her?'

'Well, I could come back at the end of the week, after I've done me jobs. I need to tell our Frank it's all sorted first. But I'll not force her.' Mabel pulls herself up tall.

'I'll be sure and have her ready for you, no messing.' Mary inclines her head meaningfully. 'Well, Ginnie? What do you say to your sister?'

Ginnie turns a watery gaze towards her sister. 'Thank you for asking me to share your home... Mabel.'

'Then, you'll come?'

Ginnie nods slowly. 'I'll come with you at the end of the week, if you'll have me?'

'Course I will.' Mabel rises quickly, relieved the meeting is over. She straightens her coat and places her hat back on her head, glancing at Ginnie once more before following Mary through the door.

When Mary returns, Ginnie rounds on her. 'I thought we were friends.'

'Oh, my love. Course I want you to stay, but I've got no right to do that.'

'Just tell her you need me.'

'You were always going on about her not visiting. She's offering you a home and you're still not happy. What do you really want?'

Tears fill Ginnie's eyes. 'I'm happier now than I've ever been and I'm going to lose it all over again. How can I leave you and Sam?'

'Listen to me, Ginnie.' Mary holds Ginnie's head with both hands, forcing her to look. 'This good time that you're talking about won't last. What happens if something you've got no control over changes? Like when Sam left? And, you don't need to worry about him, by the way; he'll come after you soon as ever he can, mark my words.' She holds on to Ginnie's hand. 'I've got to do what's best for you in the long run. Leave this place. Make something of yourself while you can. You won't regret it. I know that because, you see, when I was your age, nobody came for me.'

'You mean you was—'

'Yes, I was here. I didn't have any family and so when I was old enough to work, I was sent to the Big House. I tried for jobs in-service for a time, but it didn't work out, so I went back. After a while they sent me here to take care of the young folk. I've never known anywhere else.'

'But you was married…'

'I'll tell you something I've never told nobody else, Ginnie. But you mustn't tell a soul.'

Ginnie crosses her heart and hopes to die.

'I was never married.'

Ginnie's mouth falls open.

'I pretended I got married when I was in-service, to get this job. I couldn't get anything else. I thought it'd help if I was a respectable, married woman.'

'And you've kept it secret all these years?'

'I've never told a soul. It's too late for me now, Ginnie. But not for you.' Mary smiles and holds both Ginnie's hands between her own. 'Don't be angry, Ginnie. While there's a breath left in my body, I'm damned if I'm going to let you go through what I went through. You might even thank me for it one day.'

# Chapter Sixteen

## A Carpetbag and A Doll

**Haddon – May 1914**

Ginnie catches Sam at teatime as they come out of the dining hall. Although he's washed his hands, there's dirt under his fingernails and a black mark across his forehead where he must have rubbed sweat from his eyes. Mabel's visit is preying on her mind. She follows him from the crowded hall.

'I need to tell you something.' She doesn't know what she's going to say but she'll feel better once she's said it. Nothing can be as bad as this horrible sinking feeling in the pit of her belly. 'Veg patch. Half an hour.'

He nods and disappears with the rest of the lads.

She wanders into the kitchen and ignores the sinks full of bowls, dirty cutlery, and the piles of pans she certainly won't miss in her new life. She tries rehearsing what she's going to say to him. Should she just come out with it? Will he miss her as much as she missed him when he went away?

She can't wait any longer. She slips out of her apron and heads for the back door. Once outside, she hurries down the yard and picks her way carefully over the grass and undergrowth in the bright early evening sun. Sam is lurking between the bushes at the back of the tater patch.

'Hiya Sam.'

He wipes his hands down his trousers. 'You're early. What's up?'

'I couldn't wait. Quick...' She grabs his hand and leads him to the small wall between the compost heap and the tool shed.

'It's not every day a lad has a wench telling him she canna wait.' His grin stretches from ear to ear.

She sits on the wall and picks nervously at her fingers. 'I don't know what to say now I'm here.'

He steadies her hands, his face suddenly serious. 'Ginnie, if it's that bad, it's best to just get it over with.'

'It's good and bad. At least, I'd like to think there is good in it.' She feels cold stone through her dress, and shivers. 'Dunno what you'll think.'

'You shouldn't have come out here without putting on something to keep warm. It's not summer yet, duck. "Ne'er cast a clout till May is out." Did yer Ma never tell yer?'

He sits beside her, his arm around her shoulders, waiting for her to say something. That's another thing she likes about him. He doesn't push her into saying something until she's good and ready. She's so comfortable in his arms. How she longs to put everything else out of her mind and stay there forever.

She takes a deep breath. 'My big sister's come looking for me.'

He whistles. 'That's a turn-up. Did she say why she's never been to see yer in all this time?'

'Well... she's got married and she's got a baby on the way, though you can't really tell yet.'

He whistles again. 'Bet you didn't expect that.'

'No.' Her bright and cheerful voice has gone and a choked voice has taken over. 'Mabel wants me to go and live with her, Sam. I didn't expect that neither.'

'Live with her? In a house?'

'Course it's in a house. Where else could it be?' Ginnie automatically puts her hand on his shoulder. 'I've got to go away, Sam – at the end of the week, probably.'

'Says who?'

'Mary says, when someone gives you a place to stay, you have leave. Mabel wants me to go and live with her and her husband, and help them with their new baby, when it's born.'

'She wants you to work for her?'

'Well, I shall have to help her. Doing what I do here pretty much, except I'll be doing it for her instead.' The words rush out. 'You… you've been right good to me. I've just found out and I'm all topsy-turvy. It means I can get out of here. I might even get a job. Mary says I should be grateful something good's happening for a change.'

She watches confusion and hurt take turns to run across his face.

'You're just going to bugger off somewhere without me?' He pushes her away and turns his back. 'I came back here because of you.' He chews some broken skin from his finger.

'I've got no choice, Sam. It won't be long until you get out, and you can come find me.'

'You won't want to know me when you leave here. You'll get some big ideas and forget about me, the boy from the workhouse.'

'That's not fair. I didn't forget you when you went away, did I?' She thumps his shoulder again and again until he answers. 'Did I? Did I?'

'No, you didn't. But I went to another workhouse. You'll be free to do whatever you want.'

'Well, I'm not likely to forget *you*, am I?'

He hangs his head sheepishly and throws a stone at the broken fence a few feet away. And then another.

'Not when we've talked of getting wed.' She manages a wobbly smile. 'I know it was only pretend, but I'll never forget you. Think about that. You're my best friend, and always will be.' She gives him the biggest of hugs and squeezes his arms.

'Hey up, you're half killing me. Lay off, will yer?'

Suddenly they're laughing.

'Promise you won't forget me, Ginnie?'

She picks up his hand, lays a kiss on it and holds it against her cheek. 'I promise you, Sam White. I'll never forget you. Cross my heart and hope to die.' She licks her finger and draws a big cross on her chest.

'Hey, don't do that. You don't know what might happen.'

'I'm saying it 'cos it's true.' She holds his gaze, determined not to be the first to look away. 'You won't forget me, will you?' Her heart pounds hard, leaving no room for her lungs. 'Promise me, Sam.'

He crosses his heart and her heart sings.

'I promise, Ginnie love.'

'You'll get out of here soon. My sister's name is Mabel Farmer now, and she lives over Burslem somewhere. I'll find out where and you'll have to keep saying it over and over till you remember it. It's not that big a place. You can get a job, look for somewhere to stay. Oh, Sam, it could be so good. Don't you see?'

'I'll do that all right. And you'll wait for me?'

She hardly dares to breathe. 'Course I will, forever.'

His face closes in on her. A light kiss, gentle and sweet, brushes her lips and sends shivers up and down her spine. When he pulls away it's like part of her has gone too. She takes her time opening her eyes, wanting this moment to go on forever. She has caught a glimpse of a future she can look forward to.

'I should go. Mary needs me to sort some things for her before I leave.'

'Stay a while. It's not fair. When are you going?'

'Friday.'

'That soon? Bugger, bugger.' He throws another stone hard and hits the fence with a resounding thud. 'I suppose that's that, then.'

'Oh, Sam.'

He's on his feet, hugging her. She stays in his arms as long as she dares, then breaks away.

'Mary's going to give me some new clothes tonight. Nice ones like they wear outside.' She gives a self-conscious laugh. 'I suppose the clothes I came in will be too small now, because I've grown a fair bit, haven't I?' She twirls in front of him, wanting him to watch, to keep a picture of her fixed in his head that he will never forget.

He ruffles the top of her head and laughs. 'You haven't grown very much at all from where I'm standing.'

She swings out her arm to slap him, but he's already running. His long legs are so much faster than hers. He waves to her and disappears at the far end of the walled garden. She stays in the veg patch, where she can be closest to him, and lets the tears come.

Dabbing her eyes one last time, and praying she won't meet anyone on the way, she hurries into the house to finish her final tasks. She can't begin to explain the way she feels at this moment.

But she has no time at all to think about the future. Mary sees to that.

–

Thursday evening comes soon enough. She's hardly seen Sam and is surprised Mary hasn't shown more compassion. He has taught her a new game using string and a spinning top, but she can't concentrate. She prefers to watch so she doesn't have to take her eyes off him.

*How will it feel living in a small house with only two people and a baby? Less work, certainly. But a sick baby and smelly nappies?* Suppose she doesn't get on with Mabel, or her husband takes a dislike to her?

Sam catches up with her as she's sorting out bedding in the laundry.

'How're you feeling, duck? You look miles away already.'

'Dunno, Sam.' She has tried to feel excited about living with her sister, and a husband she's never met, and being free to do whatever she chooses. 'I can't picture the future at all. Last night

Mary asked me if I was looking forward to it but I said good things are often followed by bad.'

She walks a few paces and turns to face him. 'How did you really feel when you went away?'

'The honest truth? Petrified. But I was going to another workhouse. You're going to live with yer sister.'

'Yeah, a sister I haven't seen since I was eleven who couldn't be bothered to visit me. Why now, Sam? If I knew the answer, I'd be much happier.'

'If she was just somebody what had walked in off the street, then you should be worried. But she's your kin, Ginnie. Doesn't that make a difference?'

*Perhaps he's right*, she thinks. After all, she isn't being sent out into the world with nothing. 'I'm being silly. It'll all be fine. I'll miss you so much.'

'All I want is for you to be happy, Ginnie. I'll come for you. Wild horses won't stop me.'

'You've got the paper with Mabel's address, haven't you? Keep it safe so as you know where to find me. Even if you can't read it, you can show it to someone who can.'

'I'll get it tattooed on me forehead if you want me to?'

'This is important, Sam.'

'I'm joking. Come back and see us soon as you can.'

'I'll be back before you know it,' she smiles. 'But if you get out first, come and find me. Maybe a neighbour will let you board with them. Oh, Sam, think how wonderful that will be. We'll be free to do anything.'

–

'Ginnie dear, come and sit with me for a while.'

It's evening and the first time Mary has invited Ginnie into her room for anything other than to give her instructions.

'Don't look so surprised. I am in need of company and I haven't got you for much longer.'

She feels quite grown up sitting in Mary's room taking tea. They chat about everything, and nothing. Ginnie is surprised how much younger Mary looks when she laughs.

'I've put some clothes on your bed for tomorrow. They're not much cop but they'll do for starters. A couple of dresses, a pair of good strong boots, and a decent coat so's you don't catch your death. Oh, and I've put a couple of extra pairs of drawers out so you've got spares for washing days. There's this too.'

Mary holds out a carpetbag in a rich red tapestry with a blue pattern threaded through. 'It'll hold all your tranklements.'

'My what?' Ginnie takes the bag and opens it but there's nothing inside. It feels sturdy and looks almost new, well looked after.

'Tranklements. Your bits and pieces. I don't like calling belongings "bits and pieces". It makes them sound worthless. "Tranklements" sounds much nicer.'

'It's much too nice to give away. I might not be able to give it back to you. Are you sure?'

'Course I'm sure. A woman I used to know gave it to me a long time ago and now I'm giving it to you.'

There's a lump in Ginnie's throat.

'I'll nip upstairs and get my things. It won't take long.'

She rushes out of the room, not knowing if she can hold back any longer. Upstairs, she piles everything into her arms, takes a deep breath, and makes her way carefully down the stairs to Mary's room.

She folds up the spare dress Mary has given her and lays it on top of the underclothes on the table. These are followed by a comb with broken teeth, a lump of coal wrapped in a bit of rag so as it doesn't get the other stuff dirty, a couple of dried flowers, a red shottie, a red ribbon, and a small patchwork purse.

Mary looks quizzical. 'What's all that?'

'My tranklements.'

She picks up each item, one at a time. 'It's the story of my life. The cobble of coal, I picked up from the drive at the Big

House the day Father told me he was going to wed again. See the beautiful shine on the cut side?' She turns it over in the palm of her hand so that Mary can see the light from the lamp reflected off the hewn sides. 'Don't worry, I've washed it, so's it won't get the bag dirty. The comb,' she blinks a couple of times and sniffs, 'was Clara's, and Sam gave me the shottie. The purse was a present Clara made the Christmas before she died.'

'Oh!' Mary is lost for words.

'They'll always remind me of this place.'

'But you didn't like it. You kept yourself to yourself most of the time.'

'But I was a child when I came. Now it's as much my home as my real one was, especially with you, and Sam.'

'The flowers are from your mam's grave, aren't they?'

Ginnie nods. She can't tell Mary about the buttercup. That's between her and Sam.

Mary glances inside the bag again. 'And the ribbon?'

Ginnie picks it up and holds it in front of her, showing off its length of colour. 'It belonged to our Mabel. She was arguing with her friend about it one night and gave it to me before we left, a keepsake so's I wouldn't forget her. Like I said, this bag will hold the story of my life and I'll treasure it always. I only wish I had my book – my Sunday School prize.'

Mary is silent. Together, they gaze at Ginnie's bag of belongings.

'My life's not worth very much, is it?'

'Well, I never, Ginnie love.' Mary's voice wobbles. 'It'll be a bag full of memories, and that's so much better than lots of fancy things we might take for granted. An unwritten diary.' She takes hold of Ginnie's hands. 'You've turned out well, duckie. I'll be lost without you, but I'll not stand in your way when it comes to you having a chance of a better life.'

'I could be happy staying here,' Ginnie says wistfully.

'You may think that now, but you'll look back on this moment and wish you'd made a different choice. Mark my words. The world will be open to you to do whatever you want to. There's plenty of room in the bag for more memories, Ginnie.'

It still feels wrong to be leaving but talking has drawn her attention to new possibilities. How many more tranklements can she add to the bag – new, happy memories?

'Build the life you want, Ginnie. It won't be long before young Sam comes knocking on your door. I'd bet my life on it.'

Ginnie grins broadly. 'Oh, I do hope so.'

Mary points at the carpetbag. 'And that's another special keepsake. At least, I hope it is?'

'It means even more to me now. You've looked after me these last few years and now your carpetbag is looking after my tranklements. That makes it special. Oh, Mary, I wish I had something to give you. I wish *you* were my big sister.'

Tears fill Mary's eyes as they cling together. 'That's the best present you could've given me, duckie. You'll come see me, won't you? Tell me how you're getting on?'

'I will. I *will*.'

She drops a kiss on Mary's cheek and has another glance inside the bag. It holds everything she possesses yet it's near on empty. *No*, she chides herself, *do as Mary says and think how much more it could hold.*

'How're you feeling, Ginnie? Really feeling, I mean?'

'I don't know. Excited. Scared. Sad about the people I'm leaving behind. Happy to think I'll be part of a family again. Curious to see how I get on with Mabel and her husband. I feel like laughing and crying at the same time.'

'You'll be fine. Anyone would be proud to be your sister.'

Now Ginnie's crying. This evening Mary has been more caring than she has ever been. Even when Clara died, Mary had kept herself to herself. Ginnie tries to talk, about Haddon, Sam, Mabel, but it all comes out wrong.

She tries again. 'When I first came, I hated it. Well, you know that more than anyone.' She can feel the blush coming. 'I blamed Haddon, the Big House, my father for being here. But I came to realise that it doesn't matter where you are. It's people that matter.'

'Don't lose that, Ginnie, and you'll never be alone again.'

Upstairs later, she looks again at the dresses Mary has given her. They feel considerably lighter than those she's used to wearing. Nothing fancy – one almost reaches her ankles and is cut in a pale green woollen material. It's softer than the coarse roughness of her workhouse dresses and a whole lot prettier, with little tiny pleats sown into the bodice and showing off her steadily growing figure. It'll need shortening. The yellow flowery one's a little tight around her arms and rather short but will do for the time being. She will wear it tomorrow, for the start of her new life. A black coat, black boater, and black-laced boots complete her outfit.

When she tries on the boots and wiggles her toes, her feet feel trapped after the openness of her clogs.

–

After breakfast she asks Sam to repeat Mabel's address to check he has it fixed in his mind. As an additional precaution, she tells Mary to test him too. The worry that they'll lose touch once she's on the outside is very real. The nightmares are back, of being all alone, of searching for someone. She's convinced it's Sam she's looking for. He's the only person in the whole world she can't bear to part with.

She paces up and down the girls' bedroom. And then, because she can stand it no longer, she folds her coat over her arm, grabs her hat and the handles of the carpetbag, and casts one last glance around the room that has been her home for the last three years.

A seed of excitement is growing inside her. New challenges lie ahead, but she's not on her own any more. She will soon be part of a family again, and she has Sam, who she hopes will join her before too long. The rest of her life is about to begin.

She'll be in charge of her own destiny. She has come through the worst period of her life and things will get better from now on.

Sam is waiting at the bottom of the stairs.

'Where've you been? I thought I was going to leave without seeing you.' Her voice sounds sharp and now he's standing in front of her, she doesn't know what else to say. She certainly can't tell him how she feels about leaving because those feelings are mostly down to him. He'd probably say she's proper daft.

'I've made you a present,' he bursts out. His eyes refuse to meet hers. It's good to know that he isn't his usual self too.

He thrusts a parcel wrapped in red cloth at her. 'Here, you'd best have it. It won't do me no good.' His laugh peters out almost before it begins.

'A present?' She claps her hands. 'Oh, Sam, thank you so much.'

She unfolds the cloth to find a small wooden doll. It has strands of brown wool for hair and a lop-sided smile. It's wearing a deep red dress made from the same material as the wrapping, with tucks in the bodice, long sleeves, little bows around the hem, and a frilly white petticoat. Black painted boots cover her over-sized feet.

'Mary made the dress, but I did the rest.'

She isn't the most beautiful doll Ginnie has ever seen, but she's certainly the most special. The dress is so pretty she would love one just like it for herself, and the black boots are like the ones she's wearing.

She tries to smile to stop a sob working its way into the back of her throat. The only other doll she's ever had was the one Mother took to the pawn shop all that time ago.

He watches anxiously. 'Don't you like it?'

Her eyes have grown misty. 'She's beautiful. The best present I've ever had. And she's all mine. She's another tranklement to keep in my carpetbag.'

'What d'yer mean?'

'It's what you call your special things. Something I was talking about with Mary last night. Oh, I'll miss you so much.' She shakes his arms with each word as if the words by themselves aren't strong enough.

'You really like it? '

She nods until she thinks her head'll fall off her shoulders.

' 'S'all right then. And whenever you look at her, you'll think of me?'

'Every day, Sam.' She reaches up and kisses him on his cheek. If his face turns any redder it might burst. 'Every day.'

'Look at you, all done up like a proper lady.'

Ginnie can see the pride and, dare she say it, love in his eyes and smiles as she thinks a lady might smile. 'I feel like a lady. I'll try to find a job for you and I'll come back soon as ever I can.'

*How can I say goodbye? Should I kiss him?* A fleeting shadow crosses his face and she sees what he sees – a lady and a workhouse boy, and already everything has changed.

'And you've got a good pair of legs on yer.'

He lurches forward, plants a long kiss on her lips and bolts through the door. She touches her mouth with her fingers and tears flow. She hugs the doll and gently pulls the woollen hair over its shoulders. *She's beautiful.* Carefully, she places it in her bag of treasures, imagining him sitting whittling away at the wood to create it, just for her.

For want of something to do, she slips on her coat.

She's standing so close to the front door that when the bell rings, it very nearly pierces her ear drums. Mary appears from the kitchen, wiping her hands on her apron as Mabel steps through the door.

'Well, hello again, Miss. Its right good to see you, isn't it Ginnie?'

'Yes,' says Ginnie, breathless. 'Hello, Mabel.'

'We've got everything ready for her, Mrs Higgins.'

Ginnie bends down and searches through her bag as if checking she has everything.

Mary glances from one to the other, tutting. 'It's going be a quiet kitchen in your house if you two lasses can't find something to say to each other.'

Mabel turns to Ginnie. 'Ready?'

Ginnie takes a trembling breath. 'Sorry for what I said the other day. I didn't mean it.'

'Must've come as a bit of a shock. It's an adventure of a sort, isn't it?'

'Course it is.' Mary folds her arms under her small breasts like she always does when she gets upset.

Ginnie nods back, her bottom lip quivering as she fights to keep control. Her eyes sweep along the hall wistfully, but Sam is nowhere in sight.

She picks up her bag and turns to follow Mabel out of the house. She had hoped he'd be there to see her leave.

'Wait!'

Ginnie turns hopefully, but it's Mary who runs to her. She throws her arms around Ginnie and pulls her close, stroking her head all the while. 'I won't half miss you, darling girl. You've been a good lass and helped me no end. Be a good girl for your sister now.'

'Where's Sam?'

'Oh, you know lads can't show their feelings like us girls. He'll be missing you already. But don't you fret. I'll keep an eye on him.' Mary kisses her and pushes her away again. 'Ta-ra, Ginnie.'

The door bangs shut, leaving Ginnie and Mabel standing on the steps, alone. Mabel holds out her hand. 'Who's Sam?'

'My best friend.'

Mabel links her arm. 'I'm sure you'll make lots of new friends now.'

Together they walk down the dirt path to the road. Ginnie takes a long look at the place that has seen the good times and the bad in her life. Today, there's excitement about the future, but how much better she would feel if Sam was coming with her.

197

There is a movement at an upstairs window.

Sam.

She pulls free of Mabel's arm and concentrates hard on the darkness behind the glass.

'We need to get a move on, Ginnie.' Mabel pulls her forwards.

Ginnie gives him a huge smile, although she doubts he'll see it, and waves frantically with her free arm. He *is* there to see her off after all. He puts his hand to the glass but doesn't wave.

'It's Sam. Up there in the window.'

Mabel peers in the direction she points, but the window's empty again. With a big sigh, Ginnie turns her back on Haddon House for the last time.

'Ginnie! Come on.'

They turn the corner and head down the hill towards Burslem.

Ginnie's excitement is growing. She's going home. Yes, she'd had second thoughts when Mabel came for her but as Mary had said, it was natural, given the circumstances.

Her future will be tinged with sadness until she sees Sam again, but with him by her side, she can face anything.

She breathes in the air. It tastes of a kind of freedom.

## Chapter Seventeen

### After Haddon – July 1914

Ginnie had asked Mabel if she could go to Haddon earlier in the week and she had grudgingly agreed. Part of her had expected Mabel to change her mind, but she was as good as her word. It vexed Ginnie that Mabel couldn't or wouldn't, understand why she wanted to visit Haddon. True friendship was the one good thing to come out of such a place; where someone took you as you were, and for no other reason. What did Mabel think she'd done for all those years? Maybe in the future, the less her sister knew, the better for everyone.

Sam had been on her mind continually ever since. She grinned at how surprised he'd be when she turned up. She wanted to see his face light up and know it was for her alone.

Everywhere was bright with sunshine. She couldn't stop smiling and people smiled back as they passed. It never happened when she was dressed in her workhouse clothes. It was good to be taking her own two feet where she wanted them to go. Those who had never been shut away didn't know what it felt like to have that freedom taken away.

Haddon House still looked like home. She may not have had the best of lives, but she had friends inside she could call upon who would always look out for her. How had she let so much time pass?

Still, she was about to see Sam, and everything would be wonderful again. She hurried up to the front door, pulled her coat tidy, checked her hat was sitting straight, and rang the bell.

The door opened straightaway. It was Ada Barlow, the last girl to share her bed. Her blank eyes widened like saucers as she recognised the visitor.

'Oh, it's you, Ginnie. You don't half look smart. I hardly knowed you.'

'Can I come in and have a word with Sam?'

'Sam?'

'Sam White. My friend what was sent away 'cos he had fits?'

'Oh, you won't find him here no more.'

'Why? What d'yer mean?'

There must have been panic written on her face, for Ada clapped a hand over her mouth.

'Me and my big mouth. He wasn't taken bad, Ginnie. They sent just him to help out at the Big House 'cos they're short. Went a couple of weeks ago.'

'And he definitely hasn't had another fit?'

'Don't think so. I never heard nothing about it if he did. They just come one day and told him as he had to go.'

Ginnie swallowed hard. Her belly returned to its rightful place and she could breathe again. She was glad it was Ada at the door and not some unknown nobody.

'I have to see him, Ada. Can I speak to Mrs Higgins? She'll know what I should do.' She tried to peep over Ada's shoulder, but Ada put out a hand.

'Hang on, her's up at the Big House with some kids what have been took poorly. She's not been gone long. She'll be a while yet.'

'I'll come back and see her later then. Ada, I've got to see Sam.'

'What's it like outside ...'

'Ada?' A voice bellowed from somewhere inside the house.

Ada rolled her eyes. 'Sorry Ginnie, got to go. I'll tell Mrs Higgins as you've been asking for her. I'll not forget, never fear. Oh, and I've got a job meself—'

'Ada? Where in heaven's name *is* that girl?'

The voice from within was growing louder.

'Sorry, Ginnie. Coming!'

With a shrug of the shoulders Ada disappeared and the door banged shut, leaving Ginnie standing on the step trying to slow down her heart which had begun to gallop the moment Ada had said that Sam was not there. It had been a relief to be told he was at the Big House, but today's visit had meant so much and, once more, her efforts had been thwarted.

★★★

'German troops are pouring into Belgium to get at France. Ultimatums and all sorts are flying round. That's it, then.' Frank threw the newspaper down onto his knees. 'We'll be at war before you know it 'cos we've agreed to support little Belgium. And all because of that Duke what was killed.'

Mabel glanced up from her darning. 'What's it got to do with us?'

'Don't you see? If the Germans go through Belgium, we'll have to go over to help them, and that means war, you mark my words.'

Ginnie locked eyes with Mabel. England being nearly at war with distant countries across the sea sounded ridiculous and a little scary. Men at work talked of war as some big adventure but Ginnie had seen Fred the tow-er being sick down by the privies yesterday.

Frank's head was back in the paper the moment he'd swallowed his last mouthful of lobby. Ginnie doubted he even knew what he'd eaten.

'But it's Wakes Week,' said Mabel. 'What about them what's gone to the seaside who've saved their hard-earned wages so as they can can go to Blackpool and dance in the Tower Ballroom or the Winter Gardens?'

He glanced over the top of the newspaper. 'War's more important than folks' holidays, love. They're already asking for volunteers, by the way, just in case.'

'Don't even think about it, Frank.'

He lifted the paper so they couldn't see his face. 'Nowt's settled till it's settled.'

★★★

It was early morning. Through half-open curtains Ginnie could see people gathering in the street. Talking and occasional shouts had lured her out of bed. Women, arms folded, talked in low voices while men punched the air with their fists, calling all Germans unmentionable names.

Her door blasted wide open and Mabel fell into the room.

'We're at war, Ginnie duck.' She paced up and down beside the bed. 'You can't stay up here when there's a war on.'

'So, it's really happening?'

'I've just been in the street talking to her next door. We've been at war since eleven o'clock last night. Papers came out early.'

Frank had shown them where the fighting would likely be on a map he'd borrowed, but Ginnie had found it difficult to gauge whether or not she should be worried. It was all so far away. Surely something would stop it happening.

She followed Mabel downstairs and out through the front door. People danced jigs while others, full of doom, went on about how food prices would shoot up, and who was going to spend on pots when there was a war on. War wasn't just about soldiers fighting across the sea.

The more they heard, the more Mabel was convinced that Frank would head off to Hanley Post Office and sign up straightaway. Ginnie didn't think so; he talked a lot but, like Mabel, his talk didn't usually lead to much action. Sam was a different kettle of fish. Thank goodness he wasn't old enough to enlist. He would want to get the job done rather than talk about the ins and outs of whether and how to do it.

*The Staffordshire Sentinel* carried a huge advertisement about King and Country needing unmarried men to sign up. Some reservists had already packed their bags. It was only fair that them who had no families to support got to go first, Mabel said.

For the time being, Frank was safe.

'If they send our men to war it will be up to us women to keep the country going,' said Constance, later. 'Mrs Pankhurst has called for an end to all violence. She says we suffragettes have to pull together to "fight a common foe". It'll be our chance to show Parliament that our country will be safe with us.' The green eyes positively glowed.

If Sam had been old enough to fight, Ginnie would have been in pieces. Ginnie crossed her fingers behind her back. All she could do was to hope the war would be over before she had to cross that bridge.

\*\*\*

The first of Ginnie's acquaintances to go to war was Fred the Tow-er. He, along with some of his mates, was in the territorials and was put on active service immediately. For the first time since she had known him, he'd stopped whistling. His eyes were red when he walked through The Shop with his coat over his arm. Ginnie wondered whether he'd been led on by his mates and now it was all too real. Women crowded around him, making such a fuss. One even threw her arms round him and smothered him with kisses.

'You'll do us proud, Fred.'

'Them wenches won't half take a shine to you when yer come back a soldier, mark my words young man.'

Pat shook him by the hand. 'Good on yer, lad.'

They all sang, 'For He's a Jolly Good Fellow', and patted his back until he almost choked. It was enough to turn any lad's head. Fred looked full of himself by the time he had to go to his regimental headquarters, wherever and whatever that was.

Elsie had tears in her eyes as he disappeared through the door. 'He lives down our street. How his poor mam's going to cope I don't know. He's her only lad. Turned eighteen last Christmas. Just started bringing home a man's wage an' all.' She shook her head. 'Such a nice lad.'

That made him four years older than Ginnie. Surely the army wanted men who could hold their own in a fight, not boys like

Fred? A picture appeared involuntarily before her eyes; Sam dressed in a uniform, grown into a man. Given half a chance he'd be off, she just knew it. She'd have to pray like mad that it'd be over by then.

Three left after snapping time. The rest of the workers couldn't afford to lose more time and had to be satisfied with a pat on the back and a cheer.

Frank was full of it when he got home. He'd heard that the trains coming through from Manchester and up north were packed with soldiers. Such jollity, singing and telling jokes, anyone would've thought they were off to some huge football match.

'With so much camaraderie, we're bound to win,' he said, his eyes alight. 'I'd be hopping on the next train if I wasn't married.'

'Well, it's a good job you are, Frank Farmer. You should be thankful you've got somebody to talk some sense into that thick skull of yours.' Mabel's hands moved protectively to the bump at her stomach. 'Do you want to go and get yourself killed?'

'We got right on our side.'

'And that makes it proper then, does it?' she quipped, bending to pick up a towel to fold. 'I bet them Germans are saying same thing an' all.'

Frank jumped to his feet, eyes blazing, and banged the table with his fist, startling them both.

'Wash your bloody mouth out, woman! I'll not have no wife of mine siding with scum like that.'

'I'm not siding with 'em, Frank. It's just ... with the baby com—'

'I said shut up, I don't want to hear no more.' He threw the paper down and sank into a chair, arms folded, eyes closed, but he couldn't sit still. He hit a balled fist against his open hand again and again and each smack cracked in the quietness of the room. When he stopped, his face had taken on a pale, hunted look. He stood in front of the grate, in silence.

Ginnie gave Mabel a quick smile and ran lightly upstairs. She was not about to get into an argument, that was for sure. This sort of talk must be going on in houses across the country, she thought. Blokes and lads talking of going off to fight for their country. Wives and sweethearts begging them not to go. They were probably both right. Pray God the war wouldn't go on too long.

## Chapter Eighteen

### After Haddon – July 1914

Another two weeks passed before she was able to return to Haddon. Straight after Sunday dinner she scooted up there. Even so, it took time to cover the two miles. She told Mabel she was going to visit Constance in case she took against her going back to Haddon so soon. Frank would take great delight in stopping her if he'd an inkling. She was sure Mary could arrange for her to see Sam, write a letter even.

This time the door was answered by a strange, elderly woman with a tight mouth showing hardly any lips.

Ginnie swallowed with difficulty. 'Please can I have a word with Mrs Higgins?'

'Mrs Higgins? No, you can't. Her passed on last week.'

She moved to close the door but Ginnie thrust out a hand to stop her. 'Passed on where?'

'Passed over. She's dead. Can't think of any other way of saying it, duckie.'

'Passed away? But, but… she can't. She was up at the Big House two weeks ago. Ada said so.'

'Aye and it was that what took her an' all. She hadn't been at all well, so they say. And young Ada shouldn't be speaking out of turn. I'll give her sharp shrift, make no mistake.' The woman spat on the path and folded her arms. 'Hers gone, duck.'

Ginnie's mouth dried in an instant, her tongue too big for the space available. She slid down the wall. Arms caught her beneath her armpits and lowered her gently to the step.

'There, there, lass, sit yourself down afore you fall. I didn't mean to be so narky. I've had a bad day.' A kindly look crossed the woman's face. 'No point upsetting yer'sen. Her's probably gone to a far better place than this one. Although I can't say much 'cos I didn't know her.'

They sat together on the step, both staring into the distance while fluffy clouds raced across the warm blue sky. Ginnie blinked away tears. The pain inside was almost too much. Was she to lose everybody she cared about? Was she cursed?

'What happened?' She addressed the question to the clouds.

'They think it was the influenza. When I found out, I very nearly didn't come, I don't mind telling yer. Didn't want to go catching nothing. But they gave me an extra tanner, and me tea. Well, you can't afford to turn yer nose up at that. Reckon as they was desperate. I mean, looking after a bunch of kids what's got nowt and likely as not'll end up in the Big House. Who in their right mind would come and work here and stay for any longer than they have to?'

Mary would have. She would've done anything to help the kids in her charge. Ginnie was lucky to have known her.

Ginnie returned to the reason for her call. 'Do you know Sam White?'

'Oh, aye, he's a good lad.'

'He's been sent to the Big House, I'm told. How can I speak to him?'

'Can't help you there, duckie. All's I can say is that he'll probably stay there, given his age.'

Ginnie could scream. Would nothing ever go right for her in this world?

'What's a nice wench like you wanting with anybody what lives here, any road?'

Ginnie glanced up at the building behind, the red bricks and empty windows. 'I lived here once, but everything's changed.' A dark cloud had blotted out the sun. She wiped her wet eyes with the back of her hand.

'Well, I shouldn't go telling nobody. Seems as you've gone up in the world, and if you want to stay that way, you'll keep yer lips buttoned, mark my words.' She rubbed her hands, and then slapped her knees. 'Gotta go, now. Funeral's at the St John's Church, one o'clock on Tuesday, if you've a mind to go. Sorry I can't be more help, duckie. Best gerroff home.'

The voice was still soft, but the kindly smile had gone. Ginnie got to her feet. 'Please don't blame Ada for talking to me. She's a friend. I had to know.'

The woman gave her a quick pat on the head, stretched, and disappeared into the house giving Ginnie no choice but to leave.

Poor Mary had deserved so much more. But then, so had Clara. In her experience, the best people rarely got what they deserved. She resolved to go to the funeral. Like as not there'd be precious few people to pray for Mary's soul. It was the least she could do, even if her wages were docked for having time off.

She kicked a small stone and thrust her hands in her pocket. How was she going to get a message to Sam if he was in the Big House? Dare she just walk up to the door and ask for him, bold as brass? She walked past Chamberlain's deep in thought. Why did they even send him there when he had a job at Haddon?

Was this what love felt like? She remembered the day they talked about getting wed, and her first, sweet little kiss. They were just kids back then.

Ginnie closed her eyes and could almost feel the lightest of touches on her mouth, and then came the ache again, below her stomach. She hugged herself because there was no one else to do it for her.

She would speak to Constance, who was bound to know how to contact him. Constance didn't know, but she undertook to find out without delay.

Ginnie was discovering that patience was one of the most difficult lessons to learn, and that all she could do was wait, and hope to speak to him soon.

Ginnie walked to the church where Mary's funeral was taking place. Pavements were awash with puddles from the rain, which had started the moment she'd stuck her head out the door. A cold wetness seeped around the toes on her left foot. She took off her shoe to find the sole worn away around her big toe.

'Damn. Damn. *Damn.*' She grabbed hold of the wall around the church and tried to slide wet toes back into her shoe. The rain was getting heavier. Water trickled down her neck.

'Bleeding rain,' she shouted at the sky. 'Can't you just lay off while I get my shoe back on?' She felt her face flush. She knew better than to swear in the shade of the church.

'Ginnie?'

She hadn't heard anyone behind her. She turned and tried to make out the face under the bonnet that had appeared alongside her.

'Ada, is that you?'

'Hiya Ginnie.'

'It's right good to see yer.' Ginnie thrust the shoe back onto her foot and threw her arms around the girl. 'Blasted hole in me shoe. Have you come for Mary's funeral?'

Ada nodded.

'I came to Haddon again last week, to ask for Mary, and a new woman answered the door. I told her you'd said Mary was at the Big House. She said she was going to have words with you for talking to me. She told me about Mary.' Tears came quickly to Ginnie's eyes.

'Gorra job. I was going to tell you when you came to Haddon but the old battle-axe was in a foul mood.'

'I didn't get you into trouble, did I?'

'No. Am in-service now. Started working for a doctor up Hanley yesterday.'

'My word, you've gone up in the world.'

'I was lucky. He wanted somebody quick 'cos his other wench got herself in the family way. I was the only one as could start quick.' She shrugged her shoulders.

'That's wonderful.'

'Seems a real nice chap an' all, always smiling. I dropped on lucky.'

Ginnie wasn't too sure. 'The other girl, was she married?'

'No and it caused a bit of a stir, I think. That's why she had to go so quick, what with him being an unmarried gentleman.'

Ginnie bit her lip. 'You will be careful, Ada, won't you?'

'What do you mean?'

Ginnie had no idea how to explain men's urges. She was only just beginning to find out herself. Lust wasn't something people talked about. A couple of the girls working on the potbank had left recently because they were expecting. Neither of them had husbands, nor men friends as far as Ginnie knew.

'Just don't let him get too friendly.'

'What do you take me for, Ginnie? I'm a good girl, I am.'

Ginnie nearly burst out laughing at the horror written on Ada's face. 'Course you are, but not all men are good. It does no harm to think on.'

'I know you mean well. Shall we go in?'

They made their way into the quiet holiness of the church. Six people were sitting in the first couple of rows. Superintendent Hardcastle and Mrs Hardcastle sat in the front row, with Gladys Piper in the second row and three others Ginnie didn't recognise sat in a group on the other side of the aisle.

Ginnie walked towards Gladys who was sitting dabbing her eyes with a handkerchief. She looked up and smiled. Ginnie reached out to hold her hand and her eyes welled up again. She was just about to speak when the organ began to play sombre music and the coffin moved slowly towards the altar. The priest said prayers and the congregation sang two hymns, but it was only the priest's steady voice that Ginnie could hear.

As the coffin moved into the churchyard, Superintendent Hardcastle inclined his head towards Ginnie and to Gladys, but never spoke. A final prayer was said at the grave as the coffin was lowered, and slowly covered with soil.

The rain had stopped. Ginnie and Ada made their way to the gate and gave each other a hug, a comfort for what they had lost.

'I'd best get walking. Got a fair way to go,' said Ada, wiping her eyes.

'See you around then?'

'I'd like that.' Ginnie huddled into her coat, increasingly aware of her cold feet. She didn't know which would be worse – to have church full of grieving people or a nearly empty one with a different type of sadness.

In her bedroom later, she said a few words of her own prayers, as she had done at her mother's funeral.

–

The hammering on the front door was so hard that Ginnie was surprised it didn't give way under the strain. A second bout followed.

Ginnie rose quickly as Mabel struggled to her feet. 'I'll get it. Sit yourself down.'

She opened the door to find Constance, fist raised, about to start hammering again. 'Constance, whatever's the matter? Are you all right?'

'I have news. I couldn't wait to tell you.'

'What's going on? Oh, I didn't see you, Miss.' Overawed to see a lady outside her door, Mabel pushed Ginnie out of the way. 'Don't leave her in the street, ask the young lady in. So sorry, Miss; I don't know what she's thinking.'

Ginnie was on tenterhooks, annoyed with Mabel for interrupting her message about Sam.

'Thank you, Mrs... Farmer, isn't it?' said Constance, with one of her most enchanting smiles.

Mabel's hand clutched her neck. 'What can we do for you, Miss—?'

'I'm pleased to meet you at last, Mrs Farmer. My name is Constance Copeland. I've come with a message for Ginnie.'

'For our Ginnie? Oh, my word. Won't you take a seat in the parlour, Miss Copeland?' Mabel ushered her in. 'Could we get you a cup of tea, or something?'

'No, thank you, I can't stay. But please,' she smiled her broadest smile, 'Call me Constance.'

Mabel nodded several times and disappeared into the scullery without another word. Frank was in there having a shave. Voices could be heard arguing through the thin walls.

Ginnie closed the front room door and the shouting dulled. She rolled her eyes.

'Mother has been in touch with Superintendent Hardcastle. Sam will be discharged any day. A number of staff have volunteered their services to the Army and the workhouse doesn't have the wherewithal to continue with so many inmates. People like Sam are being discharged if they have somewhere to go.'

Ginnie collapsed into the chair opposite. 'I saw Mr Hardcastle yesterday at Mary's funeral and he never said. How can he? How much does—? I mean where?'

'It's all arranged with the superintendent.' Constance sat back, gloating like a cat with a bucket of cream.

Ginnie jumped up and threw her arms around her. 'I don't know what to say. I can't... When?' It was touch and go whether she was going to laugh or cry. There was still the little matter of a job and somewhere to live. She pulled away.

'We don't know exactly. I've asked Mother if we might offer him a bed until we can find more permanent lodgings for him.'

The tears Ginnie had tried to hold back gushed forward. 'You would do that for us?'

'Ginnie! For goodness' sake, I shall drown if you carry on.' But Constance was smiling. 'Fortunately for Sam there are likely to be plenty of jobs soon.'

'Because of the war?' Ginnie shook her head. 'It's horrible that Sam might benefit because others have been sent to fight, but it's happening already. More men from Chamberlain's went off today.'

'Mother's heard that the war will be all over by Christmas. They'll soon be back, which will be a relief to everyone, I'm sure, but *The Sentinel* says there has been heavy fighting north of Brussels and have printed the first lists of wounded and casualties.'

'I'm glad Sam isn't old enough. Is that bad of me?'

'Of course not. It shows you care.'

It was good to confide in someone who didn't look down on him.

Shortly after that, Constance left. Ginnie let her out and returned to the back room where Mabel stood, arms folded.

'Since when have you been hobnobbing with a toff? Who is she?'

Ginnie couldn't hide the grin that had spread from ear to ear. 'She came to Haddon with her mother one time. A Workhouse Friend they're called. She's been doing something in the town, and I've been helping her. She says her mother can help to get Sam out.'

Mabel's mouth fell open. 'She knows?'

'She's returning a favour for a friend,' said Ginnie, smugly.

## Chapter Nineteen

**October 1914**

Frank had taken to reading war updates out loud from *The Sentinel* each evening. He could think of nothing else. Needing no reminder, Mabel focused on her knitting pattern. Perhaps now was a good time to take herself out for the afternoon, maybe to go to Hanley where all the shops were. She couldn't visit Sam, because she hadn't heard from Constance.

'I've done all me jobs, Mabel. Pots washed, washing's done and put away. Oh, and I've swept the kitchen floor again.'

'Good girl. Don't know what we'd do without you. Do you, Frank?'

'Humph.' He hardly lifted his nose from the paper.

'I thought I might go out for an afternoon at the weekend.' She deserved it after all. She'd hardly had any time to herself since starting to work.

Mabel's eyes went from Ginnie to Frank, and back to Ginnie.

'Me and Frank are going to see Mrs Harding on Saturday. She's the midwife what's looking after this little mite. Won't be long now.' Her hands went automatically to her stomach, which had grown substantially. 'You can go on Sunday.'

Ginnie nodded, finding it hard to hide her disappointment. Going on Sunday would mean all the shops would be shut. Not that she had any money to spend, but it would've been nice to look around. She'll just have to think of somewhere else to go. 'And I want you back here before Frank goes out.'

Mabel picked up her knitting again and started to count the stitches, putting an end to further conversation.

Ginnie hummed as she put the finishing touches to the dress she was making. It had cost next to nothing because it was another too-tight dress to which she had added panels from a too-long one, a trick she had learned at Haddon, and it had turned out quite well.

She still hadn't forgiven Frank for taking her hard-earned cash and Mabel, never the kindest of people, was often argumentative. She wondered if all older sisters were like that.

Finished at last, she uttered a huge sigh and leaned back on the chair. As always happened, the moment she stopped concentrating, Sam entered her mind and a smile spread across her face. She hoped that Constance would be in touch soon.

She looked around for something to do, needing to keep busy. The grate in the front room hadn't been used for a while with it being summer.

She had cleaned it when she arrived, so it wasn't dirty. The range was clean, and she had no idea what Mabel had in mind for tea so she couldn't even make a start on that. A pot of tea wouldn't go amiss, she thought, and the pot could be steeping for their return.

The ticking clock clunked on a sideboard free of dust. Five-and-twenty past five. Mabel and Frank hadn't returned from their visit to Mrs Harding. Most of the babies born at this end of town had passed through her hands and Mabel was leaving nothing to chance.

Frank still took money out of her wages on a Friday, but Mabel must've had a word with him because he wasn't so bossy about it. Ginnie always took out a few coppers before she got home – not so much as he'd notice – and hid them until she could put them with the rest of her treasures in her carpetbag. She had discovered a rip in the lining at the bottom and she slid her purse underneath the flap in case anyone should peep inside.

She ran her fingers through her hair, now loosened, and felt grit beneath her fingernails. She might wash it in the sink because she'd missed out on bath night last night. She climbed the stairs to peer in the mirror, something she still wasn't used to doing.

Surprised to find her bedroom door open, she glanced quickly around, before diving under the bed to check her carpetbag.

*He wouldn't, would he?*

Everything was exactly as she'd left it. A shuddering breath escaped as she sat back on her heels. She would always think the worst of Frank; she couldn't help it.

She glanced through her door to the closed one opposite, itching to see inside the room Mabel shared with Frank. No harm in having a peep, was there? It might help her to get to know more about her sister.

She turned the knob and pushed the door with the tips of her fingers. The room gave the impression of being smaller than her own, with the double bed and the huge wardrobe almost covering one wall. The iron bedstead looked hard and uncomfortable and the mattress old and flat – an invitation to nightmares rather than sweet dreams.

The chest of drawers had a small, but bright mirror in the middle. Mabel's hairbrush and comb were placed at exactly the right spot and the bristles and teeth weren't clogged up with hair. Having seen the state of the rest of the house when she first came, she couldn't believe this room was so different; she'd never entered the room because she had not been asked to clean it. Was this the real Mabel and the Mabel downstairs with the dust, the flaky paintwork, and the dirty windows was just a shadow, or was it the other way around? Whatever she knew, or thought she knew, might have to be unknowed. *People are ever so complicated.*

She wandered about the room, looking and touching. Ginnie glanced in the mirror and chocolate brown eyes stared back. If it wasn't for her bushy eyebrows she would be quite pretty. Not beautiful – that would be vain, and a sin. If she was taller, she would glide as she walked and put on airs and graces like the decorating-end girls.

She was about to leave when her eyes lit on the wardrobe again. The key was in the lock. She reached out – and stopped. Opening the wardrobe was definitely peeking into things she had no right to see, but she couldn't stop herself. She turned the key and opened one of the doors, cringing at the squeak that followed. Three dresses she hadn't seen before and two coats hung in the middle of the rail. Beyond the coats was the dark cotton dress Mabel wore to church. It felt so soft, much better quality than the likes of Mabel could afford. The dark clothes on the left of the dresses must be Frank's.

The three dresses were draped like curtains around a large box on the floor of the wardrobe. She slid them along the rail, trying to remember exactly where they had been before she moved them, and lifted the lid of the box. It was stuffed full of baby clothes, enough to dress a whole hospital full of babies, and varying in size and quality.

She lifted them out one by one. Most were not much bigger than dolls clothes. She sniffed into their softness. Had Mabel been expecting before? Or had they been given to her by lots of people? She hadn't mentioned any other babies but if she *had* lost one it was no wonder she was a bit worked up and anxious about being on her own, and why Frank was so protective.

The banging of the front door pulled her back from her discoveries. Someone had come into the house. She slipped the bundle back into the box, drew back the dresses, and locked the wardrobe door. She closed the bedroom door and stepped onto the landing. Back in her own room, she picked up her comb and pulled it smartly through her hair and descended the stairs.

'That you Ginnie?'

It was Frank.

'Mabel's called at the shop for tea.'

His eyes wandered down to her hands which she was rubbing, conscious that they felt sweaty.

'It's just you and me, then.'

'I'll start—'

'No, you won't.' He caught her arm. 'You'll stay here. You're… what? Fourteen and a half was it? Quite the young lady.'

She tried to shake his hand away, but his large, thick fingers closed tightly.

'This is my house and I say whether you can stay.' He pulled her close until she could feel the tickle of his whiskers on her cheek. 'So you'd better be nice to me.'

'I'll… I'll tell Mab—'

Frank pushed her elbow up her back. She yelped at the unexpected pain. He relaxed his grip at the sound, as his lips brushed her forehead. 'I don't think so. You wouldn't dare.'

She could smell drink on his breath. He couldn't have had much because he'd not long left Mabel. Had he planned this, or had it just come to him, her being alone? She forced herself to relax momentarily and his hand slackened in response.

She stamped on his foot with all her might.

'Hell and damnation!' His eyes glittered. 'You little bugger.'

She almost laughed at the wide-eyed shock on his face. 'Yes, and I'll kick you where it hurts if you ever try that again,' she panted, determined to give him what for and leave him in no doubt that she was capable of defending herself.

He made a move towards her, arm raised. He was going to hit her. She snatched up the broom from beside the door and swung it in front of her.

He stopped. 'I'll make you regret you did that.'

'And I'll tell Mabel if you dare touch me.'

She jabbed the brush towards him. He stepped back.

The front door opened and in walked Mabel, shocking them both. Neither had heard her arrive.

'There you are. You're a funny colour, Ginnie. Are you all right? Sit down, for goodness' sake. You can sweep the floor later.'

'I tried to stop her, but she wanted to do it,' said Frank.

Ginnie sank thankfully into a chair, her breath coming quickly. 'I'll go for that walk as soon as we've had dinner tomorrow,' she blurted out, for something to say.

A look of surprise crossed Mabel's face. 'Just as long as Frank's about.'

Frank shrugged and thumped his way up the stairs.

There was Mabel's anxiety again. The box in the wardrobe might hold an explanation of her concern for the baby, but she couldn't mention it. And she had to keep quiet about Frank's behaviour too. How could she tell Mabel what had just happened?

Sometimes half knowing something was more dangerous than knowing it all.

–

A knock on the door pulled Ginnie out of her reverie. She'd been dreaming of walking with Sam in the park and around the town, just being with him. She had written his name, S-A-M jerkily on a piece of scrap paper and had absentmindedly drawn little hearts around it. She folded up the paper, slipped it down the lining of the carpetbag, and hurried downstairs to answer the door but Mabel had beaten her to it.

'Good Afternoon, Miss Constance,' she heard Mabel say, unwilling or unable to drop the 'Miss'.

Constance stepped smartly into the house and was followed by a tall man wearing a cap which he immediately removed.

Ginnie's smile went from ear to ear. 'Sam! Sam! I can't believe it.' She almost pushed a shocked Mabel out of the way.

'Hello lass. It's grand to see yer.'

His arms went around her. Conscious of what Mabel must be thinking, she wriggled free and coughed to give herself time to think. Constance, on the other hand, was quite delighted with the outcome of her surprise.

Ginnie stepped back and turned to Mabel. 'You know Constance, and this is Sam. He's a friend.'

Dressed in smart trousers without holes, a scarf about his neck, and a cap that fitted, he very nearly took her breath away. She wanted to squeeze him tight but for now was content just to gaze at him.

'I should *hope* he's a friend, after that greeting.' Mabel nodded towards him.

'Sam, this is my sister, Mabel.'

He held out his hand. 'How do, Mrs…'

Mabel shook his hand with the lightest of touches. 'Mabel'll do, lad. You'd best come in.' She withdrew her hand and it went protectively to her stomach. The smile that had greeted Constance had all but disappeared. She led their visitors to the back room leaving Ginnie to close the front door. Ginnie followed Sam, who was walking with a bit of a limp. She frowned. *Surely he's not in trouble already?*

'Will you have a cup of tea, Miss Constance?'

Mabel held herself aloof, much to Ginnie's acute embarrassment.

'Thank you, Mabel, and do please call me Constance. Sam, come and sit beside me.' Constance patted the seat next to her, giving Mabel no option but to include him in her hospitality.

'Will you have a cup of tea… Sam?'

'Thanks, Mam.' He sat down glancing around the room, his hands playing with the cap. 'Fine house you've got. Ginnie's lucky to have you look after her.'

Ginnie was sure that he could've been Sam from anywhere except from Haddon House and Mabel would have been more courteous towards him. Her nostrils flared with indignation. She glanced at Constance who shook her head imperceptibly, warning her to keep her mouth shut. Constance knew more about the world; she could have them eating out of her hands in no time. Ginnie held her tongue.

Mabel went to make the tea, leaving Ginnie free to talk. 'It's been a long time, Sam. I went to Haddon to see you, but you were helping out at the Big House. Did they tell you I came?'

'You did?'

'Course. Promised, didn't I?'

'Nobody said nothing.'

'I spoke to an old woman, not Mary. She said you were at the Big House, probably for good.'

He reached over and took her hand. The touch of his coarse, dirt-lined fingers sent goose pimples up and down her arms.

'I would've come soon as I could. I was working on greens for a bit 'cos I knew about them. That, and stone-breaking, for the roads. Back-breaking work it was.'

He grinned again and her heart turned right over. If she had any doubts at all about her feelings, they were dashed away in that moment. Even now, she couldn't believe he was actually here, in Mabel's house, about to drink tea.

Mabel returned with a wooden tray full of cups and saucers and distributed them. When she could think of nothing else to do, she sat down, reluctantly.

'Sam's got a job down the pit,' Constance chimed up. 'So many of their men have already joined up even though the government's calling it a reserved occupation and they didn't need to. They're short-handed, and Sam was willing to do anything, weren't you, Sam?'

'How's your leg?'

Sam frowned. 'How'd yer know about me leg?'

'You're limping a little.'

'Bruised me ankle, that's all. Be right as rain in no time. Am starting work on Monday, so it'll have to be.'

Everyone went quiet. His eyes said he wanted to talk to her. She squirmed in her seat, feeling on display with both Mabel and Constance watching her every movement, for very different reasons.

Constance finished her tea in no time at all and stood up. 'We mustn't take up your precious time, Mabel. We just wanted

Ginnie to know that Sam is back where he belongs. Ginnie, you must come to see me soon.' Her eyes slid towards Sam and she winked. 'How about on Saturday? Is the afternoon all right with you?'

Ginnie was certain that Constance had planned to set up a meeting so that Mabel wouldn't be able to stop her from seeing Sam.

'Wonderful. I mean, that'll be fine, won't it, Mabel? I'll get everything finished by then, I promise.'

Mabel wiped her free hand on her skirt and prepared to shake hands with Constance, unable to say no.

Not for the first time Ginnie wished she could be more like Constance.

# Chapter Twenty

October 1914

It was gone three when Ginnie got to see Sam on Saturday. She had positively flown around The Shop to complete her work and the silly smile she had been wearing all morning had not gone unnoticed. Nor had the singing. She wasn't the best singer in The Potteries, but she was sure she was the happiest.

It was her first visit to the house where Constance lived. With three floors, Holmorton Lodge was impressive. All the windows were evenly spaced out as if they had been drawn by a child. It was at the top of the hill out of Burslem and she arrived panting with the effort of it all. She bent over, holding her sides, to catch her breath and then, calmly as she could, rapped the knocker three times.

A girl dressed in black, opened the door.

'Good afternoon, Miss, can I help you?'

'I... I'm here to see Miss... I mean, I am here to see Constance. I'm a friend.' *A friend who has every right to knock on the front door of a house such as this*, she reminded herself. The arrival of a servant had thrown her.

The girl swept the door open. Ginnie felt under scrutiny but refused to be intimidated. She held her head high and walked across black and white tiles into a large hallway.

'Who was it at the door, Alice— oh.'

Agatha Copeland crossed the hall leaning heavily on her walking stick. She looked older that Ginnie remembered.

'Thank you, Alice,' said Mrs Copeland. She turned to Ginnie. 'You must be—'

'I'm Ginnie, Mrs Copeland. I've come to see Constance.'

'Of course, she's expecting you.' She inclined her head. 'And she has another visitor, you'll be pleased to know.'

With a hint of a smile, she continued towards the stairs.

A door on the right opened and Constance rushed out, arms wide. 'Ginnie! Lovely to see you. That'll be all, thank you, Alice,' she said over her shoulder. The girl in black melted away with a rustle of skirts.

'You told her? Mrs Copeland?'

'I did. Mother's very progressive in matters of the heart and politics. Alice is from the workhouse, you know. But Father – now he's a very different kettle of fish. Finds it difficult to communicate with people who are... different.'

Constance grabbed a shocked Ginnie's hand and whisked her through to somewhere she called the 'morning room'. It appeared empty but the moment she crossed the threshold, Sam rose from a wing-backed chair. She ran into his arms and squeezed him so hard he protested lest he should lose the ability to breathe. They burst into laughter although Ginnie could not have said why except that she was out of Mabel's sight and felt light-headed with joy.

'You will have lots to talk about, so I'll not intrude. Take a stroll in the garden, if you wish. I've left the door open. I shall catch up with some needlework in the parlour. Just ring the bell when you're ready, and I'll come back.' She clapped her hands and closed the door behind her with the broadest of smiles.

Ginnie felt overcome with shyness. When Mabel took her away from Haddon, she had thought she was grown up, but she wasn't. Back then, she had mourned the loss of friendship. But it wasn't friendship she longed for now, but something deeper. She feared she had left Sam, the boy, behind and that the man he was becoming didn't feel the same way about her.

It was when he returned to the chair that she noticed the limp again. 'So, how *did* you hurt your leg?'

'It's nowt.' He turned away, embarrassed.

'Come on Sam, what have you done?'

He fiddled with the cap he held in his hands and shrugged. 'I thought I'd twisted it, but it's only bruised.' He stared at his feet. The words came out in a rush. 'If you must know… I got a bit tipsy when they told me word had come from Miss Constance. She turned up with clothes and said as she'd got me some digs the other side of Burslem. She'd even put five shillings in the coat pocket. So, I had a drink to calm me nerves. Didn't know what else to do with meself. And like I said, it's only bruised.'

'You were drinking?'

'Just a couple. I couldn't believe that Miss Constance was asking for me, saying as you were her friend. What would you have done?'

The scene played out in Ginnie's mind – the astonishment that would've crossed his face – and she reminded herself how she had felt when she had met up with Constance again. Laughter gurgled in her throat.

And that was it. They were Ginnie and Sam again. Two people who had been split up and, with the help of a dear friend, had found each other again.

–

At work the following Monday she was like the cat that got the cream. George gave her odd looks. She would keep him guessing and that would irritate him more than anything. She couldn't help the grin that had attached itself to her face for most of the morning. Elsie had noticed too.

'What are you playing at, Ginnie?' she said as she headed down The Shop. 'You've got our George proper put out.'

Ginnie's smile became a huge grin. 'I don't know what you mean.'

'Come off it. You know exactly what I'm talking about. You're hiding something and it's to do with this young man what you've never spoke of till now.'

'Is it?' Ginnie refused to be drawn and took considerable pleasure in raising Elsie's own frustrations at not finding out more. She was about to walk away, but Elsie put a hand on her arm.

'I hope you know what you're doing. George's not a one to get on the wrong side of.'

'I've done nowt wrong.'

'Go easy on the lad. He's not that bad when you get used to him.'

Elsie was warning her off but then saying he wasn't a bad lad. She couldn't have it both ways. Ginnie couldn't help smiling at Elsie thinking something was going on between her and George.

'What are you pair up to?'

George came up behind them, making Ginnie jump. She hoped he hadn't heard them talking. Everything had been going along just fine recently and she didn't want anything to change that.

'That's for you to find out, me lad.' Elsie winked at Ginnie, her smile returning.

It was obvious he thought he was the subject of their chatter and the fact they wouldn't confirm or deny it only added to his belief. He grinned suddenly. The smile was somehow sweet, not suspicious. It gave Ginnie a glimpse of the real George under that armour of jokes he usually wore. Maybe he wasn't so bad after all.

-

Sam found the work in the pit hard; the heat, the long trek through dark caverns lit only by lamps, the physical labour of hewing out the coal, the red eyes frosted with coal dust. He, who loved the land and all things growing, never complained about not seeing the sun but Ginnie knew what it cost him to be buried beneath the earth all day.

As the year rolled on, they delighted in each other's company. Often, they acted like big kids. It was good to be alive.

They went out walking most weekends, strolling slowly up to the top of Burslem and back to Market Square. Sometimes they would stand outside Burslem Picture Palace on Waterloo Road and wish they could see the films, but money was too precious to waste on a couple of hours enjoyment. Besides, most of the films had no sound – just music or words on the bottom of the picture. What use was that when neither of them could read?

She introduced him to the park and watched the light of joy in his eyes as they roamed the flower beds. Once a week, after payday, they would head towards the crowd gathered around the bandstand listening to the music. It was lovely on a good dry night to arrive with no worries of having a black-streaked face wetted with soot-laden rain. The music brought tears to Ginnie's eyes and her feet twitched as if they were born to dance. Nothing could be more perfect.

Even the war across the sea was going well. Throughout October, *The Sentinel* was full of encouraging news from France and Belgium – headlines talked of early victories, the eve of liberation of French soil, and a Glorious British Stand against the Huns.

# Chapter Twenty-One

**November 1914**

'Ginnie, quick. Mabel's baby's coming.'

Sal, the youngster from next door, grabbed Ginnie's arm and dragged her through the front door. 'Her's been asking for you for ages. Says to tell yer her waters have broke.'

Ginnie couldn't breathe. 'But she's not due till the end of the month... has somebody gone for Mrs Harding?'

'Don't suppose a couple of weeks'll make a scrap of difference. Mum says baby'll come when baby's good and ready.'

Ginnie thought back to that embarrassing conversation with Mary but she was sure they never talked about babies who had decided they were ready to enter this world.

'Mabel said as her only lives a few streets away, so Mum sent our Billy to get her.'

The curtains were closed and the house in darkness even though it was only late afternoon in the middle of November. A scream sent her running for the stairs.

'Coming, Mabel,' she shouted, throwing off her coat and pounding up the stairs to find Mrs Scott, Sally's mother, leaning over Mabel, wiping her bright red face with a towel. *At least she'll know what to do, thank the Lord*, thought Ginnie.

'Took yer time, didn't yer?' Mabel panted.

Ginnie clung to the doorknob.

'Where the hell's Frank?' Mabel closed her eyes, her forehead wet with effort. Mrs Scott soaked a cloth in water and wiped it gently.

Ginnie was panting too. She, who'd never even put a nappy on a baby, was expected to help deliver her sister's precious bundle. The contraction ended. Mabel shrank back to become her sister again.

'I'm frightened.' She reached for Ginnie's hand. 'It's going to be all right, isn't it?'

'Everything's going to be fine, Mabel,' Ginnie squeaked. 'Mrs Harding'll be here any minute.'

Her eyes pleaded for confirmation, but Mrs Scott only shrugged, sending goose pimples up and down Ginnie's cold arms.

Mabel bellowed. 'Billy's been gone ages. Doesn't anybody care about my baby?'

Ginnie was at a loss. She didn't hear the door open. Somebody pushed hard against her. She staggered, momentarily losing her balance. She was about to give them a piece of her mind but stopped as the welcome figure of Mrs Harding bustled up to take hold of Mabel's hand. Ginnie sent up a quick prayer of relief.

Mrs Harding took in everything.

'Dunner werrit lass, yer only having a babbie. Most natural thing in the world.'

Mabel was beyond listening. In a less than patient voice the midwife said firmly, and without shouting, 'Mrs Farmer, will you please stop yelling and think about what I told you to do.'

Ginnie choked behind her hand trying to hide her spreading grin. This loud-mouthed woman was just what Mabel needed. Not much taller than Ginnie and twice as fat, she was grim of face and would stand no nonsense.

'Find Frank,' Ginnie whispered to Billy who had followed Mrs Harding and was lurking in the doorway. 'If you're going to scarper, you may as well do something useful.'

Billy's scared face lit up with an infectious grin. Ginnie smiled back, mouthed a quick thank you, and turned her concentration to Mabel who was sounding more and more like a fishwife.

Another scream and Mabel fell back onto the bed whimpering as the pain eased. 'Hold my hand, Ginnie.'

The midwife scrutinised her. 'You Ginnie?'

Unable to speak to this woman who could order Mabel to shut up and get away with it, Ginnie just nodded.

'Ever seen a babbie born?'

Ginnie shook her head.

Taking hold of Ginnie's hand, she covered Mabel's with it. 'You'll have to do. Talk to her and tell her to push when I say.'

Mabel squeezed her hand so hard when the next contraction came that Ginnie cried out and received a glare from Mrs Harding.

'Right now, push Mabel, push girl.'

Ginnie repeated the words, squeezing Mabel's hand as she did.

A bounding on the stairs and Frank burst into the room, breathless. He panicked when he saw the look of thunder on Mrs Harding's face and the terror in his wife's eyes.

'Get him out of here!' hollered Mrs Harding. 'It ain't right.'

He didn't need telling twice.

'And plenty of boiling water, if you please,' she shouted at his retreating back.

'Frank, don't you dare go. I need you here,' screamed Mabel, ready to climb out of bed and haul him back. Mrs Harding laid a hand on her shoulder, forcing her back onto the bed and then banged the door shut with her ample backside in case Frank should take it into his head to obey his wife. It appeared that Frank was more terrified of her than he was of Mabel, for he didn't return.

Another scream returned Ginnie's attention to her sister. 'Am still here, Mabel. It'll soon be over.'

'You a doctor now?' screeched Mabel, glaring at Ginnie.

Ginnie glanced at the midwife, who smiled for the first time. Ginnie relaxed until the next squeeze crushed her hand.

'Come on, gal. Push. Hard as you can.'

Mabel strained hard, pushing her chin into her chest, sweat pouring down her bright red face.

'And relax.'

The midwife's head disappeared behind Mabel's bent legs as she stared into her privates.

'I can't do it no more.' Mabel's body sank, her eyes closed.

'Head's crowning. Won't be long now.'

'Hear that, Mabel?' Ginnie held Mabel's hand close to her. 'Come on, Mabel. The baby's coming.'

Another scream. Another crushing of fingers.

'Push, girl. Push.' The midwife's head had disappeared completely.

Mabel held Ginnie's eyes with her own. Suddenly, the hand relaxed. The room went quiet.

Mrs Harding clucked from the opposite side of the bed as a lusty cry filled the room.

'Mother, you have a beautiful baby daughter.' She passed over a bundle of blanket, from which tiny fingers could be seen waving in time with the welcome cries of a newborn.

Mabel laughed and cried when Mrs Harding laid the screaming mite on her bloated stomach.

Little Florrie Farmer came into the world at seven o'clock on the evening of the 11th November 1914. Never had Ginnie felt so drained but so utterly satisfied. It was a wonder that such a tiny scrap could grow into a whole person.

'I've got a baby girl. Look at her tiny hands. Isn't she gorgeous?' Mabel glanced up. 'Where's Frank? I want Frank.'

Ginnie opened the door. Frank was sitting on the top of the stairs, staring at the wall. He got to his feet in slow motion and threw a quick glance at Mrs Harding, who was busily taking care of all the bloodied bedclothes. Full of smiles and happy that the women's work was done, she graciously allowed him back into the room.

'We've got a daughter, Frank. Our very own, at last. Isn't she beautiful?' Mabel burst into tears.

He clasped his cap tightly to his chest, his eyes glued on the baby.

'Go on Father, you'll have to do it sometime. May as well be now.' In one expert movement Mrs Harding scooped the bundle from Mabel and transferred her to Frank, cutting across his path as he tried to back away.

'But I might drop her.'

The baby landed in his arms. He held her as if she was a pan of hot food and stared at the little girl who would be totally dependent on him from this day forward. And cried.

Ginnie swore she would never be afraid of him again.

'I never thought as it would happen, Frank.' Tears welled up again in Mabel's eyes. 'Not after...' She burst into tears.

'Look at her tiny fingernails,' he whispered, passing his little finger between the jerking hands.

'We can leave 'em to it now, lass.' The midwife took a last lingering look and beckoned Ginnie out of the room.

Ginnie busied herself preparing tea for everyone. There would be time to say her own hello's later when Frank went off to wet the baby's head.

Later, in the quiet peacefulness of her own room, Ginnie slumped onto the bed, and couldn't for the life of her stop smiling. There was no doubt about it. That baby was a right bonnie little thing.

–

It was surprising how much work the new baby created. Mabel took to her bed and seemed to believe that Ginnie had nothing better to do than to be at her beck and call, but Ginnie didn't care. Frank had insisted Mabel put her feet up and she was not to do any work in the house. Shopping was out of the question until Mabel had been churched and received a blessing for the safe delivery of the child. All the housekeeping therefore had to be fitted in when Ginnie came home from work. However, she *did* get to cuddle Florrie as a reward. Half-forgotten lullabies sent the baby off to sleep when they were on their own. It would be nice to have a house full of babies when she was older. The actual birthings, she refused to think about.

They were sitting together, in Mabel's bedroom, knitting socks for the war effort. Little Florrie was asleep in her crib next to Mabel. On the whole she was a good baby, but, like her mother, was prone to temper tantrums from time to time. Ginnie watched Mabel's eyes stray to the cot as if she needed a constant update on the baby. It would be good for Mabel to have someone else think about, for a change.

'Sorry I've been a bit nowty with the baby coming, an' all.' Mabel bit her lip. 'I wish Mother was here. She'd know what to do. When I look at Florrie, I worry that I'm not good enough.'

Ginnie gazed into space. Mother seemed quite close at that moment, just out of reach. Looking after a tiny thing like Florrie, who could do nothing but cry, eat and sleep *was* frightening. Thank goodness Florrie wasn't her responsibility.

'I think, maybe, I should tell you about something that happened before you came to us.'

'You don't have to. I didn't realise what a difficult time it was.'

'I want to tell. S'only right. But you mustn't tell a soul.' Mabel took a deep breath. 'Florrie's not my first.'

Ginnie's heart missed a beat.

'But…' Mabel swallowed, '… she's the first baby what's lived.'

Ginnie gasped and lowered her needles. Those baby clothes weren't meant for Florrie. She was right.

'I met Frank at the picture house. I was with my mates and he was a friend of a friend. We got on well and it wasn't long before we was courting…' Her face turned bright red. 'And… well, I found out I was in the family way. Oh, we'd talked of getting wed before that, but… well we had to bring it forward, quick. Father could've killed Frank. He wouldn't speak to me till I was wed. He said I was a disgrace to the family.'

Ginnie's eyes never moved from Mabel's face.

Mabel continued. 'We got wed and I started to show soon after. A couple of mothers from round about knew we were short of money and setting up on our own. They gave us some baby stuff. Clothes, nappies and the like. It was so nice of them, I cried. Then…'

She stopped. Her eyes filled with silent tears. 'And then I lost my baby…' Mabel's voice became little more than a whisper.

Ginnie's eyes filled. She jumped up and threw her arms around Mabel. It was some time before either moved. Mabel's laziness, her worry over being left alone, Frank's concern about Ginnie helping her, the box of clothes – all made perfect sense. Even Frank's behaviour in taking her first week's pay, she could now understand.

'No wonder you needed help. But you needn't worry. Florrie's here and she's got her mummy and daddy, and her Aunty Ginnie to look out for her.'

## Chapter Twenty-Two

**August 1915**

On the whole, Pat O'Malley was a good boss. Maybe Ginnie not being a boy had turned out better than he'd expected. He still kept her on her toes but was always fair and timely with her wages. A year on, and she was still doing the job that nobody wanted, despite it being a job for the young folk and her no longer being the youngest in The Shop.

She kept an eye on people. Working next to the jolleyer gave her the opportunity to question his mouldrunner, a chatty sort, who didn't mind her asking questions. Girls and women workers did pretty much as they were told and none of them worked the machines. During the time she had been there, all the boys had moved on to better paid jobs, or into the army when they were old enough. Wounded soldiers took over as they became available. If she ever had the chance of working the machines, jolleying would have been her first choice.

Her eyes lit on Elsie, who had become quite approachable over the matter of George. After snapping time, she caught Elsie on her own. Elsie gave her such a nice smile as she passed that Ginnie decided to take a chance. She heaved a board of moulds on to her shoulder and followed her to the drying room.

'Oh, my poor back.' Elsie laid her board on the bench and deftly collected the empties. 'It's getting late. Not long to go now, thank the Lord.'

They scrambled out of the fiery heat and banged the door shut. Beads of sweat formed on Elsie's brow and her face had a crimson glow which she wiped with the back of her arm as she turned to go back to her bench.

'Elsie?' Ginnie spoke quietly. She was in two minds whether to say anything, but she'd built herself up. It was now or never. 'Do you think the bosses would let me have a go at jolleying?' she whispered.

Elsie waggled a finger in her ear as if trying to clear wax. 'Yer what, lass?'

'I wish I could have a go at the… jolleying machine.' Ginnie's voice dried to a whisper. 'I'd like to be a jolleyer one day, that's all.'

Elsie's face changed from confusion to a wide grin.

Too late, Ginnie realised Elsie had been joking when she'd asked Ginnie to repeat herself.

'Oh, my Lord, now I've heard everything.' Elsie slapped her thigh and doubled up with laughter. 'Our Ginnie, you don't half take the biscuit, duckie.'

'What's so funny?' Her face tightened. She hadn't seen any girls working the machines, but surely that didn't mean they couldn't. Why shouldn't she be the first? But the world didn't want people to be different. Look how they treated the suffragettes. She'd made a mistake in opening up to Elsie; that much was obvious. 'Please don't tell anyone.'

It was too good a story to keep quiet.

'Listen, you lot. Our Ginnie here only wants to be a jolleyer. What'll she think of next?' Elsie guffawed with laughter and wiped her streaming eyes. She placed a hand on Ginnie's shoulder and, in a low voice said, 'Seriously, them's is men's jobs. You'll thank me for telling you one day.'

Women hid smirks behind clay-covered hands and some laughed outright. Ginnie galloped to Pat's bench and snatched the next set of moulds almost before he had time to lay them down and even *he* had a broad grin on his face. With her board full, she hastened to the drying room, her eyes fixed on the floor to avoid scurrilous eyes. She had tended this dream ever since she'd first seen the machine. How it worked, she had no idea – the jollyer had once confessed that he didn't know either, although on reflection, he might have been having her on too – but it made beautifully smooth cups and bowls.

So much for her shattered dreams.

A couple of the women curtsied as she flew by. For once Ginnie was glad the heat of the drying room masked her flaming cheeks.

For the whole day George bowed low as she passed and each time her face burned all over again. Today, he was making a point of being around. She struggled into her coat at the end of the day and emerged to find him waiting for her.

He drew her aside. 'Ginnie, you can't go around saying as you want to be a jolleyer. Ideas above yer station, that's what it's called. They...' he gestured vaguely to the room, '... won't like it.'

His face had an earnest look about it and she was about to thank him for his concern.

'Besides, everybody knows as wenches don't have the brains to operate machinery,' he grinned.

She swung her fist at him.

'Only joking, honest,' he cried in mock alarm.

'Women are just as good as men, George Mountford.'

'How come there aren't more women doing them sort of jobs then?'

'Because they don't get the chance, that's why. Because of the likes of you.'

'Women doing men's work'll bring wages down and blokes have families to feed.'

'There's plenty of women what's got families and no husband. And there'll be even more after the war's over. Have you thought about that?'

She flounced off, nose in the air, keenly aware that several pairs of eyes followed her. What was the point in getting the vote if women didn't have dreams of bettering themselves?

Working the machines wouldn't be as tiring as mouldrunning and, once she had learned to control it, she was convinced she could be as good as any man.

She would keep her daft ideas to herself in future. She wouldn't stop having dreams, she just shouldn't talk about them.

–

Although George made fun of her, she didn't think he hated her any more. Occasionally he got a bit shirty, but he seemed well settled in mould making – for the time being.

He was still a Jack the Lad – Ginnie was of the opinion he couldn't stop himself. This morning he was flirting with two old women working in The Shop and they weren't half lapping it up. When his master's back was turned, George made an excuse to wander over and find some reason to squeeze by them, causing red faces and silly grins. Squeals of, 'Gerroff with yer,' were followed by more giggling. Both women were twice his age. Ginnie couldn't help watching and wishing she had some of their bottle.

He caught her eye. Unknowingly, she was staring at him. When she realised, she turned away quickly. Hearing footsteps walking towards her, she ducked near the bench to pick up some fallen clay to excuse her flustered appearance. He whistled above her, and when she rose, her head brushed his hand and sent a shock through her whole body. She felt like a trapped animal waiting for a hunter to pounce.

She pretended she didn't care. She wasn't full of saucy comments like the others, but she was getting there. When someone spilled half a bucket of slip on her newly scrubbed floor the other week, she had noted admiration on his face when she gave them a bit of lip. Not that what *he* thought was important.

'Ginnie lass, keep me waiting any longer and I'll have to dock yer wages,' Pat growled behind her.

'Coming.'

She hastened over to him, throwing a sharp frown at George. 'Is the lad giving you a hard time?'

Pat's whispered question surprised her. She shook her head quickly, picked up the waiting moulds and turned towards the drying room. George stared at her. Had she got something on her face? She lifted her hand and stopped. If there *was* clay on her face, touching it would only make it worse. Maybe he wasn't used to being ignored. There was something about him. Excitement? Danger? She certainly never knew what he was going to say or do next. Her body responded with violent flushes, a tingling of her skin as if it was on fire, a catching of her breath. She disliked this power of his but her body had a mind of its own. Even if she was interested – which she definitely wasn't – but if she was, there'd be no point because he was the same with all the wenches. And anyway, she had Sam.

Sam was different, special. Sam would do nothing to hurt her. He would always be there for her – the kindest, most gentle person she knew.

When the bell rang everybody downed tools as usual and there was much talking and laughter. It was the end of the working week and they had money in their pockets. Surprisingly, Pat clapped his hands and, as one, they all shut up and gathered around him. He was well-respected and was not one for making unnecessary conversation, particularly at clocking-off time.

Ginnie edged forward. She could read his face well now and her heart sank. In these troubled times, people wanted to know their jobs were safe. They may not be the best jobs in the world, but they were jobs when all was said and done. Nobody liked traipsing around looking for work. Factories had closed because workers were fighting overseas. Money was tight and nobody wanted to buy the ware. She was under no illusions. Anybody could do mouldrunning.

He cast an eye over each of them, waiting for silence. 'Am off to join the war effort. I want you all to know before some bugger else tells yer.'

Ginnie gave a yelp. It hadn't entered her head that Pat would consider joining up. He looked too old and his face was too pale. The place wouldn't be the same without him. Typical of him to wait until knocking-off time. He knew that once he opened his mouth his name would be on everybody's lips and that would be the end of work for the day.

'I'm not wed so likely I'll be called any time soon. Reckoned as I might as well go sooner as wait for it to happen. Them bloody Huns are still battling around that place called Ypres, what we call Wipers, and playing dirty an' all trying to gas us out. But we wunner let the buggers win.'

He was the first of the bosses to go.

–

The day after Pat left, she arrived at the usual time to get The Shop ready and stared at his empty bench. Her fingers slid around the long-handled machine she had kept supplied with moulds for a year, and some. How long would it be before he would come back to take up his rightful place? It would feel strange to have someone else barking after her to get a move on.

She filled the pail with water and picked up the brush to wipe the bench again, feeling its rough contours. By the time she'd finished, it was spotless.

George got Pat's job. For the duration of the war, he was told, if he proved himself capable. He was on the young side, but the bosses didn't have much choice. Working with him turned out better than expected. Now he was a boss, he gave up many of his laddish ways, much to the disappointment of some of the women. Only time would tell if he'd be able to keep it up.

–

'More men are needed to join up,' said Frank, scanning through *The Sentinel*. 'They say unmarried men between eighteen and forty-one will have to join up if they pass a medical.'

'Well thanks be to God you're married with a kid,' said Mabel. 'Sounds sensible to me.'

Frank said nothing more and Ginnie couldn't tell whether it was disappointment or relief she heard in his voice.

Ginnie tried to imagine what she would feel like if she knew she could be compelled to join the army to face an enemy on foreign soil. To be the one to leave, instead of the one left behind.

The word 'war' was plastered everywhere. Blackboards outside shops told of shortages. No milk, no beer, no cigarettes, all due to the war.

Frank read out reports each evening, reckoning it would only be a matter of time before married blokes got called up too. Ginnie couldn't tell by his face how he felt about it. When men got together there was camaraderie, and possibly a touch of bravado for who knew what was going on in their minds when they went home to their families? Who would keep the families safe for the men to come home to? No wonder Mabel was on edge and short-tempered.

It was a rare sight these days to see a man in civvies walking down the street. People stared, trying to work out what was stopping them from fighting. At least the men in wheelchairs, on crutches, and the blind had nothing to explain. Suffragettes, who had abandoned their political fight for the duration of the war, challenged men to 'take up the shilling and fight' or be handed a white feather of shame.

Frank talked about joining up. 'Think of the wages, Mabel. Separation Allowance, they call it. I'll get more than I do down the pots.'

'Don't talk daft. What good's wages going be if you go and get yourself killed? Tell me that, Frank Farmer, 'cos I can't make no sense of it.'

'Them Huns'll not get me, love. I can take care of myself. I'll show the buggers what it is to fight.'

'Don't you dare!'

Maybe he was saying it because Mabel wouldn't let him go and so he felt safe in talking as he did, acting determined, egged on by his mates.

–

In March 1916, Ginnie's world turned upside down. A knock came on the front door. When Ginnie opened it, she was met by a strained-looking Sam. They hadn't arranged to meet so it had to be important. Silently, she stood aside to let him in. He took off his cap and stepped past her without looking at her. Neither spoke until they had reached the kitchen.

He stood before her, moving nervously from foot to foot.

'What have you gone and done, Sam White?'

'What d'yer mean?'

'Whatever it is you've come to say, I'm not going to like it, am I?'

'Never could keep anything from you, could I?' He bit his lip and took a deep breath. 'I went to Hanley Post Office this morning and I… I joined the army…' A hint of a wobble touched the corner of his mouth.

She shook her head. 'But you… you're only sixteen, or thereabouts.' She paced away. 'You're a boy, grown up like a man.'

'The army needs men, Ginnie. Don't I look like a man to you?'

She looked at him and tried to see, not Sam, but the person he was – tall and muscular, his firm clear look. Oh, yes, she could imagine him in uniform, and he would look every inch the man he was growing into. In all honesty, she couldn't say no. There was little of the boy she had known standing in front of her, but it didn't make it right.

'Them suffragettes are calling on all men to go and fight. Constance doesn't have a go at me 'cos she knows I'm not old enough.' He took hold of both her hands and carried on in a softer voice. 'We've got to fight, to make things right. Them Germans won't give up until they've taken over the world. How could we forgive ourselves if we don't fight?'

'But you're working down the pit. You don't have to go.'

'The pit's not for me, Ginnie, duck. I need the open air, space. Leave the pit to someone as canna fight.'

She pulled her hands away and paced up and down. 'You'd be lying.'

'But I look old enough. You don't know what it's like being stared at when you walk down the street. People want to ask why I'm still here when their menfolk have gone. I've got no proof of when I was born. I *could* be old enough for all I know. Sixteen? Seventeen? Eighteen? What does it matter? I know what I need to do – in here.' He slapped his chest. 'You do see, don't you?'

No, she didn't. What she saw before her was Sam, her Sam, who had become a man in front of her very eyes, and she hadn't noticed. Her head sank onto her chest. It didn't matter what she said; he would go, she had no doubt.

'When? Do you know where?'

'I'm waiting for a letter. But you won't get rid of me easily. I'll always find you.'

She stared into his eyes, seeing tiny versions of herself reflected back. 'I know, Sam. And I'll always be waiting.'

Her arms crept up around his neck. His earnest gaze was her undoing. Wasn't that why she loved him so much? It was part of who he was. She stared at her feet, not wanting him to see the tears welling up.

He slid his hand under her chin and gently lifted it so that she had to look at him. His face blurred as it closed in. For the briefest of moments there was longing, and then his lips touched hers. This was like no other kiss. It was firm, yet gentle. A kiss from a man to the woman in his life. She didn't know why her body should ache for him, but it did.

'I want to see you every day before you go, Sam White. Do you hear?'

When he didn't speak, she turned towards him. And there it was, his shy, but beautiful grin. She smiled back. There was nothing else she could do.

-

Her shyness returned when he came to say goodbye before going off to do his basic training somewhere near a place called Stafford. He looked so smart, all dressed up in clothes supplied by Constance from one of her mother's charities, but he wasn't her Sam any more. He was a man leaving her to do a man's job.

'You *will* be careful, won't you?'

'I'm only going to be learning soldiering. There'll be no Germans about, not yet, any road. Might be all over before I get out there.'

Neither of them believed that, but it lightened the mood.

'You know what I mean.'

'Course I will. Got you to think about, haven't I?'

That night she cried into her pillow, muffling the sound so that no one would hear. In need of comfort, she scrambled out of bed and delved into her carpetbag. She pulled out Clara, the doll he'd made for her when she left Haddon, and which she had named for her special friend who had died so young. So many times she had got him back, only to lose him again. Would it always be like this? Now that she was grown up the hurt travelled even more deeply inside her.

Then, in May, the government said married men would also be conscripted, and no man was safe.

# Chapter Twenty-Three

**July 1916**

Sam had been in Ginnie's thoughts every day since he had left. Where was he? How was he? How soon she would see him again? The weeks dragged. Days bled into one another becoming difficult to tell apart.

Earlier in the month, the Allies had advanced into enemy territory at a place on the River Somme – wherever that was. *The Sentinel* said, 'the day goes well for England and France,' which was a damn good job, considering the number of telegrams received at work and in their street. It said that the guns of the Western Front were even heard in Holland, and that's a different country.

–

Out of the blue, George asked Ginnie to go to Burslem Picture Palace with him. She was at a loose end and he didn't have a regular girl he was walking out with, as far as she knew. Word travelled quickly on the potbank and she would've heard about it. She felt sorry for him and couldn't think of a reason not to keep him company. She had done a lot of babysitting of Florrie so Mabel and Frank could spend time together before he got called up so it would be good to go out and enjoy herself.

Sat in the floor-level seats, Ginnie could glance up at the small balcony covering three sides of the theatre. She soon lost herself in the silent film although it was difficult to follow when she couldn't read the words. George whispered odd words in her ear but avoided too much talking which might annoy other people.

Afterwards, they walked home with a couple of George's mates and two girls she hadn't met before, Iris and Susan. They were older and George seemed to grow more manly in their company. Ginnie soon felt out of her depth.

'Look, Ginnie. I'm sorry for having a go at you when you started at Chamberlain's. I should never have done it. I was surprised, that's all, you starting to work there. I honestly thought you'd come for my job.'

After all this time, she was surprised by his apology. He didn't strike her as the type to admit any faults.

'Come down the pub and let's grab ourselves a pint,' someone shouted.

Iris and Susan cheered and tottered across the cobbled street and in through the side door of the Red Lion, followed closely by their friends.

George beckoned to Ginnie. 'Come on. Show there's no hard feelings. I'm trying to make it up to you.'

She hung back. 'I can't go in there. I'm only sixteen and a half.' The girls had obviously done it many times before. Maybe they were old enough. She didn't know.

'Don't be daft. Nobody'll see you. And if they do, they'll be too drunk to care.'

He gave her a gentle push and she had no choice but to follow the others.

It was dark inside. Her eyes watered and smoke filled her nostrils. The smell of drink gagged at the back of her throat and caused her to cough every few minutes even though she tried to hold them back. The more she tried to stop, the worse it seemed to get.

Iris, with the low-cut dress showing beneath her open coat, frowned. 'Wherever did you find this one, George? Can't you get her to shut up? She's giving me a bleeding headache.'

Susan laughed. 'She shouldn't be out this late.'

George turned his back on them so they wouldn't hear. 'You're showing me up, Ginnie,' he hissed. 'Give it a rest, for Christ's sake.'

His mates pulled grotesque faces.

She thought of making excuses to leave but, aside from George's moans and her coughing, she was actually enjoying being treated as a grown up. A drink she hadn't asked for was put into her hands. She had no idea what it was, and she didn't like to ask. It would probably mean nothing to her anyway. She left it as long as possible before taking a sip. When she did, it set her throat on fire and she coughed a whole lot more. After another groan from George she took only the tiniest of sips. It wasn't so bad. She grew warm inside. The coughing stopped.

She watched their lips moving but couldn't hear the words above the noise around them. It didn't matter; she hadn't got a lot to say and was happy just to sit and sip her drink.

George downed his ale and got up, nodding in the direction of the door. Stumbling as the world slipped from under her feet, she burst out laughing and the world swam the other way. They made their way slowly towards the door. Someone patted her backside. She turned sharply but people were sandwiched together, her eyes swam and she couldn't make out who it was. She stumbled through the door and down the stone steps. A highly polished carriage was waiting for someone. She stretched out a hand to touch it. She wanted to ride in it and tried to tell George, but he grabbed her hand and pulled her along the street where staying upright, even on two legs, took a great deal of concentration.

The quietness of the night pressed against her head like a bandage pulled tight. A drum banged inside her brain. She rubbed her eyes and tried to be the girl who had gone into the pub, but her legs didn't belong to her and the pavement was too far away. It helped her brain to follow where he led.

He stopped in a dark doorway and pulled her to him. Her eyes opened wide as his arms locked about her. She tensed. The others had disappeared. They were alone. The quietness made her head throb.

'I want to kiss you, Ginnie. I gave you a good time, didn't I?'

His head came towards her, his lips firm and strong. He held her so tightly, she could scarcely breathe. It was nothing like the warm, tender kisses she received from Sam. Her body grew excited and, for a moment, she returned it. He leaned against her, rubbed his body against hers, her arms held tightly against her sides.

His strength suddenly frightened her. She tried to move away, he followed. There was a wall at her back and something gritty scraping her scalp. She was trapped.

She shook her head to avoid his slobbering kisses. 'No, no, please George. No.'

She tried to push him away.

He didn't hear or he didn't want to hear.

He didn't stop or wouldn't stop.

'Let me go! George…' Her fists pounding his chest and her struggles were ineffectual.

'Don't be daft. You know you want this.' His lips covered her face with little kisses. 'You owe me.'

'No… No I don't. Leave me alone.' She twisted her head away to avoid his lips.

He laughed.

She drew up her knee and, fuelled by a level of anger she didn't know she possessed, she kneed him where it hurt most.

'AGGGh rrrrgh.' He doubled up and let her go. 'Bitch! What did you do that for? You wanted it as much as me. I thought you was coughing because you wanted to get me on my own.' His breath came in short bursts, his eyes bright and hot as he covered his privates.

'It's all about you, isn't it?' Tears stung her eyes. 'I wasn't coughing on purpose and I didn't want to get you on your own. I don't owe you anything. I told you to stop, and you wouldn't listen. Leave me alone.'

She turned and ran.

Her wobbly legs had gone. Her head was clear. She ran all the way home, stopping now and again to catch her breath and to check over her shoulder. Bile rose into the back of her throat. She prayed she would get home before she was sick and, as Mabel's house came into view, she gulped with relief, holding her chest as she fought for control.

She couldn't go in like this. Her head jerked back and forth as she glanced up and down the street. Apart from someone crossing at the far end, it was empty.

When she could breathe normally, she crossed the road and leaned against Mabel's front door. She felt dirty. She should never have agreed to go to the rotten pub. How would she bear to look at him at work after this? Since when did buying a drink mean buying someone's body too? She had told him to stop —and he hadn't.

In the safety of her bedroom, the tears fell. She pulled Sam's doll out of the carpetbag and dived into bed, pulling the blankets tightly around her. But when she closed her eyes, the panic came back, and clutching Clara made it worse. She had betrayed Sam.

A line had been crossed.

–

The next morning her face felt bruised and tender, her lips swollen, and her head banged as if something inside was trying to get out. She thought about crying off work. The sickness hadn't gone away, and her head felt as if it might split open. But she had to go; she couldn't afford not to.

Why hadn't he listened when she said no? As she dressed, she turned over all she could remember of the evening, asking herself whether, at any time, she *had* led him on. She had momentarily returned his kisses. Did that count? Her chin trembled with the shame of it.

She remained upstairs for as long as she dared, hoping that Mabel was due for a lie-in.

'God you look awful, our Ginnie. Whatever were you up to last night?' Mabel stopped feeding Florrie and stared at her.

'Nothing. Have to go, I'm late.' She struggled into her coat; her sleeves seemed to have been sewn together.

'What about your breakfast?'

Mabel's voice was too loud. Ginnie couldn't face eating. Thoughts of making up her snapping made her gag. 'Haven't got time. See you later.'

Ginnie escaped through the front door and shot down the street but slowed up because her brains hurt even more. How on earth would she cope, feeling like this?

George tried to speak to her several times and eventually caught her on her way back from the privy. She had stopped still, holding her thumping head, wishing the day was over. She sensed rather than saw him. He blocked her path, hands on hips, sneering. She tried to push past him.

'Had a good time…' he murmured close to her ear, '… didn't we?'

She'd expected him to have a go at her earlier, in full view, where everyone could see and hear. Maybe he didn't want people to know she had turned him down. She backed away.

'Look, I'm sorry about last night, but we were having a good time, weren't we?'

'Stay away from me.'

His eyes hardened. 'I could've told everybody. Told them how you like to have a good time, but don't like to give anything in return. Not very nice, is it?'

'I didn't know that having a drink meant you could do what you want with me. I would never have gone with you.'

'Come off it, Ginnie, I'm not made of money. You came because you wanted to.' He took off his cap and ran dusty fingers through his hair.

She stared back, unable to hide her disgust. 'I went because I felt sorry for you.'

His fist came up towards her face. 'Don't you *ever, ever* feel sorry for me.'

She ducked. She'd definitely hit a raw spot. Her legs trembled, but she stood her ground. He would *not* threaten her. His hand fell to his side. He walked off without turning around.

She leaned against the wall, sweat pouring from her. Steadying her ragged breath, she walked back into The Shop and let it be known, quietly, that it was her time of the month, knowing that the women would ask no more questions. She escaped at dinnertime, saying she had to pick up something for her stomach, which was true, in a way.

She was still dazed as she thought over the morning's events. His anger when she said she felt sorry for him truly shocked her. These last two days had shown a violent nature she hadn't seen before. It seemed he was as much her enemy now as he had been when they first met.

—

'Ginnie!'

The footsteps behind her got louder and quicker as she walked home from work. She turned, ready to run, but it was Sam. She hadn't expected him back from training so soon or she'd never have gone out with George. She felt queasy. If Sam hadn't grabbed hold of her arm, she would've fallen flat out on the pavement.

'Ginnie? Are you all right?'

His anxious face swam into view. She put her hand to her head. He guided her to a low wall and gently pushed her down.

'When did you get back?'

He brushed aside her comment. 'You look like you've seen a ghost, lass.'

'I thought… I thought you was George.' The words were out before she could stop them.

'George Mountford? What's he got to do with it?'

Sam's eyes narrowed and his hand tightened on her arm. She squealed.

He let go straight away. 'What's he done?'

'I went— some of us from work went to the Picture Palace and then the pub… I didn't want to be the only one not to.'

'And…' His face was still flushed and showed no chance of calming.

'And… I was… Well, I was sick if you must know.'

His mouth twitched into a crooked smile. 'You mean you got drunk?'

'No!'

Her protestations didn't stop the grin.

'What would you call it then? Oh, Ginnie, you can be funny at times. I'm not getting at you. Everybody gets drunk sometime in their lives.'

He patted her head like she was a kid. Forgetting her headache, she stood tall and, hands on hips, shouted, 'That's all you know, Sam White. I'd have been all right if he hadn't…'

'He *did* do something then?'

Her anger fizzled out. 'It was nothing.'

'Tell me, Ginnie. What's he done to yer?' He shook her arm. 'Tell me, Ginnie.'

'He… he kissed me.'

Sam's face turned black as thunder. He let go of her so quickly, she almost fell over. 'You let him kiss you?'

'No! Course not.'

'You just said he did.'

His eyes glinted, his neck muscles tense, as if he was fighting for control.

She took a step back. 'I said *he* kissed *me*. There's a big difference and if you can't see that, Sam White, then there's nothing more to be said.'

She flounced off, wishing her head didn't hurt so much.

In bed later, she regretted being so childish. She should have stayed and talked to him properly, like Constance would've done. It wasn't his fault. He had borne the brunt of her frustration, and guilt that, for a few seconds, she had returned George's kiss.

–

The following evening, there was a knock on the door. Ginnie was on her own so she had no alternative but to answer it. Sam stood there, cap in hand, with a sheepish grin on his face. She waited for him to speak although it took some effort on her part.

'Hello, lass. I was looking forward to seeing you so much; it wasn't supposed to happen like it did. I'm sorry.'

'I'm right glad to see you too. I shouldn't have walked off like that.' She gave him a shy smile. 'Want to go for a walk?'

'I'd like that.'

She threw on her hat and coat and closed the door behind her. As they walked down the street, she tried to think of something to say.

'So, when *did* you get back?' It sounded lame but it was a start.

'Yesterday. I came straight round to yours, but I reckoned you were at work. So, I waited. And then I saw you.' He held up his hand as she was about to speak. 'Forget about yesterday. Whatever happened between you and George is nowt to do with me.'

'But it wasn't what you thin—'

'Listen, Ginnie. It's up to you what you do and who you drink with. But,' he stopped momentarily, 'if I hear as George Mountford, or anybody else, for that matter, has laid so much as a finger on yer'

'He won't, Sam. I told him straight.'

'We're all right then?'

She hooked her arm through his. 'Course we are. If that's all right with you?'

'There's nothing I want more.'

He pulled her to him and kissed her right on the lips, hard at first, and then more gently. It wasn't the same as it was with George; it felt good to be there.

'We're not kids any more, Ginnie. I'll be a soldier when I go back. Kids don't feel the way I feel about you.'

She gave him the broadest of smiles. She thought back to her feelings when Sam had been sent away from Haddon, the sense of loss and uncertainty that had clouded every day. She remembered the day he came back, how he had twirled her in the air and the joy welling up deep inside that she couldn't contain. But those were as nothing compared to the way she felt now. She may be only sixteen-and-a-half, but she knew in that moment, that she wanted to spend the rest of her life with him.

–

A brown envelope came through the door addressed, unusually, to *Mrs* Farmer. Mabel turned it upside down and round about, as if trying to see through the envelope to the letter inside. After concluding that second sight was not one of her talents, she took out a kitchen knife and carefully slit the envelope open. 'Wonder what they want?' she said, almost to herself.

'What who wants?' Ginnie carried on mending her work apron, which had somehow got caught up on a bench and had a tear along the hem.

'The workhouse.'

'Is it about me?' Ginnie would've snatched it off Mabel if she had been able to read.

'Oh!' Mabel's hand went to her throat.

'It's me… isn't it?' The words fell over themselves.

'Shut up, Ginnie. Not everything is about you.'

Mabel skimmed the words and glanced up at last. 'Father was took bad in the night. He's passed away. It was quick, they say. His heart. No time to get in touch. He's gone, Ginnie.' Her bottom lip trembled.

Ginnie felt choked. She had been so angry with him over Mother's funeral, and then waiting, hoping he'd get back in touch. She always meant to go back to see him but there was never enough time. Now, it was too late.

'He never did marry that workhouse woman,' Mabel said. She sighed. 'Perhaps I should've taken our Florrie to see him. But Frank said not to 'cos Father never liked him. Still, he'll be with Mother now.'

'They're asking if it's a pauper's burial we'll be needing.'

*He didn't deserve that*, Ginnie thought. Burial in an unmarked grave along with poor folk who had no one was a terrible way to end a life.

'He was so proud Mother hadn't had a pauper's funeral.' Mabel sat down, still staring at the letter. 'We owe it to him to see him taken care of properly. I'll go and see the undertaker tomorrow. He'll know what to do. They sorted out Mother's.'

Ginnie was thrust right back to that day when Mabel and her Father had left the church together not knowing that she was there, in her loneliness, to witness Mother's last journey. With Mary's help, she had held their own secret service after Father and Mabel left. It had been the day she had discovered Mary's own past and Ginnie owed it to her to keep quiet. She'd held her tongue then, and she held it now.

'Father thought you were too young for the funeral. You know about our brother Joseph, don't you? I told you he died when he was a nipper? Broke Father's heart when he had to go to the funeral. Nearly fell in the grave when he fainted. He never forgot about burying little Joseph and said a graveyard was no place for a kid. He was a broken man for ages afterwards.'

'You mean he wasn't ashamed of me?'

'Course not. Maybe I should've said something. You should have been there.'

'Happen I should've,' she murmured. A lump stuck in Ginnie's throat. It was too late now to wish she had questioned Father more and taken less notice of her own pride. She was just as bad as he was.

The funeral took place on a bright, sunny August day, not dank and dark as it was when her mother was laid to rest. This time she was linking arms with Mabel, supporting each other.

'Just you and me now, duckie,' said Mabel.

'Just me and you.'

Like Mother, he was buried in St John's churchyard, a small stone marking the place. They couldn't afford anything more. Ginnie took a carnation out of the posy they placed beside the headstone to put with the one from Mother's grave.

'I'd like us to visit Mother,' Ginnie said softly. 'As a family.'

Mabel glanced around. 'I don't know as I could find it, now.'

'I think it's near a tree isn't it?'

'Yes, I think I remem— Ginnie, how did you know that?'

Ginnie marched forward a few paces so as to keep her face hidden and pretended to scan the stones. 'I don't know. That is… I meant she would've liked one nearby.' It sounded feeble but she hoped it would be enough to take Mabel's mind off her lapse. Sure enough, Mabel merely nodded to herself and it wasn't referred to again. After much wandering they found it, small in comparison with the stones around about.

'Florence Jones, wife and mother, born 1871, died 1913,' read Mabel in a whisper, even though there was no one else to hear. 'Three years past. It's all gone so quick.'

Ginnie didn't think so. 'I wish she was still here.'

She blew a kiss onto her hand and placed it gently against the cold, rough stone.

# Chapter Twenty-Four

**August 1916**

'Guess what? I'm getting married.'

Constance had appeared on the doorstep and the words were out before the door was properly open, her green eyes as bright as a cat's. Ginnie pulled her through the door and closed it with a bang. Mabel had taken Florrie to the shops, hoping to get something for tea.

'I haven't seen you for ages. When? Oh, my word.'

Together, they danced around the kitchen.

'What wonderful news for a change. Is it Matthew? You never said you were serious.'

'Of course it's Matthew, but it all happened so quickly. He wants us to get married when he comes home in September. His unit's going overseas. So, he said, why not just get married?' She turned around, grinning from ear to ear. 'And I said yes.'

'How romantic… I think.'

Constance laughed at her confusion and unpinned her hat.

'You know Sam's doing his basic training?' Ginnie sagged, unable to maintain her excitement for Constance at the thought.

'I heard, but surely he isn't old enough?' Constance pulled Ginnie down beside her, holding on to her hand.

'He looks old enough to fight and it bothers him so yes, he's done his basic training. He said his place is out there. He doesn't actually know when he was born, so that doesn't help.'

When she had a family, she would want to protect them from the horrors of the world, give them the love and care she'd missed out on: a mother who was there for them, a father, brothers and sisters, and a home where they could be together and want for nothing.

'So, tell me about Matthew,' she said, trying to change the subject back to Constance and her good news. 'You've not said much so far.'

'Well, his name is Matthew Roundswell. He's twenty-seven, and quite handsome. Did I tell you he's a captain in the army?' Her face flushed. 'Father's taken with him because he believes Matthew will stop me getting into mischief with the suffragettes again when the war's over. Matthew believes women should have the vote. He's perfect.' She swooned dramatically.

'Isn't he a bit old?'

Constance became serious. 'Honestly, the rest were just boys by comparison. He's so knowledgeable about everything. I can't believe it. It's all happened so quickly, and so romantic. Me, soon to be a married woman!' She clapped her hands gleefully.

'You make it sound as if he's the latest in a long line. Well I hope you'll both be very happy.'

'It will be a quick wedding. Nothing fancy. But I want you and Sam to come. 16th September, at twelve o'clock. Will Sam be able to? It's only a month away.'

'He should finish his training at the end of the month, so I can ask him. Mind you, I've nowt to wear and we can't talk proper like your friends. Might be best if we stop away, all things considered.'

'Ginnie Jones, you'll do no such thing. There's no one I want there more, except Mother and Father, of course. That goes without saying. I'll find you something to wear so you needn't worry. It's going to be just a few friends for a meal. We plan to have a couple of days in Manchester on our own,' she flushed prettily, 'before he goes back to his regiment.'

'Am tickled pink for you.' She gave Constance a big hug. 'Sorry!' She jumped back, astounded by her forwardness. 'I hope he's good enough for yer. Yer such a bonnie wench.'

Constance clapped her hands. 'That's what I love about you, Ginnie. You can't help showing your feelings. The people I know are too busy thinking about themselves, rather than being happy for someone else's good fortune. Promise me you'll stay just as you are?'

'I can't promise that because I want to change. I want a good job where people don't take me for granted. I don't want to keep quiet… you showed me how it feels to talk to people and persuade them that you are right… with your suffragettes. *I* want to be like that. I want to work the machines in the potbank and not be told I can't because I'm a girl – or a woman, for that matter.'

'Good for you. There's no harm in that. But stay true to yourself along the way.'

'I want to earn lots of money so as I'm never dependent on the parish… or anybody.'

'That's just how I feel. I am a person in my own right. Our husbands should not be our keepers.' Constance's nose pointed skywards.

They burst into fits of laughter.

'We aren't really that different, are we?' said Constance. 'Have you forgiven Sam for joining up? He wanted to do what he thought was right too.'

'Even though he might get himself killed?'

'Oh, Ginnie.' Constance walked a few paces and turned. 'That's what every wife, mother and sweetheart will say before the war's out. Men and boys like Matthew and Sam are fighting for what they believe in. We have to let them go… and be proud of them. We must keep the country going and, when they come home, they will see that we believe in ourselves. They'll have to give us the vote. We'll work together and the country will be the better for it.'

'I don't care about the blasted vote. I care about what's best for Sam and how to keep him alive.'

Constance bit her lip. 'It's not just about the vote. We want our young men to live the life they want to, with us fully supporting them. And that means their mental and their physical state. How do you think Sam would feel if he didn't do what he considered to be his duty? He's got a man's values. In ordinary times, it would be good for both of you.' She turned and sat on the edge of her seat. 'But these are not ordinary times. Sam was ready and that's what's important.'

'Do you really believe that?'

'We have to, Ginnie, otherwise we'll never get through it.'

–

It was a day Ginnie would never forget. Tuesday, 5 September 1916. The day the official-looking envelope popped through the door. It was propped up on the table when she got home. Her eyes were drawn to it like an animal who knew there was something different in his space.

'Can't take me eyes off it,' said Mabel.

'Why don't you open it?'

'It's addressed to Frank. It makes it all real, and it won't go away.'

'I would want to know—'

'Since when have you been such a know-it-all? You don't know nothing at all.'

Ginnie's hands grew cold. She opened her mouth but couldn't find her voice. Instead, she backed towards the door. Mabel crumpled and burst into tears. Ginnie put aside her fear of being pushed away and gave her sister a hug. The fight had gone out of Mabel as quickly as it had come.

'I've been so scared, knowing it was only a matter of time. I never meant to get at you, our Ginnie. It's this crazy world what's getting to me.'

Ginnie was no longer the little girl needing the contact of another. She was old enough to be a giver of comfort. She patted Mabel's back gently. 'There, there, you're right… I don't know what I'd do in your place.' *But I will do very soon*, she thought sadly. She tried her best to make conversation, but Mabel answered with the barest of interest.

Another hour passed before they heard Frank's familiar whistle. Mabel's eyes filled with tears. Ginnie got to her feet and stood with a hand on Mabel's shoulder. Mabel's hand crept up to cover hers.

As he came upon them, standing together, he stopped whistling, 'Whatever's the matter with the pair of you? Have you been blarting?'

Mabel picked up the envelope, twisting it between her fingers. 'This come in the post today. It's for you.'

As if in slow motion, he laid his snapping bag down on the table, his eyes transfixed on the envelope. He took it with the tips of his fingers as if the contents might burn him. The silence grew louder, frozen in time like a photograph. Raised voices came through the wall from next door. Ginnie could almost make out who was speaking.

Frank's mouth opened and closed like a fish. When he looked up, his face was ashen. Ginnie wished she had an excuse to remove herself – something to do, somewhere to hide – but Mabel still had a hold of her hand and wasn't about to let go.

With a huge sigh, Frank lowered himself on to a chair by the table and stared at the address for what seemed like ages, and then glanced up and stared at the window.

'Me papers.'

'Must be.'

He banged the envelope on the edge of the table a few times until it was bent in the middle, creased and dog-eared. Then, he threw it onto the table and dashed to the outside privy.

Ten minutes later he was back, still pale but with bright, red eyes. Ginnie and Mabel hadn't moved. He lowered himself into his chair.

'Where's me tea then?'

'Tell them you can't go,' Mabel burst out. 'They'll understand, you with a young kid an' all?'

He stared at the fire-grate.

'Open it, Frank. I've been that worried ever since it came.'

'Well, you can wait a bit longer. A man can't open a letter like that on an empty belly.'

They were half-way through a silent tea when he threw down his fork, picked up the envelope and savagely ripped it open. He glanced at the letter then cast it to one side. He pushed his chair back and stumbled out of the kitchen, shaking his head. Mabel snatched up the letter.

'Next week. Christ almighty, he's going next week, Ginnie.' Her hand went to her throat. Unsteadily, she followed Frank outside.

Ginnie watched the two of them in the yard. A picture of two people standing in the same position flashed into her mind: Mother and Father, when she and Mabel were told he was going blind. The sadness and terror of those days came flooding back and made her belly ache. She climbed the stairs to her room. The grief was theirs to work through, but she would be there when she was needed.

Since Florrie had arrived, Frank hadn't bothered her and neither of them had spoken about his earlier behaviour. Seeing him like this, she could almost feel sorry for him. His overly enthusiastic talk was only surface deep. She thought about others who had laughed and joked about the future and wondered how many of them were hiding their true feelings and being sick in the privy.

-

'Suppose it goes on for years? Florrie won't recognise you when you come back. And if you don't come back, what then?'

'I've got no bloody choice, have I? The way you're going on sounds like you've already made up your mind I won't be coming back. That's really cheered me up no end. Where's your faith, woman?'

'They said they was calling up them with no responsibilities. They can't expect you to go with such a young baby.'

'It's all changed. Them's me call-up papers.' He shook them under Mabel's nose. 'It doesn't matter if you're married with ten babies now. Any road, Arthur and some mates from the works are going too. Best I go with those I know'll cover my back.'

'But what about us?'

'You got Ginnie.'

'We'll cope, Mabel. Till Frank comes back,' said Ginnie, softly.

Frank smiled his thanks, which surprised her. She was glad they were on good terms at last, even though – and maybe because – he was leaving them.

Ginnie put an arm around Mabel and felt the muscles in her sister's shoulders tighten with resolve before she pulled away and continued folding the washing.

'Suppose that's that, then. You just go off with the lads and no doubt you'll put us out of your mind just like you always do.'

Sam gone. Now Frank.

It was strange at first, knowing he wasn't just down the road at the Flying Horse, and that he could be in real danger at any moment. The world had changed in an instant. Sharing her life with Mabel and Florrie, all girls together, was so much better, even if Florrie was only a tot. They shared more and took things in turns because Mabel didn't need to show off to Frank.

Ginnie and Sam took a stroll around the town. He'd got leave for Constance's wedding because his regiment would soon be going overseas. Glad of each other's company, they held hands when no one was looking. They hadn't talked of courting yet. Ginnie supposed they were too young, but she wished they were. She had never felt so proud in his company.

She cast little glances at him, wanting him to notice but at the same time, hoping he didn't.

'Mabel's read in the paper that we've invented a new sort of weapon they call a tank. Like a car with guns, but much bigger. The papers say it's revolutionary and may shorten the war.'

*Maybe Sam won't have to go, or if he does go it might not be for long*, she thought.

She suggested a walk in the park to take her mind off it all, needing its colourful freshness to lift her soul. He grinned the special grin he kept for her.

'Fine day for a walk, Ginnie.'

She stiffened as she recognised George's voice coming up behind them. Bumping into *him* was the last thing she wanted. It would be all round The Shop in the morning that she'd been seen with a man. Ginnie held her space between the two of them. Neither was smiling.

She put a hand on Sam's arm as if to hold him back. He didn't say anything, but his arm felt taunt as a spring, and his hands were held in a tight ball ready for a fight.

George sniggered. 'The mouldrunner and the workhouse boy.'

Ginnie stood tall, her face cold, copying the look she often saw on Constance's face when she wanted to appear in charge of a situation. 'Whatever we're up to is nothing to do with you.'

She grabbed hold of Sam's arm and propelled him forward, the undercurrent between the two of them tangible. The less that was said, the better, as far as she was concerned.

'I can take a hint.' George gave a quick nod. 'Oh, I enjoyed our night out by the way. Glad you… *enjoyed* it too.'

Sam made a move towards him. George backed off, the smirk disappearing swiftly.

'I don't want no trouble, Sam.' She put a hand on his chest and then turned to George. 'Leave us be.'

George gave a supercilious grin. 'I'll see you on Monday.' With a nonchalant salute, he turned and sauntered off.

Sam rounded on Ginnie. 'Why did you stop me? I could've given him a thick ear.'

'That's exactly why I did it, Sam White. *I've* got to work with him, not you.'

'He's nowt but a layabout. He needs teaching a lesson.'

'I don't want the pair of you fighting. You'll be doing enough of that soon.'

They walked on in silence, their easy-going friendliness had all but disappeared, leaving her with more regrets about her night out with George. She shouldn't be arguing with Sam when they had so little time left. *Damn George for his interference.*

–

The day of Constance's wedding dawned surprisingly warm for the middle of September. Ginnie had sat up for a whole week making alterations to the dress she was to wear: a light blue serge, with a fuller skirt than she was used to, in honour of the momentous occasion. A long, fitted jacket showing off her slim waist and a very nice hat and a pair of boots from the pawn shop, completed her outfit.

Sam turned up early, dressed smartly in dark trousers and jacket, his hair cut short, army-style. His right eye was bruised, and a cut on his lip looked angry. Ginnie frowned, and he put a finger to his lips. 'Not now.'

All the way into the town, Ginnie waited for him to speak. When she could wait no longer, she spoke out. 'So, what have you been up to? Fighting, by the looks of it?'

'Bumped into the cupboard door. Looks worse than it is.' He was silent again.

She waited for more, but they had arrived at the church.

Ginnie had never been to a wedding before. All those people, people with good jobs, people with money. What would they think of a mouldrunner, and a miner soon to be soldier, with a black eye and split lip?

Constance walked towards them.

Sam removed his cap and gave Ginnie's hand a squeeze. 'Dunner werrit. It's you she wants to see today. She dunner care what we look like. We done our best. Can't do no better.'

Ginnie smiled gratefully.

Constance had never looked so lovely. White lace framed her face and a green stone, matching her eyes, nestled at her throat. Her silk dress billowed out in a little train edged with tiny white bows. How could she have organised it all in such a short time? Even so, the woman who could stand in front of a group of people and persuade them into believing all women should have the vote, looked agitated. Her small posy of flowers run through with green ribbon, moved from hand to hand and her overly bright eyes were outlined with dark circles.

Surprisingly, it was Matthew who was standing by her side and not her father. Neither appeared ready for the most exciting day of their lives. Something had passed between them.

Ginnie flashed a sharp look at Constance. 'You're... beautiful,' was all she could say. 'What's—'

'Don't, Ginnie. Everything's fine.' Constance took hold of Ginnie's hands and pulled her close. 'If you say anything, I shall cry.' She raised her voice again. 'Go in you two, unless you intend to walk in behind the bride and groom!'

She pulled away and turned to Matthew. Holding out her arm and, with her back ramrod-straight, she walked away and never looked back.

'Something bad's happened, Sam. Her's almost in tears.'

She took his arm and they made their way inside. Two bouquets of flowers adorned the first pews, but there was little else to welcome the wedding in the austere building. For as long as Ginnie had known her, Constance had been strong and well-balanced. What had upset her on this happiest of days?

In view of their late arrival, they took a pew near the back of the church and waited. A minute or two later the organist started to play the wedding march, and everyone stood up. The bride and groom made their way to the altar, both had their eyes to the front, and neither wore a trace of a smile.

They halted at the altar. Matthew let go of her arm and took her hand. He was too far away for Ginnie to see his face. She could only hope that he was in a better frame of mind.

The priest's voice rang out, clear and strong. 'Dearly beloved, we are gathered together here in the sight of God, and in the face of this congregation, to join together this Man and this Woman in holy matrimony.'

A shiver ran up and down Ginnie's spine. She reached out to hold Sam's hand. From the look she'd seen on Constance's face, she could've been going to a funeral rather than her own marriage.

'… If there is anybody here present who knows of any just impediment why these two people should not be joined in marriage speak now, or forever hold your peace.'

'I do.'

A murmur, rising in intensity, flew around the church as speculation grew. People's heads swivelled one way and the other, trying to identify who had spoken.

'I do.' The words came from the front.

It was Matthew. He stepped away from Constance. 'I can't do it.'

'But you said—'

Ginnie had to concentrate hard to hear the words.

'I know what I said… but I can't.'

The priest ushered the couple to the vestry and out of public view. The door closed momentarily and opened again. Conversation stopped instantly.

The priest cleared his throat. 'Unfortunately, there will be a slight delay in proceedings. We would ask you to bear with us and we will be with you as soon as we can.' He gave a quick nod to the organist and, as the music started, disappeared back into the vestry. The door closed with a resounding bang, resulting in an outburst of chatter as his words sank in. Mrs Copeland rose painfully and, relying on her walking stick, moved towards the vestry to join her stricken daughter.

Ginnie's hands had gone straight to her hot cheeks, as she wished desperately that she could comfort her friend. 'Poor Constance, she's such a lovely person, so kind, happy, and intelligent. Why would Matthew change his mind in church, of all places?'

'Cruel, I'd say. To let her down at the altar—'

'I hate him for this.'

'Maybe it can be sorted.' said Sam.

From the look on his face, she doubted he had ever changed his mind about anything. And even if he did, would Constance still want to marry him?

They sat for ages until the door opened again and Matthew walked out. He straightened his jacket and came to stand before the congregation, all eyes on him. Taking his time, he gazed around with a solemn face, as if maximising the effect.

'There will be no wedding today.'

He waited until the gasps and protestations had died away. 'My friends…' He took hold of the lapels of his jacket and breathed in steadily, as if delivering some great speech in a court of law. '… It is unfortunate, but something has come to light very recently which makes it impossible for my marriage to go ahead. Many of you have travelled to get here and I can only apologise and wish I had been made party to the information sooner to avoid this… embarrassment. Good day to you all.'

He strode down the aisle and out of the church, speaking to no one.

Ginnie and Sam stared at each other, shocked to the core. Poor Constance must be mortified. The only thing Ginnie could think of was her admission that she had been to prison. But, surely, that wouldn't have been enough to put an end to the wedding in such a terrible fashion?

One by one, the guests left. Ginnie and Sam remained seated, waiting for Constance to reappear. The echoes of feet on the stone floor died slowly away as the guests made their way out of the church and into the sunshine.

Soon, they were alone in an empty church.

–

Eventually, the door opened, and a tearful Constance emerged. Ginnie jumped to her feet, clutching the bible she'd forgotten she was holding. Behind Constance came her parents – her father blustering, his arms flailing around him doing the talking his mouth wasn't quick enough to utter.

'Look where your fine talking and unladylike behaviour have got you, Constance. I told you no good would come of taking up with those women. Did you listen? Oh, no, you had to go your own way, didn't you? How will we live this down? I should wash my hands of you.'

Her mother's head was held high, strong and not broken as she took Constance's arm in hers. 'Might I suggest, Edwin, that you keep your thoughts to yourself until they can be discussed in private?' As they drew level with Ginnie and Sam, a pinched expression crossed his face. He clenched his jaw, unwilling to speak to them.

Constance retraced the steps she had taken earlier. Her stark green eyes swam with pain in a face devoid of colour. She rushed into Ginnie's arms as the threatened tears broke free. There was no need for words, just a shared bearing of pain.

Ginnie guided her to a pew at the back of the church and held her hand. She slipped a snowy white handkerchief to Constance, thankful that she had come prepared, although it was supposed to be for herself and not the bride.

Sam tapped Ginnie's shoulder, muttered something about fresh air, and disappeared through the door, leaving Ginnie alone with Constance.

'I need some air too,' said Mrs Copeland and held out a hand to her husband. To Ginnie she mimed a 'thank you' above her daughter's head as she left.

The two were alone and crying over a ceremony of love that had not taken place. The handkerchief had turned into a not-so-white damp rag.

'You were right. I should've told him about prison. It seems Matthew can just about cope with me handing out leaflets for the mad women who are fighting for the right to vote, but he can't have his family besmirched by someone who has been to prison for her beliefs. It happened when I was in London, so it was never reported in *The Sentinel*. A so-called friend broke it to him a couple of days ago.'

'Oh, no.'

Ginnie couldn't believe her ears; that Matthew had known about it but left it until now to destroy the woman he was supposed to love?

Constance lifted her head, her body shaking. 'He said he could have tried to understand if I had told him. Instead, he felt I was being underhand. I swear I was only carrying out Father's wishes by keeping it quiet, and I told him so. Matthew said I should think more about my future husband instead. He's not the man I thought he was, Ginnie.'

'Good job you found out now then.'

Ginnie was having difficulty containing the anger building up inside. Matthew had deliberately and cold-heartedly shamed Constance in front of their friends and she hated him for it.

'Last night, he said he was willing to go through with the wedding.' Constance sniffed and burst into tears again.

'Look, if he could leave you at the altar like that, he isn't definitely isn't the man for you. And he has to be more than *willing*. You want someone who will love you for who you are; friendly, funny, beautiful, and helpful. Look what you've done for me and Sam.'

Constance gave a watery smile. 'Thank goodness I have you both.'

They clasped each other, the threatened tears still not far away but, for now, managed by friendship.

Soon after, a gentleman called Uncle James, Mrs Copeland's brother, arrived to collect Constance. Ginnie said she would walk home and waved an exhausted Constance off. When she had gone, Ginnie collapsed on to the stone church wall and closed her eyes.

The more she thought about it, the more convinced she was that Constance had had a lucky escape. If Matthew couldn't forgive her for something that happened when she was younger, and part of what she believed in, how could they ever be truly happy?

Sam appeared at her side. 'You all right, Ginnie?' He waited for her to speak.

'Oh, Sam, how do you ever know that what you're doing in the world is right?'

'Dunno, lass. You have to trust yer'sen and hope as you've thought it all through, I suppose.'

She laid her head against his shoulder.

'And, if it all goes belly up, I guess we have to learn from it so's we don't make the same mistake again.'

# Chapter Twenty-Five

## January 1917

Pat O'Malley was back on leave before heading overseas. He didn't know where he was going to when he went back, he said. He would say no more about it when he stopped by the factory.

When Frank came home for Christmas having completed his basic training, he looked smart, keen, fit and work-ready in his uniform. Mabel paraded him around the town, hanging on his arm while Ginnie pushed the pram. He now talked about war as a great adventure, how he was going to do his bit and let the Huns know who was boss. When he was asked what sort of training he had done he tapped the side of his nose and changed the subject. And him only a private! But Ginnie had seen enough eyes filled with fear and panic to glimpse a boy's fright within the man.

He was due to leave in a week's time, for somewhere Ginnie hadn't heard of – Cannock Chase. She didn't even know if it was in England. From there, as likely as not, he'll be sent overseas.

She believed he'd put the bad bits out of his mind so he could cope. When Mabel was alone with Ginnie, she alternated from anger at the government for getting them into this mess, to despair for herself, and a future with no father for two-year-old Florrie.

In the early days, many believed they would be home for Christmas. How much worse was it for those about to leave with no idea when this war would end?

Everyone had determined to make the most of the soldiers coming back that Christmas in 1916. Maybe for some it would be the last they would see of their loved ones. Sam had said he'd write, or rather, get someone to write for him, so she wouldn't feel lonely. Ginnie didn't know whether she liked the idea of someone else being privy to their private conversations. Then again, she didn't know who she would ask to read his letters to her. By rights it should have been Mabel, but Ginnie couldn't broach the subject, knowing what she thought about Sam and Haddon House.

Dare she ask Constance, and risk losing her friendship?

On a cold and blustery January day in 1917, Frank returned to his unit and the light which had shone out of Mabel when he was home, extinguished. It was as if she had put her whole self into giving him a good Christmas and was now merely going through the motions of living.

'He'll be all right.' Ginnie wished there was more she could say.

'My husband's gone to war and might never come back. Me and our Florrie'll be all on our own.' She sniffed hard, fighting to keep control.

'But you've got me too.' Ginnie bit her lip and told herself Mabel was upset and didn't mean it. People often hit out at those closest to them. She believed they were closer now than they had ever been but she worried about Mabel's ability to cope until Frank came home again.

She spoke to Constance about Mabel on her next visit. She didn't mean to and she felt guilty for speaking out when she had promised to keep it a secret. It had been on her mind all day, and it just came out.

'It's nothing but—'

'For goodness' sake, Ginnie, I want to know what's wrong.'

'It's not me. It's our Mabel. You know Frank's gone? He's done his training and gone back, and Mabel's petrified about being on her own.'

'Poor Mabel. She must be frantic.'

'She's worried the little mite won't know him when he comes back. Anything might happen over there.'

'And I think I've got problems.'

'Florrie's not her first, Constance.' Ginnie blurted out.

'It's not? But she hasn't got any other children.'

'She hasn't. Not living ones, any road.'

'You mean… Oh, poor woman.'

'That's why she took me out of the workhouse this time. She needed help with the house and bringing in an extra bob or two.'

'No wonder she's like she is.'

Ginnie nodded. 'I don't know what to say to her, Constance. I never knew her when she lost her baby, so I don't know how she coped. All I can say is, that she's petrified of being on her own now in case something happens to our Florrie. How can I help her?'

'By being there for her. Let her see she's got you. You know a great deal about life between you. You'll cope. You both will.'

–

She couldn't escape the bad times at the factory, either. Only yesterday Elsie had received a telegram to say her husband was missing, presumed dead. She had gone into work because she didn't want to be on her own, thinking about him all the while. Everyone was full of sympathy, but soon ran out of things to say and Elsie couldn't stop crying into the pots. In the end, she was told to go home.

At clocking-off time, Ginnie donned her coat and started on her way. George fell into step with her. They hadn't spoken much since the falling out. He had apologised again for his behaviour, blaming it on the drink. Ginnie didn't know what to believe. Her mind was with Elsie, going home to an empty house that might never see her husband again. In a way, it was a relief talking to George – somebody who wasn't expecting news from the Front.

'Poor Elsie must be ever so lonely, not knowing whether her husband's coming back. It's almost worse than him being killed.'

'How can you say that? While he's missing, there's got to be some hope.'

'Supposing she never finds out?'

'Early days yet.'

'Every day's a struggle; how she can bear it.?' She stopped and kicked a stone into the gutter. *If it had been Sam, I'd be going out of my mind too.* But she couldn't talk to George about Sam. She tore her thoughts from him. 'It won't be long before they send Frank out there. He's done his basic training. Mabel's at her wits end.'

George put his hand on her arm and stopped her. Surprised, she looked up at him.

He stroked a stray lock of hair out of her eyes and stared for a moment. In a quiet voice, he said, 'I hope there's somebody like you what's waiting for me when I come back.'

'You mean…'

'I've been called up. I'm eighteen, just turned. Didn't think my papers would come so soon.' He kicked a stone and somewhere a bottle smashed. He grinned. 'Don't suppose I could do that again. D'yer think it's a good omen?'

'When?'

'Start my training next week. You might get to use them damn machines you used to keep harping on about.'

'But I don't want to get on because you men are giving up your lives overseas.'

'Hey, less of that kind of talk. You'll have me quaking in me boots.' He laid a hand on her shoulder and turned her to face him. 'Ginnie, I—'

'What?'

'I know we haven't always seen eye to eye, but do you think you could see your way to thinking about me while I'm gone? I know I'm not the only one on your mind.'

So, that was why he wanted to make things better between them. She couldn't believe it that he, George Mountford, was pleading with her to think about him.

Her thoughts flashed back to the sun shining on Sam in the veg patch, as she remembered him stopping turning the soil to lean on his shovel and watch her make buttercup chains... and the silly idea that buttercups could foretell whether she was going to get wed. And his response: 'I'll marry yer,' he'd said.

'Where've you gone, Ginnie? You're miles away. Will you be sorry to see me go?'

Her daydream dissolved into tiny pieces and, try as she might, she couldn't get it back again.

He didn't wait for an answer. 'Anyway, it'd mean a lot if I knew someone was thinking about me, missing me, even. A bloke would find it pretty lonely out there knowing nobody cares whether he comes back or not.'

She tried to make light of it. 'I bet there's plenty of girls who would wait for you, George. Them lot at the potbank love you to tease. What about Marge?'

'Marge? What's she got to do with it? She's not my type at all.'

'What is your type?'

He put his head on one side and grinned sheepishly.

'I'm serious about Marge. Anyone can see she likes you.'

'This isn't about liking, Ginnie. It's about caring when I'm there or not. I've watched your face when bad news is dished out. I'd like to think you'd be that caring if it was me they were talking about.'

This wasn't the George she had spent the last few years avoiding – hating, at times. 'Course I'll think about you. I think about everyone as goes to war. I know as we had our differences in the past, but we can be friends, can't we?'

'Friends?'

'Ye… es?'

'You've still got your mind on him, haven't you? Workhouse boy? What's he got that I haven't?'

'He's my special friend and always will be, George, whether you like it or not.'

'But he left you. Soon as he could he was off, and him only being back a few weeks. Doesn't that tell you something?'

'It tells me he's got courage. He joined up. Didn't have to, but he did it. He knows what's right and wrong and he's willing to fight for it.'

A wince crossed his face. 'Guess I asked for that.'

She didn't answer.

'I'll see you around, Ginnie Jones.'

Before she could say anything, he leaned forward and planted a kiss in the middle of her forehead.

'A present, to think about,' he grinned and wandered off whistling, leaving her open-mouthed.

During his last week, relations between them were strained but she couldn't have done things differently. He would never replace Sam in her heart. She couldn't believe that, after everything that had passed between them, he could even think she would choose him. Better he knew now.

He was back to the same old George, buttering up the wenches and playing tricks on those who couldn't do anything about it. Ginnie was an old hand now and happily gave him a piece of her mind when she had to. The women who had egged on his laddish behaviour now told him to bugger off. He whispered something in Marge's ear. With a bright pink face, she swung out a pretend punch which he dodged successfully but tripped and knocked over a girl carrying a couple of moulds. The new jiggerer swore at him and said he hoped the army could cope with him. George shook his fist at Marge as if it was her fault.

'I'll get her back for that, mark my words,' he murmured in Ginnie's ear as he passed her, wiping a hand across his mouth.

'Careful, George. Don't do something you might regret.'

Later in the afternoon, when most of them had forgotten, he struck back. Fascinated, Ginnie watched as he crept up behind Marge, pretended to trip and threw a half-full bucket of water over her. Dripping wet, and spying him laughing, she hurled abuse at him through her clay-matted hair. Ginnie couldn't help but laugh and he gave her a wink before sidling off out of sight. She straightened her face as she caught a scowl from Marge.

–

'Heard from your husband yet, Elsie?'

Ginnie felt awkward asking but she had to say something. Maybe Elsie wanted the chance to speak of him. She had no family as far as Ginnie was aware, so who could she talk to?

Elsie shook her head. A haunted look came into her eyes. 'I keep thinking about him. Wondering if he's lying somewhere, on his own, injured. Nightmares are the worst. Sometimes I wake up screaming so hard, me throat's on fire. Do you think he's thinking of me, Ginnie?'

'You must be on his mind all the time. He'll be keeping his head down, waiting for the right moment. Thinking of you'll keep him strong.'

'Hope so. You're a good girl, Ginnie. I'm afraid I've got a confession to make.'

'What about?'

'Well, I was on me way out a few months back and something was going on in the yard. I was leaving early because I had a bit of…' she coloured momentarily, '…women's trouble.'

Ginnie nodded wondering where the conversation was heading.

'When I got out there, there was a group of lads, three, I think. They was talking to another lad – tall, handsome with lovely blue eyes.'

Ginnie's ears burned. Sam… hanging around Chamberlain's?

'I think he was your young man, Ginnie.'

'When was—?'

'Just before that posh wedding you went to.'

Ginnie's eyes widened. 'Sam was here before the wedding? He can't have been. Why would he come to Chamberlain's and not wait to see me?'

'There was a bit of a… fight.'

'Fight?'

'Him, and George Mountford.'

'What… why?'

'I think you'd know more about that than me, duck.' Elsie's voice came quietly. 'Seemed as your Sam was warning him off.'

'They were fighting about me?'

Elsie nodded and smiled. 'You've grown into a bonny young woman, Ginnie. Why wouldn't they fight over you?'

'What happened?'

'I think the lads had gone out for a smoke and your Sam was waiting. George joined them. Sam said he wanted no trouble, just a word with George. George was swaggering, you know how he does, probably 'cos he'd got his mates from the warehouse with him and your Sam was on his own. George stood between his mates and Sam, legs apart, arms folded. He just laughed and so did his mates. Sam shouted, that George was as much a pain in the arse as he had been at school. It made me chuckle I can tell yer. I had to cover my mouth so's to keep quiet.

'George wanted to know why he was hanging around where he wasn't wanted. Sam said as you were really upset when George came on to yer. Frightened yer even.' Elsie looked at her keenly. 'You never said you had any problems with him, Ginnie. George said as you were all over him after he'd taken you to the Picture House and had a drink afterwards. Sam said he wasn't looking for trouble and told him to leave you alone 'cos you wasn't interested, and you'll be courting him when he gets back.'

Ginnie's face was aflame. All of this fuss, and she'd known nothing about it.

'George was taunting him, saying while the cat's away the mice'll play. He asked Sam if he was scared of losing yer. Then they all made a move towards Sam and he backed away. He didn't want a fight, but the lads laughed and ran at him. Two of them thumped him on the back. George punched him in the face and split his lip. Caught his eye too. Then Sam thumped George and caught him in the ribs. He doubled up, and Sam scarpered.'

'They never said nothing to me.' Her mind went back to the day of the wedding and Sam's cut lip. He said he'd bumped into a cupboard door. 'Why didn't you say something sooner?'

'Not my place. After Sam ran off, George saw me. Told me to keep my gob shut, if I knew what was good for me. That it was just a bit of fun. Didn't seem much fun to me, mind. Now he's gone off to war, I thought you ought to know. Sam never mentioned it?'

'No, he didn't.' Ginnie's nostrils flared. How dared George have a go at Sam like that? And why on earth hadn't Sam said anything?

Elsie patted her back. 'Sounds like you've got yourself a good'un in Sam, Ginnie. My man's a bit like that; doesn't say much but what he says is worth listening to.'

Ginnie smiled ruefully. 'Sam's not one for making a fuss even though there are times when he should, for his own good.'

'When he comes back, you should get him into that church before somebody else does, my girl!'

–

Ginnie made a point of visiting Constance whenever Mabel could spare her and because it was Constance, Mabel had no objections. The visits went smoothly, although Constance was still not herself. She hadn't seen Matthew since he jilted her. She assumed he'd re-joined his regiment long ago and was now overseas. Gaunt-looking, she would stare vacantly into the fire. It was only when the time came to say goodbye, and Constance squeezed her hand, that Ginnie would be satisfied that her visit had not been in vain.

It was now February and Ginnie had arranged to call because she was going to teach Constance the art of knitting socks to send overseas. It was half past two and Ginnie was a few minutes early. One look at Constance told Ginnie that her sadness and depression had changed to anger and determination.

'I've come to a decision.' She took out a handkerchief from the pocket of her skirt, and dabbed her eyes, sniffing to clear her nose. She got to her feet and paced the room.

Ginnie sat back, waiting. Nothing Constance said would surprise her.

Constance sat down beside her, her eyes holding a gleam that hadn't been there earlier, her words coming quickly. 'I've spent enough time on that man. I need a challenge. I need a job.'

'A job?' She didn't see Constance as a woman in need of a wage.

'Yes, and I know just the right one. I've put in a request to become a clippie.'

'A… a clippie?'

'You know, the person who takes your money and gives you your ticket on the tram?'

'*You*… work on… a tram?' Ginnie couldn't have been more shocked if Constance had said she was learning to fly.

'Most definitely. The WSPU have a list of women who have come forward and I've put my name down too.'

Ginnie had seen occasional women conductresses at the back of the tramcars recently but never for one moment saw it as a place her friend would consider. Nursing, or office work, perhaps. Something befitting a lady. 'Are you sure it's what you want?'

Constance nodded vigorously. 'And shall I tell you why?'

She carried on without stopping, clearly not looking for an answer. Ginnie was going to be told anyway.

'I want to do something different. Men's work. You should know that feeling better than me, Ginnie. Women are doing all sorts of things while the men are away. They could easily operate the machines you talk about. I want to do something totally unexpected – to show Matthew I really don't care about his high and mighty family. The woman he might have married has got the ability and wherewithal to take on men and to win. Father won't be too happy, of course. Serve him right for telling me to keep quiet in the first place.' She nodded firmly as if to seal the conclusion. 'And another thing: "Constance" is a bit of a mouthful for a clippie. So, I shall be "Connie" from now on. It'll be great fun.' These final words were accompanied by thrusting her hands onto her hips, to make the point most strongly.

Ginnie clapped her hands and burst out laughing.

-

Ginnie received her first ever letter from Sam in April 1917. She snatched it from the sideboard where Mabel had left it for her and ran upstairs to be on her own.

The address on the envelope was written in large letters. She turned it back and forth, revelling in the feel of it. Taking a small pair of scissors out of her mending basket she slit the envelope carefully to reveal the letter inside, folded in half and half again. It was short, just a page and a half long and it had her address at the top. It started, 'Dear Ginnie.' That much, she knew. The rest of the joined-up scrawl was difficult to read. She drew her finger along each line and tried to make the letters into words as she had been taught years ago. She attempted to spell out the words by making the sounds of each of the letters. She could recognise more than she had thought, but big gaps left her frustrated. She wanted to read every word. How could she reply otherwise?

She had got by without reading much, until now. How many times had she avoided Clara's efforts to help by involving Sam or going missing just as Clara came to capture her? But

Clara wasn't strong enough. Why hadn't Mary forced her to try harder?

She knew she wasn't being fair. She had nobody to blame but herself. Mother might have let her keep her Sunday School prize if she had been able to read. When Sam was sent away from Haddon, she could have written to him and maybe she wouldn't have felt so lonely. The only way she could communicate with him now was through letters. Even her ambitions to better herself could amount to naught if she couldn't read. The fault lay firmly at her door.

Someone warned her ages ago that she would regret not making the effort. But she *would* learn; she would sit down every single night and do what she had to do. But she needed help. She would ask Constance – Connie – this very day.

As soon as she could get away, she hurried across the town and up the hill towards Sneyd. She rang the doorbell repeatedly, but no one answered. The street was bare. Ginnie tapped her foot impatiently as she ran through the possible places Connie could be. She tried the square, where they had given out pamphlets, and several of the shops Connie frequented, receiving funny looks from shopkeepers. She hung around the tram stop in the Main Street, with no success.

When Ginnie arrived home, Mabel decided to pop next door to see Mrs Scott – something to do with the socks they were knitting for the war effort – and Ginnie was left to supervise Florrie.

The whole world seemed determined she wouldn't read Sam's letter today. She slipped the letter into her carpetbag.

Ironing was something she could usefully do to take her mind off everything. She warmed the iron on the grate and started on Florrie's dresses as being the most urgent, but her mind wasn't really on the job. A singeing, burning smell soon broke into her thoughts. She wafted away the smoke to reveal a black-rimmed hole in the leg of Frank's trousers. Burnt steam hit the back of her throat.

'Bugger, bugger, bugger!' she cried out.

'Bugger, bugger, bugger?' piped up Florrie.

Ginnie bit her lip. She'd forgotten that Florrie liked to play houses under the table. Forgotten also Florrie's habit of asking questions about new words.

'Bugger is a very bad word and little girls mustn't say it.' She squatted down on her haunches and looked into the wide eyes staring back. 'Promise me never to say that word. It's only bad girls what talk that way.'

'Bad girl?' Florrie repeated blankly.

'Yes, I am a naughty Aunty Ginnie.' She smacked the back of her hand and smiled. Florrie chuckled and carried on playing with the two boxes which had now become a shop, happy in her own world. With a bit of luck, she might have forgotten by the time Mabel got home.

Once she had put Florrie to bed, Ginnie fell asleep in the chair by the fire and woke to find the coals had long since lost their heat. She rubbed her eyes as yawn followed yawn and rose automatically to put the kettle on.

'Anybody would think you've been working all day, Ginnie. You only do a few hours on Saturdays. Whatever's got into you?' said Mabel from the other chair.

Ginnie jumped. She hadn't heard Mabel return and felt guilty to be caught napping. 'Nothing much. Been for a walk.'

'I can soon find something for you to do if you can manage to stay awake for long enough?'

Ginnie shrugged, pondering on what Sam might have written as the tea brewed. She still felt too embarrassed to tell Mabel although, the more she thought about it, the more she doubted the wisdom of involving Connie too. Dare she risk owning up to anyone that she couldn't read?

# Chapter Twenty-Six

*More Letters*

**May 1917**

Another letter arrived, and Ginnie still hadn't spoken to anyone. Connie had been busy with her new job. If only she had owned up at the beginning, she wouldn't be in this pickle. Yes, and if she *had* spoken out at the beginning, she might not have been able to count Constance among her friends, said the voice inside her head.

She hated the possibility that Sam would think she didn't care and the thought of everyone sitting reading letters from home, and him waiting to hear from her, brought tears to her eyes. All because she was too stupid to write back and too worried about everyone knowing her business. She no longer cared what others thought. It was Sam that mattered; he deserved a reply.

She threw on her coat and left the house before she had chance to change her mind. By the time she arrived at Connie's she was flushed, hot, sweaty, and the soles of her feet were aching. She bent over to catch her breath just as Alice answered her knock.

'Miss Ginnie—'

'I need… to speak to Connie… Constance, Alice. Please tell her,' she gasped, holding her sides but managing a grimace of a smile.

'Whatever's the matter, Ginnie? Are you unwell?' Connie hurried towards her.

Ginnie reached for her hand. 'Please, Connie. I have to see you.'

'Come inside, quickly.'

Connie all but pulled her through to what might have been their parlour. It wasn't a room she had been in before. It was large and its walls were lined with shelf after shelf of books. Ginnie doubted they had any pictures at all.

Connie sat in a large chair beside a small table where she placed a book and indicated Ginnie should sit opposite. 'What's wrong and how can I help?'

'I've had a letter...' Ginnie blurted out. '... well... two letters, and I've been meaning to talk to you since the first one came, but I didn't and now that I've got another one, I'm worried something's wrong and don't want him to think I don't care—'

Connie held up her hand. 'Slow down, my love. My head's spinning.'

Ginnie held up her hand and took a deep breath. 'I... I've had two letters from Sam. Well, they *are* from Sam, but he hasn't written them.' Seeing the blank look cross her friend's face, she slowed down. 'He can't read or write. Somebody has to help him.'

Connie flushed delicately. 'I see.'

Ginnie stopped talking and tried to read Constance's face.

'My dear girl, I'm not shocked. Just surprised I didn't know.'

'It's something you learn to keep to yourself very early on. You get picked on and laughed at.' Ginnie's voice was almost a whisper.

Connie nodded. She laid her hand on Ginnie's knee and waited until Ginnie was able to look at her. 'So, how can I help?' Her voice was every bit as quiet as Ginnie's but, somehow, it held encouragement and strength.

'We-ell,' Ginnie started again. 'I've got these letters and they're really important to me but... I...' The words drained away. Flames of red shot from her neck to her cheeks. She lowered her head, unable to go on.

'You mean you…you can't—' Connie faltered.

'I can't…' She closed her eyes, swallowed, and tried again. '…I can't… read, neither.'

'Oh, you poor love. I should've realised what you meant instead of forcing you to speak of it.'

Ginnie tensed. 'Like I said, when you're ashamed to admit something, it's surprising how much you can hide.'

'But you went to school at Haddon House… everybody did.'

'I was laughed at and made to feel a fool. Mr Latham made me stand in the dunces' corner with the younger kids. I felt… this small.' She spaced out an inch between her finger and thumb, then dashed away an escaping tear. She stood up to her full height. 'I got more out of helping Mary Higgins. She needed me as much as I needed her.'

'I'm so terribly sorry you were put into such a terrible position.'

'Clara tried to teach me. I even tried to hide from her so's I didn't have to sit like an overgrown kid pointing at the words. She was younger than me and she'd been in Haddon all her life.'

'Does your sister know?'

Ginnie shook her head. 'She looks down on Haddon House because it belongs to the workhouse. She doesn't want me to have anything to do with them no more. She says I've gone up in the world.' Ginnie snorted. 'I can't give her another reason to dislike Sam. They were just getting to know one another before he went to war.'

'But you hid it so well. The reading, I mean.'

'I pretended to read, but I asked questions in such a way that her and Frank would tell me what the papers said. Didn't need to read much else. Until now.'

'What about my pamphlet? Oh, I remember – you took it away to read later.'

'When I got home, I asked our Mabel what she thought of it. So I'll understand if you throw me out.'

'…because you can't read?'

Ginnie's eyes glistened but she sat upright.

'Listen to me.' Connie grabbed her shoulders. 'I would never throw you out. Do you hear me? Darling Ginnie, don't you realise how important you are to me?'

'You really mean that?'

'When I'm with you I can be myself. Believe me, it's not always the case.' The smile disappeared.

*She's thinking of Matthew*, Ginnie realised. She relaxed into the chair. She had confronted her demon and won. Shyly, she held out the dog-eared letters. 'Would you…?'

'Of course.' Connie took them and, after a quick nod from Ginnie, opened the first one.

March 1917

Dear Ginnie

I hope this letter finds you well, lass. I know we can't be sure of anything these days, but it would be nice to think of you sitting in front of the fire reading about my doings over here. I am feeling well, although I don't know where we will sleep tonight. All I can tell you is, so far so good. I have been told to expect to have the runs from time to time, but not to worry about it. It's part of a soldier's life. We have been here since I got back learning about guns and marching and the like. We've run miles and for once I'm glad of all the hard work I've done because I am fitter than most of the other blokes here. Some can scarce walk a mile before running out of steam. We don't know when we will move nor where we will move to. As far as France is concerned, we just want to get the job done and come home.

My mate, Stevo, wrote this letter. He's happy to help out, although he says I ought to learn so as I can do it for myself. I think he's worried about what I might ask him to write. I will send you word as often as I can, so I hope someone is helping you. Don't be afraid to ask, Ginnie. You don't know how much it means to me knowing as you are back home reading this.

From your friend
Sam

Connie looked up. 'That's a lovely letter.'

Ginnie could imagine him sitting somewhere thinking hard what to write. How much had come from Stevo, she couldn't begin to know, but she could sense Sam speaking to her directly in parts. The letter was dated March, and it was now the beginning of May. What must he be thinking?

'Would you like me to carry on?'

'Yes, please.' Ginnie clasped her hands together.

Connie smiled and opened the second letter. The paper crinkled as she unfolded it.

April 1917
Dear Ginnie

I am writing to say that I am quite well and hope this letter finds you well too. We are in Belgium. Fighting has been heavy and there's been lots of rain. I thought it rained hard in England, but being in trenches you live in it, day in day out.

We have just heard that we are off to xxxx tomorrow, so I wanted to let you know. From there we will head for xxxx. I hope it'll be sunny. We leave for xxxx on xxxx and hope to meet up with the xxxx units soon after. Don't worry about me, Ginnie. I promise to keep my head down and stay safe. Have you heard from anybody else? It's funny to think that blokes from Burslem might be in the next town and I'll never know. We are working towards ending this war. The sooner that's done, the sooner we can all come home. Hopefully it won't be long now.

I hope you are well and are missing me as much as I am missing you. It keeps all of us going, knowing that you lassies are waiting for us back home. Yesterday, Stevo found out he had become a dad for the first time. He can't talk of nothing else. Pity as he can't see the little mite. Called him Stephen John, for his father and grandfather. We have even more to fight for now.

Take care, lass.

Love

Sam

PS Did you get my letter? You feel a long way away tonight.

PPS I have heard that our letters are being censored so I don't know that this letter will make a lot of sense to you. I am sorry about that.

He sounded tired but he had signed it, 'Love, Sam' for the first time. That must mean something. He felt closer now. With her eyes closed, she could picture him, sitting on the chair where Connie was sitting. He could probably say more in a letter than he would ever admit to if he was sat beside her.

'Thank you so much but I must get back. Our Mabel'll be wondering where I am.' She clasped the letters to her chest.

'Maybe I can help. I don't wish to be presumptuous...' Connie hesitated, '... I want to help, if you'll let me. I would be more than happy to teach you to read. If you like? I'm happy to get together whenever I'm not working.'

Ginnie shook her head slowly. 'I'm such a dunce. Clara tried and didn't get anywhere.'

'Oh, I don't give up very easily.' Connie smiled.

'When you see how stupid—'

'You're not. It's because I'm your friend that I want to help, Ginnie. I promise it won't make any difference to us.'

She had no reason to doubt what Connie was saying. And judging by the way Connie acted during the Votes for Women meetings, she wouldn't be put off by anything.

'If you're sure…'

'That's settled, then. Come here on Saturday and we'll make a start. I'll help you to write back to him too. Looks like we shall be a little busy for a while.'

–

Ginnie very nearly didn't go. Her seventeen-year-old self felt a rawness deep inside when she thought of sitting at someone's knee like a kid, fingering words to get them to make some sense. Neither did she deserve sympathy for a problem of her own making.

She tapped on Connie's front door, trying not to make too much noise. Almost immediately, Connie appeared in the hall, arms full of bedclothes.

'Ginnie, my dear, do go and wash your face. It's all black and you look as if you've been down the pit all day.'

In Ginnie's heightened state, and if the words had come from anyone else, they might've rankled, but Ginnie did as she was bid. The towel in the bathroom was thick and she buried her face in its clean freshness, hoping she didn't smear it with sooty wetness.

'That's much better,' Connie said as Ginnie returned. 'But you look a trifle peaky. You're not ill, are you?'

Connie waved her into the room full of books which, Ginnie discovered, was called the library. It was spick and span apart from two piles of books set out on the table beside one of the two chairs. The air disappeared out of Ginnie's lungs. 'You haven't half been busy,' she squeaked.

'They're all my favourites. I'm so looking forward to introducing them to you.' Connie drew up another chair. 'I read most of them at school so they're not dreadfully complicated.'

She bit her lip, flushing madly. 'Sorry, that wasn't how it was meant to come out.'

Ginnie took up the first book off the pile and flicked through the pages. She put it down quickly and picked up another, with fewer pages, and then another, her heart sinking with each one. None of them had pictures. She licked her lips, her mouth dry.

Connie watched her keenly. 'They're all wonderful stories, but we can start with something else if you prefer? I have others upstairs…'

Once more Ginnie wondered if this really was a good idea. 'I can't read nothing like these,' she blurted out, wringing her hands. 'I need kids' books, with pictures. Nowt fancy. I'll have enough trouble picking up the words and remembering them without concentrating on the story an' all.'

'I'm so sorry. I was worried about upsetting you. It looks like I've managed to do that anyway. Do forgive me.'

'Oh, don't mind me, I'm a bag of nerves.' Ginnie fidgeted. 'I would like you to help me, honest I would.'

'And I should be honoured… very pleased to help. And if you see a book you would like to read, we will start with that. In the meantime, we still have your letters… and we can start by writing back to Sam?'

Ginnie nodded furiously. They composed a reply to Sam and, together, they copied it out again so that Ginnie could use it for reading practice.

> May 1917
>
> Dear Sam
>
> Thank you for your letters. I am sorry it has taken ages to send one to you. Connie is helping me now so I will be able to write back more quickly in future. She is also helping me with my reading, and it might start to make sense at last.
>
> I was so happy to get the letters even though you can't tell me much. I can picture you telling

Stevo so he could write down the words. Your letters make me feel close to you. I am using them for reading practice, as well as mine to you. I will know every word by heart.

I hope you and Stevo are well and taking care of yourselves. I hate to think of you over there so close to the Germans. Please be careful and stay safe. I was happy to hear the news about Stevo becoming a father. What a pity he can't come back home to see his son.

That's all for now. Write back soon so that I can practice my reading. Stay safe. There, I've said it twice because I mean it.

Love Ginnie

PS Constance is calling herself Connie now and she says hello too.

She was pleased with her very first letter, although Connie had written it. It sounded quite grown up. Connie folded it, slipped it into an envelope, and gave her the second copy. Ginnie promised to practice reading at home, learn the words and copy them for herself as neatly as she could. Sometimes there were long gaps between the letters and it was all she could do to carry on, but with Connie's support she persevered.

In the quiet of Connie's house, she was able to concentrate. The work was hard but not threatening. She started by spelling out the letters that made up the words. She took each letter from Sam and re-wrote the contents without joining the letters and copied from Connie's books too. The words stayed in her mind if she had written them herself. Gradually, it started to make some sense. Connie didn't laugh, raise her voice, sigh, or try to rush her. Instead, she smiled, encouraged, cajoled and congratulated. With considerable patience, she placed her hand over Ginnie's to guide her through the forest of words.

Ginnie grew relaxed. The end of her finger was no longer white when she traced her way across the page. They had disagreements, and Ginnie grew frustrated when the words wouldn't come, but the fear had gone. Importantly, she kept going back.

There was a long break before the next two letters arrived. It was a day she was due to have her lesson, so she stuffed them into her pocket without opening them. The handwriting was different on one. Maybe Stevo wasn't around and Sam had got someone else to write it. She didn't want to think about the alternative. The arrival of new letters took a load off her mind.

They went straight to the library and Connie started to read.

July 1917
My Dear Ginnie

'Sounds as if poor Sam is missing you, Ginnie.' Connie chuckled and started again.

July 1917
My Dear Ginnie

We have been in xxxx for a while and we haven't been able to post letters, so I hope this one finds you well. I got your letter and am glad Constance is helping you. Fancy calling herself Connie, after all this time.

The sounds of the guns seem never ending, day and night. I think about you all the time, Ginnie, love. Stevo laughs at me but you should hear him go on about his little nipper. He said he was going to scratch out that last bit when I'm not looking and I'll be none the wiser. He's promised to teach me a bit of writing when we are not so busy.

I don't know when I will get the chance to see you again. They say we need reinforcements and might drop back behind the lines. Maybe we will get a chance sooner or later.

Stay safe, duck

Your loving Sam

PS Just heard we have got some men joining us from xxxx tomorrow. There might be a xxxxxxx coming.

She wondered what was about to happen. It was August now so, whatever it was, had already happened.

'Please God he's safe. It's funny how I can hear him saying the words inside my head, as if he's speaking to me from the past.'

Connie nodded and picked up the other letter. 'The writing's different on this one.'

'I thought that too. He must've asked somebody else to write it for him. I hope Stevo is... well. I feel as if I know him too.'

'Thank you for allowing me to share them with you. It's a privilege.' Connie smiled broadly, opening the final letter. Constance studied the envelope and then the letter and looked up. 'It's from England,' was all she said.

Aldershot,
England
July 1917
Dear Ginnie

I always start letters 'Dear so and so'. I am calling you 'Dear Ginnie' because I don't know what else to call you. I don't really think Dear is the right word in the circumstances, but never mind.

You don't know me and I am sorry that I have to write you this. I never wanted to but I have been forced into it. It wouldn't be fair if you don't know. I thought as he would tell you himself, but I bet he hasn't and you deserve to know. It's only right—

Connie broke off but continued to read without speaking. She looked up, troubled. 'I don't think I should be reading this.' She thrust the letter towards Ginnie, unable to meet her eyes.

'What do you mean? You've got to.'

'It's… well… it's a bit delicate.'

'But you have to.'

'Can't you get Mabel to read it to you?'

Ginnie's face tightened. 'I told you. Mabel doesn't know I can't read. Tell me, Connie. Please?'

'You won't like it.'

'He's all right, isn't he?'

'The letter isn't from Sam.'

'But it must be. I don't know anyone else.' Suddenly, she thought of George. What on earth was in the letter that had so clearly upset her friend? 'Connie – please tell me. I can't wait any longer.'

'Very well. But don't say I didn't warn you.'

> … When the war is over, Sam is coming to live with me. He's told me that you and him are friends. He talks about you a lot and doesn't want to let you down. He says he will tell you when he sees you, but I'm not sure he will. Well, I'm having his baby so he hasn't got much say in the matter. We will get married when he comes home. I'm sure you won't want to live with him now you know he loves me.
>
> Yours respectfully
> Annie Kent

By the end of the letter, Connie was whispering. She threw the hand holding the letter down on to her knee. 'Ginnie, I'm so sorry.'

'I don't understand. Sam wouldn't… he just wouldn't. We were waiting for each other.' He wouldn't do this to her. Not her Sam. He crossed his heart. That meant… *Oh, no God, please, no.*

'You're both so young, Ginnie. Fighting in the army has made him grow up quickly. He's not the same Sam who got on that train. Although, I have to say I'm surprised.'

Ginnie couldn't have stood up to save her life. She opened and closed her eyes, just like she did when she was a child, to see if she could make the nightmare go away.

And the biggest joke of all? She couldn't damn well read it for herself.

She ran to the bathroom.

And retched.

*How could he do this?*

She stood in the silence, twisting her hands. She needed air. Space to be on her own. To regain control of her breathing.

Taking a deep breath, she walked back into the library. Constance was standing by the window with the letter in her hand. She turned.

'Sam wouldn't get a woman pregnant, Ginnie. He wouldn't do that to you.'

'Why would a strange woman write and tell me a pack of lies? How would she have my name and address if he didn't tell her?'

'Maybe it's some terrible joke?'

'We were just kids. Maybe I read too much into it and it wasn't meant to be.'

Ginnie tried to sound grown up but she had expected Sam to be part of her life forever and now her heart was quietly breaking. 'I'm sorry you had to read it to me but thank you anyway.'

'We should send another letter to him, to see if we can't sort out what's going on.'

'Oh, no – I couldn't.'

'Yes, you could. You don't have to come straight out with it. We'll just say that you've received his letters, and ask if he knows an Annie Kent, from Aldershot, who has also written to you.'

Ginnie agreed. She folded up the letters carefully and returned them to her pocket. She made her excuses and left. Closing the gate behind her, she almost retched again.

What if the letter was wrong? What if Annie Kent had got the wrong man, the wrong family? Innocent until proved guilty, and all that. The Sam she knew wouldn't do this to her. He just wouldn't.

-

Over the next few weeks the jumble of letters became words, and the words became meaningful. She knew more words than she'd thought. No longer did she have to try to remember them; they came into her head without her thinking. She didn't even have to point to them. She had needed something to concentrate on, to take her mind off Annie Kent, and reading was the perfect solution. With Connie's help, she had sent a letter asking Sam if he knew Annie Kent but, once it had been posted, she found herself not wanting an answer. But the same question played over and over in her mind: *how did Annie Kent know where to send the letter?*

The first time Ginnie read *Peter Pan* by herself, she broke down and sobbed. Connie didn't say where she had found the book, but it had colour pictures and the green cover had faded slightly.

'It's such a lovely story, isn't it? I know it's for kids but I'm sure I shall like it even when I'm old.' Ginnie wiped away her tears and laid the book on the table.

'It's one of my favourites too,' said Connie. 'I remember sitting on the bed and wishing I could fly.' She coloured a little. 'When I was quite a bit younger.'

'Peter reminds me of Sam...' Ginnie mused. '... but Sam's not so naughty.'

The room filled with laughter.

'I always wanted to read but the words just wouldn't stay in my head. How come I suddenly can? It must be your good teaching.' She sat back in the chair for a moment, grinning.

'When you were in school, you were forced. You got uptight and anxious?'

Ginnie nodded.

'Well, we're reading together, and enjoying it. We both want to do it and we're sharing the experience, so it's very different.'

'I'm comfortable sitting here with you. I don't feel as you'll laugh behind my back. I love stories. They take my mind off things. I want to read and read.' She picked up some of the books Connie had put out for her to look at next and read out the titles on their spines slowly. '*The Secret Garden. The Railway Children, What Katy Did*. And don't forget one of those books you had when we first started.'

'*Pride and Prejudice* is my favourite.'

'Then that's what I want to read – when you think I'm ready.'

Connie picked up her hand and looked into her eyes, deadly serious. 'I promise I will never, ever laugh at you. You're making such progress. I'm so proud of you.'

And, when another letter came at the beginning of September, there were no words she couldn't read. Oddly, this one *was* from George.

August 1917

Dear Ginnie

How is life back in the real world? It's crummy out here. Can't tell you where, but they don't speak English. Hope you're looking after yourself. I can't wait to see you again. Hope you are thinking about me as much as I'm thinking of you.

I'm sorry about what I said, and what I did, Ginnie. Put it down to be being worried about leaving home, and taking to drink, and leaving you too. Things could have been better between us before I went, I know that, but I hope that we can start all over again. I promise that we can work everything work out. I really like you, Ginnie. You mean a lot to me.

You were right to feel sorry for me. There isn't anyone else in my life and I was frightened, Ginnie, yes – frightened that I would die over here and no one back home would know, or care.

I hope you are able to find someone you can trust to read this to you. I want to say more but it will have to wait until I come back.

I'll write again soon.

Yours

George

It was surprising to hear from him. She sat back, the letter still in her hands. He made it sound as if they were real friends. Not a bit like the George Mountford of old. She remembered Elsie's words about his fight with Sam. She was still angry with him, but she could hear the loneliness in his words, and was surprised by his thoughtfulness about her needing to find someone she could trust to read it to her. She took the letter upstairs and sat on the bed to read it again. It wasn't so much to do with what it said, or who it was from. It was more about her ability to read it for herself.

# Chapter Twenty-Seven

**September 1917**

Mabel received a short note saying that Frank expected to go to The Front any day. By the time it arrived, it was already three weeks old. She stammered as she read it out, clutching at her throat. Florrie, in a world of her own, was sitting under the table talking to her dolls. Ginnie's heart quickened. Frank wasn't up to much but to Mabel he was as good as any other man most of the time.

Newspapers were full of stories of success for Allied troops, about objectives won, prisoners taken and the fruitlessness facing the enemy. Over the summer, news had come of a major offensive in Flanders, described as the greatest battle of the war, east of Ypres where so much of the war has already taken place. *The Sentinel* spoke of a number of villages being taken, with some British casualties, near a place called Passchendaele. The prisoners captured numbered in thousands with the Germans suffering severe casualties; soldiers had been killed, wounded, gassed.

Ginnie gazed through the window. Although her eyes focused on the houses opposite, her mind was with those count-less men fighting overseas. Sam and Frank, Fred the Tow-er, Pat and others from Chamberlain's – people who had crossed her path, some more fleetingly than others. How many would live to cross her path again?

Just when there was hope that 1917 would see the end of the war, the Huns increased their attacks on England. What did it matter if things were going well in France and Belgium if the Germans were turning their Zeppelins towards us?

A lack of workers and not enough sales had caused the closure of some potbanks but Chamberlain's had said it would stay open for the time being. One nearby potbank closed only last week and some of the women had moved to Chamberlain's. She hoped they didn't send too many. It sounded selfish, but it was only her wages keeping their heads above water. She had no idea how much money Frank sent home and Mabel never talked about it.

When the two of them settled up on a Friday night, it was usually Ginnie giving over her board and nothing much coming back her way. Trips to the grocer's after work, even now, were not part of her contribution. Ginnie didn't want to upset Mabel but she had begun to wonder how long she could, or should, put up with it.

Today was no different. She had called to get the last of the week's bread rations on the way home and was later than usual. She shouted a greeting as she walked in. The house had an empty, dead feel about it. Mabel never said she was going anywhere so it was surprising for her to be out so late because of getting Florrie's tea.

Ginnie sang her way through to the kitchen.

A body sat at the table, in the twilight. The notes died on Ginnie's lips. She almost let out a scream when a croaky voice spoke out.

'Dunner werrit, it's only me.' Mabel struggled to her feet. She wiped her face and blew her nose noisily.

'Whatever's the matt—' Ginnie dropped the bag she was carrying and ran around the table. 'Is summat the matter with our Florrie?'

The paper in Mabel's hand fluttered to the floor in the silence. For a long moment neither spoke.

'Is it Fr—?'

That started Mabel off again. Ginnie's legs wobbled and her knees buckled under her. She made a grab for the table and winced at the harsh grating sound as its legs slid sharply across the floor. She steadied herself, not taking her eyes off Mabel. Almost every day now, women were in tears over loved ones killed, or listed as 'Missing, Presumed Dead'. Horrible words, final but with no ending. Nobody believed it would happen to them; it was the only way they could get through it.

Today it was happening here, in their own home. 'Is he—?'

Ginnie moved towards her but Mabel raised her hand, her chest heaving. 'Don't. If you start feeling sorry for me. I'm sure I'll—'

Ginnie stopped.

Mabel stooped to pick up the paper and played with it, turning it round and round, staring at the wall. Then she looked at Ginnie again and the pain in her eyes brought a lump to Ginnie's throat.

'He's gone. Dead. No messing with my Frank… oh no.' She shook her head and grimaced as if she had something bad in her mouth. Her voice became a whisper. 'What shall I do without him?'

'Does it say he's definitely…' Ginnie couldn't bring herself to say the word.

Mabel's shoulders sank. ' "Killed in Action" is what it says.'

Her voice sounded harsh in the quietness, before the tears came.

Ginnie threw her arms about her sister and Mabel clung so tightly Ginnie had to force herself away to breathe. Trembling bones shook beneath her hands.

'How'll we cope, Ginnie?' She was quiet for a moment then shook her head. 'Didn't I tell him this would happen? Oh, but he knew best. Always did.' She closed her eyes and held the letter close. 'You won't leave me, Ginnie, will you?'

'Course I'm not leaving you. We'll sort something out.' She lit the lamp and turned towards the kettle steeping on the grate. 'When did it come?'

'About three. I've been sitting here ever since. What time is it?' Her hands went automatically to her hair as she tried to tidy herself and wiped her wet, red eyes.

'Nearly six thirty. What about our Florrie?'

'She's all right. I gave her a bit of something. She's fast asleep.'

Ginnie forced the cup of tea into Mabel's hands and guided her to a chair.

'I didn't go shopping today.' Mabel stared at the floor. 'I was about to pop out when they came with— there's now't for tea.'

'I picked up the bread, but I couldn't eat a thing. I'd choke if I tried.'

There was more bad news at work. Like Frank, Pat O'Malley had gone to fight for his country, even though he'd never been outside The Potteries. He too had been killed in action. Poor Pat; he was a good man. She would never forget him.

Elsie's face looked pale. She patted Ginnie's shoulder and gently touched her cheek, wiping away a tear she didn't know was there. As far as Ginnie knew, Elsie was still waiting for news of her husband. And no news from Sam. Keeping her brain busy was the only way she could bear emptiness in her heart.

–

It was Mabel's idea to go for a walk to get a bit of air that Saturday afternoon. It was good to be out in a balmy, late September breeze. They each held one of Florrie's small hands as she walked between them.

A group of women were having a natter near to an old poster of Kitchener's accusatory pointing hand hanging on the door of the town hall.

'Your Country Needs You?' cried out Mabel, letting go of Florrie's hand and running towards the town hall. 'Damn you for making me a widow,' she screamed. She snatched it off the door and tore it in half.

'Mabel! You'll have the bobbies after us.' Ginnie, holding on to Florrie as best she could, tried to pull her back. 'Please come away. We'll be in so much trouble.'

It was like showing a red rag to a bull.

'Do you really think I care?'

The breeze carried the scraps of paper across the square and two small girls began to fight over who could catch them. Florrie burst into tears as Ginnie tried her best to drag Mabel away.

A bobby charged across the street, waving a truncheon. Ginnie planted herself between the irate constable and Mabel.

'Sorry, sir, she doesn't mean it.'

'Don't you dare go apologising for me, Ginnie Jones. And don't say I don't mean it. Oh, I mean it all right.' Mabel's voice continued to rise.

'Shush, shush. Please, Mabel.'

Fearful for Mabel's sanity, and hearing the panic rising in her own voice, Ginnie turned to the policeman. 'She's just had bad news. You know how it is, sir?'

He glared at them but quickly took note of the desolation written across Mabel's screwed-up face as Ginnie fought to hold on to her flailing arms, willing him to see the grief-stricken woman below the anger.

Ginnie gave her sister one last shake. 'Who's going to take care of Florrie if *you* get locked up? Look at her, Mabel. Look!'

At last, Mabel seemed to come to her senses. Her eyes darkened with pain, and she crumpled against Ginnie's shoulder, letting the tears run unchecked down her cheeks.

'Please...?' The word leaving Ginnie's lips was nothing more than a whisper.

'I won't report her this time, lass. But keep her under control else I'll have to take her in.'

*Damn them all for making men and young lads feel guilty about staying behind, and for bringing such heartache to their families,* Ginnie thought, even though it may have been unpatriotic. Out loud, she said, 'Yes, sir, I will.'

'It's his own bloody fault. Stupid bugger. I told him he'd go and get himself killed, and what does he do? He goes anyway. He goes, and leaves me, and look at her... she's so small—'

'Hush, Mabel don't.'

All signs of anger evaporated. Mabel doubled up. 'I told him, Ginnie. I told him, I told him.'

'I know you did. But he *had* to go. You know that.'

With their arms linked and Ginnie gripping Florrie's tiny hand, they made slow, stumbling progress back home through streets empty of young folk. Never a day went by now when Ginnie didn't hear someone sobbing for a lost brother, son, dad, lover, or friend. She didn't know where Sam was. All she knew was he was out there somewhere.

*Please, God, keep him safe.*

-

As 1918 rolled in, there were reports of Allied victories and towns reclaimed, and another letter from Sam. A lump formed in her throat. She needed to be alone to read it. Was he missing her as much as she missed him? Had Annie Kent told him about the baby? Annie had sent her letter in August and hadn't given any idea when it was due; it might already have happened, and this letter could be telling her that he'd become a father. Her Sam – a father.

But he wasn't *her* Sam any more. And each thought drove a knife deeper into Ginnie's heart.

She grabbed her coat and slipped the letter into a pocket. She headed out towards Burslem Park. Not even Connie could help her through this mess. She sat on the nearest seat to the entrance staring at the leafless trees. There was no birdsong. A strange quiet hung in the air as if the park was waiting for something. She pulled her coat tightly around her to keep out the dampness carried on the wind. Too late, she remembered her hat was still sitting on the table where she'd left it.

She rummaged in her pocket for the letter. It was Stevo's writing, thank goodness.

A picture came to mind, of Florrie when she was born, such a tiny mite. Sam would never turn his back on his own kin. If he knew about the baby, she would lose him for certain. She was forced to take deep breaths to ease the knots in her back and her neck.

She ripped the envelope open and started to read.

January 1918
    Dearest Ginnie,
    Sorry for not writing sooner and this letter is going to be short as well. I just wanted you to know that me and Stevo are ok. We've been under fire off and on forever. I don't know what you've been told back home but we've welcomed the parcels and all look forward to wearing new socks. It's surprising how quickly socks rot and fall to pieces. Keep sending them.
    I live in hope that I can send you some good news soon because of xxxxxxx xxxxx.
    Look after yourself.
    Yours
    Sam
    xx

She sat back and let the letter fall onto her knees. He was alive. No mention of Annie, or the baby, and nothing to worry about, according to Sam. No news was good news. If only she could convince herself, she could keep him close for a little bit longer.

–

Connie turned up on the doorstep in her clippie uniform, eyes bright with tears, but grinning broadly, Ginnie wasn't sure whether to laugh or cry.

'My word, you look might smart.'

'Have you seen the newspapers?'

'Not for a couple of days. Why?'

'We've got the vote! Just think, women will vote in the next election.'

Connie grabbed her hands and had her dancing a jig before she knew it. 'Hang on. Hang on. You mean *we've* all got the vote? All women?'

Connie's nose wrinkled and her shoulders shrugged. 'Not strictly speaking. It's a bit more complicated.'

'Why? Have we got it or not?' Ginnie couldn't make head nor tail of Connie's words.

'Parliament has given women over thirty, with property, the vote, to be exact.'

'Why not all women? Why should owning a house even matter?'

'Well, it'll come eventually. We must look on the bright side. They've acknowledged that we have the brains and can do any job as well as a man. When the war's over we'll convince them you don't *need* money to have brains. We'll keep pushing.'

The following day, Elsie received a telegram. Her husband had died in a POW camp in northern Germany.

Good news, tinged with bad, as always.

# Chapter Twenty-Eight

## The Telegram

**June 1918**

Ginnie still hankered after jiggering work but, at eighteen, she was much wiser. The only person she spoke to about her future was Connie.

'All women should have ambitions.' Connie laid down her needles thoughtfully. They were knitting yet more socks and scarves to send overseas.

Ginnie wondered what was coming next. Connie was like a dog with a bone when she had something on her mind.

'I've been thinking.'

Ginnie smothered a chuckle. 'Tell me something new.'

'What's so funny?'

'Nothing.' Ginnie tried to set her face straight. 'What's on your mind?'

'No pottery manufacturer is going to employ you on those machines you talk about, and you don't want to be a mouldrunner all your life. Am I right?'

'You think I should give up?'

'Of course not.' The green eyes flashed. 'You should re-think your ambitions.'

'What do you mean?'

'You never thought you would learn to read but you're reading now.'

'Not very well—'

'Don't say that. You're reading and that's the important point. Doesn't that give you encouragement?'

'For what?'

'Oh, come on, Ginnie. There are jobs you've never thought about. Even if you remain with Chamberlain's you don't have to stay in the clay-end.'

She was right as usual. Never once had Ginnie thought about leaving the clay-end. Not even in the darkest times.

'And you don't have to stay at Chamberlain's. What about other potbanks, other industries? The world's so much bigger than you can imagine. Who'd have thought of me becoming a clippie?'

They laughed and joked about all the jobs they could possibly do, but it set Ginnie thinking on the way home. She *was* guilty of letting things happen to her. Learning to work the jolleying and jiggering machines felt exciting because they were part of the world she knew.

On Monday, instead of hurrying to work with her head down thinking of nothing in particular, she stopped outside the gates and watched the scurrying workers in their single-minded determination to get to work on time. Most of the people at large at that time of the day worked in the clay-end, and were dressed in old, dark trousers and a coat, if they were lucky – drab-looking women in drab coats displaying long, clay-spattered aprons. Men working in the office were not on the street at this time. It would be another hour at least before their work began. Could it be that the cleaner the job, the later you started to work?

She glanced up at the bottle oven, noting its smooth curved outer lining of red bricks. She had asked about the types of jobs to be found in the different parts of the factory and her eyes had been opened. She tried to guess the jobs the workers did by the clothes they wore. Men in long aprons carrying saggars into the kiln for firing, the dippers, the fettlers, other jobs she hadn't heard of. And then there was the clean-end, the decorating end where patterns were smoothed on to the ware before heading for glost firing. Some of the ware was painted by hand in other potbanks, the more pricey ones. And then there were overlookers and packers getting the ware ready for sale to shops all over the place.

She'd never given any of them a thought, until now. It was quite scary to realise that she should look for change rather than expect change to come looking for her.

–

'Connie, I want to look like you.'

Ginnie burst out laughing at the startled face sitting opposite.

'Well, not exactly like you. What I mean is, I want people to take me seriously. I'm not a child. Dotty at work is having a baby and she's only seventeen.'

'I hope *that* isn't among your current plans?'

Ginnie flushed violently. 'No, 'course not. But I do want to be taken seriously. I want to be smart and confident, like Sarah when she used to stand on her box in the marketplace. Like you when you got people to take the pamphlets. You were the one who said I should look to better myself. Well, first of all I need to look the part.'

'But what you wear doesn't make you intelligent.'

'If I look good, I might feel more confident.'

'And you think I can help you to choose?'

'Well, if I find something that looks good, I can run up a copy. I can't afford to buy anything at the moment.'

Connie, her head on one side, thought for a moment. 'I see what you mean. I think I can help.' She screwed up her mouth in a most unbecoming manner. 'Why don't you come over next week and we'll have a look through my closet?'

'Oh, I didn't mean for you to—'

'I know, but I have lots of clothes I've hardly ever worn. We're not too different in size, although you will likely have to shorten the length. I'm still a few inches taller than you.'

'Connie, you're so good to me.'

At last she was working towards something. She'd learned to read and was concentrating on writing which was coming along quicker than she had thought possible. Time to work on her next ambition – a job she could be proud of. She didn't know what it would be just at the moment, but she was sure she would recognise it when she saw it.

–

Mabel was working through *The Sentinel*. She'd taken over reading the names of the missing and the dead from Frank. Ginnie was quite happy to let her because Mabel would sometimes fill in the story of each, whether he was married, where his mum and dad lived, and who might be waiting for his return.

'Oh, my word…'

She looked up from the newspaper, her face pale. Her hand strayed to her mouth. 'What's that lad's name? The one you carried a torch for in that place… Sam… White, was it?'

Mabel never referred to Haddon, by name or otherwise, so mentioning Sam's name at all was unusual. Doing so while reading the newspaper was deeply disturbing. A coldness crept into Ginnie's bones. She had stuffed the letter from Annie Kent deep into the carpetbag although her eyes were drawn towards it whenever she entered her bedroom. It was as if the letter was slowly burning a hole in the tapestry.

'Yes… Sam White…' she whispered.

Slowly, Mabel lowered her newspaper and the pages crackled as it encountered her knees. 'Ginnie love?'

Ginnie had never seen so much compassion on Mabel's drawn face. 'Maybe I should get cracking with them pots.' She jumped up, refusing to make eye contact. She had to get away. 'They won't wash themselves.'

'Hang on, love.' Mabel caught hold of her hand. 'Sit yourself down.'

Ginnie did as she was bid, sitting on the very edge of her seat, ready to take flight if it should be needed.

'The paper… says he's…missing.'

The words hissed in the quiet of the back kitchen. The clock ticked. Ginnie lifted a trembling hand to move a hair out of her eyes. Her forehead felt clammy to the touch although she could have sworn she was shivering. She snatched the newspaper and scanned the casualty lists of the dead, the wounded, the gassed, the missing.

'I know I always said as you could do better, but I didn't mean it.'

Those few words were the closest to an apology Ginnie was likely to receive.

'And Sam White's a common name. Happen it might not be your Sam. And he's missing, not…'

Ginnie sprang to her feet. 'I have to go.'

She rushed up the stairs and slammed the bedroom door, sinking down onto her knees beside the bed. She felt sick. Sam was goodness knows where, alive or… or not, and maybe having a baby he would never see with this Annie person. Could she go through the rest of her life never seeing him again, wondering whether he ever loved her? She didn't want him to die. Better he should live with Annie Kent and his baby.

*Please God, don't let him die.*

She skimmed through *The Sentinel*, hardly able to pick out the words as she blinked away her tears. In Flanders there were major battles on two sections of the Allied Front: the Aisne River and Ypres. Fresh German forces had succeeded in crossing the river during the night, causing Allied troops to fall back. Soldiers came under attack from the Huns with tanks and gas shells. Germans boasted of holding 25,000 prisoners. North Midlands troops were involved, the paper said.

Of course, Sam might not have been anywhere near but it brought home to her the plight of the soldiers. How could these men come back home unaffected by what they had seen and done in the name of duty?

That night stretched on and on and she couldn't sleep when Sam was out there, all alone, among the Germans. She awoke hollow-eyed and walked as if enclosed in an 'awake-nightmare', as she used to call them, glad to go to work and force her mind to concentrate on getting the moulds to and from the drying room. Bad news was almost a daily occurrence. Women she didn't know patted her shoulder as she went by.

The following day a telegram arrived addressed to Miss Ginnie Jones, care of Mrs Mabel Farmer.

'I'll take it upstairs,' she said in a stony voice. With heavy limbs she climbed the stairs, dreading the point at which she would reach her room and make the decision to open the envelope. She sat on her bed and stared at the envelope, understanding now why it had taken Frank so long to open his call-up papers.

She opened the envelope with great care and read the words she hoped never to see.

Samuel White (Private)
Missing in Action – 30 May 1918

It was ages ago. Surely she'd have known the precise moment Sam was in trouble? They were soulmates. She could conjure him up in her mind and the image was so strong she could almost reach out and touch him. She would know.

She was quiet again when she went into work the next day and refused to mention the telegram. Elsie asked more than once if she was feeling all right. Ginnie inclined her head and carried on. Not ready to talk, she shot through the door when the knocking-off bell rang, before she could be asked any awkward questions.

At teatime, she caught Mabel watching her, maybe comparing Ginnie's experience with her own. But Sam could be still alive; Mabel knew Frank was dead. Nothing could change that. It sounded terrible, but it was the only thing Ginnie could cling to. Any minute Sam could come walking through the door. But, in her mind, there was a shadowy shape of a woman standing by his shoulder, a woman who had more of a claim on him than she had. She so wanted, needed, that rotten letter to be wrong. One thing she still couldn't let go – Annie Kent must've got her name and address from somewhere.

Her mind turned to others who had not returned, Frank, Pat, even Fred the Tow-er. Lost lives, and for what? Years of living hand to mouth, lost jobs, rich getting richer and the poor getting poorer. Some said the whole country might never recover.

That night, she tossed and turned, fighting with the sheets to get herself comfortable. She hadn't shed a tear all day. Not a one. She tried to sleep. That was when the dream came back.

> Draughts blowing through the station. Keep warm. Echoes, noises bustling. Trains come and trains go. Platforms clear. More people come. The window of the stationmaster's office… A blurred me looking back. A train. An engine, a hiss of steam. A tunnel of bodies. A nightmare tunnel. A scream. A burning throat. Looking for somebody – Sam?

Her nightgown was damp. Her cheeks. Her hands. A scream rose in her chest, ready to explode through her mouth. It was a good job that Florrie had slept with Mabel since Frank's passing.

All her life the nightmares insisted she was searching for something, someone. She tossed and turned, burrowing into the bedclothes but the nightmare carried on.

> Ginnie? Ginnie? Sam's voice. Bodies everywhere. Sam! Sam! An arm waving. He's here. He's here. Sam

She awoke with a start, her heart racing. Panting. She expected her face to feel tight, but it didn't. She wasn't running away at all.

She was searching – for Sam. Running – to Sam. The monster was the war that had taken him away. Dear God, the nightmare she'd had since she went into Haddon House wasn't out to get her. She wasn't running away at all – she was running *to* Sam. She just hadn't understood until now. The realisation brought with it a sense of well-being; the tightness in her shoulders had gone and a warm tiredness had invaded her body. The nightmare was still there but she was no longer frightened. He was coming home. She was sure of it. She would not lie down and accept what life threw at her. If she had to fight Annie Kent for him then she would. In the dream, he was coming home. She had to cling to that above all else.

Her eyes smarted and her body swayed, faint with relief. Shakily, she climbed out of bed and took Clara out of the carpetbag and stood beside the window, leaning cold elbows on the sill. She watched faintly glowing stars and, hugging Clara, wondered if those same stars were shining on Sam at that very moment.

There was still no end in sight, but Ginnie slept soundly that night.

–

Just lately, Mabel had started dolling herself up to go out. She had got herself a job at a factory making insulators for telegraph poles and the like, critical for communications, she was told when she went looking for a job. She worked nights mostly and so money was less tight. She'd run up a new dress from a couple of old curtains and bought a pair of going-out shoes from the pawn shop.

Watching Mabel putting lipstick on for work one night, Ginnie lifted an eyebrow. Mabel was doing her best to avoid looking at her and Ginnie resolved to find out what was going on. She waited until Mabel was almost ready to leave and then, hands on hips, barred the way to the front door.

'Is there something I should know, Mabel?'

'What d'yer mean?'

'You, off to work all done up to the nines? What d'yer think I mean?'

'Give over, Ginnie, I'm in a rush and I have washing to put away.'

Ginnie folded her arms. 'And I'm staying right here until you tell me.'

'I was going to tell yer, but what with the news about Sam, it didn't seem right.'

'If you've got something to say, Mabel, say it. I don't like being kept in the dark.'

With a pink face Mabel muttered, 'There's this bloke—'

'A man?'

'Blokes usually are men.' Mabel gave an exaggerated sigh. 'There's this bloke what's started at the Co-op. I think he's taken a shine to me, that's all.'

Ginnie whistled. 'You mean *you* fancy him?'

Mabel's face became a motley shade of purple. 'Nothing's going on. It's far too soon for that. But it makes me feel good. So, will you shift out of my way so's I can get a move on? Otherwise, I'll be late, and it'll be your fault.'

'Only if you promise to tell me everything when you come home.'

Mabel couldn't wipe the smile off her face. She looked surprisingly good, and slightly nervous. Ginnie had almost forgotten that Mabel was more or less the same age as Connie. She came over much older.

'There'll be nowt to tell.'

Ginnie folded her arms and raised an eyebrow again.

'But, if there *is* anything to tell, you'll be the first to know. Now shift out of me way, will yer?'

The house became quiet again. Ginnie stared around the room; the same room she had lived in for the last four years. During that time, she'd gone from being an ex-workhouse girl to a sister, to a mouldrunner, doing the job nobody wanted.

She'd found Sam, only to lose him again twice, possibly to Annie Kent, and then, maybe, to a God who never answered her prayers. Yes, this room had seen a lot. She was pleased for Mabel, she really was. But how ironic that Mabel should find someone just as *she* might be about to lose Sam, either to the war, or to Annie Kent.

# Chapter Twenty-Nine

*A Job Offer, a Union Jack and Letters*

## September 1918

'Ginnie? Ginnie Jones?'

She was deep in thought, walking past the Queen's Hall. She checked the newspapers night after night hoping to see, what? Something about Sam, to bring him closer? Reading of the horrors as battles played out across Europe only made everything ten times worse.

A woman stopped in front of her. The girl who had once shared her bed and complained of chilblains appeared to be quite the young lady now.

'Ada Barlow! You're looking well.'

'Can't complain. Got a job at Royal Edward's a couple of months back. Doing all right for meself.'

'It didn't work out at the doctor's?'

Ada snorted. 'You were right about him, dirty old beggar. Couldn't keep his hands to himself. Chased me round the table a couple of times. Got a kick out of being the master, if you know what I mean.'

Ginnie was in a hurry. Mabel was expecting her home an hour since, but her curiosity was raised. 'So, what are you doing at Royal Edward's?'

'Am transferring.'

'Trans…what?'

'Trans-fe-ring. I decorate the ware with transfers. Well, small plates so far. Good job an' all.'

Ginnie's ears perked up. 'That's in the clean-end, isn't it?'

'Yes. Bet you could get a job there an' all if you tried.'

'D'yer think so?'

'I wrote and told them it's what I've always wanted, and they believed me,' Ada grinned. Then her face straightened. 'Mind you, it *is* what I've always wanted so I wasn't telling no fibs.'

Ada was always one for the full truth, slow of mind but warm-natured and kind.

They parted soon after. Ginnie's thoughts overflowed with ideas. She had to keep herself busy otherwise she would fall apart waiting for news of Sam. She would do something positive; she would ask Connie to help her put together a letter, with no mistakes, asking for a job at Royal Edward's Pottery Manufacturers Ltd, and she would send it off straightaway before she could change her mind.

Connie thought it an excellent plan and immediately whisked her upstairs to rummage through her vast wardrobe. Dress after dress, which might be appropriate attire to wear when going for a job in the clean-end, were laid out on the bed for inspection. They settled on a dark navy skirt, with a matching jacket edged with white braiding as being smart, but not overly dressy.

Ginnie stared at the mirror. The young woman looking back at her had a neat, trim figure and an air of confident reliability – the very look she wanted. No longer a child, but a full-grown woman who could be relied upon to decorate pottery to meet their high standards.

They spent the next hour thinking what Ginnie might say to impress them sufficiently to offer her a job. She went home to spend the evening altering the skirt, with her head spinning.

She was over the moon to receive a letter by return of post inviting her for an appointment. She presented herself outside Royal Edward's two weeks later. It was a bright and sunny day, a good omen, she thought. Although the butterflies were back in her belly, she was convinced she was doing the right thing. She had to try.

Royal Edward's was a well-kept and imposing potbank standing on the edge of Burslem with a reputation for producing pottery to grace the best tables in the land. It was not called 'Royal' lightly. The room she was taken to was larger than The Shop at Chamberlain's and full of work benches of chattering women. They wore no bonnets and their aprons were white and not spotted with clay.

Everyone stopped talking as Ginnie followed the woman who had collected her from the lodge. She was reminded of being the new girl on her first day at school. She clutched the little bag lent to her by Connie and pressed it against her chest. Then, head high and chin out, she followed the smartly dressed woman to a small room no bigger than the desk it held.

The woman gestured to Ginnie to sit which she did, thankfully, and went on to outline the work done in the busy Decorating Shop. She would begin, she was told, as an enameller, shading in outlines printed on the pottery. If her work was satisfactory, she may be moved on to transferring and ultimately on to freehand painting if she showed exceptional aptitude. It all sounded wonderful. Better than her wildest dreams. Some of Ginnie's excitement must have rubbed off onto the woman opposite because she was smiling too.

Ginnie did her best to answer all the questions fired at her: what was her favourite subject at school, why did she want to leave her current job, why did she want to work at Royal Edward's Pottery Manufacturers Ltd? Surprisingly, she was only a little nervous and the easiest question was the last. The smile on the woman's face encouraged her to speak out. She wanted to make something more beautiful than it was before she had decorated it. She'd talked about the magnificent ware she had seen in the shops but kept to herself her lack of money to buy.

Suddenly, it was all over and she was outside the door again, being ushered back towards the lodge.

'If we wish to take things further, we will let you know, Miss…?'

'Miss Jones, Ginnie Jones.'

The woman nodded and turned on her heel without another word.

And that was that.

—

'Come on, Ginnie. We're going out.' Connie appeared at the front door, dressed for walking. 'I'm not about to let you stay at home worrying about Sam and whether Royal Edward's are going to give you a job. You need taking out of yourself. We are going to the Picture Palace to see a film called *A Pottery Girl's Romance.*'

'I don't really feel up to it. I don't think I've got the job. It's been ages.'

'Oh, Ginnie, it's early days yet. Never mind how you feel now. You'll enjoy the film.'

Ginnie frowned. 'I'm not sure…'

'It's been made here, in Burslem, with local people. We might recognise someone. It'll be such fun.'

'A moving picture about Burslem. Who'd have thought it?'

She had only ever been to the Picture Palace once and that was with George on that fateful day. A flicker of excitement ignited in her. She *should* go and rid herself of the horrible thoughts of George forcing himself on her.

'It starts tonight so go and put on your best dress. Quickly now,' Connie added.

Ginnie wanted to ask if the film might be sad. It *was*, but she had taken a handkerchief with her – *and* now she could read every word! The smell of the disinfectant that had been sprayed around the cinema before the performance stuck in her throat and was a clear reminder of the vigilance needed to avoid the deadly flu still circulating. It was a pity that *A Pottery Girl's Romance* also reminded her of her experience with George.

The end of September arrived and still no word from Sam. Every day there were reports of Allied victories and

German defeats. Only yesterday she had read something in *The Sentinel* about German peace terms. On 29th September North Midlands troops had stormed the Hindenburg defences near St Quentin, taking thousands of prisoners and that little village of Passchendaele had been retaken. They called it 'a glorious weekend'. *Where on earth were they sending all those prisoners? Surely the end must come soon.*

–

Ginnie wasn't keen on reading letters from someone whose handwriting she didn't recognise since receiving the one from Annie Kent. So, when such a letter *did* arrive, she was tempted to throw it straight in the fire but curiosity stopped her. The address on the envelope was neatly written and had no overseas postmarks. She took a kitchen knife from the drawer and carefully slit it open to reveal an equally well-penned letter on white paper. She licked her lips and forced her brain to concentrate.

> 22nd September 1918
>
> Dear Miss Jones
>
> Thank you for visiting Royal Edward's Pottery Manufacturers on the 10th inst. After careful consideration I would like to offer you a position as a Transferrer within our Decorating Shop. If you would care to...

She squealed with delight and danced on the spot. Mabel came running in from the garden and pulled up short when she saw the letter in Ginnie's hand.

'I've got it. I've got the job!'

Mabel stared at Ginnie as if she was going loopy and it reminded her that she had kept it quiet. Only Connie knew, and possibly Sam, if he had received her last letter.

'I've got myself a job with Royal Edward's, transferring.'

'My, my. You didn't half give me a fright.'

'They want me to start… oh, I never got that far.' She read through the rest of the letter. 'They want me to start a week come Monday. Oh, I can't believe it.'

'You've done well, our Ginnie. I'll give you that.' Mabel smiled and gave her a hug.

Mouldrunner Ginnie Jones would be working in the clean-end at last. She let out a loud whoop. It was all down to Connie and her teaching.

—

'It most certainly is not down to me,' said Connie later. 'Who went to see them and convinced them? I knew you could do it. I'm very proud of you.'

'I don't see how when I couldn't see for myself.'

'Sometimes all that's required is a little push. I did nothing more.' Her green eyes twinkled.

Ginnie threw her arms around Connie and thanked her lucky stars for the day Connie had re-entered her life. No longer would she be Ginnie Jones, doing the job that nobody wanted at Chamberlain's Pottery, but Ginnie Jones, decorator at Royal Edward's Pottery Manufacturers. She would need a new set of clothes – no, better make that two sets, for when one was in the wash. Royal Edward's had made her feel welcome during the interview, talking of things she could do rather than continuous warnings on what would happen if she should fail.

She said her goodbyes at Chamberlain's with only a touch of regret. Mouldrunning, she could well do without. It was people Ginnie would miss. Elsie, at first difficult, had become a friend, and she gave Ginnie a hug and planted a kiss on her cheek. There were a couple of others she would miss too. It would probably be best to forget George, given his mood changes. It was a pity. Sometimes he could be quite nice.

Her first day at Royal Edward's was an experience. She waited at the lodge for someone to collect her. It was not the woman with whom she'd had the interview, but a young woman wearing a bibbed, white apron. Her hair was twisted into one long plait down her back. And, best of all, she was clean. She introduced herself as Selina, 'After my mother,' she said, as if apologising.

'It's a beautiful name.'

The girl smiled. 'Thank you for that, Ginnie. I'll be sitting next to you and will teach you.'

Ginnie grinned back, delighted. Here was another friend and she could feel it in her bones that they would get on just fine.

She settled into the new routine well, learned quickly, and got on with the job. Selina praised her nimbleness and Ginnie had never felt so proud. Some patterns were complicated to cut out and took all her attention. At first the transfers were difficult to control and the ends of her fingers too wet to feel the delicate patterns. The tissue had to be laid on the ware, centred and rubbed with a hard, bristled brush to transfer the pattern to the pottery. It was then washed in a big, square sink to remove the paper, dipped in glaze and sent for firing to make the decoration permanent. She was responsible for her own work, unless an overlooker pulled her up over inferior ware. At the end of the day her hands were sore and her wrists ached, but she didn't regret it. Not for one minute.

–

The Germans were in retreat and Western Flanders was almost entirely out of German hands!

The Allies had entered Cambrai and talks of German surrender were growing ever stronger. It was good news at last. *It was funny*, thought Ginnie, *how some French and Belgian towns had become more well-known than many English cities*. Ginnie didn't know where they were but even the smallest of places seemed important.

And then it was over. The armistice was signed at five a.m. on 11th November 1918 – Florrie's birthday, as it happened –

and hostilities on all fronts ended at eleven o'clock. The Kaiser had abdicated and was a fugitive, and call-up notices had been cancelled. Connie said the boys would soon be home and no one else would have to have to prepare themselves for war.

People crowded the streets. Children ran around waving Union Jacks and church bells pealed the whole day. It was the sounds that Ginnie noticed most of all. The Potteries had awoken from a terrible nightmare. As darkness fell, shops were lit up for the first time since the war started. She hadn't seen the town alive with lights before, even if it was for only one night. It seemed such a happy place, she couldn't keep the smile off her face. When she lived with her parents, she'd been too young to be out at night and at Haddon, she hadn't been allowed through the door after lights out.

Mothers, husbands and girlfriends would soon be hearing from their loved ones, many after weeks of silence and know, at last, that they were safe. For those who had lost someone, this time would be bitter-sweet.

There was still no word from Sam. But he would be coming home soon – her dream said so and she was clinging to the hope it brought. In the blackest moments, she remembered Elsie's husband. He had been missing and now he was dead. Maybe she was acting like a kid to place so much faith in a dream. Maybe it was time she grew up.

That evening she sat, with the curtains wide open, gazing through the bedroom window. The need to feel the freedom of the wind on her face overwhelmed her. She donned her outside clothes left hanging over a chair and tiptoed to the door. Turning the knob very slowly, she crept downstairs. The keys were hanging in their usual place.

She listened. Nobody stirred.

A moment later she was outside. The air was cool, and the wind brisk on her face. She took deep breaths and relaxed into herself so completely she could almost shout for the sheer joy of freedom. She could hear singing and music coming from the

# Chapter Thirty

## The Book

**March 1919**

Two months after her nineteenth birthday, Ginnie was on her way home and having a conversation inside her head. Now that the war was over, she had a burning desire to put the past aside, to start rebuilding what the war had taken away. The reading and writing lessons with Connie had opened up her mind. She had taken charge of her future and was no longer content to let *it* take hold of her. She had already begun with the new job but there was still her non-existent social life to sort out.

She was not prepared to let go of her dream of Sam's homecoming. Many of the soldiers had returned but, even now, some were still finding their way home. She would give him all the time in the world, if only he'd come back. What did it matter about Annie Kent and her baby? But it did matter because she knew in her heart that Sam would be honourable in all things, otherwise, he wouldn't be her Sam.

She was tormented with new dreams in which she fought with a woman she couldn't see, a shadow, while Sam was lying in the mud in some foreign field, alone, crying out her name. That's when she always woke up to discover the tears on her face were real.

She had been working at Royal Edward's for nearly six months now and had settled in easily. She could believe she was almost happy. It made her think of Connie. Sadly, her job as a clippie had ended with the end of the war. It was now her turn to wonder where her future lay.

'Can I walk you home?'

It was the first time she'd seen George since he had returned. He didn't look much different from when he went away in 1917. He had the same cheeky grin and jokey nature, but his face held a trace of uncertainty. No doubt he'd soon have women eating out of his hands. A good-looking man like him wouldn't stay on the shelf for long, not when there were two or three girls after every bloke. The war had seen to that.

Mabel had started saying that beggars couldn't be choosers, and if Ginnie got too fussy, she'd end up an old maid, scraping along as best she could. Ginnie sometimes wondered if she was being pig-headed in insisting she wait for Sam, just to prove Mabel wrong. But she knew why she couldn't be content with somebody else, someone like George: she didn't love him.

'You got what you wanted then, Ginnie. A new job.'

They were statements rather than questions. She nodded at him and smiled. 'How are you, George – and how's life at Chamberlain's?'

'Same as always. Did you know they've given me Pat's old job for keeps?'

'Good on you, George. Congratulations.'

They walked on and it was a few moments before George began to speak. He looked serious.

'Hoped I'd see you around.'

'I'm pretty well settled now, too,' she said.

He stared into her eyes. 'You've turned into a smart-looking wench.'

She couldn't get over his behaviour and the un-asked-for compliments. She wondered if she would always ask herself what he wanted in exchange. She was sure he would've kissed her if she hadn't moved away. She didn't say anything.

'But then again, you always were. Especially with that dreamy look you often have. You looked miles away just then.'

330

'I was.'

His face was pale and for once he didn't fill the silence with empty words and jokes. 'You know I think an awful lot of you, Ginnie. And I know I've been a pain in the backside to you from time to time, but it was only because I was jealous. I couldn't believe I'd fallen for you, knowing where you came from.'

She lifted her head sharply.

'I'm trying to be truthful, Ginnie. It's a compliment. Despite what I knew about your past, I still wanted you. I swear it's true. And now I want to make it up to you. I want you to be my girl, Ginnie. I very much want us to start courting.'

Never ever had she suspected she would hear those words from the mouth of George Mountford. And he looked sober enough. Nowhere near as confident as he usually was. She almost felt sorry for him.

In the past he'd made it plain he didn't like her, and now he was talking of *courting*? He wasn't the type to be tied to one girl; he thought too much of himself for that. Besides, she wasn't ready to put Sam out of her mind. Not yet.

She scuffed her boot on the pavement. She'd never knowingly led him on and wasn't about to, despite what Mabel said. 'I can't, George. I'm sorry.'

'What do you mean, you can't?'

'Just that. I'm really flattered, but you know I'm waiting for Sam.'

His eyebrows climbed up into his hair and he pulled away. 'You'd still choose him over me?'

'I already have,' she said softly. 'A long time ago.'

'Isn't he missing? I know you still care for him; I'm not that insensitive. But you can't still think he's coming back – not after all this time?'

'He promised, and I believe him. He doesn't tell no lies neither.'

George smiled faintly. 'He may not have had much choice.'

'Shut up, will yer?' She slapped his arm.

He grabbed her hands and pulled her towards him. 'Just how long are you going to give him? Are you really prepared to wait for ever? Ask yourself why he isn't here now. The war's over. Don't you think he would've come rushing back if he was coming? He's been gone nearly three years, Ginnie. Three whole years. Even if he is still alive… anything could've happened.'

His face was flushed with sincerity, but she wouldn't change her mind. 'I'm sorry, George.'

'Then you're a fool, Ginnie Jones. That's what you are. But you'll give up. And when you do, I'll be waiting. And that's my promise to you.'

The pain on his face told her he was hurting. She even began to wonder if she might come to regret her fine words and putting all that faith into a dream.

—

The High Street was busy and it took longer than usual to walk its length. Staring into shop windows was all Ginnie could afford do most of the time, but today she had been paid and needed a new coat. True, her new job brought in extra wages, but she was still intent on saving all she could.

Her favourite shop was still the pawnbroker's even though it held bad memories. She sometimes wondered if she would recognise stuff that years ago belonged to her family. No doubt their belongings were long gone – bought, or buried as rubbish. Mr Cox sold all sorts and she liked to make up stories about who had pawned them.

The bell tinkled as she opened the door. Mr Cox glanced over his spectacles and nodded in acknowledgement. She only dared to go in once or twice a month for fear of being labelled a thief because she very rarely bought, just odds and sods, coppers worth.

She picked up a chain, dusty and dulled with age, from which hung a lovely green stone. The stone was almost half as big as the nail on her little finger and was probably worth more money than she could possibly imagine. No one in these parts would have the money to buy such an expensive-looking thing. It would look good around Connie's neck, although she doubted her friend had *ever* frequented Mr Cox's shop.

Most of the good stuff was on show. She picked up a gold bracelet decorated with coloured stones, with earrings to match. It was probably worth more than a whole year's wages. Mr Cox watched surreptitiously, as if expecting her to rob him. He should know better. She wouldn't have the nerve to come in here again if she did that. She only wanted to touch, and to daydream.

Sometimes, he brought out new boxes. Not new stock, just dusty boxes with damaged lids that hadn't seen the light of day since entering the shop. She loved to rummage through the boxes of weird tranklements, the use of most of which she could only guess at. She put the lid on the last box, satisfied there was nothing to persuade her to part with her money.

And then she saw it.

She would've recognised it anywhere. It was in a box in the corner along with other books, but this one had partly fallen out as if waiting for her alone. She reached over a rocking horse and a huge drum and, with a trembling hand, dragged towards her, *The Children's Book of Parables*, with its painting of Jesus on the cover. She opened it carefully. There, at the top of the inside cover, was a faint scribble: *To Miss G. Jones, For attendance. January 1911*.

In her mind's eye she saw the Ginnie she used to be, walking down the aisle to collect her prize, so worried, and yet so proud. She wiped her eyes on her sleeve and silently started to read 'The Prodigal Son' until her face was dry and she could make her way over to Mr Cox.

Needless to say, she didn't buy the new coat.

Back in her room at Mabel's, she fulfilled the promise she had made to herself. She wanted the words to go on and on, for the sheer joy of reading. She would tell Mabel soon enough, but not yet. This moment belonged to her and her alone.

Her mind turned to Sam. She knew she would have to come to terms with him not being around sooner or later. She still hadn't been properly courted yet. Only George and Elsie knew she wouldn't take up with anyone else because she was in love with a lad from the workhouse who hadn't come back from the war and wasn't likely to after all this time. Somewhere deep down, she knew that, but the bloody-mindedness she had inherited from Father wouldn't let her walk that path yet.

She watched others, jealous they had someone to care about, to touch, to share things with. She wanted somebody in her life, someone who loved her and wanted to be with her through thick and thin. She had seen George a few times since he'd come back, as a friend, but she could never love him. He didn't sweep her off her feet or make her go weak at the knees as she did when she thought of Sam.

−

It was an unusually sunny day for the time of year, and she had been out walking by herself. In her mind, she was with Sam, holding hands and talking about all the things they could do now the war was over. Try as she might, though, she couldn't break free from the ever-present shadow of Annie Kent and her baby. She turned her face towards the sun and took deep breaths. She had to be strong. Thanks to Connie, she was more confident now than she had ever been.

Perhaps she could take Mabel and Florrie for a walk later and enjoy the cool sun before it disappeared behind the skyline. For the first time in four and a half years they could look forward to a summer with no talk of war. She was even singing as she opened the back door.

'Hi Mabel. I'm home.'

All was quiet. Surprised, Ginnie popped her head around the kitchen door. Mabel sat in a chair, beaming. Her eyes swung from Ginnie to the chair facing her. Ginnie's eyes followed.

A man rose. A tall man with dark curls. A man whose body she recognised even though she couldn't see his face. When he turned towards her, her heart almost catapulted out of her chest.

It was a good job she had laid down her posy of blue-bells mixed with early primroses for otherwise, sure as eggs is eggs, she would have thrown them everywhere. She screamed. Choked. Laughed. Cried. His beautiful blue eyes were overly bright but sunken, with traces of shadows that would take time to fade. Her breath couldn't come fast enough. He held out his hands, the rough hands of a man who had worked hard for a long time. He drew her close. How scrawny he felt.

'Oh, Sam…'

He laid a finger on her mouth. 'I know you'll have plenty of questions, Ginnie love, and I'll do me best to answer them, but can I just tell you what it means to me to see you again? There were times I thought I never would.'

'Am… am I dreaming, Sam?'

His arms pinned hers to her sides. 'Hope not. I want you fully awake when I kiss you.'

His voice was deep and husky. She was hardly aware of Mabel's embarrassed little cough. Even when Mabel got to her feet and called Florrie to come with her, Ginnie hardly noticed. The door closed softly behind them and she was alone with him.

'What… how… when?'

*The baby! Ask him about the baby.*

'I'm here, Ginnie, and I'm never going to leave you again. Never, ever.'

When it came, the longed-for kiss took her breath clean out of her lungs. She wanted the touch of his lips, the feel of them, the joy of them to stay with her and when they parted, it felt as if she was losing him all over again.

'When did you get back—'

'—Did you get my letter?'

They laughed as their words mingled.

'I never got no letter saying as you were coming back, if that's what you mean. They said you were missing in action. Oh, Sam, it was horrible. I couldn't bear it.' She pulled away from him so she could gaze hungrily at his face once more.

'I sent a letter, Ginnie. Soon as I was freed.'

'Freed?'

'I was a prisoner for a while.'

'You – a prisoner?'

'In a place called Dortmund, somewhere in Germany. That's when I got my gammy leg.' He pointed to a walking stick beside the chair.

They sat opposite each other, still holding hands.

'I didn't get no letter about you being a prisoner, Sam. I got others.' Her face felt tight.

'You didn't? Well, I came back just soon as I could. Thousands of us were trying to get home. We had to make our way as best we could. German shops ran out of food. Didn't have enough for themselves never mind us POW's.'

'What… why… how?'

He laughed out loud. 'So many questions, me duck.' His face sobered. 'All in good time, Ginnie. All in good time.'

She couldn't return the laugh. There was too much unsaid between them. Now that she had calmed, she could look at him properly: his crooked grin, the lines around his eyes, the deep hollow cheeks, and the shaking hand resting on his knee.

His eyes followed hers and the smile left his face. 'I can't tell you no lies, Ginnie love. It was bad out there. I can't talk about it right now, but I will. I'll tell you so as you'll understand why I might've changed a bit.'

'If only you'd written, Sam. Stevo would…'

'Stevo's dead, Ginnie. Bloody went and died on the way home.' His voice broke. Swallowing, he patted his top pocket.

'Got a letter here for his missus. I was in hospital for a fair time after that. Didn't know where I was or how long I was there for. All I thought about was getting back to you.'

'Oh, Sam.'

Her heart twisted until she couldn't bear to breathe. He'd said as much as he could. To come through two and a half years of the most awful experiences imaginable with a friend only to have him die on the way home – what could she possibly say that would comfort him? It was inconceivable to compare the deaths of loved ones and friends that had stood by you when times were hard, but she did have an inkling of the pain he must have been under.

'There's so much I want to ask you. Just to see you sat in front of me, though, is enough. Somebody said, "missing" meant dead, but I wouldn't believe it. If you were dead, I think I would've known.'

*Ask him about Annie.*

He stood up and pulled her into his arms, putting an end to her talk. But so much was firing off in her brain. She pushed him away even as she noted the look of surprise cross his face, but she could wait no longer.

'Sam, can I ask you about Annie Kent?' she blurted out and watched his face intently. 'Everything else can wait, but what can you tell me about her?'

'Who's Annie Kent?' His face was blank.

'You know her very well, or so I've been told.'

His confusion looked genuine enough, no sign of embarrassment, no red face. Nothing. 'You don't know her?'

He shook his head, eyes narrowed. 'Where's this going, Ginnie? You say you've been told I know her? Says who?'

'She did.' Did the name really mean nothing to /him? 'Wait here.'

She ran upstairs, her heart racing. *Why did the blasted woman send the letter?* She burrowed into the carpetbag and pulled it out, tattered around the edges now. She walked slowly down the stairs and into the back kitchen, pressing the envelope against her chest to straighten the creases. She thrust it at him and held her breath.

Confused, he took the letter. 'What's this?'

Ginnie couldn't take her eyes off him. If he didn't know anything about it, where had it come from, and who on earth could Annie Kent be?

He glanced over it. 'If you want me to read all this, Ginnie duck, we'll need to get your Mabel. Stevo helped me with me reading but after we was prisoners, I stopped.'

She sank down beside him. His eyes opened wide as she started to read but then she concentrated on the letter. She finished reading and kept her head down, unable to look at him.

'What a load of… what the bloody hell…Where did you get this… this *rubbish* from?'

'Came in the post. I wrote to you to ask who she was.'

'I never got nothing about no Annie Kent.' He paused. 'Are you saying as you believe it?'

She got to her feet unsteadily. 'At first I didn't, Sam. But how did she know me if you hadn't told her? How did she get my address? That's what I kept asking myself.'

'I swear to you, on my life, Ginnie I don't know anybody called Annie Kent and never have.'

The truth lay bare, written on his face. Of that, she had no doubt.

'But if I get hold of her, she'll wish she'd never heard of you.'

'But that's not true is it?' She sat down beside him again and covered his balled-up fist with her hand. 'You couldn't show violence to any woman.'

Gently, she rubbed the now relaxed fist. 'That's why—'

She shut up quickly. She'd nearly said that was why she loved him. Instead, she snuggled up against him and hid her face in his jacket.

It was too soon. Too much unsaid.

'Doubt we'll ever find out. But it doesn't matter now.'

338

## Chapter Thirty-One

**April 1919**

Sam was happy to hear all about her new job and how well she was doing, but he refused to go back to mining – too many memories of what needed to be forgotten, he said. He would find work somewhere outside, where he could taste freedom, at a farm, or maybe Burslem Park.

Connie came to visit as soon as she heard Sam was back and had promised he could have a bed at Holmorton Lodge until he could find somewhere to board. Gaiety such as Ginnie had never known before filled the house. Even Mabel's new bloke was there. He had a nice way with him and Ginnie thought he would do all right by her sister, and he'd be good for Florrie. It was late by the time everyone left. Mabel put Florrie to bed and left them alone.

Sam sat with his arm around Ginnie, eyes closed. With her head on his chest, she felt the steady rhythm of his heart.

He started to talk.

'Me and Stevo, we were real pals by the time we got out there, Ginnie. And we'd look out for one another. We had to. I suppose the workhouse helped me get through it. Some of the blokes struggled, you know, in here.' He tapped his head and sighed. 'They were quiet, kept themselves to themselves. I say, Ginnie duck, we may've been dragged up as kids, but we learned to survive.' He stared into the dying embers in the grate.

Ginnie held him silently.

'I could tell you what it was like in the trenches, but I don't think I could ever find the words to describe it so as you'd understand. There was times when we chatted away as if we'd got all day to ourselves. Out in the open with the wind fresh on our faces. Them what'd been there a long time talked about how green it used to be, with fields and trees, like England, only warmer. I might've liked it then. Blokes said it was like being on holiday with the lads. They didn't have times like that before the war. Too busy working every hour in the factories.'

His voice trailed off. Ginnie heard him gulp. She didn't move a muscle. She might regret hearing what he was about to say but she would it regret it even more if he didn't speak.

'We never saw that, Ginnie. By the time we landed, the fields were mud baths – bare ground, where nothing was growing. We had hard winters. Snow, rain for weeks. In some of the old trenches it was like drowning in sludge. You had trouble hanging on to your boots. God help you if you lost your balance. You stayed in your wet muddy clothes until you was relieved. And then there were rats.'

He shuddered violently and moved his legs as if he could see them scurrying around his feet.

'Food wasn't safe from the buggers. What we didn't eat straightaway, we hung up out of their way – or used it as bait to catch them.'

Ginnie shivered in spite of herself, wanting to be strong for his sake but the horrors he had seen, and was still facing deep inside, broke her heart. He was nineteen and had lived through so much.

She lifted her head. He still had one arm around her, so she clasped the other firmly. Her mouth was dry as she waited for him to carry on. It was the only thing she could do for him.

'When we walked into the first camp, it was daylight. A group of men walked towards us, slowly, with some shuffling going on. I thought that maybe they were going for a rest. Maybe they'd been up all night. They got closer, and then I could see why they were walking an arm's length away from each other. They were blinded and were holding on to the shoulder of the man in front. We found out later they'd been gassed. As we passed by, we couldn't take our eyes off them. They were kids, Ginnie. Just like me. And I wanted to run, as far away as I could and throw my guts up. I really didn't know which would be worse: staying put or being shot for desertion. That night I curled up on the wooden slats and bawled my eyes out. That was the last time I cried – until Stevo.

'You want to believe you was one of the lucky ones, not one of the voices shouting from the craters in no man's land. Screams, cries, mutterings that might have been prayers, the last words from those too far away to be rescued. Some of the men in the trenches had to be held back. The voices got inside their heads. They were all for going over the top just to get rid of them. We tried to stop them… save them. When it's one of your own…'

He shook his head, the tears uncontrollable.

Never had Ginnie seen such torment. Her mind flew back to Frank. How had *he* coped? Did he know anything of those last few minutes, maybe clinging on to life until death was the only option? She squeezed Sam's hand and gently smoothed out his fisted fingers.

'During the worst of the fighting, our company grew smaller and we were re-grouped. Can you imagine that? Not enough of us left to form a company. At first it was thought they'd deserted – we found some of them, wounded or worse.'

He got to his feet and reached for his stick, pacing the room, with agitation playing across his cheeks. He turned to face her, swallowing the nerves away. 'I'm sorry to talk this way. You shouldn't have to hear it. I'm so sorry.'

He hung his head limply and she rushed into his arms.

They stood together, Ginnie's arms holding him up, willing her strength into him. She wanted to cry all the tears she had held back until this moment. But he needed her and she had to hold on for a little longer. Hold on until she could cry alone for the Sam she used to know.

'You were taken prisoner...' she said softly. 'Did you feel safe?'

'So many of us, Ginnie. The Huns didn't know where to put us all. We never gave up. Lots were wounded, but we would've carried on fighting. Some of us were put to work behind the lines, digging holes for the dead, layer after layer. We were desperate for food and drink, and still more men were coming. I've seen men scooping water out of ditches and eating tater peelings was a luxury.'

Ginnie couldn't help her gasp at the power of the body to do whatever was necessary to stay alive.

'They took our greatcoats. All we had was blankets to cover our heads and shoulders. Mind you, the work kept us warm until nine at night. In the coal mine we hauled loaded trucks along underground and if we didn't reach our quota we were beaten with shovels and pickaxe handles. Underground constantly and always hungry. No fresh air, no sun, no light apart from the lamps, if you was lucky. You could see by the look in the eyes of some men that they'd started to die inside.

'When the armistice came, they weren't ready. We were all desperate to get home by Christmas but there wasn't enough transport, food, clothes even. More of us were dying. Even Stevo...' his voice broke and when he started to speak again his voice was cracked as the words stuck in his throat. '... even Stevo, on our way home. We'd walked for days. We tried to get food, but there was little to be had. The locals gave us what they could spare. When we got to the coast, we were put in a transit camp to sail back to England. Flu was rife. Both of us went down with it... only Stevo didn't...'

He held her so tightly she had to gasp for air. She imagined clouds marching across the Burslem sky just as they would march over the devastation that was northern France and Belgium. She couldn't possibly see and feel the horror he was describing to her, but it began to feel as if the traumas of her life had been preparing her to build the strength for this moment.

Gradually, the shaking in his body slowed and stopped. She didn't let go. She left it to him to decide when to pull away.

Finally, he lifted his head and rubbed his eyes and cheeks to stem the wetness still gathering.

'Sorry, Ginnie love. Not cried like that since—'

'You've nothing to say sorry for, Sam White.' She lifted his hands to her lips and kissed each one and held them in hers, giving them life again.

He left soon after to stay with a neighbour for the night, after which he would stay with Connie until he found somewhere to board more permanently. Ginnie had offered to sleep with Mabel and Florrie so that he could have her bed, but he wouldn't hear of it.

Ginnie tumbled on to her bed, drained and numb. Listening to Sam had been the hardest thing she had ever done. The boy that had been such a big part of her life was gone. Who could live through such agonies and remain the same? George had said nothing but, then again, they weren't close, even though George thought they were. Even further back, she wondered how many of those boys who had wandered around the clay-end in their flat caps had come home to people like her and wished with all their hearts for the childhood they should have had.

A flame was lit, a burning anger was steadily growing inside her. She pounded at her pillow, over and over until it burst and covered her with soft, white feathers.

The tears she had held back flowed without mercy.

## Chapter Thirty-Two

*A Diary of Memories*

**April 1919**

Ginnie was feeling exhausted. It had been two days since Sam had opened up to her. Two days of pain and off-loading her devastation at Sam's story. Mabel hadn't asked her any questions but had sat with her, no doubt thinking of her own loss.

Saturday night soon came and Mabel was getting Florrie ready for bed. There was a bang on the front door. Ginnie jumped up to answer it.

The bang came again, more insistently.

'*Coming!* For goodness' sake, hold your horses.'

'Ginnie? Open the door. It's me.'

*George.*

Her heart sank. She didn't know if she could cope with him tonight. Maybe she could invite him into the front room to talk quietly about whatever it was he's so desperate to talk about. Better to be in control than have him shouting on the doorstep. She opened the door a couple of inches and his face filled the gap.

'Ginnie! Open up.'

'What do you want?'

'Need to talk – *hic* – talk to you.'

'You're drunk.'

'Might be. Please, Ginnie.' He thrust his foot into the gap and, as she made out his hunched shoulder, his weight forced the door and sent it crashing against the wall.

The possibility of staying in control flew through the window.

'Hey, you can't do that.'

Mabel's anxious face appeared around the door to the kitchen. 'What's going on? You all right, our Ginnie?' Florrie's little head peeped through her skirts with a finger in her mouth.

Ginnie flashed a warning look at George as he collapsed unsteadily into a chair. 'I'm fine. It's George Mountford. Someone I used to work with at Chamberlain's needing a word.'

'At this time of night? Who the hell does he think he is? Barging into our house like—?'

'Won't be long, I promise.' Ginnie shepherded a muttering Mabel back into the kitchen and closed the door firmly. Folding her arms, Ginnie turned back to George and hissed, 'Whatever's got into you – apart from the drink?'

He jumped up and pulled her towards him.

Caught by surprise, she didn't back away.

'I knew it,' he gloated, grinning from ear to ear. 'You wanted me to come calling on you, didn't you?'

'What *are* you going on about?'

'You were having me on about Sam, weren't you? I've seen you staring at me when you pass me in the town. You don't look like that at a bloke you're not interested in.'

She'd never looked at him in a special way or given him any encouragement – quite the opposite, in fact. 'George… I was hoping you'd get talking to Marge. You've played tricks on her in the past. I thought you liked her. Wanted to get her attention.'

'That old tub. Why should I want to get together with the likes of her, for Christ's sake?'

His astonishment sounded genuine. She pulled herself out of his grasp. 'I… I thought you needed someone…' Her voice fell quiet.

His face developed a grin that seemed to grow as she continued to look at him.

'Yes…Yes, I do. *You*, you stupid wench! We could be so good together. I can't let you throw your life away waiting for someone who's been missing for six months.'

'But Sam isn't…'

He stood up unsteadily. His arms went around her again. He kissed her hard, as if to stem the flow of words coming out of her mouth. He pushed her back to the chair with a strength she hadn't thought possible. She forced her head to turn away to escape his roving lips, afraid to cry out for fear of upsetting little Florrie in the next room. The strength of his drink-laden attack at the pub filled her head. It had taken so much effort to push him away.

Ginnie twisted out of his grasp and lurched for the poker, swinging it in front of her as if it was a sword. She would use it if she had to.

George's eyes opened wide, became clear and focused, then shocked, as if he'd come out of a nightmare.

'Ginnie, what are you doing, for heaven's sake?' He stepped away. 'I'm s-sorry. Don't know what came over me. You hate me that much?' He sank into a chair.

'How can I not hate you? You're drunk, you're selfish, and a bully. You only listen when it suits.'

His face paled as her words sank in. She lowered the poker but kept a hold of it. 'You don't love me, George. What really gets to you is that you can't cope with me not caring for you. I've only ever tried to help you after what you said when you went to war – about having no one to write to you.'

His mouth opened but no words came out. He slumped forward, his head in his hands, his fingers sliding through his hair. 'Christ…what have I done?'

Slowly, she laid the poker on the table beside her where she could pick it up swiftly if she needed to. She thought she heard movement in the kitchen, but there was none – although she would swear that Mabel was waiting with a weapon of her own on the other side of the door.

'Bloody Sam White. He's been inside your head all these years. You could never let him go, could you?'

She shook her head, slowly. 'No, I couldn't.'

He laughed, a grotesque laugh that wasn't funny in the least. 'I thought I could win over some workhouse boy who'll never have two ha'pennies to rub together. After all, you were nowt but a kid and I'd always had a way with wenches. I thought I could make you love me.' He fixed his gaze on his hands, locked together. 'But you don't know the half of it, Ginnie.'

He seemed to want to speak, and then he changed his mind, at war with himself. 'Remember when you told me you was waiting for him?'

'Yes.'

'I did see him. Me and the lads was having a laugh outside Chamberlain's and he came asking for you. I told him we was courting, you and me.'

She remembered what Elsie had said, about them fighting around the time of the wedding.

'Sam looked like a tramp, Ginnie, I swear. He's not good enough for you.' He turned his head towards the window, unable to look her in the eye. 'Wouldn't let it drop. So me and a couple of others... thumped him. I told him that if he ever came near you, I'd tan the backside off him.'

'I know.'

He frowned. 'When did he tell you?'

'He didn't. It was somebody else.'

'Why did you have to fall for him when you could've had me, Ginnie?' His cry was heartfelt as his finger battered his chest. 'I tried to hate you, but I couldn't. So, I tried to make you want me and it all kept going wrong. I couldn't take no chances of you seeing him again. I told him to get out of Burslem.' He looked her straight in the eye. 'He wasn't afraid of me, you know. He only thought of you.'

Part of her felt sorry for him, for the torture he was putting himself through. His eyes were dull and empty.

She laid her hand on his arm and he jumped as if the move had burnt a hole in his jacket. She took a step backwards.

'There's something else I may as well get off me chest, but yer not going to like it.'

'You don't have to say any more.'

'Might as well. I can't hate myself any more than I do now.' Unsteadily, he got to his feet and crossed to the window. With his back to her, he carried on. 'The letter you got from Annie Kent…'

'How d'yer know about that?'

'Because it was me.'

'What do yer mean… it was you?'

'I wrote it.'

'But who's Annie Kent?'

'I made her up.'

'Why, for heaven's sake? What about the baby?'

'No Annie Kent. No baby. I thought that if he was carrying on with somebody, you'd drop him. Guess I got that wrong too. I followed you around in case he'd come back to stay. Never suspected that toff, the fancy woman, whatever her name is, was in on it too. I *did* start a dalliance with Marge so's you'd be jealous. Then my call-up papers came through and I didn't know how I could leave you here, on yer own, in case he came back before me.'

All the heartache over Annie Kent, the baby, all lies? Her brain buzzed. Her mouth opened and shut but no words came out. She'd never really doubted Sam. Well, maybe just a tiny bit. But the baby, alive in her thoughts, had really got to her. The grief she'd suffered, the time she had spent tossing and turning, trying to get out of her mind the picture of Sam cuddling a child of his own body…Her lips curled and a new hardness tightened around her heart. All the pity, the guilt, the feeling she might have led George on, dissolved in that instant.

'I think you'd better leave.'

He straightened his coat and stared at her as if he was stocking up images before he could let her go. Slowly, he headed towards

348

the front door. As he turned the knob, he stared straight at her. 'That's the problem when you love the wrong person, isn't it? You don't know how lucky you are, lass. Well, I say that. It's all a bit pointless now, isn't it?'

'What d'yer mean?'

'Like I said before, you can't wait for him forever.'

'He's back, George. He was here yesterday.'

As he stared at her his face slowly changed. 'He isn't…'

She shook her head. 'No, George. He's very much alive. Goodbye, George. I never want to see you again.'

He clung to the door as if all the strength and power had drained out of him. His mouth opened and closed but no words came. His eyes pleaded with her. She stared straight through him as if he didn't exist.

When the door closed behind him, she sank into a chair, shaking violently.

Annie Kent and her baby would take some time to disappear from her mind, but her struggles were finally over.

–

The Sunday service ended. Everyone filed into the aisles and queued patiently towards the door of the church, the men smartly dressed, rather than khaki-clad. Amid all the celebrations and excitement, the full realisation of what had happened over the last few days was becoming clearer in Ginnie's mind. Everything she had ever wanted was within her grasp. She, who had never had choices in life, now had hope.

Suddenly, she felt incredibly nervous. In her experience, all good things were followed by bad. When things had gone badly, she was able to make an excuse because most of it wasn't her fault. Dare she take on this wonderful new future? A future she had shaped and chosen for herself. It was an awesome responsibility. How could she live with herself it all went wrong?

She glanced sideways at Sam who was leaning on his stick and concentrating on where he put his feet on the uneven pathway.

'How are you today?' Her mouth was so dry she could hardly get her words out. They sounded stilted and distant. Sam didn't seem to notice.

'Not so bad. What about you?'

She turned to face him, looking for signs of pain or injury. The twinkle was still there but it was masked by something deeper, darker, a mirror to the terrors he'd lived through. They could never go back to the boy and girl they had once been, but she was happy to look at him, sit with him, touch him.

'Oh, Sam.' She *would* take a chance on the future. She had earned the right to it. She threw her arms around him. He held her tightly, but she wasn't complaining. His lips were buried in her hair and they just stood together taking comfort in the touch of each other, the closeness.

He struggled to speak. 'You kept me going out there, you know. I wasn't going to let no Hun stop me from coming back to yer.'

She laughed and was in danger of becoming hysterical but managed to calm herself. The tension burst, like a bubble.

'You with yer new job at Royal Edward's. You gone up in the world, my girl. Done well.'

Those few words sounded wonderful. Here she was, sitting talking to him, as if it was the most natural thing in the world. 'Did you find any saucy French women in your travels?' She was joking, but still held her breath.

'Course not. You're the *only* one for me. Always will be.'

Her eyes filled with all the remembrances of those terrible months when she didn't know when, or if, he would come back to her.

'You don't believe me?'

'Course I do. I just want to hear you say it.'

Goose pimples spread everywhere. Her whole body felt alive with longing. His face turned and moved to meet hers, closer and closer until it became a blur. She closed her eyes. His lips touched hers and it felt like an explosion inside her head. When he pulled away, she opened her eyes, wanting more of him.

'So, you don't believe the letter from this Annie Kent?'

'No. I think we can forget about her.' The sooner Annie Kent was banished from their minds, the better. Better that Sam never discovered the truth.

'No chance. I want to know who's been upsetting yer and give her a piece of my mind. Spiteful bugger.'

'Sam, it's not important. We've got each other. Pity someone who has to make up stories like that, for I'm sure that's all it was.'

He looked as if he didn't believe her. Then sighed.

'You're right, I suppose.'

His eyes wandered over the graves surrounding them and his face became solemn. She wondered if, in his head, he was somewhere in France, thinking of Stevo, and all the lives buried there. She ached for him.

His lips brushed the sadness from her face. 'I do love you.'

'I love hearing you say it, and I love you too, more than anything.'

They sat down on a wooden bench under a tree that held the beginnings of new life among its branches. His arm came around her and they sat, comfortable in their world.

'By the way, d'yer see anything of George Mountford?'

She tried to speak calmly. 'As far as I know, he's back at Chamberlain's. I don't get to see any of them now.' She played with a button on her coat and took a quick glance under her eyelashes. 'Have *you* seen him?' She held her breath.

'Not for a while, thank the Lord.'

'Why do you say that?'

'We had a slight… disagreement before I went overseas.'

'I know. Elsie from Chamberlain's told me. She was there when it happened. George told her to say nothing, but she felt she had to.'

'Why didn't you tell me?'

'You had to work with the sod. He's still as much a pain in the arse as he was at school.'

Ginnie's mouth twitched. That was Sam all over.

'When I got back from the colony, I was over the moon, even though I say so meself. You'd grown up a fair bit while I was away and I think we both had feelings, grown-up feelings, even though we were so young. Remember that daft game we played when we was kids when we made plans to get wed? At least, you thought it was daft, but I knew different. I knew you were the wench for me even back then, but I didn't want to scare you off. You was barely old enough to know what you wanted. And yer Mother had just passed on. I had to bide me time.'

He smiled shyly. 'I think I'm done waiting.'

–

They arrived back at Mabel's and stood together on the doorstep. He opened his arms and, not caring who was there to see, she threw herself into them, revelling in their strength while knowing that from now on, he'd never let her go. And her promise to him? That she'd never want him to.

Her lips were every bit as hungry for him as he was for her.

The door opened. Mabel had her hat and coat on ready for work. 'I thought it was you, Ginnie. You're late.'

Sam pulled away, his face flushed.

Mabel had a wry smile on her face.

'Sorry, we got a bit carried away there, Mrs Farmer. And if we're late then it's my fault.'

'It's all right, Sam.' Mabel gave him a warm smile. 'And I've told you before to call me Mabel, otherwise you'll make me feel like Ginnie's mother. Am off to work now, Ginnie. You'll remember to feed our Florrie, won't you?'

Ginnie's cup was overflowing. When the mood took a hold of her, she was still afraid that something might come along to spoil it, and she could see just by looking at Sam's face when nightmares had fought with his need to sleep. It was early days for both of them, but she was sure they'd get there in the end.

'Did I tell you I kept a diary when you was away?' said Ginnie, dreamily. 'It started at Haddon. I wanted to remember the good times and the bad.'

'How did you manage that? I mean what with yer reading and writing an' all?'

'My diary wasn't written. It was about *things*… my tranklements. I think I might have mentioned them when I left Haddon?'

He shrugged. 'Don't remember. Is that a made-up word?'

'I suppose it was made up sometime. Tranklements are just bits and pieces, special things. Reminders of people and places. It's what Mary called them. They don't mean anything to nobody else, just to me.'

'Sounds grand. Would you show me? You don't have to, if you don't want to.'

She hesitated. 'It'll probably look like a pile of junk to you.'

Even after all this time the carpetbag wasn't all that heavy, although many new tranklements had been added. Memories, of themselves, don't weigh much. The heaviness came with the feelings they left behind.

She placed the bag on the table and opened it. Sam's letters were on the top, along with the letter from Royal Edward's offering her the job and the telegram telling her Sam was missing. She set them down beside the bag. Out came *The Children's Book of Parables*, a suffragette pamphlet, a piece of coal, a red shottie, a purse with the letter G in the corner, a tanner, a piece of red ribbon, and a broken comb, and a Union Jack from the end of the war.

'The carpetbag is one of my treasures an' all.' She picked it up and ran a hand over the tapestry, featuring a winged horse and a woman from the olden days, stroking the rich leather handles. 'Do you remember Mary giving it to me?' She stopped momentarily. 'Poor Mary. Like I said, nothing worth looking at.' Her fingers ran over each of the treasures in turn, reminding herself of their feel, her mind far away in the past. Each with its own story.

Sam didn't touch. After all, they weren't his *to* touch. He pointed at the book. 'That looks grand.'

'It's me Sunday School Prize from before Haddon. I promised myself I'd read it one day. And look…'

She opened the book at the parable of 'The Prodigal Son', and inside were three flowers, a buttercup and two carnations, flattened and colourless, but perfectly preserved.

'The buttercup – you saved it.'

She nodded tremulously. 'It meant a lot to me.' She felt breathless at the raw emotion in his face. His eyes darkened, and she could see a faint throbbing in his cheek.

'You know what will happen now – what we promised the buttercup.'

Her bottom lip trembled. She wasn't going to cry. Not yet.

'Ginnie? Will you marry me? We'll have to save a bob or two f—'

'Yes. Yes. Oh Sam, yes!'

She threw herself into his arms. Never had anywhere felt so safe and, when she glanced up at him, he looked so proud she burst into tears.

He wiped them away, gently.

'Just goes to show what you can do, doesn't it? Will yer… you know, teach me, so's I can read it too? I want to be clever, better meself, just like you.'

'Course I will. But you don't have to be clever to read, Sam. I found that out.'

'What about the carnations?'

'One's from Mother's grave. The other from Father's.'

'I do love you, Ginnie Jones,' he said, stroking her hair gently.

Ginnie's eyes shone. 'And, last of all…' She reached into the bag and brought out her doll, Clara, and hugged her.

'You kept her.'

Ginnie stroked Clara's hair and tidied her dress. 'And that's my very best tranklement of all. I love you, Sam White.'

# A Letter from Lynn

I am so excited to have my debut novel published by Hera Books. This novel has been in my head since I began researching my family tree double-figure years ago. I can't believe I am now the author of a book and have a second on the way. My thanks to Keshini Naidoo and Lindsey Mooney at Hera Books, my editor, Jennie Ayres and to you, Dear Reader, for choosing to read it. As a debut author, I would love for you to pass on your thoughts in a review and to help other like-minded readers discover life in the Staffordshire Potteries.

The novel, inspired by my grandma, began as a short story. The short story became the prologue to my published novel – writers throw nothing away! I spent most of my life in and around Stoke-on-Trent, and went to school in Burslem, the setting for the novel. Many of the family have worked 'on the pots'. Although living in Orkney, I am always a 'Stokie' at heart.

Experiences gained in childhood resonate throughout our lives; our ambitions change and what we think we want no longer applies. In the early twentieth century poverty and loneliness were facts of life. The workhouse and poor relief were the only means of survival for many people. Add to that illiteracy and the circle is complete. Even today, people survive by hiding their failings until something gives them the confidence to ask for help. I was a Volunteer Adult Literacy Tutor and, I suppose, was a little like Constance at first, aching to pass on my love of reading to others.

I hope you have enjoyed reading about Ginnie, Sam, and Connie. Catch up with them again in the second book in the series, due out next year, where Connie takes centre stage.

You can find me on my social media pages:

www.facebook.com/lynnjohnsonauthor
twitter: @lynnjohnsonjots
email: lynnjohnsonauthor@gmail.com
website: www.lynnjohnsonauthor.com

Thanks again for choosing my book
Very best wishes
Lynn Johnson

# Acknowledgements

This book has been a long time in the making. The move from writing stodgy reports to creative fiction, is a big one. I had a lot to learn and took advantage of the opportunities offered by the wonderful Romantic Novelists Association and their fantastic New Writers' Scheme. I am indebted to their dedicated readers who gave my novel a good workout. My heartfelt thanks go to Keshini Naidoo and Lindsey Mooney of Hera Books for having faith in me.

Stromness Writing Group have supported me and have lived Ginnie's story, in all its guises, as it has evolved and the Work in Progress Group offered sound advice on 'showing, not telling!' To all of you, individually and collectively, I send my thanks.

Beta Readers are invaluable to authors and I thank Jacqui Rogers, Suzy Kelly, Amy Louise Blaney, Louise Graham, Liz Coward, Anne Booth, and Peter Urpeth, (of HI-Arts and Creative Scotland) who have all given their time over the years. There are many others who have met Ginnie and Sam along the way and I am grateful for their input.

Any novel set in a period of history not lived by the writer relies heavily on research to ground it in the period. I thank Stoke-on-Trent Archives for their support of my long-distance requests. To get a really good idea of Ginnie's background, the Gladstone Pottery Museum, Stoke-on-Trent is a living experience of 'the job that nobody wants'. Another highlight has to be the Southwell Workhouse in Nottinghamshire, operated by the National Trust. An excellent insight into a woman's place in the pottery industry was obtained from

Jacqueline Sarsby's fascinating book: *Missuses and Mouldrunners: An Oral History of Women Pottery Workers at Work and at Home.* Another invaluable source of information is the wonderful www.workhouses.org. Any mistakes in interpreting the wealth of information collected are all my own.

All of the places mentioned in the novel are real, although street names are fictional. Haddon Workhouse is based on the Burslem and Wolstanton Workhouse, with its separate hostel for children, in Stoke-on-Trent. The individual towns mentioned are all real, but the pottery manufacturers, Chamberlain's and Royal Edward's are fictional. Langho Colony, near to Manchester, actually existed although Sam's story is fictional, and *Langho Colony, Langho Centre 1906 – 1984: a contextual Study of Manchester's Public Institution for People with Epilepsy* by Jean Barclay proved a very useful source.

Finally, my thanks go to my family – my mother who started me on this journey and my two sisters, Carol Blood and Pat Beresford, who have kept me there. Last, but not least, is my lovely husband, Michael who has encouraged me every step of the way and without whom this journey would never have been completed.